BLESS THIS HOUSE

NORAH LOFTS

BLESS THIS HOUSE

DOUBLEDAY & COMPANY, INC.

GARDEN CITY, NEW YORK

With the exception of actual historical personages, the characters are entirely the product of the author's imagination and have no relation to any person in real life.

This is the story of Merravay, a moderately sized house in South Suffolk which was built in 1577 by men who, though primarily concerned with earning their bread, found in their work the only outlet for their creative instinct. Therefore they made it beautiful, with a beauty to which some of those who came after were susceptible and others immune.

This is the story of those who built it, those who loved it, those who hated it, those who bought it with money, those who paid for it in other coin.

Such a story, spanning the years between the two Elizabeths, if made continuous, would be too long, so here, in a series of significant episodes, in each of which the house itself plays a part, is offered the history of Merravay.

Contents

BLESS THIS HOUSE

The Apprentice

W E—that is my Uncle Francis and I—finished the building of Tom Rowhedge's new house at Merravay on the last Sunday in October in the year 1577.

The weather had changed that day and it was bright and clear with a hint of frost in the air. It was still sunny when, at midafternoon, Uncle Francis stepped back to survey the last bit of the work that had fallen to his share, the carving of the great newel post at the stair foot. I knew he had finished although I had my back to him and did not look round. I heard him grunt as he straightened himself; heard his foot on the floor as he stepped back; heard the sound of his horny hands rubbing together with satisfaction. Presently he spoke,

"Well, Jonathan boy, thass done. And though I say it, as sound and pretty a job as any I ever see."

I said, "Umm," behind my teeth. If he wanted praise for his work, I thought, let him look elsewhere. Not that praise would be lacking, for every bit of his skill and craftsmanship had gone into that staircase, and it was a job any man might rightly be proud of. He waited for a moment as though expectant of some further response from me, but I went on with my own last job, the fitting of the wide seat into the space under the big window on the far side of the hall. I hoped that he would go away, go home and leave me in peace. My thoughts, though far from pleasant, were preferable to his company.

He moved over to the place where our rush baskets yawned on the floor. I heard the clank of his tools as he laid them away, and then the gurgle of ale as he drank from the wooden bottle.

"Are you dry?"

"No," I said.

He fumbled about in the bag in which we carried our noon pieces.

There was food in it, for he had eaten lightly at noon, being anxious to get back to his newel post, and I, not to be outdone, had also gone back to work with my hunger unsatisfied. I now heard the squeak of a knife against the crisp crust of the loaf, and then the moister sound of an onion being sliced.

"Care for a bite, then?" he asked.

"No."

He chumbled his food in his usual noisy way.

"How long do you reckon it'll take you to finish?"

If I said a short time he would wait for me; if I said a long one he would offer to help me.

"I don't know," I said.

He strolled over towards me, wiping his mouth on the back of his hand.

"You keep on at that rate, boy, and you gotta hour's work. Thass where you're weak, yet, Jonathan—reckoning up a job. You want to be able to cast your eye over a job and reckon exactly how long it'll take; otherwise when a customer say, 'How much,' you'd be all at sea, like. You'll hev to go a bit more careful when you get this end near the brickwork, don't you'll skin your knuckles. And you know I *still* think them pegs is cut a mite short. I quite see there ain't the wear and tear on a window seat that there is on stairs, still you want a job to last. Every peg in them stairs . . ." he turned and looked at his handiwork ". . . is six inches long. Ah, them stairs'll be there, sound as they are today, when your children's children are old 'uns with children of their own."

Wonderful! I thought. Tom Rowhedge's children and theirs, and theirs scampering up and down, all safe and secure because every peg in "them" stairs is six inches long and driven by an honest man. Oh for God's sake go away and leave me alone! With my teeth on edge I waited for him to say that he'd give me a hand. However, when he spoke he said,

"I'll just go and hev a look at that well cover; then there's another little job I wanta do. I'll be back time you're finished. On'y go a bit wary-like when you get to the corner. Once knew a man bark his knuckles on a new wall that hadn't had time to get friendly and a rare lot of trouble he had. His fingers was stiff to the end of his days."

"I'm always careful," I said shortly.

He left me. I heard the big door beyond the screen open and close, sweetly for all it was so newly hung.

Well, God be thanked, I thought, that's over. These last two months when Uncle Francis and I had been working alone in Tom's house had been about as much as I could endure. But it was over; when the last of my too-short, new-fashioned pegs was driven home Tom's house would stand, sound and beautiful, all ready for occupation.

I had only two more to drive when a chance glance through the window showed me Uncle Francis, with a short axe in his hand, striding away across the cleared space which was to be the garden and in which there was already a sundial, like the hub of a wheel, with tiny young box hedges radiating out like spokes, marking off the beds where next year the flowers would bloom. He jumped, nimble as a boy, across the dividing ditch, and set off across the meadow in the direction of Layer Wood. This afternoon the lowering sun shone on the thinned blazing leaves of the beeches, and the contrast between them and the few dark firs that grew amongst them was as startling and lovely as it was in the spring of the year when the firs looked black against the bright translucent young green. Wondering what in the world he was up to now, I drove home my last two pegs and laid my tools away. Then I lifted the ale bottle and shook it. It was empty. Quite reasonably, when I said I wasn't thirsty, Uncle Francis had drained it. I was reminded of one of the hateful old sayings which he quoted at me when I was a child and refused something and then regretted it. "He who will not when he may, when he would he shall have nothing." My uncle was never at a loss for a proverb and he produced every one as though it were mint-new.

Setting the empty bottle back in the basket, I remembered another of his silly sayings, "More ways of killing a cat than choking it with butter." Most applicable in my case because I had just remembered where I could get myself a drink. At Easter time, just before the bricklayers, the tilers, the plasterers, and ordinary carpenters had finished their work and were about to leave, Tom Rowhedge had paid us a day's visit and had stumped about all over the house, laughing and shouting, wildly excited, extremely pleased with all he saw. He had brought food with him, a whole ham, a great silverside of beef, a barrel of ale, a butt of wine, and a little keg of French brandy. There'd been a hilarious feast.

I was sick that day and although I hoped nobody had noticed me when I crept away, Tom had; and next morning, very early on his way back to Bywater, where his ship lay, he had halted his horse by our house and, without dismounting, rapped on the door. I opened it. He looked down at me and said,

"I was sorry you took sick, Jon. You still look a bit green; have a care to yourself. What I came to tell you was—they finished all but the brandy and that I laid by for you when you feel better. It's in the buttery cupboard and the key's under the beam. I must go. God keep you, Jon. I'll see you at Christmas."

He rode off into the mist of the August morning, leaving me with this new bit of his kindness lying like lead in my sick belly.

Now I took from the basket the horn cup which Uncle Francis had not troubled to use when he drank, and I carried it along, through the passage that led to the kitchen quarters, into the buttery, which smelt clean and fresh of new wood and new whitewash. I found the key and opened the cupboard and there was the little keg. I drew myself a cupful of the brandy and sipped it, somewhat disappointed. I had never tasted brandy before; the duty on it was heavy and put it beyond the means of workingmen, but I had heard about it and had expected something wonderful. And plainly Tom had thought he was doing me a special favour when he hid it for me. I thought it lacked the flavour of good ale and it hadn't the same mouth-filling quality; one's thirst didn't leap to welcome it and there was something rather choky about it. However, it was something to drink; and as it went down it was warming. I was grateful for that because I'd been working hard and grown hot, and the buttery, placed on the north side of the house for coolness, struck me with a sudden chill. So I emptied the cup and filled it again. And then, quite suddenly I understood why people who could afford it would buy brandy whatever the duty on it. I felt warm and light and taken out of myself. I could look back and regard all that had happened to me as though it had happened to another person. Nothing hurt any more. Everything was very clear and bright, but it was like a story, or like—if one could imagine such a thing—a series of vivid pictures in which people moved and talked . . . and I watched, understanding, sympathising, one with the person whose story it was, and yet detached and un-hurt.

I suppose it was natural, since I was sitting in Tom Rowhedge's house, drinking Tom Rowhedge's brandy, that I should begin my remembering, or my recalling, or my re-seeing, with my first meeting with him. I'd seen him before because we were both at King Edward VI's Grammar School; but he was a lordly great boy of thirteen and I was a lowly worm of eight, so between us there was a great gulf fixed, a gulf wider and deeper and more carefully guarded than any which the adult world knows, a gulf neither of us would have dreamed of crossing even if we had been blood brothers. The sight of him walking with his father into the little apothecary's shop which my father kept in the Friargate, and which I was "minding" on this August morning during my first holiday, covered me with the blushing confusion only experienced by schoolboys. It was made all the worse because I had just then a private and particular reason for trying to appear indispensable to my father but I knew I couldn't serve Mr. Rowhedge nimbly and satisfactorily under Tom's eye, so I weakly rang the bell which summonsed Father. He came and quickly served Mr. Rowhedge with the horse pills he wanted.

"Your boy, Martin?" he asked.

"Aye, and a right helpful little fellow," said Father.

Tom's father eyed me as though I were an animal he thought of purchasing but had doubts about.

"Bit pingling looking, ain't he? Either you work him too hard, Martin, or else you give him the wrong physic." It was understandable that old Rowhedge, accustomed to looking at Tom, and perhaps to catching sight of his own reflection in a polished pan, should think that I looked very small and pale, for their faces—very much alike—were broad and red and shining with health.

"He isn't much of an advertisement for my trade, certainly," said Father in his precise way. "But apart from his little trouble—and that is mending—he's healthy enough. He seldom ails." Please God, I begged, don't let the great oaf ask what is my little trouble! "And he has a head on him," Father went on fatuously. "Doing well up at the school, aren't you, Jon boy?" Oh horror upon horror! In front of a big boy, too.

"Tell you what, Martin," said Mr. Rowhedge, "it'd do him the world of good to come out to Slipwell till th'end of the holiday. Famous good air out at Slipwell. A chestful of that and a bellyful of good farm food'd make a new boy of him."

My face felt redder than a poppy. The man meant well, of course, but I resented his remarks about my appearance and I was embarrassed beyond measure at the suggestion that I should go and stay in Tom Rowhedge's house. Good heavens, he might be obliged to speak to me.

"What d'you say, Jon? Would you like that?" Father was never the man to make up another person's mind for him.

I looked helplessly at Tom; and he was grinning at me.

"You could be my crew," he said. "I want somebody small and light."

That was nothing less than an order. So I nodded, being beyond speech.

"You can ride back ahind of Tom," said Mr. Rowhedge. "The cob'll never notice your weight!"

The holiday thus carelessly suggested changed not the course but the flavour of my life. Not because of anything in itself but because it forestalled and prevented me from asking Father to let me leave school. I'd had a half year at King Edward's School and that was quite enough for me. I was almost certain that I had only to tell Father what it was really like and he would not wish me to remain.

But the holiday had slipped away without ever presenting me with the ideal opportunity for stating my case; Father was very busy. He had his shop and his workroom; he had his hobby, which was helping an eccentric old neighbour to set up and work a little printing press upon which they aimed, one day, to print Greaves' *Herbal*, and he had also to do all that was done on the domestic side. My mother had died when I was very small and Father's experience with hired help had been discouraging. So, being anxious to have his whole attention for my horrifying tale, I had avoided all those occasions when it seemed likely that he would say, "Don't bother me at the moment, Jon boy," or "Oh yes. Yes. Yes, I'm listening," when it was obvious that he was doing nothing of the sort. I had concentrated upon helping him, so earnestly, so devotedly, that he would deem me indispensable. And my reward for that was to be in the shop when the Rowhedges came in, and to be whisked off to Slipwell all in a minute and finally find myself, at the end of the holiday, riding back to school behind Tom. I'd hesitated and I'd lost.

By the time that school closed for Christmas the idea of leaving would have filled me with dismay.

The change was in me, not in the school. The rising bell still clanged at six in the morning; we still washed in cold water, seven or eight to a basin and woe betide him whose ablutions were scamped; we still hurried down to the great cold classroom and did two hours' work before attaining the dubious comfort of breakfast, a hunk of bread thinly smeared with lardy fat and a mug of the sourest flattest liquid ever called ale. No item of the routine varied. After breakfast we were turned into the yard to warm ourselves with rough play, and the bullies were busy, the tricksters played their practical jokes. Then we worked again until midday, each misunderstanding, each mistake, each scrap of detected inattention calling into play the formidable birch that Dr. Trudgett always carried under his left arm, whence it could, in the blink of an eye, be transferred to his right hand, which, for all it looked thin and frail, was as strong as a blacksmith's.

When I had planned my school-leaving campaign I had especially meant to emphasise the difference between the Dr. Trudgett whom my Father knew and liked and the Dr. Trudgett whom the classroom knew and feared. For many years Father had had dealings with the schoolmaster because, when King Edward had established the school on the site of the old Abbey of St. Dunstan, the first headmaster had saved from ruin the little herb garden which the monks had tended. In later days this had become a source of steady income to his successors, for most of the herb gardens attached to the monasteries and nunneries had been allowed to perish through lack of care, and in my day apothecaries and physicians from as far away as London sent to Baildon for their supplies. It was through buying herbs from the school garden that Father first got in touch with Dr. Trudgett, whom he came to admire very much, saying —and this was high praise—that he was a most enlightened man. And I can believe that, standing in the evening light amongst the sweet-smelling herbs, discoursing upon this subject and that, Dr. Trudgett showed to advantage. Possibly Father showed to advantage too; for when the idea of sending me to school was mooted, Dr. Trudgett welcomed it, despite my disability, which Father in his honest way felt bound to mention.

"I have enough healthy ploughboys," he said. "And more than a few good scholars have been subject to just such fits as you describe in your boy."

He had added that most boys came to school too late and that in his opinion I should begin at once. And so I went to school after the Christmas in the year when I was eight.

But Father had never seen Dr. Trudgett in the classroom. Never heard him say to some pallid, trembling blunderer,

"You cannot reckon seven times eight! That must be mended, sir. Bend over and count aloud."

Seven times eight is fifty-six, and fifty-six strokes from Dr. Trudgett's birch would set the blood running from a boy's breeches.

That was the kind of thing I had intended to tell Father. But I never did. For as soon as I entered upon my second half year, having in the first mastered the painful rudiments, I found that I had the makings of a scholar. There is no vanity in that statement; it is a quotation from Dr. Trudgett's own dictum.

Within a week of our return to school I went to the head of the bench, and I stayed there. Before Michaelmas I moved to the next, where nobody was less than twelve years old. I was fuddled at first but I was so eager, so desperate to get along with this fascinating business of learning, that I even ventured to hold up my arm and ask for enlightenment when I did not understand. And more than once Dr. Trudgett would say, "That is an intelligent question!" and he would explain painstakingly.

Within the classroom all began to go well; and outside, too, in the yard, on the holding of forty acres where we worked for Dr. Trudgett's benefit in the afternoon, and in the big dormitory at night, things were better. I mean for me. And thanks for that were due to Tom Rowhedge. I might now be roaring ahead with the trivium, that is grammar, logic, and rhetoric, and rather more than holding my own with the quadrivium, though my arithmetic was faulty yet, but I was still a small boy, weak-fisted, and a born butt for fools because of my funny fits. But after that holiday, when I had been the meek, easily ordered "crew" of the boat that Tom had built and loved to sail on the river at Slipwell, he had assumed a kind of responsibility for me. By doing so he showed not merely physical courage but a boldness of spirit, a disregard for custom and tradition. He was thirteen years old, very big and strong for his age, but he was not yet amongst the biggest of the boys and he was a lamentably poor scholar. He still had his way to make in his own sphere. Any other big boy would have withdrawn himself and ignored me once we were back at school; but Tom did not. And one day, finding me in trouble, he said, "Leave him alone or you'll have me to reckon with." The boys who were bullying me were bigger than Tom and higher up in the school. But they were taken by surprise at his unorthodoxy, and remembered his reputation as a fighter. They jeered, of course, to cover their discomfiture but they drifted off without having accomplished their purpose, which was to see if I could be teased into having a fit. And after that I noticed a great lessening in the torment to which I had been subjected.

I don't think I could have been teased into a fit. Nobody teased me, that I can remember, when I lived at home with Father, and there I had fits pretty frequently. In those days they took me unaware. There would be a kind of crackling sound, like that of a stick fire newly lighted, in my ears, and a flash or two of light before my eyes. Then the shutter came down, and there was darkness. When I came round I felt a little weak and dizzy, but quite all right, except that once I had almost bitten my tongue through. After that—I suppose I was about six years old then—at the first crackle I used to thrust my thumb into my mouth and wait, looking like a thumb-sucking zany until the shutter fell. And soon I was wary enough to seek privacy at the first warning sign. At school, of course, that wasn't always possible, and to the louts my fits were a source of amusement. Dr. Trudgett, on the other hand, one day when I had one in his presence and came round, dizzy and apologetic, said,

"Don't worry about it, Borage. I've always been inclined to think that the Apostle Paul was similarly afflicted. He speaks often of a bodily weakness and men have been at pains to name it, attributing to him everything from lameness to lung sickness. But I think the clue lies in his experience on the road to Damascus. Tell me, do you see a great light?"

"Not a great light, sir. A feeble flash or two."

"And do you hear voices?"

"No voices, sir. Only a faint crackling."

"Well, you are young. And you are not an apostle. And you are not a saint. And probably I am talking nonsense. I merely wished to point out to you that your ailment is no reason for shame; nor for idleness. . . ."

I certainly was not idle, though that was small credit to me. I learned as naturally, as eagerly, and with as much pleasure as other boys played. When I returned to school after the Christmas when I was ten years old I was placed on the top bench but one and I vowed to myself that by Easter I would deserve, even though I did not attain, a remove. Tom Rowhedge, who before Christmas had occupied the very seat in which I now sat, did not return to school, having realised his dream of going to sea. His father, with three elder sons to work the farm and share it, was anxious that he should seek a livelihood elsewhere and had sent him to school with the intention of making a merchant of him. But Tom chose for himself and the old man had promised that when he was as much at home on the sea as he was on land, he would buy and fit out a ship for him.

It was February and I was halfway up the bench and with six weeks still to go before Easter when it happened.

The usher, Master Richards, was taking the evening class when the message came for me to go to Dr. Trudgett's room. Boys near me whispered their jibes or their commiserations, according to their nature, and indicated by dumb show what I might expect when I got there. But walking along the dim passage which in the old days had been a cloister, I could not, search my mind as I might, hit upon any fault or any offence serious enough to rate my being called out from evening study. Even my arithmetic—always shaky—had seemed correct when I checked my answers with those of a boy who very seldom made a miscalculation. Still one never knew . . .

Dr. Trudgett was not alone in his grim little room; I was aware of that though I did not look at the visitor. I took a swift glance at my master's face and saw that something had upset him. He had a pale face as a rule, but anger always painted a thin pink glaze over his cheekbones. It was there now, and I dropped my eyes quickly and stood looking down at my own feet while my trepidation mounted. However, Dr. Trudgett spoke kindly,

"Come in, boy." He turned on the stranger and said, "Well, here he is, and you can see for yourself what I said. He's not cut out for manual labour. He has a modicum of brains, though. I had hopes for him."

"Had," not "have"; even then I noticed the tense.

I looked up, this time at the other man. He was a big, thickset fellow, clad in the drab-coloured homespun which workmen wear on Sundays and holidays, when they discard their working clothes. His deeply tanned face was heavily furrowed and wore a brooding look; the frown-scars on his brow, the way the thick eyebrows jutted and knotted, prepared one for a glance of some ferocity, yet his eyes, surprisingly light and blue, had a mild and kindly look.

"I'm your uncle, Francis Sheply," he said, "and I'm afraid I've brung you bad news."

I had never heard of him in my life; I was unaware that I had any relatives at all.

"Yes," said Dr. Trudgett. "Perhaps you'd better sit down, Borage."

More puzzled than ever, I took the chair he indicated and sat down on its edge, glancing from one face to another, waiting for one man or the other to break the bad news whatever it might be. I hadn't a suspicion, even then. "Your father is dead," said my uncle. "It seem he cut his thumb a while back and never heeded it, but it turned to blood poisoning and his end come very sudden. He on'y just had time to send for me and bid me care for you. And that, my boy, I'm right ready to do." He gave me a smile of kind reassurance which lighted his dark face strangely, and then he looked at Dr. Trudgett and added firmly, "According to my lights."

Dr. Trudgett ignored this and came and laid his hand on my shoulder. "You've sustained a heavy loss, Jonathan. You have my sympathy." His hand increased its pressure for a second before it withdrew. "Cry if you want to," he said. "There's easement in tears."

But there were no tears in me just then. I sat there with every feeling in me stunned, save only a half-fearful curiosity. Dr. Trudgett moved towards the window embrasure and with a jerk of his head indicated that my uncle should follow him.

"About this other business," he began in a low voice, "we must beware of making a hasty decision. And one thing to remember is that the lad is subject to fits. It seems to me that your plan for him would offer certain risks."

"He'll be under my eye. And he might well take a fit when he was sharpening a quill! There's another thing, too. For a boy like that a quiet outdoor life might work a cure. Too much striving indoors and fretting his brain may be the root of the trouble."

"Nonsense!" ejaculated Dr. Trudgett. But it seemed to me that even *he* had realised that Uncle Francis Sheply was not a man to be turned by direct opposition. He said more persuasively,

"Let us defer the matter for a while, say until the end of the half year. That can do no harm. And if you are thinking of the cost—as I can well understand you may be—think no more of it. Martin Borage chose to pay the fee but there are provisions in the foundation for poor scholars and there would be no difficulty, no difficulty at all."

" 'Tisn't the cost. The boy is no pauper. Martin Borage had money saved and owned his freehold. There'll be enough to set Jonathan up in business when the time comes."

This simple—and interesting—statement seemed to set fire to Dr. Trudgett's always easily inflammable temper.

"Then in God's name, man, *why* do you suggest taking him away?"

"Because, on his deathbed, Martin Borage sent for me and I gave him my solemn promise to handle the boy as though he was my own. Martin Borage and me was never friends, but the boy is my sister's child and therefore my flesh and blood, halfway at least. So I give my word, and my boy he is from this day forward. And no boy of mine would spend his young years sitting on a school bench."

"Why not?"

"Because I don't hold with it." That was the first time I heard those words fall from my uncle's tongue and I did not understand their deadly significance. I sat there, apparently disregarded, with my head in my hands, listening avidly; and I knew now roughly what the argument was about. I trusted Dr. Trudgett to rout Francis Sheply. I didn't know then that when Francis Sheply said, "I don't hold with it," there was no more to be said.

Dr. Trudgett, equally ignorant, said,

"And what, pray, do you mean by *that?* Why do you not hold with schooling?"

"I never said I didn't hold with schooling. I said I didn't hold with a boy of mine heving schooling. There've been schoolmen since the beginning. But 'tis plain to me that things was better, aye, a far sight better, when learning was kept where it belonged, to the great and the godly that was born to it in the station of life to which God had called them." (The smooth, pat, cultured phrase sounded strange on his rough tongue.) "To my mind things hev gone wrong through them that should be butchers and blacksmiths and shepherds getting a little learning and getting blown up with pride and argufying about what they don't wholly understand nor hev proper respect for."

"I *see*," said Dr. Trudgett drily. So did I. I knew at that moment what my uncle was; a backward-looking, would-be Papist. To him and to his sort Thomas Wolsey was a butcher, Thomas Cromwell a blacksmith. I understood why my uncle and my father had never been friends; I'd heard my father and his crony the printer talk about my uncle's kind; unprogressive, reactionary, people whose cardinal belief was, "As it was in the beginning so it shall be, henceforth and forever more." Years and years ago there'd been a lot of them, thirty thousand of them in the north of England had actually rebelled against the King. The Old Men and the New Men had come to blows and the Old Men had been defeated. But in lonely places, in a few stubborn minds the old fires, carefully hidden, still smouldered.

I waited now for Dr. Trudgett, with his shrewd wit and sharp tongue, to put my uncle in his place. He began with one of those calm, oblique statements which so often presaged devastating rage in the classroom.

"You are indeed a bold man to say that to *me!*"

But before he could proceed my uncle cut in with,

"Aye. And I'm sorry to run down in your hearing the trade you make your bread by. 'Tis as aggravating, I do see, as though somebody should say to me that carpentering and joining was a wicked waste of time. Just the same, feeling and thinking as I do about all this here new learning and the making of bad schoolmen out of what might hev been good workmen, I can on'y do my duty as I see it; and that is to take and make a good craftsman out of Jonathan here, same as I would my own boy."

Afterwards, thinking it over, as I did endlessly, I wondered whether Dr. Trudgett was conscious, as I was, of the blow dealt to his dignity and authority by the opening words of that speech. Without—I am sure— wittingly intending to do so, this rough country carpenter had reduced Dr. Trudgett to his own level, a man with a living to earn. He stripped him of his gown, of his birch, and under cover of a half apology, said, "If everybody thought as I think, you'd starve!" Whether Dr. Trudgett saw it as I saw it I never knew. Certainly he did not turn and rend my uncle as I had expected and hoped he would. He said, still in a reasonable voice,

"But he is not your boy; that must be remembered. His father sent him to school and so far as we can tell intended him to remain there. His wishes should be considered. Also I think, the boy's own. He is very young but his understanding is beyond his years. This is hardly the time perhaps . . . the news has been a blow to him. Really, I do feel that this should all be left for the moment. Why must such an important matter be decided this evening?"

"Thass a full day's walk from Nettleton to Baildon," said my uncle simply. "Altogether, time I see Martin Borage decently buried and get meself home again I'll hev lost five days' work. I don't want to hev to come back in the summer and go on argufying about what to my mind is plain at this minute. As for the dead man's wishes, 'twasn't you he sent hotfoot for as soon as he knew he was dying; 'twas for me. And though, poor man, he was past saying much, maybe sending for me had meaning. There's many a man," said Uncle Francis firmly, "that hev lived in error, die knowing the old ways is best; and maybe Martin Borage at the end knew it too. Otherwise why did he send for me, a day's walk away and no friend of his?"

"He was probably not in his right mind," said Dr. Trudgett sharply.

My uncle swung round; he brought one of his great hands, clenched into a fist, down on the end of the table.

"There you are!" he cried. "Thass the way it go now. Tossing the words hither and thither, spinning a web as sticky as a spider's to catch a man's wits in. He was out of his mind, you say; because when he was dying he saw how he'd been wrong with his pills and his potions and his new learning and his printing and his sending his boy to be stuffed up with pride. With his last breath, with his eyes darkening, a man incline to repentance—else why send for me that was dead set agin all *he* believed in. And so he's out of his mind. That'll do, sir; there's nought more to be said. I see how the wind blow here, and it is as I allust suspected. No fit place for the boy I hev took for my own." He moved around the table and touched my arm. "Come along, Jonathan. Thass time we was moving. Go fetch your duds, if you want 'em. You're coming home to bide with me and your aunt and I promise you it on't be our fault if you ain't happy there."

I moved my arm away from his hand and stood up.

"I don't want to go with you," I said. I turned to my master, "Please, sir, permit me to stay here."

"With the best will in the world, boy," said Dr. Trudgett. He bit his lip and beat his finger tips on the table; he seemed to be thinking deeply and rapidly. My uncle drew back a little. One could see how the deep grooves on each side of his mouth had been carved; his smile, no longer kindly, deepened them.

"As an orphan," said Dr. Trudgett quietly, "Jonathan now falls under the jurisdiction of the Justices. It is too late now, but tomorrow morning I will consult Mr. Aldridge upon this matter. I am prepared to abide by his decision. And you?"

The sardonic smile on my uncle's face deepened.

"That hare on't run, sir. 'Twas Mr. Aldridge himself that Mr. Turnbull the attorney called in to witness the will he'd drawed up in such a hurry. I can give you the wording. 'I appoint the brother of my wife, deceased, Francis Sheply, carpenter, of Nettleton in this county, to act as guardian to my son Jonathan and to hold for him, in trust, for the which he shall answer in the day of Judgement, such property as I die possessed of, until he shall come of age.' Thass plain enough, ain't it? And time the attorney did the writing I said, 'Martin, rest easy about the boy; he shall be to me as my own.' But, of course, if you doubt my word and hev a fancy to waste your time, and mine, we'll beat it out in front of the Justices."

"I hardly think you would have invented that legal phrasing. Well, in the circumstances . . ." He turned to me. "I'm sorry, Jonathan. You have the makings of a scholar and could have been a credit to the school. It's a very great pity." He stood for a moment, looking directly into my eyes with his boring gaze, and when he spoke again it was in his brisk, bracing schoolroom manner. "We mustn't waste energy on idle regrets, my boy. You *can* read, you've had a thorough grounding, such as few people attain. And man who can read has a door open in his mind which no one but himself can close again. Keep yours open. I hope you'll remember something of what you have learned, and I hope too that you will so apply yourself to your new trade that your uncle's prejudice against schooling for common people withers away."

The words were so final, so completely valedictory, that the expostulations and protests forming in my mind died away. There is something frightening in the sight of someone whom one has regarded as omnipotent suddenly yielding to a superior authority.

"I believe you already possess a book of your own. A *printed* book, is it not?"

"Yes, sir. A Gospel of St. Matthew."

Dr. Trudgett went over to the cupboard where his own books, a dozen or so of them, lay, and after some deliberation selected a chunky little book, clumsily bound in a linen cover.

"My father gave me this," said my master. "He wrote it and made it himself. He was bedridden many years. He devised this plan for making me *wish* to read Latin for pleasure. See . . . each story begins in English and then, at the turning point of the tale, goes on in Latin. I hope the day will come, my dear boy, when you will read on and never notice the change of language. And now I see that your uncle is impatient. Go and collect your belongings."

They were few enough. A change of linen, a spare pair of shoes, my printed Testament, and a sea shell given me by Tom Rowhedge as a parting present. I owned a knife, too, and a foot rule, and several quills, and a dozen coloured marbles; but they were in the classroom and I did not intend to risk, for their sake, the open question from Master Richards, "What are you about, Borage?" and the whispered questions of the boys. I laid my spare shirt flat on the floor, piled my goods on it

23

and made a bundle. I remembered my cloak and retrieved it from the pegs in the dormitory passage. All the time something in my mind, relentless and sterile as the knock of a passing bell, kept saying, "This is the end, the end, the end."

On my way back to the room where my uncle waited I passed a little slit window where one June evening, towards the end of my first half year, when I was miserably unhappy and fully determined not to come back after the holidays, I had stood and looked out and seen my father, with his big basket on his arm, going across the yard towards the herb garden to collect his supplies. The sight had called to mind happy summer evenings in the past when I had been with him; and I had cried a few hot tears of homesickness and self-pity which I had imagined came from affection. Now I stood by the same window and suddenly, great boy though I was, I was crying again. And now I was wise enough to realise that I was not weeping for my father, who had always been so kind to me. For that I blamed Francis Sheply. If he had come with his news and gone again without interfering with me . . . then I should have had tears to spare.

II

If, during my first wretched half year at King Edward's, Uncle Francis had arrived and whisked me away, I should probably have settled down in Nettleton and thought myself happy and lucky. My uncle lived very comfortably indeed. The cottage had been built by my grandfather, and stood, with the adjoining workshop, in two acres of ground. We had our own cow, a number of pigs, a good many hens and ducks and geese; the garden produced all, and more, that we needed in the way of fruit and vegetables; and my Aunt Mary devoted her entire life to the management of her household. Except to go to church on Sunday morning she never set foot outside her own domain. She had no contacts with the outer world; Uncle Francis did what little marketing was needed, and even over so personal a matter as a new pair of shoes she would say, "When you pass Jim Farrow's next time, my man, bespeak my winter shoes; and tell him to allow for the growth of my bunion." And presently my uncle or I would fetch home the shoes and she would try them on and say, "They do very well. Thank you." She spoke less than any woman I ever knew; in fact she never made an unnecessary remark and for days on end would only open her mouth to say, "Supper's ready" or "Would you like some more?" On the evening, when we arrived at the cottage, tired and hungry, Uncle Francis said to her,

"Martin Borage is dead. This is his boy, Jonathan. I brung him home to live with us," and she looked at me—quite kindly—and said,

"He's welcome. I'll set another place."

I am not sure that she ever knew my name. She fed me and washed and mended my clothes, looked after me tenderly when I chanced to be sick, addressed me as "you" and referred to me always as "the boy." For all the impact I made on her I might have been a new bit of livestock Uncle Francis had brought home. And at first so far as I was concerned she might have been livestock too, an animal, domesticated, superlatively well trained: later on I found myself wondering about her. Had she once been otherwise? Had she come to this cottage a lively, ordinary, pretty young bride? (That she had, once, been very pretty, was obvious even yet.) And had she perhaps had likes and dislikes, a personality of her own; and had she come up against the deadly, overpowering character of my uncle and suffered a defeat, and retreated and taken refuge in making herself simply another of his tools? Was her silence, her complete negation, a defence? After I had repeatedly battered myself against his never-to-be-shaken, never-to-be-ruffled, so reasonable unreasonableness, I did sometimes wonder. I did sometimes consider following her example. Why speak, for instance, when what you said was without effect? Why not give in, become just another useful, inanimate tool?

It seemed plain to me, from the very first, that I should never be a good carpenter, even with the best will in the world. Material, the dead stuff I worked with, was against me. I might cut two pieces of wood, cut them with the greatest care, each, say, four inches long; when I had them nailed together—not when I measured them tentatively, mind—one would be slightly longer than the other, and the protruberant edge could never be neatly sliced off because it would develop an unsuspected knot, or go splintery. With even so simple a business beyond me, with every tool I handled going blunt or demented or purely vicious, my life was misery; and always there was Uncle Francis looming up, kindly, watchful, determined. "Now look, boy. You wanta take your hammer . . ."—or "your saw" or "your chisel"—"like this and put your hand so . . ."; and I used to think furiously, It isn't *my* hammer; damn you, it's your damned hammer; take your damned hammer, damn you, and do your own damned job. (My repertoire of abuse, even mental abuse, was pretty restricted.)

One day, irritated past caution, I said,

"Now do you see? Can't you realise that never in my life shall I be a good carpenter? I just haven't the aptitude. Please, please, Uncle Francis, let me go back to school and do something I *can* do."

"Don't talk so silly," he said placidly. "Didn't they ever teach you at school—if at first you don't succeed, try, try, agin. If not they oughta. Come on now, you give your mind to it. Thass really the trouble with you, you know. Your heart ain't here, yet. You still would rather be a half-baked clerk going round ready to sell your soul for a bit of scribe-work, than a master carpenter like I mean you to be."

"And what right," I asked hotly, "have *you* to choose what I should be?"

"Every right. You was left to me to bring up as my own."

25

"That was a mistake," I said, putting into words the certainty which I had fingered over many times. "My father was frightened. He was dying, suddenly, and he wanted to be sure that I had a home and somebody to look after me. That was all he meant. He wanted *you* to take *his* place, not that *I* should take the place of the son *you* never had! Can't you see that? My father cared about people being able to read and write . . . he'd turn in his grave to know that I was wasting my life here banging silly nails into bits of wood."

"Now half you a minute." (That was one of his irritating country expressions, meaning "Wait half a minute.") "You got this all wrong, boy. Look here. As you say I never had no son of me own, and many a time I hev wondered why God should see fit to hev me childless, when I hev a house, and a holding, and a good honest trade to pass on. And many a time I hev thought of taking a boy to rear and bring up in my craft. But something hev allust bin agin that idea. Then suddenly there is my own sister's boy handed to me. And maybe as you say your father was frightened, as well he might be, called to meet his God with all his sins on him; but he was in his right mind; so why, as I said to the man to his face, why didn't he hand you over to your Dr. Trudgett or leave you and his bit of money to the Justices to take care of? I know why. God guided him. God knew that you and me would fit in like a neat bit of dovetail. I saw that plain. And nobody, least of all you, my boy, can tell me any different."

Firm conviction is a contagious thing; and so is . . . well, what can one call it? . . . superstition? I know I stood there with my face still hot with fury and felt a cold finger trail down my spine. Stated with such confidence, the idea was just feasible enough to be uncomfortable.

It made *me* so negligible. Here's a boy for Martin Borage to send to school and take pride in. Right about turn! Here, Francis Sheply, is the boy you always wanted, a boy to train to be a carpenter!

But what about me?

Dr. Trudgett had often pointed out the distinction between the theories that were, as he termed it, "susceptible to proof" and those which were not, and later that day it struck me that Uncle Francis' theory about my destiny fell into the former class. So that evening after supper—it was early summer by this time and the daylight lingered—I stuffed my bilingual *Tales from Boccaccio* into my jerkin and, with my Testament under my arm, strolled out, saying that I was going to Layer Wood to read. To have taken two books would have aroused suspicion but the one visible one under my arm merely provoked Uncle Francis' dry comment that at this rate I should soon know it off by heart.

I walked to the wood, found the path, and started to run. The path was a short cut from Nettleton to Clevely and when I emerged from the wood, close to Rawley's farm, I was near the main road to Baildon. I walked again when I was near enough to Rawley's to be under observation, and then, once on the road, ran again as though the devil were after me. I walked through Minsham, then ran again, and so continued through the thickening darkness. I was more than halfway to Baildon before I was thoroughly exhausted. Then I lay down in a dry ditch and slept until the light of the new day, and the chorus of bird song which greeted it, waked me.

I was in Baildon, washing my hands and face and smoothing my hair over the horse trough in the Friargate just before nine o'clock, and at the school gate as the bell rang for the beginning of the morning class. I couldn't have timed it better. I was in the passage, just outside Dr. Trudgett's study door, when he emerged, settling the birch under his arm, twitching his gown into place, on his way to the classroom.

I said, "Sir."

He halted, looked at me for a second without recognition, and then said, "Ha, Borage! So you've come back, eh?"

"Yes, sir," I gasped; and then, because I knew he was impatient and time was short and this no place for beating about the bush and being diffident and deferential, I gabbled on. I told him that I couldn't bear life at Nettleton, couldn't bear being a carpenter; please, I said, please, couldn't I come back; couldn't he, wouldn't he, take me in and if my uncle came in search of me, say that I wasn't there.

"Dear me," he said, when I had gabbled myself to a standstill, "in one respect you tell the truth, at least. That your mind is withering. In good truth, that is so. I always thought you were a sensible fellow. And now you invite me, *me,* to conspire with you in the telling of a lie, and what is worse a stupid lie! How could I hide you, as you so flippantly suggest? To begin with you would have to re-enter as a poor scholar, and your qualifications for that estate would involve the submittance of your name, your antecedents, and circumstances to the Justices and the Governors. Besides, do you seriously imagine that when your uncle raised the hue and cry for you I should perjure myself on your behalf. Really, Borage, it is a plan of which any intelligent boy on the bottom form would be ashamed!"

"It was all I could think of," I mumbled.

"The obvious thing, I suppose. So obvious that your uncle and guardian is probably at the gate this moment! Come in here a moment." He opened the door of his room. "Now, tell me truly—is it merely that you dislike the work, the way of life, or is he unkind to you? Are you ill fed? Ill treated?"

"Oh no," I said, rather wildly, because his suggestion that my uncle might already be on my trail threw me into a panic. "He's kind to me. It's just that I don't like it there. I don't want to be a carpenter. I want to come back to school. I want to go on learning. I'd rather be here and be beaten every day for misconstruing or miscalculations than do woodwork with my *kind* uncle."

"Few of them," said Dr. Trudgett, jerking his head in the direction of the schoolroom, "would agree with you." He brooded for a moment. "It does all seem a pity, a very great pity indeed. I was grieved at the time, I remember. But your uncle is within his rights and honestly, Borage, there is nothing *I* can do. In Utopia, I suppose, education will be compulsory and men like your uncle will gnash their teeth in vain . . . but this is not Utopia. How old are you, Borage?"

"Thirteen in November."

"Eight years to wait. In eight years you will be of age and your own man." He scowled, trying to remember. "And your uncle mentioned a little property. Look," he said, and his expression lightened, "I do believe that you are one of those rare people who do seek after learning, and wish to pursue it. If you can practise your reading and not let your mind rust, it would not be too late in eight years' time. Come back to me then. You'll be twenty-one in November—providing I am still alive we will spend the Christmas holiday together; we'll work fourteen hours a day. And then you shall go to Cambridge. The Master of Peterhouse is an old friend of mine. . . . It shall be managed, Borage. Tell me, can you remember when you were five . . . anything that happened when you were about that age?"

"Why yes, sir. On the day itself I broke a precious flask in my father's workroom and I remember him saying that were it not my birthday I should go supperless to bed for meddling."

"And that seems long ago?"

"No, sir. When I speak of it, it seems like yesterday."

"Well, that was eight years ago. In a similar length of time you will be free to sate your hunger for learning. And now you must go back and do your duty by your uncle, thanking God that he is, as you say, kind. Many are not. Wait . . . I have another thought. Nettleton . . . of course! Simon Dodson is priest of that parish; a very learned man, though his stutter has prevented his gaining preferment. *He* could help you; he has books, ability . . . and, I doubt not, is lonely and fears as you do the withering of his mind. Have you not become acquainted? I will write to him on your behalf. Two old King Edward's boys in one small parish, and not friends? Strange!"

"But he is married, sir."

"And how should that prevent his noticing a good mind dying for lack of sustenance on his doorstep?"

"My uncle strongly disapproves of married priests, sir. On Sundays we go to church and my uncle pays his dues. But only to escape the penalties. Privately he calls Pastor Dodson 'the leader of the Geneva Jig' and outside the church door has no truck with him."

Dr. Trudgett wrinkled his brow.

"The Geneva Jig; what is that?"

"A derisive term, sir, applied to the Psalms as arranged for congregational singing by a Catholic gentleman—of Cornwall, I believe."

"A man of your uncle's mind?"

I nodded.

"I see. So closer contact with Simon Dodson would be an embarrassment to you. What a pity! Yes, yes. Come in," he cried as a timid knock sounded on the door. And there was a boy, sent by Master Richards, to ask with all respect whether the bell had been rung loud enough . . .

I knew that to the end of my days I should remember the lonely, deserted feeling which came upon me as I saw Dr. Trudgett settle the birch and twitch at his gown as he sent the boy running to say yes, of course he had heard the bell and would be in the classroom in a moment. There was a close organisation, a little society, going its way, and he had his place in it . . . and I had once had mine. But no more! I was outside of it; and I was alone. I had the thought that as I felt then the dying might feel. All this activity, all this routine in which I once had a share, is going on without me. . . . Horrible.

I stood in the yard for quite a long time. I could hear the murmur of voices, and twice the unmistakable smack of the birch. And I looked ahead at eight long years of sawing and planing, hammering and chiselling; eight years of Uncle Francis saying "I don't hold with it" and the subject being closed. I thought, I won't go back. I'll go on and I'll find another school; I'll say my name is Jon Carter or something like that and that I am an orphan. . . . I'll get in somewhere, somehow.

Of course, I was young, immature, and romantic.

I was not yet sure that Uncle Francis' theory had been disproved.

Presently I gave myself a shake and remembered that if Uncle Francis really were looking for me this would be one of the places he would search. So I trotted out of the school gate and away down the hill to the market place, from which roads led off in all directions. I intended to take the one to Colchester, which went on, I knew, to London. But by this time I was extremely hungry. The stomach has its habits and mine was used to being stuffed full of bread and bacon and home-brewed ale at seven o'clock each morning. It was now almost ten. And on the corner of the market place and the road to Colchester there was a baker's shop. A smell to make the hungry mouth water issued from the new loaves which a pleasant-faced, stout woman was taking from a big basket and laying on the shelves. I halted, sniffing. I hadn't a penny in my pocket; yet the idea of begging took a bit of getting used to. While I hesitated, the woman looked out and saw me.

"What do *you* want?" she asked; her voice far less pleasant than her face would have led one to expect.

I would have said, "Nothing," and moved on, but the thought struck me that I must get used to asking for what I wanted, what I needed, what I must have . . . and I might as well start now.

"I want a penny loaf and I have no penny."

"Oh!" she said. "Well, I have a weevilly flour bin that should be emptied and scoured out against the new lot coming in this very morning. If you like to do that for me you can have a loaf . . . when the job's done."

Such a chance might not occur again between here and Colchester, I thought, so I said I would do the job and she led me through the shop into the bakehouse, showed me the bin and the bucket and the scrubbing brush, and then stood and watched while I took off my doublet and laid it, with my books, on another bin.

"Have you run away from school?" she asked.

"No."

"Yet you ain't a Baildon boy; nor you don't look like a beggar," she mused.

"I'm on my way from one school to another, if you must know," I said.

"No need to be rude. And do well into the corners," she said. She went away to the shop; but presently she was back and stood there telling me about the accident which had happened to her husband. "So I'm single-handed," she said. "And before you go you can help me open the yard gate, then it'll be ready for the miller. But you can eat your loaf first." She inspected the bin and seemed pleased, and when she brought me the loaf she had split it and laid a piece of meat within. I wolfed it quickly and then went to help her with the gate, a tall heavy one which had sunk on its hinges and opened with the utmost difficulty. As I tugged it the last stubborn foot the woman said, "Well, ain't that timely. Here is miller." I looked out and saw the wagon; and then the miller—Jacob Woody of Nettleton.

"Well," he exclaimed, "I'll go to sea if it ain't Jon Borage. You wicked little varmint. There's your pore uncle standing at the crossroads asking everybody to cry you . . ."

I had turned as he spoke and was making for the shop, thinking that I could be through it and away up the Colchester road before he had climbed down from the wagon. But the woman had already slammed the door and was standing guard of it, saying,

"There, I knew it. I had a feeling . . ."

"By cock," said the miller, now on his feet in the gateway, "if you was mine, I'd give you a rare walloping. Up all night Francy Sheply was and half a dozen more with him, reckoning you'd took a fit. Hollering and hunting all through Layer with lanterns they was, and down by the river. And now there he stand, wasting a working day, asking everybody what pass to look out for ye and hev you cried everywhere and pass on the word. I should hope he'll give you a hiding—and here's one on account." He raised the whip he had in his hand and aimed a blow at me. Without warning the crackling, flashing darkness whirled down on me, and when I came to my senses again I was lying on the wagon floor and the wagon was rumbling into Nettleton. I'd had no time to push my thumb into my mouth and consequently my tongue was so badly bitten that I couldn't speak or eat for several days. When I could speak I said to my uncle, "I'm sorry you were alarmed about me; but I still don't see that you had the right to have me cried as though I were a stray horse."

"Oh! Well, I shall hev," he answered.

At the end of that week he had me up in front of the Justices and I was formally apprenticed to him for seven years, with four years of journeyman status to follow. Until I became twenty-three I should be, virtually, his bondsman. Incongruously enough, at the same time he moved his order for flour and meal from Jacob Woody and gave it to the miller at Clevely. Woody, when he brought me home, had said frankly that he had struck me, and Uncle Francis "didn't hold" with that.

Well, so far as any theory concerning God's intentions and man's destiny was "susceptible to proof," my uncle's idea that he and I were intended to be dovetailed together seemed to have stood the test. Halfconvinced, but even more resentful, I began to settle down.

III

I was fifteen when I made my next, rather less amateur bid for freedom. By that time I had grown a good deal and my fits came more and more rarely. Uncle Francis was fond of pointing out that he had been right about the health-giving effect of manual work. He delighted also in my increasing handiness and skill, for by this time I had had sense to see that if I must be a carpenter I might as well be a good one; there had been a time when I had done slovenly work deliberately, but that became boring in the end. I might finally have found some pleasure in my work but for the fact that Tom Rowhedge came home from sea just at the time when my uncle and I were working on a new barn at Slipwell. There again the finger of destiny might be perceptible; for Slipwell was eight or nine miles from Nettleton, and it is unlikely that Tom would ever have known that I was in Nettleton, or, knowing it, have troubled to seek me out.

Tom was now twenty, an enormous, handsome, swaggering fellow, with a darkly tanned face and a huge copper-coloured beard and thick gold rings in his ears. At no time in our lives had the five years' difference in our ages loomed so large. He had done his five years at sea—and from things he occasionally let drop in conversation I gathered that they had been years of great hardship; even Tom, who was tough and plucky, confessed that during the first months he had contemplated running away *from* sea more often than when at King Edward's he had dreamed of running away *to* sea. But he had survived and was now to reap his reward; his father was going to fit out a ship of which Tom would be master. Old Rowhedge could afford that—as well as paying other people to build his barns—because he had been made very prosperous through the peculiar thing which was happening at Slipwell. Farther to the north the coast was sinking into the sea, at Dunwich whole streets and great churches were being lost, but at Slipwell the land was rising. There were old men there who could remember their fathers recalling the time when the marshes at Slipwell were useless, wet, and reedy, and actually under water for eight months of the year. Gradually, over the last hundred or hundred and fifty years, the marshes had risen and were now useful grazing ground for sheep. True the animals were scrawny, but old Tom Rowhedge was not interested in the amount or the quality of the mutton they produced; he reared them for their wool, and since wool was in great demand just then, he was making a pretty penny.

I can only suppose that Tom, once the excitement of his home-coming had died down, was lonely and found it easier to talk to someone who had *seen* a globe and knew the difference between America and Africa, even if that someone were only a fifteen-year-old carpenter's apprentice, than to his father and brothers and the men in the village whose idea of a far distant place was Colchester or Dunwich. Whatever the reason, during the weeks when he was at home he seemed to seek my company, and often while I was working he would lounge about and talk, or even lend a hand to the job I was doing. And in the evenings we often walked together. Towards the end of his stay, softened by his friendliness, I spoke of myself and tried to tell him something of my wretched discontent. Tom, like Dr. Trudgett, asked whether my uncle was kind to me.

"Completely, entirely," I said. "But you know, Tom, you can murder a fellow by cracking his skull with an axe, and you can also do it by pushing a featherbed over him and holding it down long enough. That's how his *kindness* feels to me. I'd far rather he fetched me a clout occasionally and gave me a shabby breakfast and let me go and read with Pastor Dodson."

"Don't wish for clouts or bad food," said Tom. "But why shouldn't you read with old Dodson if you want to?"

"Because Uncle Francis doesn't hold with him! I see pretty clearly now what's in his mind. He's absolutely old-fashioned, practically a Papist you know, and he thinks all the new ways are just temporary things. So it's the duty of people who think as he does—and there are more of them than you might think—to rear up a generation of young ones with the same ideas. It'd be such a pity, wouldn't it," I said sourly, "if when the old ideas became fashionable again nobody remembered exactly what they were!"

"I can't exactly see the old ideas coming back," said Tom. "The new 'uns fit far too easy. Married clerics for example. Who'd want to go back to the old ways when it meant giving up a nice little bed-partner like Agnes Dodson. She must be at least twenty years younger than he is, wouldn't you think?"

I'd never noticed Mistress Dodson. My interest in women was still so completely childlike that I still reckoned them adorable if they handed out cake when one worked for them, and detestable if, halfway through a job, they changed their minds and wanted something altered. Also at this moment I was irritated by the switching of the conversation from the general to the particular.

"I don't know how old they are," I said. "I only know he has a lot of books, more even than Dr. Trudgett; and I'm not allowed to do more than answer him civilly if he greets me. That *does* stick in my craw. Together with a lot of other things."

"What things?" Tom asked; accepting my change of subject more good-humouredly than I had accepted his.

"Well, this apprenticeship, for instance. Seven years and then four. Positive slavery, and all over the country the system is on its last legs, and he knows it. Only the old-fashioned people bother nowadays; and a good thing, too. Don't you think it's iniquitous that until I'm twenty-three I can't get a job, or choose where I live, or get married. . . ."

"And are you anxious to get married?" Tom asked with a smile.

"Don't be silly. It's just a rotten system whereby a person who doesn't want to do a job at all is tied to it in such a way that when he gets out of bondage he's too old to do anything else. That's the old way, the good old way!"

"Aye; I can see. It's hard-tack for you. And there ain't much I can do, Jonathan. Now if you had a hankering for the sea . . ."

"But I have," I said, not with complete truth, for until Tom had returned with his wonderful stories and his fine clothes and gold rings I had never actually envied him his trade; his freedom to choose it, yes, I had envied that.

"Well then . . . if you really mean that, boy, maybe we could come to some arrangement with your uncle. It costs a bit to break or transfer indentures I believe . . ." He scowled. "But a handy boy like you, trained carpenter and all, and light in the rigging would be a very useful thing to have. And I'd see you got your sea legs, Jonathan, a damned sight easier than I did." His eyes began to sparkle with the old boyish enthusiasm I remembered.

"It needn't cost you anything," I said proudly. "My father left me fifty pounds. Uncle Francis has it locked in the chest by his bed; and every month he adds a shilling to it. It's *just* possible that if I offered him that for my freedom . . . Oh, Tom, if only he would!" It seemed, for a moment, almost likely, for Uncle Francis was, within limits, a money-minded man. He would not put money before his principles, and he was not the kind of "careful man," of whom there were many in our neighbourhood, who would live meagrely in order to save a penny, but he would, and often did, haggle for an hour over the price of a job he was to do, or of material he had to buy, and I never knew anyone get the better of him in a bargain.

That evening I suggested to Uncle Francis that he should cancel my indentures and allow me to go to sea with Tom, and in return take my fifty pounds for his own.

He laughed his rare laugh.

"You really are a silly young fool, Jon," he said. "The most I ever heard of paid for indenture breaking was twenty pounds, and that was a gentleman's son that was apprenticed to the wine trade, and both his father and two brothers older than him died in one week of the winter sickness so he must buy himself out and go to look after his manor. And here's you, my own flesh and blood, offer me fifty to do a thing I wouldn't do for ten times the money! Where'd you be in a year's time, a silly great gaby like you. Tom Rowhedge can look on the sea as a playground, soon's he's sick or sorry there's a plough waiting for him at Slipwell. You'd be just a half-timed apprentice, no more use than a half-baked loaf. You just oughta go down to Bywater one day and take a look at the old sailormen on the quay there, poor old hulks with one eye, or peg legs, or empty sleeves. They was all going to make their fortunes, once. Now they wish they'd stayed at home and learned a craft. And thass what you're going to do, boy, willy-nilly. And the day you finish, a right craftsman like me, able to hold your own with all comers, with fifty pounds in your hand, and a bit added, you'll thank me from your heart. Them that went so fast, with a three-years apprenticeship—they've cut to that now, God forgive 'em—poor handless critters that couldn't make a kitchen shelf—they'll look up to you and call you master. Aye, you'll bless the memory of your uncle that wouldn't let you runagate, wasting your substance or your time. And thass my last word, Jon," he said, his face growing sombre again.

IV

So Tom Rowhedge sailed away in quest of fortune and I stayed at home, mastering the carpenter's craft and in my spare time reading my two books, trying to keep open that door in my mind of which Dr. Trudgett had spoken, until the rather horrible day came when I realised that I was not *reading* any more; I knew my Gospel and *Tales from Boccaccio* by heart. It was useless to ask Uncle Francis to give me money to buy a new book, he didn't hold with reading. However, I was now well on into my eighteenth year; in fourteen or fifteen months I should be a journeyman, drawing a journeyman's small wage. The first thing I would buy would be a book, I thought.

And then I fell in love.

Her name was Elizabeth—Elizabeth Rawley—and she was the youngest of five pretty girls who owed no part of their charm to their ribbons and laces and such falderals, for their father was an old curmudgeon, noted for his meanness even in our parts, where "carefulness" was regarded with respectful admiration. He was very unneighbourly too, and as his farm lay on the far side of Layer Wood, on the boundary of Nettleton and Clevely, the Rawley girls were hardly known to us by sight until old Rawley fell out with the parson at Clevely over a load of hay. After that he elected to attend our church, as he was entitled to do since he had land in both parishes, though the church at Clevely was much nearer his house. We knew about the dispute concerning the hay because it was the kind of news which Uncle Francis would seize upon and drone on about as another sign of the bad new times; he sided heavily with the parson of Clevely, who, since he was unmarried, was more to his taste than our Pastor Dodson. So we were not surprised one Sunday morning to see old Rawley walk into church, looking like an angry old bear and followed by his wife and four daughters. The eldest girl had been married a year or so previously and the grudging meagre wedding feast had been a matter of gossip ever since.

It was a lovely warm summer morning and all but the elderly women were wearing light-coloured gowns or dull ones brightened by a bit of cambric or ribbon. The Rawley girls wore a kind of uniform, skimpy straight gowns of grey homespun, and plain straw bonnets. But they were young, and they were pretty, and they were new to us, and that morning there was a good deal of fidgeting and head-turning among the younger men—and some no longer young.

It happened that they were just in front of me, so close that I could smell the lavender in which those ugly dresses had been laid; and presently I noticed that although, from the back, they looked so much alike, there were differences in size and shape. And whereas three of the girls had yellow hair, one had black. Little tendrils of it crept out from under the bonnet's edge and lay, soft and curly, like little feathers against the whiteness of her neck. Unfairly, I immediately began to credit her with all the sweet smell of lavender. Then I noticed that she was the smallest and slightest of the four . . . and something began to move in my stomach, which was entirely new and rather painful and yet altogether delightful and exciting.

The moment service ended old Rawley led the way out and they all followed, looking neither right nor left, but I did catch a glimpse of the dark-haired girl's face, and it was, to my mind, the prettiest of all. The others were pink-cheeked and touched by the sun, but she was pale, pale as the windflowers which shimmered through Layer Wood in the spring.

I ceased to look forward to the moment when I should earn a wage and be able to buy a book. My forward-looking narrowed itself down to seven-day stretches between Sunday mornings. The curious feeling in my stomach grew. Presently it no longer depended upon the sight of her; it was there, all aquiver, when I thought about her.

Then there came a memorable evening when I was taking the short cut through Layer Wood. I was alone, for lately Uncle Francis had trusted me with simple jobs, and this one, the building of settles either side a hearth in a house at Clevely, was well within my scope. I was walking along a ride thickly bordered by blackberry bushes when, just ahead of me, I saw my little dark-haired girl. She was jumping and snatching at something in the bushes. I quickened my step and saw what had happened. She had hooked down a branch where the berries grew larger and in greater profusion, and the spray had sprung back, taking her crooked stick with it. As soon as she saw me she desisted from her effort to recover the stick and, turning to a lower bush, began to pick busily. It was a chance not to be missed. Yet I almost passed by because at the idea of speaking to her my heart began to thump so heavily that I went dizzy and a kind of blackness came in front of my eyes. I was reminded of my now all-but-outgrown affliction, and thought with terror —suppose I had a fit now! A thought to remember with irony later on. The dizziness did not crackle, however, nor did the darkness flash, and I finally got back enough breath to say chokingly,

"Let me try."

It was too high even for me; but I had my tools with me and it was the matter of a moment to walk into the wood, find a crooked hazel, and cut another.

"Oh thank you," she said, and smiled, and I saw how sweetly her mouth curved over her small teeth, and how long her eyelashes were. Everything in me moved towards her with pure love.

"Wait a minute," I said, and, taking the stick I had made, I hooked down the one she had lost; then there were two sticks, and two people gathering the berries.

We hardly spoke. I asked her name and she told me, Elizabeth; and the word was full of music and wonder, as though that had been the first time it had ever fallen on human ear. I told her that I had seen her in church, and she said, yes, she knew. My shyness wore off with a rapidity that astonished even me, and when the basket was full to the brim I was bold enough to ask,

"Will you be blackberrying tomorrow?"

"Oh no. Thanks to your help I have enough."

"Let's throw some away."

She was shocked. "Oh no. I couldn't do that."

"Well, what will you be doing tomorrow?"

"Making the jelly, I expect. I have the little jobs while the others help to bring in the corn."

"And what about the next night?"

"Oh . . . well, if the jelly sets I might carry some to my Aunt Thomasin. I usually do and then, later on, she gives us some of her quinces."

I knew where her aunt lived.

"If you could make it about this time on the day after tomorrow, I should be finished work and I could meet you here again. If you like," I added.

"It isn't what I like. It's Father. He'd be very cross. He'd be cross if he knew I was talking to you now."

"Why?"

"We're not allowed to talk to people, well . . . men, or boys. . . ."

"Then he shan't know. I'll meet you here, about this time, the day after tomorrow." Already that moment had a luminous golden haze around it.

"All right," she said dubiously. "But if it rained, or if the jelly didn't set or anything . . ."

I carried the basket to the edge of the wood. She was ill at ease again and finally almost snatched it from me.

The next evening but one was quite fine; but though I waited about in the ride until it was pitch-dark she didn't come; nor did she any evening for the rest of the week. And when on Sunday all the other people stood about after church, greeting one another, gossiping, exchanging the week's news, and making the most of what, for those who lived in outlying places, was the only meeting during the week, old Rawley walked straight past and away and though I was so close to Elizabeth that I could have leaned forward and kissed her, she never even glanced at me.

The next week—though my work at Clevely was done and it was awkward to manage the time—I spent the evenings in the woodland ride; and the next Sunday was as unrewarding as its predecessor. It was plain to me that some action was needed.

The following week was the Harvest Fair in Baildon. Everybody had a holiday on that day. Even Uncle Francis took the day off; not because he approved of the various devices for parting labouring men from their hard-earned coins but because the Fair was one of "the old customs" and mixed up in the merrymaking there were genuine stalls where goods and stores for the winter could be purchased at less-than-market prices. My father, who had never respected anything merely because it was old, had heartily disapproved of the Fair on account of the low prices, which, he held, were unjust to the regular shopkeepers in the town.

However, the Fair gave me an idea, because on that Sunday, staring at the little curls on Elizabeth's neck, I thought how easy it would be, if she were almost any other girl, for me to ask her to come with me to the Fair. And so an idea fell into my head.

Some kind of sentiment prevented me from parting with the book Dr. Trudgett had given me; so I sold my Testament back to the printer who had been my father's friend. He scolded me heartily until I said, "But it is useless to me now. I know every word in it by heart."

Then he ruffled the pages and asked, "Is that so, indeed? Tell me then what follows the words, 'This fellow doth not cast out devils but by Beelzebub the prince of devils.' Go on from there."

" 'And Jesus knew their thoughts and said unto them, Every kingdom that is divided against itself is brought to desolation; and every city or house divided against itself shall not stand. And if Satan cast out Satan . . .' " I went on, glib and flawless while the printer stared.

"Enough!" he said at last. "As you say, you need this no more. How come you to have such knowledge of it?"

I told him that it, and one other, had been my sole reading for five years.

"Oh then," he said, "you wish another book . . ." and began to gabble about how much he would allow on the Testament against a new one, what new ones he had, and so on.

I was furious with myself not to have thought of making an exchange before; and I was furious with myself because even then, even with my plan in mind, I *was* tempted. I wanted another book, I was hungry for one. So I said gruffly what I wanted was money for the Testament; what would he give me?

I went straight to a stall of trinkets and bought a pair of shoe buckles, very plain, but good of their kind.

Next evening I walked boldly up to Rawley's door. The lower half of it was closed, the upper half open, and when I reached it, angrily and loudly announced by the yard dog, every member of the family seated about the supper table was turned towards the opening. I saw Elizabeth's creamy pallor change to the grey-white of ashes as she recognised me; I hated myself for frightening her; I tried to shoot her a reassuring glance.

Old Matt Rawley was in the process of lifting a thick slice of brawn balanced on a thicker piece of bread towards his mouth. He arrested it just long enough to ask,

"Whadda you want?"

I held out my hand in which lay one of the shoe buckles, now somewhat battered and scratched and far from new-looking.

"On Sunday morning," I said quickly, anxious to put Elizabeth out of her torment, "I picked this up in the aisle just after you'd gone past; and I thought it might belong to one of the young ladies."

One could imagine the flutter of interest and inquiry that such an announcement, made from some distance, would cause in any other family of five women. Around the Rawley table no one said a word. And only Elizabeth moved. She leaned back in her chair with a gesture of relief.

"Whad is it?" Matt Rawley demanded.

I took that as invitation to enter. I'm in, I thought.

"Shoe buckle, ain't it?" he said, as I laid the object beside his plate. "Any of you mawthers hev such a thing?" His fierce little eyes swept round the table, as though daring any daughter of his to admit to the possession of such an ornament. One by one they said, "No, Father." Then Mrs. Rawley said,

"My Sunday shoes have buckles. May I see? No. Mine are quite different."

"Oh well," I said, "I just wondered. I'll give it to Sexton. Whoever lost it will be asking on Sunday."

"It was kind of you," said Mrs. Rawley in her quiet little voice. It was from her that the girls had their prettiness and their gentle ways.

"It was a pleasure," I said. Then I turned about to Matt who was proceeding with his supper.

"By the way," I said, "I suppose you know about your gate at the top there."

"What about it?"

"It's down, post and all. I wondered. I noticed you'd got stock in the field."

He shoved the last piece of brawn into his mouth and jumped up. "You young fool, why the hell di'n't you say so afore. Stand there blithering about a pack o'nonsense time my cows get out. Come on. You can gimme a hand."

He blundered out into the yard, muttering. "One of them brutes musta rubbed agin it. 'Twasn't very stiddy certainly but 'twas all right last time I hitched it."

And it had been all right, that is no more tumble-down than anything else on the ramshackle place, when I unhitched it. Now it lay flat, with two broken bars; and the post with its rotted end lay beside it. I'd done a thorough job there if I never did another.

"Thass past mending," Matt said. "That musta bin the devil of a shove. I wonder if the brute as did that got out." He turned and stared towards the cattle, shadowy in the gathering dusk. "They seem all right. Eight. D'you make eight? Your eyes is younger'n mine."

I agreed that there were eight. He then began to direct me how to help him prop the gate in such a way that it would form a temporary stop-gap. The broken, sagging thing was difficult to handle, but when I dropped my end and wrecked it still further Matt Rawley's temper gave way,

"You clumsy young b——, you!" he said.

I put up a good show of resentment.

"Can I help it if your gate is so rotten that it falls to pieces in my hand? You should thank me for trying, not call me names. But for my warning you, you'd have your cows in the pound by the morning."

"Thass true. Thass true, too, that but for your help I'd hev propped this up. Broke past mending now, it is, thanks to you."

"It was that before I ever touched it."

" 'Twas not. By all rights you oughta make me a new one real cheap."

"Make you a new one!" I said, and laughed.

"Ah, so you should. Call yourself a carpenter don't you? And go round breaking folkses gates!" He was well away now, scenting a shrewd bargain.

"That does sound bad," I admitted. "Well, what would you call cheap?"

"You oughta do it for nowt! I find wood and you do the work. You broke it arter all."

"One bar," I said.

We argued very happily for ten minutes and finally reached an arrangement satisfactory to us both. I was to make him a new gate in my spare time in return for sixpence and my supper. I pointed out firmly that if I came direct from my ordinary work and worked until darkness fell I should miss my meal at home; and he said,

"Damn it, I'll give you some grub."

I think that apart from the Bywater merchant who had married Caroline Rawley I was the only person ever to be invited to sit at the Rawley table. Surely a good augury!

I did not hurry over the gate and managed to spend four evenings at the farm, eating four obviously grudged suppers with Elizabeth just across the table. She never spoke, and hardly looked at me, but it was joy to see her; and on the third evening, by cutting my finger a little and walking up to the house to ask for a bit of bandage I did manage to find her in the kitchen alone; and short and furtive as the meeting was it served my purpose, for we were able to arrange not only our next meeting but a whole series of meetings for the future.

Each Saturday one of the Rawley girls went to Thomasin Griggs' lonely little cottage to clean and cook. The old woman was Matt Rawley's sister and very like him. She was a widow, childless, and possessed considerable property in Baildon. The girls took strict turns because the capricious old creature demanded it, saying that Susan was the best brass cleaner, Ellen the best washerwoman, Emma the best cook, and Elizabeth the best company. They themselves adhered as strictly as possible to the rotation because the three-mile walk through Layer Wood and a hard day's work under a carping old woman was anything but a pleasure, especially in winter. Weather was never allowed to interfere with the routine, for Matt Rawley had great hopes of his sister; hopes never justified, for when she did die she left all her property to found almshouses in Baildon for "poor respectable tradespeople"—presumably those who had paid extortionate rents for the little shops which she had owned.

So every fourth Saturday it would be possible for me to meet Elizabeth and walk home with her. And with that, being young and simple and undemanding, we were, for the moment, quite content.

We did, of course, speak about other meetings, less furtive, less far separated; but the very mention put Elizabeth into a panic. She explained to me the origin of her father's order about not speaking to men.

"He's been strict like that ever since Caroline married."

"But why?" I asked. For everyone agreed that Caroline Rawley had married marvellously well. James Braddock, a well-to-do wool chandler was surely a good match for a girl from an outlying farm, however pretty she was.

"Well, you see; Father and James Braddock had arranged that Caroline should marry him when she was seventeen, and then when the time came Caroline didn't want to. She had got to know somebody else and wanted to marry him instead. She always was headstrong and though Father was mad as a hornet she stuck out a long time. He beat her—real hard, I mean, not just a clout—she was really black and blue; and then he locked her up and every day she had just a crust and a mug of water. So, of course, in the end she had to give in. But it took a long time. And then Father said he'd see that none of the rest of us took fancies like that into our heads and we were never to look at or speak to any man. Truly, Jon dear, when you came to the door that time I felt quite *sick*. I was so afraid you might say something and he'd know. Father's beatings are nothing to laugh at."

"I can believe that," I said. "All the same, when the time comes I shall marry you, you know. It might be quite easy. When I am twenty-three I shall have a bit of money and a trade to my hand."

"But when you are twenty-three I shall be twenty-two. Father will have promised me before that!" The thought struck me dumb; and she went on calmly. "Susan is getting married at Christmas; she's very lucky, her man is young and cheerful and nice to look at. Ellen is promised, and she's not much more than a year older than I am, and though her man is old—he's got children older than Ellen—and he's bald and hasn't got many teeth, she will be well off and she will get away. Emma now will never be married at all."

"Why not?"

"Well, there are two reasons. Emma isn't . . . well, not very pretty. I don't know whether you noticed, but she isn't as pretty as Susan or Ellen. And she is a very good cook. I've never known her spoil a dish, and whatever she makes, even pease porridge, somehow tastes better than ours. So Emma is the one who is to stay at home and look after Father and Mother when they are old."

"He's got it all arranged, hasn't he?" I said savagely.

"Oh yes. Even the farm. Because we have no brother—and do you know he still throws that at Mother, oh, almost every day—that is why Susan has such a nice man chosen for her. Robin Fulger has only just a little farm but it's next to ours, and the two are going to be put together and when Father is old Robin will work them both. And when they have a boy he's to be called Rawley!" She made this announcement with a kind of pride and pleasure and plainly shared her father's satisfaction over the arrangement. To me it was just one more instance, a particularly glaring one perhaps, of the dreadful domination of the old over the young.

"What beats me," I said, "is how your father sets about his match-making. Nobody ever sees you except at church."

"There's the stall," she said, as though that explained everything. Seeing my mystification, she explained that they had a butter stall on Baildon market place each Friday. It was there that James Braddock had seen Caroline, and the bald, almost toothless man had seen Ellen.

"With Robin, Father just went and arranged with *his* father. He'd had his eye on Robin for a long time."

"Do you go to tend the stall?"

"Not yet. Ellen and Susan so far, but when Susan marries then I shall go."

"Well, after Christmas I shall play hooky and come and visit the stall sometimes," I said. But that was one of what I called my unacceptable remarks. Elizabeth seemed to fear and dread any reference to the future or to any kind of contact other than these Saturday evening walks through the wood.

"Father is there, and very watchful," she said.

Susan was married at Christmas and *she* had a proper wedding because Robin Fulger's mother insisted on it, saying she wasn't going to have her son married like a hedge tinker. After that Elizabeth went to market every Friday and I had to wait for the third Saturday—Susan's marriage did do that for us—before I could ask my searching questions. Had anyone hung about the stall and then talked to Matt Rawley? Had anyone spoken to Elizabeth, stared at her, bought more butter than seemed normal? Every Friday I could imagine the dreadful thing happening.

One spring day I did as I promised and made an excuse to go into Baildon on a Friday. I did the errands that had been entrusted to me and then went and sat in the church porch, which overlooked the market, and watched. It seemed to me that every man in Baildon that day seemed to linger and stare as he passed the stall where the two pretty girls were selling the butter and the eggs and the little cheeses. And I looked ahead, half in panic, half with assurance. In November I should be nineteen and my apprenticeship would be done. If I could get my uncle's consent to my marriage I could present myself to Matt Rawley as a suitor for Elizabeth's hand. I wasn't rich, but I had more than sixty pounds laid by, for Uncle Francis had been meticulous about adding the shilling to the coffer's store, and I had a trade. I wasn't such a hopeless suitor. What I earned during the next four years would pay for Elizabeth's food and she could share my bed. (God, what that thought called up!) And she would be a help to Aunt Mary in the house. On the other hand, if out of timidity or diffidence I waited, some oaf, some lout, some beastly bald toothless rich old man—or worse, some rich and handsome young one—would step in. And I could not lose Elizabeth now; we'd never done more than kiss one another, or walk handed, but she was part of my very vitals.

The business of speaking to my uncle went badly from the start. The idea agitated me so cruelly that at my first attempt I went down in a fit before I had given him any notion of what I wanted to talk about. It must have been eighteen months at least since I had been so taken, and I was as surprised as he was. He had the sense to push a wad of linen between my teeth, and for that I was grateful. I could at least talk when I came to myself.

I could talk, and I was calm and lucid. I said that I had found the girl I wanted to marry, but that if I waited for four years I was afraid she would be married to someone else, so please would he give me his permission to be married at once. I outlined my plans for the arrangements of bed and board.

"And who is the wench?"

"I'm afraid that there are reasons for not telling you that until I have your consent, sir."

"Somebody you're ashamed of?"

"Not at all."

"Is it Bess Whymark of The Evening Star?"

"Good God no! Never mind the name. I'll tell you when you have said yes or no to the question I asked to begin with. Will you give me your permission to get married before I finish my journeyman's time?"

"I will not."

"Why?"

"I don't hold with married journeymen. For one thing they don't tend their work properly and for another it's awkward. You talk glib as sharing your bed and this house as ain't yours to share. Hev you thought what that means? Hev you thought about your Aunt Mary who's been good to you? Hev you thought about the three young 'uns you might breed in four years? How'd they fit in in a quiet house?"

"All right," I said. "Then will you give me your permission and pay me a proper wage—you could take it out of the money you hold for me. Clapper Green's cottage is empty. I could hire that and live there. Uncle Francis, it's my very life you hold in your hands; I must get married, soon. I can't wait until I'm twenty-three."

"Hev you gone and got a girl into trouble?"

"No. Of course not. What do you think I am? Look, promise on your honour not to tell. It's Elizabeth Rawley, and you know what her father is. He'll marry her off to the first comer who makes a good bid for her. And that mustn't happen."

"Now thass what I tell you about changing times," said my uncle, bringing one hand down on his knee. "When I was young a man got a roof to his head, a bed of his own, a chair and a table, and a few pots and pans and *then* he looked round for a wench to wed. You young 'uns nowadays got no foresight, you go at things like a bull at a gate. Do you really think Matt Rawley'd let his girl marry a fellow with four years still to do at his craft and not so much as a saucepan to his name? He've done well with his wenches, Matt hev, and the one you're sick for is the pick of the bunch, you young fool. He'll hev an alderman for her; don't, I'll go to sea."

"That's just what I'm afraid of," I cried. "If you can see that, you must see why it is essential that I speak for her *now*."

"Well, lucky I'm here and hev a hold on you. I can at least stop you making that much fool of yourself. See here, Jon boy. The best plums come at the top of the tree and to get 'em you hev to hev a ladder. The time'll come maybe, I hope and trust it will, when you'll be a master carpenter with a place and a business and 'prentices of your own . . . that'll be your ladder. *Then* you can look about and pick a wench whose father'll be glad to listen to you, and treat you respectful. And that'll be seemly. But to go to Matt Rawley and ask him to give his girl to come and tuck in *here*, thass just asking him to kick your teeth in, and he *would*."

"I'd risk that. If you would just give me your permission."

"Well, I ain't give it and I shan't. I got my pride like other men; and part of it is to see you a right proper craftsman, finished and set up; not to be kicked on to Matt Rawley's dungheap for a silly handless young fool."

The mention of *his* pride went to my temper like a flame to faggot; I stormed at him, my voice rising shrill and shaky, using abusive terms I hardly knew I knew. But he was not to be moved, and I realised that the noise I was making was no more than the yelping of a newly tethered puppy, half-choked by the chain. And lest, as with a puppy, my rage die down into a whimper of self-pity and my tears come and shame me before my uncle, I was obliged to dash out of the house, leaving him in every way the victor.

V

In the September preceding my nineteenth birthday Tom Rowhedge came home again. He had been away for more than four years; and if his previous absence had changed him from boy to man, the second one had worked an even greater change. Tom came home a rich man and a hero. He'd sailed from Bywater in the ship which his father had fitted out for him and with very little else, save his wits; he came home with money in his pocket, the title deeds of Merravay in his hand, and with his fame running before him like a courier. It is true that he had sailed away a whole and handsome man and returned with a patch over an empty eye socket and an ugly scar seaming one side of his face . . . but most men would have given an eye to have had his story.

He had made two or three modestly profitable voyages to Continental ports, carrying cargoes of wool and bringing back wines and silks and spices; and, but for his kindness of heart and his easily roused enthusiasm, might have continued in that trade, one of a thousand men who followed their bent, made a living, and remained unknown. But one day, in a low tavern in Calais, he fell in with an old English sailor who said he was a Devon man, and dying, and who was trying to beg a passage home because he wanted to be buried in Totnes. Hard drinking, and the new pox which had raged through the seaports ever since the trade with Africa had been established, had made this old man a very repulsive object to look upon; and, as Tom Rowhedge confessed to me, though he felt sorry for him he didn't fancy his company "on my nice clean ship." However, pity won the day and Tom made room for the derelict, who, once aboard and sober, seemed to take a new lease of life; even his horrid sores sloughed off. He began to talk. He said he had once been John Hawkins' gunner and he could give what sounded like a first-hand account of the disaster of San Juan de Ulúa; and he did know about the trade in blackamoors. He knew where they were to be bought, and what one should look for in buying them; he knew where they should be sold, and what prices should be asked. There was, he said, a fortune to be made in the trade because the Spanish colonists in America, having worked and whipped all the Indians to death, were now working and whipping the Negroes at such a rate that the demand was enormous while the supply was small and dwindling since Spain had forbidden the colonists to buy slaves transported by any but Spanish ships, and what with the searching and the fighting that resulted, none but the hardiest and bravest of the English would engage in the trade.

"Look what happened to Jack Hawkins hisself back in '68 . . ." The old man told his tale again. But he added that there was fortune to be made even yet by those who had the pluck to take the risk. Tom's ambition and enthusiasm took light; the old man, whose name was Jabez Trengrove, decided to postpone his death for a while and make one more effort to acquire that fortune which had lured him to sea so many years before. In return for showing Tom the ropes of the new trade, and acting as gunner if necessary, he was to have a tenth of the profits. So they made all things ready and set off for Africa.

As Tom told me this story—sitting on the lid of the dower chest on which I was carving a bride's initials and the date—I realised that he combined, in an unusual degree, a kind heart and a complete lack of imagination. Brought face to face with any kind of misery, he was moved to immediate pity and to alleviating action, but misery unseen was, for him, non-existent. So he sailed off in the highest spirits in his "nice clean ship," eager to engage in the dirtiest trade on earth. But when Trengrove found the river which he remembered and had led the way ashore and Tom saw the slave stockades for the first time, "Then," he said, "I began to have my doubts." Trengrove talked him out of them. He seems to have had a glib tongue. He said that left to themselves the blacka-moors ate one another, or were eaten, either by their human enemies or by crocodiles and lions; their customs were hideous, their diseases innumerable, and their expectation of life practically negligible. In fact, he said, the best thing that could happen to them was to be shipped to America, and nothing but their hopeless ignorance made the slave trade, the stockades, the collars and the bonds necessary. If they had the sense of lice they would swarm aboard and beg to be taken away. Tom let himself be persuaded, the more easily perhaps because he was just fall-ing victim to the fever which attacks every white man on his first visit to these unhealthy places. Trengrove concluded the bargaining, loaded the blacks, and brought the ship out to sea. They were south of the Cape Verde islands, where they meant to water, when Tom was well enough to leave his bunk.

"Most of the time I was sick, Jon, I'd either been building that first little boat of mine—you remember?—or was back at King Edward's; and wherever my mind was, my nose was conscious of a most horrible stink. If I was in my boat I used to think it was the river mud; if I was at school I thought they'd burnt the pease porridge again. But that day I was clear in my mind and knew I was aboard my own ship and what in Hell the stench could be I couldn't think. . . ."

When he knew, when he had traced the dreadful smell to its source and seen in the low, stifling hold, meant for the stowing of wool bales and wine barrels, the black men and women lying closer than salt herrings in a keg, on boards thick with the slime of their own excreta; when he learned that on an average five died each day, and were tossed overboard with no more ceremony than if they were maggoty apples, his horror and indignation knew no bounds.

"But you must of knowed," Trengrove said. "You must allow for half or rather more to die. The Middle Passage sieves them out, see? The good 'uns live and the weak 'uns die and you know them you sell is good stuff. That allust have been that way and allust will."

"Not on *my* ship," Tom said.

Trengrove's one fear was that Tom would allow the slaves out of the hold. He told a terrifying tale about a slave ship where the captain had thought that exercise and fresh air might reduce the death rate. One evening the batch being exercised had turned on the unwary crew and overcome them. They'd spared only the boy who had been in the habit of bringing them water. After that the ship had drifted since there was no one capable of steering her, and finally they'd set her on fire. The boy, and the black woman whom he had been "given" as a sign of favour, had been picked up and told the tale. "You don't want that to happen, do you?" Trengrove asked.

"We'll air them ten at a time then, and have the space where the ten have been swabbed down."

"Well, that'll keep us busy till we get to Curama," Trengrove said, lightly because he was relieved.

"I shan't wait for Curama," said Tom. "I shall unload them at the first place I come to."

"Now, now," said Trengrove. "We agreed on Curama. The prices there are the best in the world."

"B—— the prices!" said Tom.

Notwithstanding the alleviation in their lot the Negroes, homesick and seasick, continued to die. And Tom continued to fret despite Trengrove's repeated assurances that they were making the passage with a phenomenally low death rate. One morning when they were still full ten degrees east of Trinidad, Tom sighted a smear on the horizon.

"Land," he said to Trengrove. "Know anything about it?"

"An island," said Trengrove laconically. "You'll see a lot of them between here and Curama."

"Spanish island?"

"Could I know? There's scores of 'em in these parts. No bigger'n peppercorns lots of 'em. Chaps that ain't got nothing else to do land on 'em sometimes and stamp about and sort of christen 'em, either with their own name or the name of their favourite saint. I daresay that little dot is to let in a manner of speaking and if you were so minded and weren't all sail set for Curama, you could land there and call it Rowhedge Island, or St. Thomas. There'd be nothing to show for it, and the next silly b—— that came along'd give *his* name. See? Islands about here mean nothing till they've been took over and built on. This is the new world, remember."

"I see," Tom said; and turning, he called out to the man at the helm to change course and steer for the smudge on the skyline.

"So you want to discover an island, do you?" asked Trengrove, jibing but good-humoured. "Well, no doubt it's been discovered before and will be again. Islands are difficult to put a mark on."

"If this one is suitable for the purpose I'll put my mark on it," Tom said.

"How?"

"I'm going to chuck the blacks on to it."

And that, despite Trengrove's frenzied protests, was exactly what he did do. He landed himself first on what he described as a dish-shaped island about as big as Nettleton parish. The little peppercorn of an island bore no sign of very recent human occupation, but men had lived there once. He found some ruined huts smothered with creepers; a spring of water with the rock under its lip worn away where at some time women had rested their vessels. The clear water teamed with fish, and there were tall trees bearing bananas—a fruit which Tom tried to describe to me.

"I landed them there, Jon, boatload by boatload, and at first they were puzzled and fearful; but when they began to understand, they were like children let loose in a cherry orchard. It was wonderful. I felt like God! They dashed into the water and splashed about and sang and swam and shouted; they shinned up the trees after the fruit. They gathered flowers and made great wreaths to hang round their necks and my neck. And I stood there and stared at them and realised what they'd cost me! After four years of being my own master I'd got a ship without a cargo, a crew to pay, a savagely angry partner, and not a penny piece in the world."

"So *then* you decided to turn pirate, Tom?"

"Well, not exactly. What I meant to do was to come back to England and either ask Father for a loan, or, if he couldn't manage it, mortgage my ship for three or four voyages. I had to pay the crew, I had to give Trengrove his percentage—he'd have gone stark staring crazy, I reckon, before we got home—he was near to raving then; so when the old *Sancta Theresa* hove in sight, it was like an answer to prayer, Jon."

It was, of course, just Tom's luck that the *Sancta Theresa* was stuffed as full as she could hold without sinking with silver from the mines at Santiago, and with treasures from Cuzco, the Inca capital which the Spaniards had been stripping for nearly twenty years and hadn't yet picked clean. There was more wealth in that one vessel than a hundred small ships like Tom's could have earned by honest trading in a hundred years.

The little *Mermaid* brought the *Sancta Theresa* into port at Plymouth like a small dingy sheep dog bringing a great gilded sheep into the fold, and there were great rejoicings. By law and tradition the greater part of the immense treasure went into the Queen's coffers, but the share which fell to Tom and Trengrove, whom he insisted upon treating as his partner because he said that but for him he would never have done more than ferry across the Channel, was enough to make them moderately rich for the rest of their lives. Neverthless Tom was astonished and immensely flattered when the Queen sent for him.

I suppose that before he dies Tom will tell the tale of that meeting a thousand times; but I was amongst the first to whom it was told, for Tom rode straight from London to Slipwell afterwards and sought me out on the second day after his arrival in order to give me the present he had bought for me in London. Strange man, he had remembered that on that evening when I poured out my heart of discontent to him, I had mentioned my great dearth of books; and riding out of London, he had stopped in Cheapside and bought me three! Malory's *Morte d'Arthur*, More's *Utopia*, and Tottel's *Miscellany*. For a moment, with them in my hand, I also felt rich. Perhaps that is why I always think of Tom's interview with the Queen (about which he proceeded to tell me) as taking place in bright sunshine.

"What was she like, Tom?" I asked.

"Not like anything, except maybe the figurehead of a ship." He said that innocently, almost unintentionally, and then, quite suddenly saw the value of it. He slapped his hand on his knee.

"But that's it exactly," he exclaimed, astonished by his own perceptiveness. "That's what she's like—the figurehead of a ship just newly painted."

"Is she beautiful?" I had by that time a measure for beauty; I had my tally stick. *My* Elizabeth was beautiful; I was eager to hear how Tom's Elizabeth stood with that measure.

"Oh no," Tom said. "Not as a woman; but then how could she be? She is old, over forty you know. But nobody in his senses would think of that! I mean . . . who asks the age of a figurehead? If it is significant, and freshly coloured . . ."

I could see that he was still a little dazed by the one leap of imagination he had ever known. So I said invitingly,

"But she was significant then?"

"Oh yes. Not like anybody you ever saw, or thought about. She sat at the end of a big room at Whitehall Palace. That is difficult to describe, too. You see, Jon, it's bigger than Nettleton church, and empty—except for the people, of course. And she sat at the end of it in a chair, with a crowd of people about; all in very bright rich clothes. Well, then somebody said my name very loud; and the lords and ladies drew back a bit, so there was all that big open space for me to walk over; and I felt, Jon, like we used to feel when old Trudgett used to say, 'Come up here, boy,' only worse. The floor seemed to rock, you know. But I got across it and went down on my knee like a fellow outside had told me to . . . and then . . ." He broke off with a laugh in which there was some embarrassment.

"Yes, Tom, then?"

"Well, she patted my head, as though I'd been a good dog that had caught a hare for the pot! And she thanked me and said several pleasant things. Then she said, 'Stand up and let us look at you.' So I stood up, and I felt a thorough fool. And she said something about being handsome and what a pity it was about this. . . ." He laid a finger to the patch and the scar. And then she must have made some sign, though I didn't mark it; for all the people skipped away except for the two guards at the door. And then she said,

" 'I would knight you, Thomas Rowhedge, if I dared, but I dare not. And lest you think me a coward for saying I dare not, I will tell you why. His Majesty of Spain has a curious habit of misconstruing my actions and chooses to think that I commission my brave men to sack his ships; a thing I have never done, in peace, and never should. It would be so *unnecessary!* You smile—you have, I see, an understanding humour! Then you will understand that to set Sir Thomas Rowhedge on the Rolls would—shall we say?—*remind* those who watch that it was Thomas Rowhedge who brought the *Sancta Theresa* to port? And just at this moment that would be unwise.' I muttered something about not looking for any reward of that nature . . . you know the sort of thing one says at such moments, and then she said, 'But you have lost an eye, my good man, and that is a great pity for your beauty is marred now.' And she stared at me as though the loss of an eye were a very great matter. I mumbled again and what I said was perfectly true, Jon—after a bit you *can* see quite well with one eye. And then she asked me where I came from, and I told her Slipwell, where Essex joins Suffolk; and she asked me what my father did and various other questions which I would have resented from anyone else. Suddenly she snapped her fingers. Her hands are longer and thinner and whiter than anyone else's and she uses them more, Jon. She snapped her fingers and said, 'On that border there is a place called Merravay, is there not?' 'Yes,' I said, 'lying between Slipwell and Nettleton. There is a ruined castle there and some acres of good land gone derelict since my Lord of Norfolk went to the Tower. . . .' I chopped off there, it being a sore subject and verging on the political. But she laughed and said, 'I see you carry your sea eye ashore with you, Tom Rowhedge! Derelict it is and that is a pity. Well, since I am reminded of that estate, and since I have it in my gift and can dispose of it without a trumpeting that will sound in the ears of Spain, Merravay is yours!' And even while I was thanking her, you know, it seemed strange that with all she has to think of and to manage and control she should remember Merravay."

"They say she never forgets anything."

Tom gave his old cheerful chuckle. "Well, *that,* as old Trudgett used to say, 'is susceptible to proof,' Jon. Because then she asked me what I should do with Merravay, and I said I should build a house there and get the land under plough again, and make a place to retire to one day. And what do you think she said? 'I shall visit you,' she said. 'Indeed a house in that quarter will be a convenience for me. There is Hengrave, in Suffolk, which is a pleasant place indeed, and Framlingham, which I dislike heartily because of its associations; and Essex is thick with great houses; but hitherto on the border accommodation has been meagre. So look for me at Merravay, Tom Rowhedge.' That was her last word, Jon. And next day a pale-faced fellow brought along all the papers, sealed and signed."

"Well," I said; and "Well" again. And then I recovered myself a little and said, "It will have to be a big, grand house, Tom."

"Not too big." He had been sitting on his old accustomed seat—the sawhorse in our workshop; now he rose and began to walk about amongst the shavings and sawdust. "After the open sea, Jon, a man doesn't crave space; he longs for something cosy and close. I'll have a small house, but everything fine in it. After all, I'm the one who has to live in it. Look, this is what I've been thinking . . . tell me what you think of this. . . ." He took a splinter of wood, brushed away the shavings and litter from a space on the floor, and began to draw on the bare earth thus exposed. "Let's say a fair-sized hall—then if she *does* come there'll be room for her, and everything—about what? Fifty feet long by twenty wide; the door coming in here, with a screen, nicely carved to keep the draught out; the stairs going up *here* to the gallery. See? Now on this side a smaller room; twenty by twenty—that's big, isn't it? Big enough for me, anyway; with a huge hearth, and I shall sit at table with my back to it. Then I'll have the kitchens directly to the rear, so that dishes come hot to table; brewhouse, washhouse, storeroom; we needn't bother about them at the moment. Then look. The stairs come up here. Nothing over the hall, I think. People are beginning to floor over the hall nowadays, for economy's sake, but I needn't bother about that. The hall goes to the roof, apart from the gallery, that is. You see I have to bear in mind that she might come, and then we'd need a gallery for the musicians. Gallery along here, and then sleeping chambers could lead off. How many would I need, Jon? Eight? Ten?"

"You couldn't get many over the one chamber and the kitchens," I said. "Unless you had another floor."

"Oh, must I? I fancied a small house."

"Then have another room here," I said, taking the stick from his hand and adding my contribution. "See, that would balance better. The big hall across the front, two rooms, each half as large as the hall, behind, and then kitchens behind them. That way, if you didn't want very big sleeping chambers, you could manage."

"One must be a fair size. Suppose she stayed the night."

"One big one then, running this way, see?" And then I suddenly remembered something which I had heard. "No, Tom," I said. "That won't do at all. This plan is working out square. And I'm told that nowadays all the new houses are being built on an E as a compliment to the Queen. And if there's a likelihood that she will visit and perhaps even spend a night here, and she gave you the land and knows the house is new-built . . . by cock, Tom, if ever a house had to be an E it is this house of yours. Now, let me see." I scrubbed my foot over the lines already drawn and set to work again. I'd never planned a house before, never indeed thought of a house in terms of planning, but it seemed to come easily to me, and in a few minutes I had it drawn out on the floor.

"There you are, Tom," I said, in a voice that betrayed my elation. "There's your E. There you have your big hall, with the gallery above, and the kitchens handy behind it. Rooms to the left and right can be many or few, large or small to suit your fancy, so long as you build forward to make the top leg and the bottom, and set the porch in the centre for the third. Turn the face of the house to the south, lad, so your buttery and larder and storerooms stand cool on the north, and at one end of the gallery above, make a great bedchamber with another window to catch the morning sun—a chamber fit for a queen."

I stared at the lines scratched in the earth and the sawdust, and out of them I saw a stately house, a beautiful house, rear itself. A poem built not with words, but with timber and glass and stone and brick. . . .

"By cock!" said Tom, clapping me on the back, "now I can *see* it. Till now I've been in the dark. I had in mind some snug little place to tuck into when I got too old to go to sea. And when I told the Queen I'd build a house I meant in time to come. But now . . ." His eyes took on a far-away look. "Ah, Jon, I see it, with every timber seasoned oak, and red bricks for the walls. Come along with me, now, and let's go see where we'll set her. . . ."

So I rode pillion behind him again, as in our boyhood days, taking the track out of the village which could only be used in fair weather and which led on through Slipwell to Bywater.

Away back in the time of the Normans there had been a castle at Merravay, and there was an old story which said that in those days the sea had covered all Slipwell and the man who reared the castle had been warned that one day the sea would come up and engulf it; the name "Merravay" was supposed to have its origin in that threat. The castle had been ruined and deserted for many generations and now all that was left was a broken tower, no more than ten feet high. In more recent times, when the land was held by the Duke of Norfolk and tilled on his behalf, labourers had lived in the tower under a roof of reeds laid flat across it. This thatch had rotted and fallen inwards like the crust of an ill-made pie, but inside the thick walls the mark of old ancient fires could still be traced; and somehow that was pitiable. And the whole place had a sad, desolate air, so that even Tom, little fanciful as he was, turned his back on the ruins and said,

"The stones can maybe be used for barn or byre; for the house I'd lief even the foundations were new."

We walked forward and came to a dip in the ground where the moat had been. The water had drained away long since and it was now no moister than a ditch, and like a ditch, was full of ferns and dead meadow-sweet. Beyond, the ground rose gently but surely.

I looked about me, seeking the likeliest site. Then I turned and faced the sad ruins again. Between them and the edge of the moat where we stood were two great trees, unlike any I had ever seen before, very sombre with their almost black foliage. I did not know their name then, but later on, while we were building, I heard somebody say that he had been told that they were cedars, probably brought home as saplings by some owner of the castle who had been on Crusade. And it is true that there was a Crusader's tomb in Nettleton church. That morning, without knowing their value or their history, I could see their virtue in relation to our plans, and I said,

"Tom, if it were my house, I'd set her between those trees. 'Twill be years before any tree you plant is grown high enough to give shade in summer or shelter in winter. And if you put the house there you'll have this space for a garden and the dip will make a boundary between garden and field. . . ."

"If she'll lay there, Jon. Let's pace it out and see. . . ."

The space was exactly right, and the ground was level there.

"But they're melancholy things," said Tom, eyeing the black trees with small favour.

"The whole place has a melancholy air," I agreed, "but that is because it has been long deserted. And when your trees have grown these can come down."

So it was decided. On the way home Tom said he would ride straight on and engage Clem Hubbard, a master mason to do the building; "And you and your uncle must care for all the woodwork, Jon."

"It would please me to have a hand on your house, Tom; but an apprentice can't pledge for his master. You must see *him* about the business."

Privately I entertained a grave doubt as to whether Uncle Francis would take kindly to the idea of working on a house that was to be built with money stolen from the Spaniards who were real Papists, on land given to Tom by a queen in whose authority my uncle barely believed. He might easily not hold with it. I was surprised when, a few days later, he came to me, rubbing his hands and saying gleefully that we had work for two years ahead, building Tom Rowhedge's new house at Merravay. Some nasty carping streak in me made me express my surprise in one of my sweet-sour remarks, and he said,

"Bless the boy, what a simpleton it is! Why even in the good days when Queen Mary sat on the throne, the English hated the Span'ards and robbed 'em whenever they could! Why, if I met a Span'ard I'd rob him myself, if for no other reason than because a Span'ard put an end to the owd ways in England."

"How do you make that out?"

"Plumb easy. 'Twas a Span'ard married Queen Mary and used her so ill that she died broken-hearted. Anybody that was half a man 'ud hev stayed by her and bred a bevy of sons to stand between the throne and the bastard. . . ."

Even for Uncle Francis, in the privacy of his home, that was very plain speaking; he knew it and checked himself and looked, for a moment, ill at ease. Encouraged by the sight of his rare discomfiture I said mercilessly,

"But that is what I meant. If you think *that* of the Queen, you must think also that Merravay was not hers to give, however you skim round the idea of Tom's deserving a reward."

"Nor I do, in a way," he said slowly. "But 'twas wasted as it was, Jon. Been laying waste these many years. Surely 'tis better in Tom's hands." He recovered from the little setback which his slip of the tongue had occasioned and became his usual, ever-right, moralising self.

"You oughta be owd enough now, boy, not to pick holes in your own blanket. Take a look round you. Whass been ordered this month? A dower chest and a coupla milking stools! We ain't had a proper big job for months and with the harvest so bad we ain't likely to get one. We should all go down on our knees and thank God for Tom Rowhedge and the fine big house that'll mean bread for us and a dozen like us for the next coupla years."

As well as being pleased with the prospect of steady work for a long time my uncle was enjoying a sense of importance; for, as Tom had told the Queen, Merravay lay about midway between Nettleton and Slipwell, and so our carpenter's shop made a convenient headquarters for the conferences which were necessary before the house was begun. Tom's loyalty, or his lack of imagination, had led him to make the thing as purely local as possible. Clem Hubbard, the master builder of Baildon had said confidently that he could build a palace or a cathedral so long as he had a free hand and a plan to go by. He put his faith, he said, in a good foundation; building, like gardening, was a matter of digging deep enough; given eight feet of sound foundation underground, you couldn't go wrong. He was exactly like my uncle in his devotion to rule-of-thumb sayings and in his faith in his own ability. My uncle, who to my knowledge had never worked on anything bigger or more important than Rowhedge's new barn, and who really specialised in small, meticulously finished work, was equally confident when he talked about kingpins and beams nine inches square. He pinned his faith in sound wood. If you stuck to oak, well seasoned, and used plenty of it, and didn't scamp your pinning, you couldn't go wrong.

There were several such meetings in the warm, apple-scented evenings of that September before Tom went back to his ship. And they were always held in our shop. Sometimes there were as many as ten of us gathered the bench; for the man who made bricks at Maldon and the man who was supplying the timber and the lead worker from Bywater who was to cast spout heads bearing a Tudor rose, the initials T R, and the date 1577—these and their sons, or their journeymen, must all have a say. And unless it happened to be Elizabeth's Saturday for visiting her aunt, I was there too. Midway through the chatter and the amicable argument we would hear the scream of the well pulley and know that Aunt Mary was hauling the jug of ale from the deeps in which it had been cooling, and presently she would come in, quiet as a ghost, with the ale and the mugs and a plate of saffron cakes and a dish of damsons.

At first, in the centre of the bench there lay the piece of paper bearing the plan which I had drawn on the floor; it was always referred to as "Jon's picture"; presently it was joined by other pictures. Tom said, "I want the bricks laid herringbone fashion, Clem," and it had fallen to me to illustrate what he meant. It was the same with the spout heads. But though they valued the "pictures" as guides in what was—had they admitted it—pretty uncharted territory, they never allowed me to feel in the least important because I had made them. Nothing *really* mattered save good deep foundations, and sound, well-seasoned timber. And as I once said to Tom, "If in the end you get a house that is anything but a glorified barn, you'll have me to thank!"

So, on the first day of October we stood in the mellow sunshine while Tom took spade in hand and cut the first sod. Then Uncle Francis came forward with a handful of salt and gravely sprinkled it in the sign of the cross over the broken soil, and said, "Bless the ground on which we build, and the house that we build." And even those of the company who thought that very old-fashioned said, "Amen." Uncle Francis, though he was a carpenter, a master man, then took spade in hand and began to dig with the best, saying as he did so, "Well begun is half done!"

Then the mass of day labourers whom Clem Hubbard had engaged fell to work and began to dig the foundations along the lines which we had previously pegged out by the plan.

In that same week Tom rode off to Plymouth, where he had left his *Mermaid* for refitting. He was returning to the Continental trade, having had, he said, his bellyful of adventure. He said he intended to crowd in as much trade as he could in the two years while Merravay was building; "For I doubt, Jon, whether, once the place is finished, I shall ever willingly leave it again."

I said then the thing that had been on the tip of my tongue many times. "When you settle down, Tom, you'll have to get married."

"I know," he said, and laughed. "The trouble with me is I like so many wenches so much! I should have been a Turk!"

"And you never saw one you preferred above all?"

"No."

"You will," I said.

"I hope so," he said quite gravely. "The house will need a mistress."

I think it was then that my feeling for Tom suffered damage. It began like the hairline crack in a plaster wall which, left untended, will widen and let in the frost and the rain until it brings the wall down. And once the thing had happened I was surprised that it hadn't happened before; but it is true that, until he spoke of installing a wife at Merravay, I had not envied him. He had and he was everything that I had not and was not, and during my first wretched year at Nettleton I had often thought, Lucky Tom to be allowed to choose his own trade, but that was all.

Nor had I envied him his luck, his money, his fame, his meeting with the Queen; in fact, because he was my friend, and always so kind to me, I had felt a vicarious pleasure in his success. None of it was an encroachment upon *me*. But now I thought, quite bitterly—Yes, *you've* only to look round and wag your finger and you can marry any girl you fancy, whereas I . . .

VI

However I saw him off pleasantly and was flattered because although my uncle and Clem Hubbard set small store by me Tom said openly, "Jon knows what I want the house to be like. We planned it together and he made me see it; so if any question arises he is to decide." And all through the next year I was tolerably happy. The work was far more interesting and absorbing than any I had ever been engaged on before; working with a number of men was a pleasant change, saving my spirit from the constant rub of my uncle's company; now and then I was able to exercise a certain authority in the making of a decision; and so far there had been no mention of anyone "speaking" for Elizabeth. She still stood, each Friday, behind the butter stall, as open for offers, had folks but known it, as the dairy stuff she sold; and I still endured agonies for great stretches of time. I would meet her on a Saturday and walk from Thomasin Griggs' cottage to within sight of Rawley's, and my first question was "Has anything happened?" So far she had always said, "Nothing"; and I could then be happy until the next Friday when she went to the stall again. And that was a childish snatch at consolation, like whistling in the dark, because I knew perfectly well that someone might make approaches to her father at any moment of those six charmed days, even at the moment when we were walking along the woodland ride, telling one another that all might yet come right. Nevertheless I always felt better between the Saturday when I saw her and the following Friday; and then there were fifteen days to wait before I saw her again.

Still, the weeks and the months flew past, all the faster for this constant looking forward, this constant awareness of time; and I was twenty. In three years I should be free. Often we spoke of that. Often Elizabeth said, "I do want to marry you, Jon. I know I like you better than I shall ever like anyone. But I couldn't stand up to Father. Even Caroline couldn't, and she was very brave." And I would remember that she had been only a child when Caroline had defied that dreadful man; the beating, the locking up on bread and water, the final capitulation had all made a deep and lasting impression on her. She couldn't be blamed for that. So I would say, "But you would let me know. I wouldn't just let you go. I'd do something!" And she would say, "Of course, Jon. I'd let you know. And now let's talk about something else."

Generally I then went on to tell her how Merravay was growing.

It grew apace. And it was beautiful. Though I say—I who made the plan and said where the windows should be set and what patterns should be carved over the hearth at which, on cold nights at sea, Tom dreamed of warming his back—it was a beautiful house. I came to love it. There were times when it seemed more mine than Tom's.

He only saw it twice. He came home in the first February, when the walls were about roof-high and the inside no more than a skeleton, and he stamped about a bit and then said to me,

"The old men have done a good job, so far. But it looks raw and kind of lonely. I think I should put the garden in hand." He looked away towards Layer Wood and grinned a little sheepishly. "It sounds a bit lordly, Jon, but I happened to fall in with an old man who had a deal to do with the laying out of the garden at Hampton. He's crippled now . . . in fact he was begging in Plymouth when I found him . . . but if one took the trouble and had him carried about . . . he still *knows* about gardens," he ended almost defiantly.

"And what is lordly about that?" I asked.

"He worked for the Queen, and for the King, Jon."

"And now he begs."

"Yes. Isn't that sad?"

"He was lucky to fall in with you," I said.

They brought the old man in easy stages to Nettleton, where Tom arranged him lodgings at The Evening Star. And my uncle made a little wheeled cart, in which for the next few months the old man sat like a goblin, directing the laying out of the garden. Nobody liked him much, for, though Tom's kindness had brought him up from the gutter, he acted in a very disdainful way towards us all, calling us Johnny Go-to-ploughs, and bumpkins. Also he always held a long staff across his knees and did not hesitate to strike out with it if anyone annoyed him or got in his way. Once he even hit out at Clem Hubbard, who had stepped on a bed of young wallflowers. But he planned a garden such as had never been seen in our parts before, where even quite big houses, such as Mr. Turnbull's at Baildon, had gardens which had grown up haphazard and were more for use than ornament.

Unfortunately for me the more Merravay grew in beauty the more I loved it, and the more I envied Tom. And every time I envied Tom I fell to brooding over what might have been my lot if my uncle had let me buy myself out and go with him to sea when he invited me. *I* might then have had some money and could have been building a house, nothing like so stately as this one, of course, but a pretty little cottage for Elizabeth. Thoughts like that were hard to bear, and on the day when Tom arrived just at Easter, bringing food and wine and brandy and making an impromptu feast, all my stomach seemed to go sour and I was sick, physically sick. (I'd heard Dr. Trudgett pour scorn upon the theory of the ascendancy of the various humours in man; but a bilious humour certainly had me that day.)

Soon after Easter the bricklayers were paid off; and then the tilers; the lead-beaters came and fixed the handsome waterspouts and the guttering and lounged about waiting for a wet day to test their work and then went away satisfied. Finally only Uncle Francis and I were left at Merravay, putting the finishing touches.

The previous Saturday had been one of those golden-haloed days which came once in three weeks for me, and the fact that it was a drear dismal drizzly day, like so many had been that month, did nothing to lower my spirits. Truth to tell I rather liked a wet Saturday night, for then I could make Elizabeth walk under my cloak for quite a bit of the road—though we must always make sure that she did not arrive home too dry-looking—and now and again when we came to a particularly splashy place in the path I would lift her over. So light and warm and fluttery she was then, like a bird.

The evening promised well. At six o'clock it was almost dark and rain was falling. I waited at my usual place, as near to the old woman's cottage as I could well be and yet remain out of sight should she look from the tiny window; and when Elizabeth, carrying her basket, rounded the corner I opened my cloak and said, "Come under," and put my arm about her as I had done on a dozen similar evenings. But this evening, instead of coming under and nestling up to me like a bird, she said,

"No, thank you, Jon," and began to walk briskly along the path.

"What's the matter?" I asked. "Is anything the matter?"

I thought she shook her head. "Well then, why won't you walk under my cloak? You'll be soaked before you get home."

She walked more quickly until she was almost running. I reached out and took her arm, but my handhold was mostly cloak and she shook me off quite easily.

"Glory to God," I said, "what is wrong with you tonight?"

And then I saw that she was crying. Even that didn't bring me to a sense of disaster, for old Thomasin Griggs took an infernal delight in tormenting her nieces and it was nothing new for Elizabeth to emerge from that cottage in tears; but ordinarily she would run to me and tell me about it and I would kiss her and talk nonsense until she cheered up again.

"Is it the old she-devil?" I asked, hurrying along just behind Elizabeth, for the path was so narrow that two people could only walk abreast if both willed it. "Tell me, honeysweet, it'll be better if you tell me. What did she do to you?" This time I had a firm hold of her arm and pulled her to a standstill, swinging her round so that I could see her face, so small and pale and sweet in her hood, and only just visible, what with the trees' shadow and the early dusk.

"It isn't her," she said in a voice that was a crying voice but still more or less familiar. Then in a wild high one that I never heard before she said, "It's you and me, and Father . . . and Tom Rowhedge."

"Tom Rowhedge," I repeated stupidly. "What's he . . . ?" Then, of course, I knew.

To him that hath shall be given, and from him that hath not shall be taken the one thing that he hath.

"Darling, try to stop crying," I said; for now she was sobbing uncontrollably and I couldn't think as clearly as I needed to.

"When did this happen? When he was home at Easter?"

"I suppose so. I don't know. I do remember that week because we had market on Thursday because of it being Good Friday week. And he came and talked to Father and then he rode beside us as far as Goose Green and Father asked him to supper. And on Easter Sunday he came again. . . ."

"You never told me," I said harshly. For it was that kind of thing which I had dreaded each time I asked her if anything had happened since I saw her last.

"I didn't know. He never said anything. Nor did Father until the night before last when we heard that Chris Huxstable had died when they cut him for the stone."

She was still sobbing wildly and twisting my hands in hers, and her last sentence was the kind of non sequitur that occurs in delirium. I thought for a moment that she was raving.

"Chris Huxstable? What's he got to do with it?"

"Father said . . . oh, Jon, this is horrible, but he said it . . . Chris Huxstable spoke for me as long ago as last Christmas. But he was sick then and didn't want to be married till he was better. If he would have married me out of hand Father said he'd have struck hands on the bargain at once, then I'd be a widow and rich. But Chris said he'd try drinking the Walsingham water, and if that didn't shift his trouble he'd be cut. So you see, Jon, Father couldn't say aye or nay to Tom Rowhedge at Easter, because Chris was still at Walsingham then. But the water didn't work and so he was cut and he died and when Father heard he just said, 'Oh. Well, my girl, you'll have Merravay instead of the tannery; and it smells sweeter.' And that, truly, was the first I knew."

"God!" I said, "I'm glad of Hell! There should be Hell for men like your father. He'd have given *you* to Chris Huxstable, who stank of rotting hides and his own corruption till you could smell him a mile off. Darling, Lisbeth darling . . ." I clutched her to me, shuddering, aghast at the thought of what she had escaped. My mind rocked. "Tom is young and clean," I said. "But he shan't have you! And Tom is my friend . . . he wouldn't want to take my sweetheart." I had a sudden flash of enlightenment. "Honeysweet, I'll wager anything in the world that Tom spoke for you out of kindness. Tom has the kindest heart in the world," I said. "He'd want to save you from Chris Huxstable." I felt her stiffen under my hands.

"Thank you for that, Jon," she said, and pulled herself away and began to walk on.

"Oh, what have I said now? Lisbeth you know I meant no offence; you know, don't you, that I think you so sweet and pretty and altogether desirable that the King—if we had a king—might well seek your favours and count himself lucky if you smiled on him. But what I said about Tom is true . . . he is kind; and I'm quite sure that if I tell him that you are my sweetheart, he will withdraw his offer."

Alas, the further I plunged the deeper I went in the mire.

"You think it was so lightly made?"

"No, no. But Tom would understand. He has so much, Lisbeth. . . . I have so little . . . nothing but my love. . . ."

All wrong, all wrong!

"If you talk him into withdrawing, then it will be another Chris Huxstable for me," she said. "And though I must bear my father's arrangements for me . . . because he is my father . . . I cannot see why you and Tom Rowhedge should bandy me about as though I was a marble. . . ." She spoke angrily and began to walk again with short, sharp steps. Some sort of madness flared in me and I said,

"I'm beginning to think you *want* to marry Tom. Is that it? Maybe you think you're like Susan—lucky?"

"When I think of Chris Huxstable I know I am!" She stopped again, and wiped the back of her hand and the cuff of her sleeve across her face. "Don't be angry, Jon. We knew all along that we could never be married, didn't we? These times together . . . they were very sweet . . . I shall always remember them; but they were like something in a song, or a story, not a bit of real life. . . ."

She sounded very old suddenly, old and wise and calm. An appalling sense of loneliness fastened down on me. She had gone over; she was now on the side of the old men who arranged things without taking any count of human feelings.

"If you're so philosophic and resigned all at once," I said unkindly, "tell me—why were you crying when I met you?"

My bleeding vanity yearned for one word of comfort to staunch its wound; I wanted her to say that she minded, too. She gave me as honest an answer as any man ever had from a woman, I think.

"I was afraid you might be angry with me, Jon. I always cry when I'm frightened."

"And for *me* you have no feeling at all?"

"Oh that isn't true. Honestly, Jon, ever since the night before last I've been thinking . . . I know it sounds a strange thing to say . . . but I wished you'd never sought me out and talked to me and walked with me, because then I should be so glad that it was Tom Rowhedge and not Chris Huxstable that I'd be the happiest girl in the world."

"Oh," I said. I stood for a moment so coldly furious that I wanted to break her in pieces, and then all at once I saw what those words implied; poor little darling! Pity for her, and self-pity, and fury, and my feeling of being deserted all churned together in my mind, and far off, like distant thunder, I heard that warning crackle.

"Run along," I said. "Somebody calling . . . your father! Go! And be happy!"

I did not see her go. I had just time to turn round and thrust my thumb into my mouth when the crackling, flashing dark, saying be happy, be happy, BE HAPPY, closed down on me.

When it cleared the rain had stopped and the moon was high and the mud of the puddle in which I had been lying had soaked to my skin.

VII

Sitting there in the freshly whitewashed buttery of Merravay, I could look back and see all my life up to that point quite clearly, and quite dispassionately. But after that there was a blur. I couldn't eat more than a few mouthfuls without sickening and I learned that there are many levels to sleep. Ordinarily one dives in and is received in the cradling depths, but it is possible to float just under the surface, to be no longer fully wakeful, to be a prey to dreams, and yet not quite asleep. I did that every night; and every day I went to Merravay and worked and sometimes my uncle would say things—like he had just said that about my children's children and the stairs at Merravay—which pressed on my hurt.

But the brandy was good. It seemed to take the place of the food which sickened and the sleep which eluded me. For the first time for a week I felt like myself. I set the cup on the shelf and stood up. I thought, well, this is Merravay, the house which I planned and Tom paid for, the house in which Elizabeth will live. I shall never come here again; so I will look over it now.

This is the hall; fifty feet by twenty as we planned, with the screen to keep out the draught of the door. And, by God, the screen carving is beautiful; solid oak carved to the delicacy of lace; the best job Uncle Francis ever did. And here is the staircase, solid and sound, every peg six inches long, and such a lovely piece of carving on the newel posts: Moses with his staff turning into a snake. . . . I told Uncle Francis that story; he can't read, he doesn't approve of reading, he really wishes back the time when nobody in a village could read except the priest—and that in Latin—and yet he liked that story, and used it; so here is Moses, looking very much like Mr. Aldridge, J.P.; just his beard I swear;

and just about the look of surprise that he would wear if his walking stick turned into a snake. But it's a fine piece of work, and I hope when the Queen comes she will notice it. Elizabeth will have to make a curtsey to the Queen. And the Queen, if she is a woman at all, will envy her complexion and probably ask if she uses rose water or witch-hazel for it. And Elizabeth will surely give her an honest answer; she's extremely honest, my Elizabeth, Tom's Elizabeth. . . .

Ah well . . . here's the room Tom dreamed of; a fine square room with a good hearth, the board above it nicely carved too, though not so magnificent a work as the Moses; this is Tudor roses, very right and proper because it was the Tudor Queen who gave Tom Merravay. And who thought of that pretty touch? Jon Borage, bless him! Never at a loss. Tudor roses in this chamber; and in the other, across the hall, there's a sailing ship. And in both rooms there's this big fair window, with a window seat. In the morning Elizabeth can sit here in the sun; and in the evening she can cross the hall and sit in the other and still have the sun. And be happy! be happy! BE HAPPY! Better not think about that.

But you want her to be happy, don't you? Of course I do. She never did me any harm. She was my little honey-sweet love, my darling, my little bird, but the plums worth gathering grow at the top and you have to have a ladder; you have to have a ladder and you haven't got a ladder have you Jon Borage you haven't you have to have a ladder.

Come on now. You're upstairs. Here is the gallery where the musicians will sit, will sit, will sit and play when the Queen comes. Will anyone notice that it is carved in the lacy pattern and matches the screen by the door? At this end of the gallery is the state bedroom. You'd better face it, you know; they'll surely use it on the wedding night. What here? Yes; here. You know, Jon Borage, you are a fool. You could have taken her maidenhead; you know you could. Any night last summer when the hawthorn was in bloom and the cuckoo was calling. What a fool, what a cuckoo you were. There was your chance! She loved you then; she used to cling to you and kiss you and walk under your cloak when it rained. If you'd taken her then . . . and she'd quickened, he'd have been glad, Matt Rawley would have been glad, to have you make an honest woman of her. Oh, but she is honest; she told me why she cried . . . hardly any other woman would have done that. And then when your uncle asked, "Have you gone and got a girl into trouble?" you could have said, "Yes," and then he would have been all agog for you to marry her. Do you see? But she was like a flower, to be handled gently. Oh yes, gently, brought to market with the bloom on her, "Fresh violets!" . . . oh the fool that you were! Cuckoo! Cuckoo!

Pass we on. Here are six bedchambers, all square and sound. There'll be a little boy one day, and his hair will be copper-coloured and his cheeks will be rosy; and there'll be a little girl with black hair and a skin of cream. And maybe Elizabeth will say, "He shall be Thomas Jonathan." Would she dare? Why not? I never did them any harm; I planned this house. He'll say, "Of course, Jonathan, good old Jonathan . . . why does he never come to see us?" And the little girl will be Elizabeth Thomasin. Why Thomasin, darling? Because and because . . . but that is a secret. Because while that cuckoo called and while that hawthorn bloomed something that might have happened didn't happen . . . because life like sleep has different levels and on one level . . . Yes, darling, on one level you belonged to me.

There'll be guests and there'll be servants.

Let's go down again. What a fine kitchen! You could roast an ox by that hearth; doubtless you will. When the Queen comes. And at this end by the little fire . . . blackberry jelly, my sweet. You'll stand here and seal the jars down with a bit of pig's bladder and you'll carry them across here into the storeroom. . . . I shall always see your little purple-stained hands dropping the glossy berries into the basket. Will you see mine? Truly, my dear, I hope not; because you always knew that we had no future. You saw what I refused to see. So make your blackberry jelly, make your curtsey, make your little boy and your little girl and be happy! be happy!

And what of me?

I was back now in the hall, in the place from which I had started, near the window farthest from the stairs. And as clearly as I had seen what life held for Tom and Elizabeth, I saw what was left for me. Nothing. Nothing for my mind, because Uncle Francy didn't hold with book learning; nothing for my heart because he didn't hold with apprentices marrying. . . . I looked down a dark, cold narrow tunnel of years, a slipway to the grave; and despair, the last, the worst, enemy of man, came upon me. I saw myself going on and on through all the changing seasons, empty-minded, empty-hearted, with just my hands busy. Stools and cupboards and coffins. Even Merravay which I had planned with joy was finished now and such a job would never come my way again. I was nothing and had nothing to hope for. . . .

And I saw, with piercing clarity, who was to blame. My uncle had taken me, spoiled and deformed me as surely as though he had sawn off my head, cut out my heart, and used my dead hands for hammers. If he had done that, in a physical sense, they would have hanged him; as it was they praised him for his charity to an orphan! The Bible was wiser . . . it bade us not to fear those who killed the body but to fear those who killed the soul. It also said that man could not live by bread alone . . . bread, years and years of earning bread, eating bread, caring, thinking, knowing nothing of anything but one's bread. It wasn't bearable. . . .

I stood there and I died.

He bustled in, carrying in his hand the lopped-off top of a fir tree.

"Had to go a long way in to get a well-shaped one," he said. His voice rang very loud and clear in my ears, the voice of someone shouting down a well. I saw him clearly too. Every line and furrow in his face and the bits of sawdust on the lock of hair that showed under his white carpenter's hat looked as huge and distinct as cobblestones.

He went over to his tool basket and took out a length of white ribbon, which he folded and hacked into lengths with his knife.

I sat down on the window seat and watched him. He propped up the little tree and began to tie the bits of ribbon to its boughs. "This is for prosperity," he said, "and this for health." He mentioned long life and happiness, fertility and charity. Then he tied the last knot to the topmost bough and said, "God bless this house."

And I sat and watched him.

"In the old days, Jon," he said, straightening himself, "every house that was reared was blessed. And who can deny it, the houses stood better and the folks were happier. You and me are alone now, boy, and there's none to mock; so though I know you don't feel about the old things as I do, we'll go now together and put the Bless-this-house on Tom Rowhedge's roof."

The old things. The old way of thinking that a carpenter's boy must stick to his bench; the old way of apprenticing boys so that the master's will was law; the old way of making girls marry the man their father chose; the old superstitions . . . the idea that an omnipotent, omniscient God would look kindly on a house because of a bit of fir tree and some ribbon knots. Horrible, obscene!

Alive I might have ventured some futile protest. But I was dead. I rose and followed him out of the house and into the yard at the back. The space was paved with stones, even as eggs, so that on wet days no one would need to don clogs to cross it. My uncle took a ladder and reared it against the back porch.

"Now you on'y hev to stand by," he said, "and when I hev it fixed you say 'Bless this House,' and Heaven'll be so pleased to see us holding to the old customs, the blessings'll come tumbling thick and fast."

He climbed up the ladder and gained the roof of the porch. After that it was easy, for the planes had been so set that a man could gain access to inspect the tiles or clear the snow from the gutter between the gables. I saw his long knobbly legs in their coarse grey hose and the seat of his soiled, baggy breeches disappear. I heard the scratch of his nailed shoes on the tiles. Then there was silence, and after a space, his voice.

"God bless this house," he said earnestly.

The stick-crackling sound began in my ears. And this time the voices about which, long ago, Dr. Trudgett had inquired did make themselves heard. First, very faint and far-away the voice of my father saying things about the chains which superstition clamped upon men; then Uncle Francy's voice saying that he didn't hold with schooling and did I think

Matt Rawley would let his daughter marry a fellow with four years still to do at his craft; and then another voice, soft, persuasive, and unrecognised. The voice of hope. . . . Yes, at this moment, when all hope was ended, there was the voice, the indomitable voice, saying to me that Elizabeth and Tom were not married yet, that there was money in the coffer, that death cancelled indentures and the world was wide.

For a moment everything seemed marvellously clear and I thought what a fool I had been not to think of this sooner. Then the darkness and the confusion which I knew so well began to close in. A darkness shot with sparks and flashes of horrid light. In one flash I saw him coming, carefully, spiderlike, along the ridge of the porch and towards the ladder. I put my left thumb in my mouth for I knew what the whirling and the darkness and the lights portended; but at the same time I laid my right hand on the ladder. The sound of its fall came sharp and hard through the crackling noises; the sound of his fall was just a soft thud. The voice in my head began to scream as it drew away into the distance.

And then it was quite dark and very quiet.

Interlude

That autumn was long remembered. Seldom, if ever before in the course of their long history, had the parishes of Nettleton, Clevely, and Slipwell been shaken by such a series of dramatic happenings.

There was first the tragedy—the almost double tragedy—at Merravay. The ladder had slipped under Francy Sheply's feet and cast him to his death; and the boy Jon, finding him thus, had been taken with a fit of such severity and length that he, too, was taken up for dead. Indeed the hastily summoned helpers who lashed planks into rough stretchers and carried them back to Nettleton were convinced that they carried two corpses.

This story, exciting enough in itself, was lent a peculiar embellishment by the behaviour of Mary Sheply, who claimed to have had a warning. Because she was so silent and unobtrusive a woman people tended to believe without question her story of how, just at sunset on the day of the tragedy, she went to fetch a last pail of water from the well, and had "a feeling" that something untoward had happened. She ignored it for a while, but when supper was ready and darkness complete and neither of her men had returned, she—who never ventured forth alone—walked into The Evening Star, looked round, and, not finding what she sought, said,

"Is there a man here who will come with me to Merravay? I have a feeling that something has happened to my husband."

On the way, accompanied by three or four kind-hearted fellows, she spoke again.

"I should have come at first warning, before it was dark."

Afterwards they took pains to assure her that even an earlier arrival could have done nothing for Francy. They said, too, how fortunate it was that she had acted in time to save Jon; for that night brought a sharp frost, and lying there with the life at such low ebb in him, he might have died too. As it was he was up and about again in time to follow his uncle to the graveyard, where the sad rites were considerably enlivened by his falling into another fit.

The account of these disasters had just reached the most outlying farm and cottage when from the centre of Nettleton village a new story began to ripple. The story of Jon Borage's almost inconceivable conduct. After all, said the gossips, he was an orphan, and Francy Sheply had been a father to him, far more dutiful and conscientious than many fathers were in these days. The gossips could name one or two men who had done less for their own children than Francy had done for Jon. And Mary had done her duty by him too. One would have expected that he would now turn about and do his bounden duty, which was obviously to stay in Nettleton and ply the carpenter's trade and keep a roof over Mary's head. But no! A most amazing thing had happened.

Francy Sheply had died on a Saturday and been buried on the following Friday. On that Friday Jon had fallen into a fit and for several days had been carefully and lovingly tended by his aunt. On Saturday he had risen from his bed and staggered to the chest where his uncle had kept his savings. The total sum amounted, they said, to just over one hundred pounds sterling. The boy had claimed fifty.

Mary Sheply, suddenly garrulous, had reported the scene.

"Jon said to me, 'This was what my father left me. Francis Sheply put it away—I hope before your eyes,' and I said, 'That is true. I saw him do it.' And then he said, 'He added a shilling for every week of toil I bore, but that I will not take. That is yours.' And I said, 'But it is yours by right, boy.' But of that he took no notice at all. He took his fifty pounds and said that now he would go to Cambridge. But when he said it he shook and trembled and his face went all awry so that I feared he would be taken with another fit. But he did not. He grew calm and told me the value of the timber and the tools and what I should ask for them; and then he kissed me and thanked me for my care of him.

"And I said, 'Do you go straight to Cambridge?'—because it was in my mind to pack him some food in a poke against the journey. And he said he had something to do first. 'If this thing had come about two years ago,' he said, 'I could have gone straight with a free heart, but now it is late.' And with that he left me."

Sympathetic hearers condoled with her, the victim of such monstrous ingratitude. But she said, "He was always longing to be elsewhere. I knew from the first; but my man was not one to be gainsaid. Now he is gone and it is better so."

This story had not reached the outskirts before another was hard on its heels. And the next happening, because it might have fallen upon any one of the villagers, took pride of place. In order to fall from a ladder one must climb one; in order to be deserted by an ingrate nephew one must adopt one; but anybody, anybody walking in the darkness alone, might be set on as Elizabeth Rawley was. And the thought "That might have been me" lends a sharp edge to one's appreciation of another's narrow escape.

Elizabeth Rawley had left her Aunt Thomasin's cottage at the usual time. As was her custom during winter she carried a small horn lantern as well as her basket. What was unusual—and this gave rise to endless speculation as to whether or not the attacker had had information or motive—was that on this evening the basket, instead of containing some trivial domestic offering, held part of Aunt Thomasin's wedding gift to her niece. Thomasin Griggs was mean and miserly, but Elizabeth was her favourite niece and the cloud of senility was thickening about the old woman's mind. All day, ever since Elizabeth had told her of her betrothal, which she did as soon as she arrived, Aunt Thomasin had been diving into chests and cupboards and bringing out articles, some worthless, some of value and piling them together, saying, "All for you, my dear; all for you." Elizabeth, before she left, had loaded her basket, leaving the rest of the pile to be carried home gradually; and being a shrewd girl, she had selected the most valuable of the goods, since there was considerable likelihood that Aunt Thomasin's mood would change and the articles return to their hiding places. So she had in the basket a fine copper skillet, a pewter meat dish, two silver spoons, a horn mug bound with silver and a three-parts-finished patchwork quilt, work upon which had outlasted the old woman's eyesight. Laden with spoil and in high spirits, she had set out for home.

Two hours later, without lantern, without basket, with her clothing torn and muddied and her mouth bruised and swollen, she staggered into the kitchen at Rawley's in a state of hysterical collapse. It was a long time before any coherent statement could be drawn from her. Questions, cosseting, and hot milk laced with a spoonful of Matt's precious hoarded brandy having failed, the father's temper gave way and he shouted at her to stop that blether and speak or he'd try what a clout would do. And so presently the story came out. A man, a stranger, had jumped out of the bushes, hit her in the mouth, knocked her down in the mud, and run off with her basket.

"And was that all?" Matt demanded.

Elizabeth nodded, putting her hands to her mouth.

"All? And enough, surely," her mother said.

It was Emma who said, "But you're over an hour late, Lisbeth. And this all sounds so quick."

"I lay dazed; and . . . having lost my lantern in the scuffle, I walked slowly," Elizabeth said. And having said that quite calmly, she broke down again; so that they saw that further questioning would be useless. Grieved as they were for the loss of the skillet, the dish, spoons, mug, and quilt, but thankful that the thief had been content with taking what was replaceable, they got her to bed.

With the first light of morning Matt Rawley walked along the woodland ride, intent upon the recovery of the lantern. Elizabeth said that when the man jumped upon her she dropped the lantern and it went out; so there was a chance it had been overlooked; and it was a good lantern, worth fourteen pence.

Such carefulness merits reward. The lantern lay there beside the path, and near by the stiff, bleached grass and some bushes with broken twigs bore out Elizabeth's story of a struggle having taken place. Matt retrieved the lantern, walked on as far as Thomasin Griggs' cottage and told her the tale, briefly, and then returned home. At some point along the path his attention was caught by a gleam of scarlet amongst the dun of the thicket; investigating, he drew out a patchwork quilt. The thief had evidently thought it too bulky, or too recognisable, and had thrown it away. Which proved him a fool; for Elizabeth had prudently rolled the two silver spoons and the mug in its heavy folds.

After that Matt walked slowly, keeping, as he said, his eyes skinned, though hardly expecting to find further treasure. He did not leave the path, or search very thoroughly, which was perhaps a pity; for everything which Elizabeth had lost was there within a stone's throw. The quilt, a bulky bundle, had not made quite such an arching flight as the other things, that was all. And on the other side of the path, in the little hazel coppice from which Jon Borage had once cut a crook for Elizabeth's blackberrying, there was something else which would have interested Matt Rawley very much.

But that lay hidden with its hopes and its despairs, its love and hatred, its frailty and its sins for almost three hundred years.

Through all the dark of that winter women feared to venture out alone and men talked sternly of what measures should be taken to suppress such sturdy beggars and vagabonds as the one whom Elizabeth Rawley had encountered.

At Christmas Tom Rowhedge came home and married Elizabeth Rawley and took up residence in his fine new house, and in the August of the following year Elizabeth, who should have known better than to indulge in such activities when heavily pregnant, slipped from the stool on which she was standing to turn her ripe cheeses on their rack. The fall precipitated the birth, and the child—a boy—was born some six or seven weeks before his time. That, of course, accounted for his frail and delicate appearance.

In June of the next year 1579 Her Majesty the Queen kept her promise to visit Merravay. Tom Rowhedge, honest man, knowing his limitations, forebore to attempt the masques and plays which other of her hosts—often less well founded than Tom—devised for her entertainment. On the lawn, now grown smooth and green, which stretched between the house and the edge of Layer Wood, he set up a Maypole; and there, until sunset, the young people of three parishes performed, under the indulgent royal eye, exactly the same ritual dances, "Gathering Peascods," "Hayman's Hoff," "Granny Go Far," as they ordinarily measured upon the village green. And when the sun was down the rural musicians moved with their fiddles and their horns and their cymbals into the gallery of the great hall and played while a mixed company sat at feast below. Tom made the one courtier speech of his life when he said,

"Your Grace commands even the seasons. Ordinarily such food and such company come together only after harvest; and then we call it a 'horkey.'"

And the Queen said, "I have never been present at a horkey and this pleases me well."

And once she looked round and pressed her long thin hands together and said, "This is the very heart of England. My thanks, Master Rowhedge, for bringing it so close to me."

In the morning, just before she rode off for Framlingham, she brought up, out of that memory of hers where nothing was ever mislaid or mislabelled, the recollection of her half-intent to knight Tom Rowhedge.

"Now I can do it and the Spanish ambassador will feel no prick. I can knight you, Master Rowhedge, for the best hospitality I have known on this journey."

That evening young Thomas Rowhedge, with a good dose of poppy-head syrup soothing his stomach, slept peacefully while in the small west-facing room his father and mother, careful folk, supped upon the remains of the feast of yesterday. Tom Rowhedge, worrying the last fragment from a chicken bone, suddenly paused and stared at the fireless hearth above which wreathed the Tudor roses which Francy Borage had carved.

"Lisbeth," he said, "I reckon that now we'll rate a crest; and I know what it shall be. My ship is the *Mermaid,* and my Maypole pleased the Queen. We'll have a mermaid with a Maypole behind her. If that is to your fancy."

Elizabeth thought that that would do very well.

And then Tom said,

"You know, all these two days Jon Borage has been in my mind. He it was that planned the house, 'fit for the Queen' as he said. I wish he could have been here to see her in it and to see . . ."

He broke off, astonished, because his wife had begun to cry in a wild, distraught fashion.

Quite understandable, of course; so much strain and excitement, for a woman in her condition. She was carrying her second child, the boy Matthew who was, in looks and liveliness, greatly to surpass his brother. Young Thomas, however, remained his mother's favourite, and largely due to her unremitting care lived to inherit Merravay, to become one of James I's original baronets, to marry late in life and beget one child, unfortunately a girl.

The Witch

YESTERDAY, when I asked Master Turnbull to add to his kindness by sending me some writing materials, he, thinking that I intended to write letters, warned me to be very careful what I wrote. He is sceptical of the charge they have brought against me and hopes for an acquittal. I am less hopeful, perhaps because I am less certain of my innocence.

Most people accused of witchcraft—and the number so charged has greatly increased in the last few years—violently and vehemently repudiate the accusation, but some, whom I privately suspect of being crazy, admit it and go to their doom muttering curses and incantations and expecting, I fear, some magical intervention at the last moment. Even those who proclaim their innocence seem to know about things which mean nothing to me; they speak of incubi, succubi, familiars, midnight brews, sabbaths, and covens; but now and then I have a troubling suspicion that these things are only the rubbish which clutter the edges of that unknown world and that maybe I missed them and went straight to the heart. Perhaps I am the only person who, asked whether she were a witch or not, could truthfully say, "I do not know." I do know that some very strange things have happened to me, or through me.

The first occurred when I was eleven years old. I was then living at Merravay with my father, Sir Thomas Rowhedge, who was almost bedridden, and my grandmother, Dame Elizabeth, who bore me a grudge because, being the only child of my father, I had been born a girl. I was very young indeed when a conversation between my father and grandmother sent me stealing into the kitchen to ask old Annie, my friend and comforter, "What is the difference between a boy and a girl?" Annie said, "They're a different shape, love," and gave me a piece of pork crackling to chew. The untimely gift and the note in her voice convinced me that of the two shapes I was the wrong one.

My grandmother was always busy with the affairs of the estate and the household, and with looking after my father, whom she loved so dearly that she was jealous of the very hound he fondled. He was busy, too, with the books he read and the poems and plays which he wrote; but he was kind and I should have spent more time with him had not my grandmother stood between us. As it was, I sought company in the kitchens and yard, and at the time of which I am writing I had found the—to my mind—perfect friend. His name was Robin and he looked after sheep. His father had been hanged for stealing and his mother had married our shepherd and had three or four children by him; there was little room for Robin in heart or home. Once he was sure that I was friendly and no spy for my grandmother he accepted my company gladly and we had merry times together. Despite his hard life he was cheerful and kind; he knew many songs and old stories; he could make wonderful whistles out of an elder twig, and he could sing like a blackbird.

One October day he told me that on the following morning he was to walk over to Ockley to fetch home two dozen sheep which my grandmother had bought from the Fennel flock. I said I would go with him and take a bag dinner; he was always hungry. I also said I would try to get a horse, then he could ride pillion to Ockley and, coming home, we would ride and tie. I was rather proud of my skill as a sheep drover.

It was a blue and gold morning with a singing wind and I was skipping blithely over the cobbles of the yard on my way to the stables when my grandmother rapped on a window and demanded to know where I was going. She was immensely annoyed. It would look well, would it not, she asked, for me to appear at Ockley as a sheep wench! And what had I in the bag? Annie had seen to it that I had a thoroughly good bag dinner; two crusty loaves, a cold pheasant, a hard Suffolk cheese, six apples, and some walnuts. "A little food," I said. But when I was back in the Ship Chamber and my grandmother took the bag from my hand and swung it so that it caught me a clout on the side of my head it did not seem so little. All day, as I sat by the spinning wheel to which she condemned me, my head rang and throbbed.

I watched Robin go trudging off alone; I knew he would have nothing in his bag but a slab of cold porridge. And he would think me faithless. He should have come back at five and I edged my wheel nearer the window so that when he came I might wave and indicate by grimaces what had happened to me; but dusk came and then full dark and still he had not come. We were at supper when someone ran in from the kitchen to say that Sheep Robin was back and that he had lost four sheep on Strawless Common, where a great dog had run out and scattered the flock. He had searched as long as the light lasted but had only rounded up twenty.

The sheep were of some breed which my grandmother had coveted for a long time and the loss sent her into a screaming fury. Carrying with her the chop bone which she had been picking, she hurried into the yard and shouted to Robin that he must go back and search again and that if he didn't bring back the sheep she would see that he was hanged as his father had been. When she returned to table my father said mildly, "That was a dire threat; the poor boy may have taken it literally."

"I meant it so," she said, and leaned over to hack herself another chop.

I spent most of that night on my knees, praying to God to help Robin to find the sheep.

I was early about, and hopeful, but he had not returned; and shortly before noon my grandmother despatched Robin's stepfather and another man to help with the search. They came back at dusk. They had found no trace of the sheep; but they had found Robin, hanging lifeless from the bough of a tree on the edge of the common.

My father was quite peevish and said, "There, what did I tell you?"

My grandmother said, "I consider it proof of guilt."

I could only think that Robin would never sing or whistle or laugh again. And he'd had such a poor life; even his last day had been darkened by disappointment. It was quite unbearable. I imagined him searching and searching, growing desperate, tired to the bone, cold, hungry, and frightened. . . .

Once safe in my own room I cried and cried. Then, remembering my prayers of the previous night, I grew savagely angry with God. "King of Kings whose power no creature is able to resist," it said; couldn't He have called those sheep back, wherever they were? "Not a sparrow falls," it said, but Robin had dangled, lifeless. And who cared? Nobody but me.

And then there came into my mind, neat and complete as though somebody had spoken it in my ear, the remark, "But you must allow for the Devil!" And then out went my candle.

There was nothing unusual about that; for though we made our own and had great stores of them my grandmother doled them out meanly and I was quite used to undressing in the dark; but the failure of my candle drew my attention to the passing of time for it had been new that night. I hurried into bed and there I began to think about the Devil.

I am trying now to be entirely honest. I did actually find *comfort* in the thought that the Devil had, on Strawless Common, defeated God. I much preferred that thought to the thought that God hadn't cared, hadn't helped Robin. I thought all the way back to the story of Eden. God, all-loving, all-wise, had surely wanted people to be happy and healthy and good; it was the Devil who spoiled it all . . . and since so many people were miserable and sickly and bad the Devil must indeed be very powerful. The lifeless, voiceless thing, lately a singing boy, which they had cut down and put under a sack in the barn to await an unhallowed crossroad grave seemed to me to prove the power of the Devil.

But I must insist that though, at that moment, I was forced to acknowledge his power that was all I did. I did not applaud it; I was indeed sorry. I was on God's side. . . .

Having pursued that line of thought to its conclusion, I began to think more practically. I was quite certain that Robin had neither lost the sheep through carelessness nor connived at their removal from the flock. But I knew how in quiet country districts like ours stories passed down from generation to generation, and I thought that what I wanted now—all I could want for Robin—was that in years to come when men told the story by fire on winter nights they should add, "And after all, those sheep were found."

Suddenly that became a matter of the utmost urgency. It sounds absurd now . . . but at that time I was only a child. . . . I reached out in the dark and took in my hand the last whistle which Robin had made for me. I said, in my mind, "Robin, I swear by this whistle that I will . . . I must prove your innocence." And then it happened. I saw as clearly as I now see this quill and this paper, a disused clay pit, so long abandoned that grass and nettles and willow-herb had grown about its slopes; and seven wind-bent young hawthorns leaned over its edge. I thought, Ah! that is the place, and in the morning I shall go there and find those sheep. And I fell asleep as though I had been poleaxed.

At first light I stole out of the house, saddled a horse, and was away. There had been a light hoarfrost and all the world was webbed over with a grey-white shining veil.

I rode blindly, making for Strawless Common, which I had never seen, but I knew its direction and I had heard it described, and roads in our parts were few. I recognised it when I arrived, a great rough stretch of common land, a space of rabbit-burrowed turf, dotted with gorse bushes, blackberry brambles, heather clumps, and stunted hawthorns. At one edge a few clod cottages stood, and the animals belonging to the cottagers, sharp-boned donkeys and cows and goats, lived on the meagre pasture of the sterile land; and beyond these unsatisfactory grazing places the common stretched away to Ockley. I realised that I might search all day every day for a week without finding what I sought; so I did what I have heard of fogbound travellers doing. I laid the reins on my horse's neck and said, "Now go."

He seemed to pick his way as daintily as a dancer, skirting a heather clump, rounding a bush, avoiding a rabbit hole; and all the time I wondered why, free of guidance, he had not turned and made for home. Certainty mounted in me as he moved, and I was not one mite surprised when at last he checked and there was a row of seven wind-bowed hawthorns, with their berries shining darkly red under the frosty cobwebs. I slipped out of the saddle, said "Stand," and walked forward, passing between the trees.

And there was the pit, full of grass, nettles, and willow-herb, and at its bottom four woolly carcasses, horribly mangled and bloody, and standing guard over them, roused from glutted slumber by my approach, was one of those great fierce herd-hounds which poor men keep . . . and keep hungry to foster their natural fierceness.

I knew with a certainty beyond all doubt that on each woolly, bloodied haunch there would be the Fennel mark, the arrow of red ochre, cancelled out by a tarry stroke . . . but I meant to see. When I faced my grandmother with the truth there must be no undermining shadow of doubt. I began to let myself down into the pit. The dog resented that. As I slid and shuffled along the slope he raised his hackles and began to circle about his kill, and when a final slither brought me to the comparatively level ground of the pit's bottom he came forward menacingly. And all at once I was furious with him. Granted he was hungry . . . he had killed Robin and was now prepared to defeat me in my determination to clear the dead boy's name. Damn him, I thought. I was armed only with a little light switch which I carried more for show than use, for my horse, well fed and well trained, needed neither stimulus nor correction. As a weapon it was negligible and evidently the dog thought so, for as I stepped forward he came on, stiff-legged, his eyes shining green, his muzzle wrinkled back to show his long fangs. And something snapped in my head.

"You devil!" I yelled at him. "I'll kill you. I'll kill you!" I raised the little switch and went forward. I saw the menace in his eyes turn to terror; the wrinkled snarl smoothed out. His tail dropped; he pivotted round on his hind legs and went tearing across the pit's bottom and scrambling up its far side.

I made sure of the marks on the wool and then turned and began to climb back towards the hawthorns. When I was almost at the top the thyme-covered hummock on which my feet were braced gave way and I was left with my hands frenziedly digging into the edge of the pit while my feet sought for hold in the raw clay. And it was then that I called to my horse, as though he were a person. "Come here," I said. And he came. "Nearer, so that I can take hold of the bridle," I said. And when I had gripped the rein I said, "Pull!"

I swear that at that moment there seemed nothing strange or unnatural about it at all. When I mounted and rode back to Merravay to face my grandmother there was nothing in my mind except simple triumph because I had proved Robin's integrity. And later on all the wonder I felt was concerned with the fact that I had had a vision of the place where the sheep lay. That the dog had feared me and the horse obeyed me did not seem strange at all. Yet it is all this talk about animals, horses and dogs, which is to be my undoing. . . . And even as I feel bound to protest that no animal has ever been my "familiar," I know full well that if on any market day I leaned from the little slit of a window which admits light and air to this cell and said to a herd of beasts on their way to the slaughterhouse, "Turn about and face the blows and go the other way," they would do it. I know they would. They would do it because I *know* they would. But does that make me a witch?

II

All through the next year each change of season reminded me of Robin and started the pain anew. I wept for him when the first lambs bleated, when the first hawthorn buds broke white, when the first cuckoo called. Fortunately for me my father, who was not without guile in his own way, countered my grandmother's complaints about what she called my "runagate behaviour" by determining to teach me to read and write. The next few years passed rapidly and without incident, at least so far as this confession is concerned.

There came the harvesttime when my grandmother said, perhaps truly, that I was too big to go and help in the fields; my part in the corn-gathering was henceforth to be confined to the baking of big flat saffron cakes known as "harvest buns" and the making of the very small small-beer which was provided for the workers at this season. Working with, and under the eye of, the old woman whose resentment towards me seemed to increase with the years was far from pleasant and I was not wholly sorry—God forgive me—when my father took one of his "summer colds" and needed all her attention. We were all used to his indispositions and the way my grandmother behaved when he was ill; and this time everything followed the ordinary pattern, even to her taking Dido, his favourite hound, by the scruff of her neck and hauling her out from under the bed and shutting her into a shed in the yard. On the third morning of my father's illness my grandmother, coming into the kitchen, reported that he was much better; and later in the day, cheered by this news and knowing that there were buns and beer in plenty, I took advantage of her peroccupation to wander out into the sunshine and presently I found myself in the harvest field. It was at some distance from the house and was part of the land known as New Holding because it had been added to the Merravay estate during the last twenty years. The women, scantily clad and wearing bright sunbonnets, followed with rakes and pitchforks and bundles of twine, shocking and stooking the corn behind the men who wielded the scythes; they laughed and sang as they worked, and almost before I knew what I was about I was amongst them, as busy and as merry as the best of them. And then, all suddenly, through the happy noise, there came the melancholy howling of the hound. I said, "My father is dead!" and, dropping the sheaf I held, I burst into tears.

They crowded about me, asking how I knew, and I must have sobbed out something about the dog. There are those who claim now to have seen a great black dog run through the stubble towards me, but that, I am perfectly sure, is nonsense. I am equally sure that those who say that at that moment they all drew away from me in terror are lying; I can clearly remember how they all crowded about me and how in a cluster we moved back to the house, where we learned that what I had said was dismally true.

There followed some weeks of unrelieved misery. Unostentatious as the bond between me and my father had been, it was real enough and his death was a loss to me in many ways. However, there is no place here for detailed description of my feelings.

Since I was a girl the title passed, naturally, to my cousin Rawley, who was the son of my grandmother's second child. About my uncle Matthew Rowhedge there was some slight mystery, darkly hinted at by Annie, who could now and then say things of startling malignancy about my grandmother. Dame Elizabeth had never been fond of or fair to her second son, though by all accounts he had been a strong, handsome, lusty boy, the sort upon whom any normal woman would have doted; apparently my grandfather had much preferred him to my father, who had been ailing and bookish even as a child. My grandfather had died untimely, gored by a bull, and soon afterwards Matthew had gone to sea and had not been seen at Merravay again. He had died in the Caribbean long ago.

I think—though I have no proof—that it was a shock to my grandmother to learn that my father had willed Merravay to Rawley. The place was not entailed and could have been left to her, or to me, but no doubt my father's sense of seemliness had demanded that the original land should go with the title. The fields and the empty house at New Holding and the recently purchased Slipwell meadows were left to my grandmother for her lifetime, and then to me; and if I married while she was alive she was to provide me with a dowry of five hundred pounds.

I was secretly grieved by the realisation that I should never own Merravay, which had always seemed to me to be the most beautiful house in the world, and I was depressed at the thought of going to live in the New Holding house with my grandmother, who now began to speak openly of the move. Only once did she express any resentment.

"I've slept in that room for fifty years and had a mind to die in it," she said.

"It is possible that Rawley might let us stay here," I said hopefully. "The house is large enough."

"I should never dream of asking a favour of him," she retorted; then she added, "Of course if he asked me to stay that would be another matter."

Rawley was at that moment on the high seas, on his way home from Bermuda. Mr. Turnbull, the attorney who had drawn up Father's will, had sent him news of his inheritance and had also made some half-hearted attempts—easily frustrated by Dame Elizabeth—to assume some authority at Merravay pending the heir's arrival.

"I am capable of continuing the management and am prepared to give an account of my stewardship," she said.

What she was not capable of doing—and vast was her annoyance—was to read the letter which eventually arrived from Rawley. Unwillingly she handed it to me. She could do the most complicated reckonings in her head or with the aid of a tally stick, and she never forgot a fact or a figure, but she had never learned to read.

Now, as I broke the seal and looked with dismay at the vile, almost illegible script, she leaned on my shoulder, breathing audibly and giving me little nips in her impatience.

"Well," she snapped, "in what manner does he write?"

I began to read the letter slowly, word by word as I deciphered it.

"Never mind that. In what *manner*, fool? Civil or cool or what?"

"Very civil, I think. . . . Oh yes, indeed. He says it will be a month or more before he has set his own affairs in order. He says he would be vastly obliged if you would 'see to and handle and manage all things' as he understands you have done in the past."

"Is there mention of Master Turnbull?"

"None."

She straightened herself and I could feel the certainty of present power and the hope of its continuance flow through her, heartening as wine.

"He sounds like a young man of good judgement. Fetch your tools, girl, and write to him straightaway."

When I came back she was holding the letter in her hand, gravely studying the marks which made no sense for her. Then she looked up at me with an expression which I had never seen turned on me before, appraising, as though I were a colt or a heifer whose value she was assessing.

"It is a pity that you are so plain and like a pikestaff," she said. "A young man of good sense might think to marry you and hold the land entire. Here take it. . . ." She pushed the letter into my hand.

"But ma'am," I began.

"I want no buts from you! Sit down and make ready to write. . . ."

For once I was grateful to her for cutting me short, for my sentence would have ended, "Rawley is married already." Then she would have demanded to know how I knew and for that I had no answer, and her suspicion that I had not read the letter properly would have been the least of the unpleasant results. But I did know! What is more I knew that Rawley's wife was in some way strange, was small and pale and beautiful, and that there was a fragrance about her, the scent of some flower I had never smelt.

III

I had seen and smelt aright. Rawley had married a Spanish girl, the daughter of a man with great estates. It had been a runaway match, for Isabella's father had had no intention of allowing his lovely daughter to marry a penniless English sailor.

I was completely enchanted by Isabella from the moment I saw her. I was just at the age when, for all I was so ugly and coltish, I was on the verge of becoming a woman, looking half longingly, half reluctantly, into the world of femininity in which Isabella moved with such grace and assurance. I had never had a sister or a girl friend; I had no memory of my mother; and my grandmother, though Annie swore that she had once been pretty and charming, had long ago put aside all the trappings of sex. So when Isabella allowed me into her room, let me look at and finger her things, let me watch her at her toilet and even brush her long black hair, I was like some earnest young apprentice in the presence of a master craftsman. And she was extravagantly kind to me, partly because she and my grandmother were at loggerheads from the start and took opposite sides in everything. Also, of course, those first months at Merravay were lonely for Isabella. Rawley had much to learn and was out on the land much of the day, spending the evenings with Dame Elizabeth, now his mentor. She had set herself to convince him that she was indispensable, and Rawley, out of his element, easy-going by nature, and, truth to tell, no match for her in wits, seemed content to consult her and lean upon her. There was no more talk of leaving Merravay, and it looked as though the old woman would attain her wish to die in the great room which was always spoken of as the "Queen's Chamber."

Rawley and Isabella came to Merravay in the winter and that year the cold was severe even for our parts. Isabella, huddled in a shawl, went shuddering about as chilled as a butterfly which has outstayed its season. My grandmother, always scant of sympathy and utterly ignorant of warmer climates, attributed Isabella's misery to the fact that she undressed to go to bed and occasionally took a bath. One should, said my grandmother, don a good flannel shift and petticoat at Michaelmas and keep them on, day and night, till Easter; that way one stored up heat.

There came an April morning when the wind veered round and the sun shone. I had been in Isabella's room, fitting on a dress which she was making for me. She sewed beautifully and had taken my wardrobe in hand. Her room was in the west "leg" of the house and at that hour, at that season, was cold and sunless. When we came out on to the gallery we stood warming ourselves in the sun and chatting. Isabella had been telling me about her distant home, which sounded like a palace to me, and I suppose it was pride and loyalty to Merravay which made me say, "You've never seen the best bedchamber here, have you? The Queen once slept in it."

Making sure that my grandmother was downstairs on her rounds of kitchen, dairy, and buttery, I opened the door of the room to which I had so often gone in fear and trembling and the certainty of punishment. I intended now to display to Isabella the grandeur and beauty of the apartment with its two great deep-set windows, its noble fireplace, its walls lined with wood so neatly and finely carved they looked as if they were hung with linen, the little dais on which the vast bed stood. Long familiarity had blinded me to the other aspects of the room. My grandmother used it for other purposes than sleeping. There were tally sticks, samples of wool and seed, specially choice medicines for all ailments, human and animal, great rolls of flannel and print for the servants' annual dole and, besides, a great medley of ill-assorted articles which had been put there to await the moment when my grandmother could give them her leisurely attention. The windows had not, I think, been opened during her occupancy and the room stank of wool, of horse liniment, and sheep-dip, and, perhaps, a little of unfastidious old woman. The fire had been allowed to go out but the sun shone in strongly and, as well as lighting up the cobwebs on the scarred old tally sticks and the general disorder, made the room as warm as summer.

"It is the most warm room of the house," Isabella said.

"And it could be beautiful," I felt compelled to add.

"The smell is that of the slave cabins," Isabella said. "Come away!"

But she had made up her mind and within a few hours the war of the Queen's Chamber had begun.

There was more to it than two women fighting for the possession of one room. What they were both after was proof of Rawley's allegiance. He loved Isabella quite fanatically; he wanted her to be warm and comfortable; he recognised her right, as mistress of the house, to the best bedchamber; but somewhere along the road Dame Elizabeth had extorted or tricked out of him a promise that so long as she stayed at Merravay and helped him she should remain in that room; and this was the lambing season, when even the toughest, most knowledgeable old shepherd did not mind asking the dame's advice and would say with topsy-turvy pride, "Ah, her's a masterpiece! 'That'll live,' she say, and live that do though I give it up for dead!"

While the fight raged there came, as there always does as soon as the poor lambs are dropped, a spell of really bitter weather, and one evening Isabella, shivering by the fire, asked me to run up to her room and bring down her little shoulder cape which was made of velvet lined with fur and which had a snug, upstanding collar.

The days were beginning to draw out into those long evenings which are so sad in cold weather and I did not take a candle. I looked into Isabella's clothes closet, sniffing the fragrance, and failed to find the cape on any peg. Then I looked into her chest and was on the point of lighting a candle to aid my search when I thought of the shelf in the closet. I reached up and my fingers touched the fur. Then I realised that something else, something hard, had come down with the cape into my hand. It was a little doll.

My first thought was sentimental and female; Isabella was going to have a baby and had made it a doll already! I knew she wanted a baby more than anything and I was glad for her. With the cape over my arm and the doll in my hand I went towards the window, beyond which the sunset sky, coldly lilac and green, was beginning to darken. Then I wondered why Isabella had made a doll so ugly . . . so exactly like my grandmother.

My grandmother still wore a great wheel ruff in the old style, a ruff which it became more and more difficult to get dressed properly as one after another of the old servants who had learnt the art died off. She also wore the stiff, padded panniers which King James I had forbidden to be worn at court, years ago, because they took up so much room. Old Annie had once told me that the ruff and the panniers were exact copies of those which Queen Elizabeth had worn when she visited Merravay and made my grandfather a knight. Perhaps, I thought, she had also said that to Isabella and perhaps Isabella, much as she disliked my grandmother, had seen the romance of that and had wished her child's first toy to link with the tradition. And then I thought, How careless! For one of Isabella's best brass-headed pins had been left in the doll, stuck in in such a fashion that the point protruded at the back of the bodice. I pulled it out and would have put it in the little pin box where it belonged, and then I remembered that by doing so I should betray the fact that I knew Isabella's secret. I was not supposed to have seen the doll at all. So I pushed the pin back, carefully, into the thickness of the panniered skirt so that the point was hidden and couldn't scratch anyone as it had so nearly scratched me.

Then I realised that the room seemed suddenly darker and colder and that I had an uncomfortable feeling of being alone, a long way from the warm, inhabited part of the house . . . and yet perhaps not quite alone! I hurried back to Isabella.

Two or three days later when my grandmother was coming downstairs she slipped and broke her thigh bone. We carried her to one of the side rooms, and, knowing the seriousness of a broken bone at her age, I felt a little sorry that she was, after all, not to die in her own chamber. However she did not die. The bone knitted, though crookedly so that she was lame and lopsided from that time on. She could no longer walk upstairs and refused to be carried; so the tally sticks and all her other treasures were brought downstairs. On level ground she could move, slowly and awkwardly, but indefatigably, and Jack Lantern made her a little cart, like a chair set on wheels, in which she could be pushed about out of doors.

After a week's scrubbing and polishing and airing the Queen's Chamber was ready for Isabella.

IV

Time passed. The confidence which I awaited from Isabella never came, and beneath all the increasingly gay social life which was beginning to enliven Merravay—for Rawley was convivial and popular—there was just a trace of discontent and anxiety; there was, each month, a day or two when Isabella was gloomy and downcast, and I would think, Poor Isabella, disappointed again!

So we came to my birthday, which was in June, and we must have a party with the Fennels, the Blackwoods, and the Headways to eat supper with us and play hide-and-seek and other merry games in the garden in the warm dusk and afterwards dance in the hall. Lady Fennel, who had a loud, hearty voice, asked me how old I was and when I said, "Sixteen," she said, "How time passes! Think, by Yule I shall be a grandmother!"

Mrs. Headway said, "Mary has lost no time! Why, she was married only at Candlemas."

"Ah, well," said Lady Fennel, "I always say a good tinder strikes first time and a damp one never will!" They laughed. I happened to look at Isabella and saw her white-rose pallor take on a tallowy hue and the bones showed in her nose.

Two nights later there was a full moon; I had no curtains to my window and the light, falling full on my bed, woke me. After a while I got up and went towards the screen which in winter stood between me and the window to exclude the draught and which in summer leaned, folded, by the wall. It would now serve to shade me from this extraordinarily vivid and strangely melancholy light. Hanging over the screen at that moment was the exquisitely made petticoat which Isabella had sewn and given me for my birthday. I had not laid it away in my press because I was waiting for some rose leaves which I was drying to be ready enough to sprinkle in its folds. It was so lovely with its delicate stitching and fine embroidery that I meant to lay it up with care to await some really special occasion. As I lifted it from the screen I thought about that special occasion . . . for most girls of my age that would mean my wedding day; but I had little hope that anyone would fall in love with me. I was so tall, so thin; and in me the Rowhedge red hair, instead of being dark chestnut, was a pale, very unbecoming russet, and it was short, very curly, and springy, so that even my grandmother had never succeeded in making a parting in it; it grew like a lamb's pelt. Also I had pale green eyes and in summer hundreds of freckles.

I was thinking these purely personal thoughts as I took the petticoat in hand, and then everything rushed out of my mind except terror. Not for myself; for Isabella. I knew in that special way of knowing that she was in danger, horrible danger. How, lying there in her own bedroom with Rawley by her side, she could be in danger of any kind I could not think; but I knew she was. Then I thought that she might be ill. My first impulse was to go running along the gallery, but even under the impact of terror some sense remained with me and I thought that if this were all nonsense and they were asleep they would hardly thank me for going to their room. But if she had been taken ill Rawley would have made a light. I ran to my window from which theirs was visible. I looked out. I don't think I even saw their window, for my eye was caught by something which moved, accompanied by a sharp black shadow, across the smooth turf of the lawn. It had almost reached the point where a deep decline separated the garden from the field. There, in old times, when the castle of Merravay was in being, the moat had lain.

The moving figure—and I was almost certain that it was Isabella—disappeared into the dip and then emerged again in the cornfield and began to move towards Layer Wood. It was Isabella, and my first thought was that she was walking in her sleep, for never consciously would *she* leave her warm bed and go wandering in the night. I had been led to believe that nothing untoward ever happened to sleepwalkers; so I wondered again why I should have the certainty that she was in peril. Then I remembered.

Years earlier, when I was very young, I had been a frequent visitor to Layer Wood, going there in search of wild flowers and the very small, very sweet wild strawberries which grew there in profusion; until one day I pushed my way through a little hazel thicket and had been so frightened, of nothing, seized with such sheer reasonless animal terror that I had dropped my basket and run home like a rabbit. Ever since I had avoided that spot, and called it, in my own mind, the Bad Place. Now Isabella was walking straight towards it.

I pushed my bare feet into my shoes and, hitching up my night shift, ran out into the moonlight. I could, at need, run like a stag and if I had stopped to put on my stockings and fasten my shoes I might have saved time. As it was, my feet, slippery with the cold sweat of fear, came out of my shoes at each step until finally I discarded the shoes altogether and ran barefoot over the sharp tufts left from the hay-scything in the field.

Isabella was in the wood when I reached her; and she was wide awake. I gasped out, "What are you doing?"

She said shortly, "A thing of importance. You must help or go away. Better I think you should go."

"I can't leave you here, alone. This is a bad place . . ."

"A right place. Now lend me your hands and stay silent or go. And never speak, never, of what you see."

I stayed; I helped. Does that make me a witch? Does a kitchen slut handing a dish, passing a spoon, thereby become a cook?

I hated it all; I hated it so much that by the time the thing was done I was well on the way to hating Isabella herself. When it was over she sat down exhausted on a fallen tree trunk, and it was I who stamped out the fire and buried the poor drained body of the little white cock who would never greet the sun again. Then I picked up the doubly sullied bowl.

"That must be broken," she said. I hesitated, for it was one of a new set and pretty, yellow with a brown rim. She took it from me and smashed it against the tree trunk. It fell into four almost even pieces. She counted them and then fitted the pieces together as though to make certain that none was missing.

"It is a pity. It will be a girl. But that is the beginning only. I shall call her by your name."

"Do you really believe . . ."

"Oh yes. It is a thing very old, brought by the slave people from Africa, but very sure. And all that was left to do, Alice; marrying Rawley, who is heretic, has made me incommunicate—not even the little saints would ask for me. But by next year this time I shall have a baby. Let us go home now."

In April of the following year the baby was born; and it was a girl. But it was not named for me; for Isabella died within half an hour of its birth and it was left to my grandmother, the only person unaffected by the tragedy, to choose the name. She chose Thomasina.

V

Rawley took refuge in drunkenness.

My grandmother bore with him patiently at first, but as the sum of months mounted she took on a censorious tone. One day she told him that *she* had always found hard work the best cure for heartbreak.

"How could you know? You never loved anything but a tally stick!" he said bitterly.

Another day she suggested—I think with good intent—that he should leave Merravay and return to the sea for a while. She said she would look after his affairs for him.

"I'm damned sure of that!" Rawley said nastily.

Things worsened between them as he grew more and more sottish, and one evening as he slumped over the supper table she snapped out,

"If you are so uxorious that being widowed makes a sot of you, the best thing you can do is to marry again."

Rawley cried out like an animal, a wordless sound of pain; then he picked up his heavy silver tankard and flung it at her. She put up her hand and by the luckiest chance caught the tankard by the handle. Setting it with exaggerated care on the table, she said coldly,

"That is exactly the action of a spoilt child whose toy has been taken away." Then with dignity, despite her limp, she walked away and Rawley lowered his head until it rested on the table.

"She shouldn't say such things to you," I said. Filled with pity I went near and laid my arm across his shoulders. I meant to comfort him as one comforts a child, and like a child he turned to me, making a little muffled sound, half groan, half sob, as he thrust his head against me. I stroked his head and said, "Poor Rawley."

Then all at once it was "Poor Alice"! I began to tremble, sharp pain transfixed me, I was dizzy, I was gasping for breath.

Rawley moved, freeing himself.

"Dear little Alice," he mumbled. "Kind. Mustn't upset yourself. Be all right." He patted me as though I were a dog, and went lurching away not to the Queen's Chamber but to a small bare room which actually *smelt* of his misery.

And that is how I fell in love with Rawley.

The pain continued in me and grew worse and added to it was a terrible shyness. I was so afraid that he might guess what I felt about him that I dared not look him in the face; I could hardly speak to him and avoided seeing him whenever I could.

The slow months passed and there came the time when rumours about Rawley and Phyllis Whymark, the girl from The Evening Star, began to creep about. Strange as it may sound I could see exactly what it was that Rawley sought and found in her; I liked her too. There had been a time when she used to drive geese up to the London market and she would come to Merravay some days before the setting-out day to dip the feet of the geese in tar, which hardened and protected them from the wear and tear of the long journey. I used to steal out to watch this process, to enjoy her easy, wryly humourous conversation and to gaze with admiration upon a girl, not much my senior, who could undertake that long hazardous journey alone. Her mother was a woman of notorious bad character, but though I wouldn't have staked a pin on Phyllis being a virgin, she wasn't a whore either, the respect with which men spoke of and to her proved *that*. With her nimble wit, earthy philosophy, and salty humour she was just the company for Rawley at that moment and she would never in any way remind him of Isabella. But for the fact that I was myself in love with him I should have regarded the affair as a blessing.

Not so my grandmother; she was scornful and furious and in her fury precipitated the very situation she dreaded, for one day she faced Rawley with the rumour, and he whipped round and said that if the idea of his having Phyl Whymark as his mistress was so shocking and repulsive the only way of mending the matter that he could think of would be that he should marry her! And despite the aching of my heart I could not deny that he could have done worse; there was something vital and vigorous about that young woman; if Rawley married her he would never miss his grandmother, for Phyl was capable of running Merravay or anything else. The very way she walked showed that.

Probably the old woman recognised her match; for as soon as she had convinced herself that Rawley meant what he said she began again to make preparations for leaving Merravay and going to New Holding. She took a high-handed attitude towards the affair, an attitude which I could but admire.

"Don't for one moment imagine," she said, "that I shall stay here working myself into my grave to keep that baseborn slut in comfort! I leave you to go to ruin at your own gait."

She began to gather her gear together, and at last there came the—to me—dreadful day when she told Jack Lantern to take out all the sacred tally sticks and burn them. I knew then that there was no hope.

Later that day she told me to make ready anything I wished to take with me to New Holding; the servants would convey the baggage next day, make fires in the house and arrange it, and we should follow on the day after.

I went up to my room feeling that life was over. I must turn my back on the man I loved, the house I loved, and go forward through the joyless days in bleak and bitter company.

Since my grandmother had decided to leave Rawley to his fate she had been less strict about candles and I went to my room with two long new ones.

I had few possessions and I was too wretched to care much what I took or what I left; but at the very bottom of my chest I came upon two things which I had hidden there because the very sight of them gave me pain. One was the petticoat which Isabella had given me on my birthday, the other was the last little whistle that Robin had ever made. I couldn't leave them behind, nor could I take them with me. I thought of the Dame's tally sticks and decided that her action was seemly. I carried my treasures over to the hearth and, taking my candle, tilted the stick so that the flame licked at the fine linen; but before it was smouldering the candle fell out of the stick, rolled away, and went out.

In the dark once more I felt my way to my chest, took up my brush and began to brush my hair; thinking as I did so about the whistle and the clay pit, about the petticoat and that night of full moon.

This is what confuses me. I performed no ritual; I said nothing; but I *thought,* and as I thought I became aware of a kind of power, something welling up in me so that instead of thinking to myself, I wish Rawley would marry me instead of Phyllis Whymark, I was thinking, breathing, willing, *being* to myself, He shan't marry Phyllis Whymark, he must marry me! I will it, it shall happen.

VI

The next day passed without event, save that my grandmother suddenly remembered a couple of silver spoons and a mug.

"They were of small value measured by all that has come into this house since," she said, "but they are mine and must go with me." That sounded reasonable enough. But when the things were found she said, "They are dear to me though I had overlooked them. They were with me in the mud that night. Then I flung them into the bushes and my father found them. A very stern man was my father; he was to blame for everything."

The idea of her ever throwing anything of value into a bush was somewhat startling, but I was too miserable to give it much heed.

Rawley did not come near us that day. Darkness fell and my grandmother and I sat down to our last supper at Merravay. I thought she looked pale and a little tired, which was not to be wondered at. We ate, with small appetite, in silence until she said abruptly,

"Chris Huxstable is dead, you know. He was cut for the stone and died. So now you'll have Merravay, my girl, and that will smell sweeter than the tannery!"

"I beg pardon, ma'am; I don't understand."

"No, well, you're young. But I give you warning. You never *have* anything. Whether it's a stinking tannery or a beautiful estate you don't have it; it has you; and when it has sucked your very marrow they'll cast you on the dung heap. That happened to me, clever as I was. But they didn't have it all their own way, you know. There was a time when I had nothing; and the few things I had I must throw away to make it look like a robbery. And it was so muddy too! But I was so happy. So happy. I've never been happy since."

I was alarmed and shocked to see that tears were running down her face. I had never seen her cry before; even when my father died she had shed her tears behind a closed door.

"I think you are feeling unwell, ma'am," I said, rising from the table and going to where she sat. "Come let me help you to your room."

She took my wrist in her thin hard old hand and I could feel the unnatural heat of it.

"You must decide," she said. "And now; there is no time to waste. Will you come or won't you? Fifty gold pieces will last a long time and I'm not without skill. You'll never lack." Her voice changed, losing its urgency, its curious echo of youth. "That is what he said, you know.

And then it was so muddy and I wondered how I could explain. But I did. I fooled them all."

"Of course," I said soothingly. "Come and lie down now."

In the kitchen, whither I went to fetch a hot brick, for the old woman's feet were as cold as her hands were hot, I found Jack Lantern trying to persuade the cook to put two hedgehogs in the oven for him. He had found them on his way back from taking our baggage to New Holding. The cook refused to have anything to do with such uncanny creatures and he went off disgruntledly muttering that he would cook them himself.

Apparently he did so, over a fire made of Dame Elizabeth's tally sticks. Later on he swore that the fire was out before he left it and went to sleep off his orgy, and that may well have been true. A spark may have flown up and started a quiet slow smouldering in the thatch of the stable while he was enjoying his strange repast. It was hours later, hard on midnight, when the glare and crackle of the fire and the screams of the frightened horses trapped in the stable roused the house.

When I reached the yard the roof of the stable was all ablaze, but all the horses save three at the far end, beyond an eight-foot-high partition, had been got out. Just over the partition a portion of the flaming roof had fallen inwards, setting fire to the partition itself. Jack Lantern had actually made one dash past the flames and attempted to drive the three horses out, but they had refused to face the blazing barrier and were now rearing and screaming against the farther wall. I could see instantly that though the partition was aflame there was still a passage between its end and the wall. The opening in normal times was wide enough to admit a man with a forkful of hay, and I knew that I could save the horses if they would just do what I told them. Darting and shrugging away from those who would have restrained me, I ran in through the opening that was arched and bordered with flame and seized the first horse by the mane. My hands were as steady as they ever were at table, my voice as calm as though I were exchanging the time of day with a passer-by. "Steady now," I said. "Trust me; there is room. Steady, you're safe with me." Three times I did it, and as I followed the last horse past the flames and into safety the whole roof, with a snarling roar, caved in. Smoke and flames and bits of blazing débris seemed to reach towards me; I lurched forward and fell into Rawley's arms.

They are saying now, of course, that I went to and fro through the flames, exalting and unhurt. That is hardly true. I suffered no serious damage, but my hair and eyebrows, like the manes and tails of the horses, were singed; and the skin of my face and arms were scorched so that it peeled off like cornhusks and left me painfully raw. They lie who say that, tempered by the fires of Hell, I emerged from a burning stable unscathed. . . .

But . . . but ought I to deny the power of the Power which had come to my aid so timely? In twenty-four hours I should have been at New Holding and Merravay might have burned to the ground without my knowing. I had willed that something should happen to take Rawley from Phyl Whymark and give him to me . . . and what I willed had come to pass.

This is no love story and these things are too intimate to set down here. It suffices to say that while they were larding my raw flesh with goose grease and then powdering over the grease with flour, so that I was most grotesquely masked, and my close pelt of hair, crisped and blackened, was flaking about like ash Rawley came and knelt by my bed and told me how he had felt when he saw that burning stable and heard that I was within. And I shall always cherish the knowledge that he was coming to me through the flames.

VII

And after that, for almost twenty years nothing strange took place. Life proceeded in normal, placid fashion. We were very happy.

I was one of Lady Fennel's "good tinder" kind. Within a year I had borne a child, a boy, whom we called Charles. He was a happy, healthy, handsome little boy and with him and Thomasina, who now seemed like my own, I was well content.

My grandmother lived only a short while after the night of the fire and was never again wholly sound of mind. At the end I had her carried up into the Queen's Chamber so that she might die there as she had wished, but it was a wasted gesture, for she seemed to imagine that she was lying in Layer Wood and complained bitterly about the mud.

Tucked away between the woods, the river, and the sea, we at Merravay led, I can now see, a life that was isolated, self-contained, and perhaps unduly complacent. It was life after the antique fashion, in which a bad batch of butter or a hailstorm that flattened a wheat field seemed of more dire importance than the disputes of bishops or the conferences of kings.

We were warned, of course. As early as the December of 1637, Sir Walter Fennel, sitting at our table, full of our food and wine, suddenly leaned forward and asked Rawley,

"Have you paid your ship-money yet?"

"Some time since. Why?"

"Pity," said Sir Walter, cracking a walnut between his fingers. "I didn't. And now I see that this Buckinghamshire fellow, Hampden, is refusing to pay and letting his case come into court. And not a penny will they get from me until I see which way the cat jumps."

"I can tell you that now," said Rawley cheerfully. "They'll make him pay—and next year put up his dues!"

"That remains to be seen," said Sir Walter. "After all Hampden rests his case upon an indisputable fact—that ship-money is illegal."

The old sailor in Rawley knew a brief resurrection.

"God above us! We've got to have ships, haven't we? And how can we have ships without money?"

"Taxes should be levied by Parliament," said Sir Walter, something stubborn and pontifical creeping into his voice.

"But we haven't had a parliament for eight years! And when you wail about ship-money you should remember, Walter, what a mass of taxes the Parliament men would have levied if they'd sat there all that time with nothing else to do."

That seemed to me a sound argument; and since Rawley was holding his own so well I forebore to say anything.

"Well . . . of course, if that is the attitude you take . . ." There was something a little ominous about Sir Walter's unfinished sentence, and although for a long time after that conversation our families continued to meet and maintain friendly relationships something sour remained and would reveal itself from time to time in remarks such as "You're a King's man, aren't you, Rawley?" or "Don't say such things in Row-hedge's house, he's Royalist, remember!"

One day Rawley said to me, "I'd give a shilling to know where Fennel gets his information. To my certain knowledge he's not been in London these last three years, yet everything that's said and done there is known at Ockley within a week—if we can believe him."

Next time I saw Lady Fennel I asked her the question and she was pleased to tell me about the weekly *Newsletter* to which Sir Walter, the Headways, and Blackwoods subscribed and shared. An enterprising fellow called Shuttle had started the scheme to supply news to country places, and the service was now so swift that a *Newsletter* sent from London on Wednesday morning reached Ockley on Saturday afternoon. I promptly ordered a copy for us, and then, when I found it to be violently anti-Royalist I also subscribed to another which was equally biassed on the other side; but though we read—or rather I read while Rawley listened, yawning—and talked about what we read the whole business seemed remote, unimportant. So unconcerned were we that when in 1640 the King did call a Parliament which promptly declared ship-money to be illegal, the first thing Rawley said was, "Now Walter will be happy! Let's ask him to supper and see his shining face!"

I also remember, quite clearly, that we were at Ockley when the news came that the Queen had left England and gone to Holland.

"That means war and nothing less," said Sir Walter. "She's off to beg, borrow, or steal money and with the powder and shot and the foreign mercenaries thus provided, the King'll shed our English blood!"

"But the Queen has gone to convey the Princess to her husband, which is reasonable enough," Rawley protested.

"The Princess is a child of ten!" Sir Walter snorted. "It's time you faced facts, Rowhedge; or do you mean to sit on the fence till you're pushed off?"

I suppose that was our intention, if we could have been said to have any at all; but in the end we were forced into taking sides. By our own son.

Charles, then aged seventeen, was at Cambridge; and one day in June we received a letter from him. Instead of the usual rather rambling amusing discourse to which we were accustomed this letter contained some terse instructions.

"Please send as quickly as possible, my mare and a sound pack horse, my warm cloak, my silver cup and ten pounds. Let young Lantern, or Bill Woods, or better still both if you can spare them come to ride with me. I am for Oxford."

"Oxford," said Rawley. "What in the Devil's name does he want with Oxford. Didn't we thrash out the question and settle on Cambridge for his learning?"

"He is going to the King," I said.

"That is nonsense! Now that I will not allow," Rawley spluttered. "This is a grown men's quarrel, whipped up by old fools. If it comes to blows let the old men give and receive them. Sit you down, Alice, and write to him bluntly and say I bid him stay where he is. Or better still, come home. Aye, that is it. If this matter of learning is so light that it can be abandoned to go gallivanting off to Oxford then the boy might just as well . . ."

I never heard the end of that sentence. I stood there with Charles' letter in my hand, and the thing which had not happened for so many years happened again. I saw my son, grown older and thinner and brown of skin, standing in a strange place. He stood between sky and sea, both blue with an intensity of blue that our skies, our seas, never knew. There was fierce, vivid sunlight, and queer trees with feathery foliage which shook out a warm spicy odour. He looked well and prosperous and assured, and something remained of his old boyish merriment, tinged now with bitterness. . . .

"Here," Rawley said, slipping his arm about me. "Bear up, Alice, don't take it so hard. He hasn't gone yet, and, by God, he shall not go! I'll ride myself to Cambridge and knock sense into his head if needs be."

"He'll go if he has set his mind to it," I said; "and if he goes he must go well equipped."

"He won't go," said Rawley stubbornly. "He won't want to go when I've had my say."

"I will come with you," I said, "to take leave of him, in case . . . And we will take what he asks for, in case . . . But of course I hope that you may persuade him."

I knew then that it was a vain hope, and when we reached Cambridge

I was more than ever certain. The whole place was in an uproar. The town and the surrounding countryside was strongly Parliamentarian but the Colleges were for the King. Behind the closed gates the young men were making ready, melting down their silverware, gathering their gear, looking to their weapons. They were all in wild, hilarious high spirits, like children about to go on some long-promised treat, and of course poor Rawley's arguments and persuasions were no more than leaves in a wind. In fact there was one moment when it seemed as though the contagious enthusiasm might make a convert of him.

Despite my inner certainty that Charles was not going to his death, that he would live to be at least thirty, I parted with him in agony, for I did not believe that I should ever see him in the flesh again. I was also miserable for Rawley's sake and wished that I could have told him what I *knew*. But that was impossible; for one thing he would have thought me mad; for another there was some deep instinct which informed me that these were not things to speak of.

All I could do as the battles of Edgehill and Newbury and Chalgrove Field followed one another was to say, "I feel in my bones that the boy has taken no harm. I should have known, Rawley. I am his mother."

VIII

At Merravay, through all these troublous times, life went on much as usual. Except for the Hattons at Mortiboys all our neighbours were inclined to the Puritan cause, but there was no fighting in our district. Since we were known to veer the other way and had a son rising rapidly in the Royalist ranks, the worst that befell us was that we were regarded a little askance and avoided, rather as though we had a case of plague in our house. Sir Walter Fennel, most Puritan of our neighbours, foreswore our company, but he still sent his mares to our Barbary stallion. With the Blackwoods we remained on cordial terms because two years before war broke out Thomasina had married young Robert Blackwood. When her first-born was christened Robert Rawley we were asked to the ceremony, and, the Royalist cause being in the ascendant at the time, we were not unwelcome to the other guests. But as time went on matters became more difficult.

For one thing, a Huntingdon squire named Oliver Cromwell came back after the first Battle of Newbury to raise new forces in East Anglia. He had said of the Parliamentarian forces, "Do you think that the spirits of such base fellows will ever be able to encounter gentlemen that have honour and courage and resolution in them," and he had vowed to raise an army of his own from men of honour and courage and resolution. In due time there came to us at Merravay a manifesto, a demand for men and money.

The moment I had it in my hand I saw—just as I had seen the clay pit, and Rawley's wife, and Charles aged thirty in a far place—a really horrid sight, a mass of mouldering bones hanging in chains above the heads of a great crowd of people all jeering and pointing, rejoicing in the grisly sight.

"From whose hand?" I asked. "Who wrote this?"

"The General's own," they told me. I drew Rawley aside and said, "Though it would be expedient now to trim our sails a trifle, have nothing to do with this man. I have a feeling that he will come to a bad end."

Rawley stared at me, astonished. "What could I have to do with him, Alice, even if he were headed for the Throne itself. With Charles on the other side!"

(This incident seems strange to remember now, when Cromwell rides so high and I lie so low. But that "eye in my hand" never saw wrong and the end is not yet!)

One day soon after that Rawley was in Baildon, in the yard of a hostelry called The Hawk In Hand, where he stabled his horse, and one of the hostlers came up and asked rather furtively, "The young master is with the King, ain't he, Sir Rawley?" We had never made a secret of that, so Rawley said, "Yes."

"Well, if ever you want to send him owt, bring it here. We've got ways of managing." And shortly after that we began to receive cryptic little messages from Charles, demanding money. We sent it, cautiously and suspiciously at first, but it always reached its destination and was always acknowledged in terms which made sense to me but would have meant nothing to anyone who had intercepted the letter. One little note, for instance, read, "Who used to be a notorious gambler? Wouldn't he put up a stake?" And that sent Rawley riding to Kit Hatton, who would have bet on which way the wind would blow tomorrow, and Kit raised two hundred pounds which went down "The Tunnel" as we called this line of communication.

Then came the second Battle of Newbury, and next time Rawley visited Baildon he found The Hawk In Hand closed down. For many weeks during that long cold winter we had no news of Charles at all and what other news we received was all discouraging.

One evening Rawley and I were sitting in the Ship Chamber when I heard a stealthy tapping at the window. I thought it might be a gull. In bad weather they came up the river and grew bold, friendly as barnyard fowls, and I often put scraps on the sill for them. I looked and saw something—too large to be a gull—move behind the pane.

"Rawley . . . there is someone by the window."

For the last week or so Rawley had been convinced that he was being watched wherever he went. He rose now in anger and said, "Spying on us at our fireside now, are they?" He went and unlatched the casement and flung it open and then stepped back with a cry. Charles put a leg over the sill.

"Dear hearts," he said, "I hope I did not alarm you." He pulled off the old woollen cap he wore and came to kiss me. All his lovely glossy curls had been shorn, and as soon as I had recovered myself I said, "Oh Charles, you look like a Roundhead."

"That was my intention. I've got so far on my looks but I dared not trust them where I was known. That is why I came to the window. Mother, can I have something to eat, at once? I've a great deal to say and I must be on my way in an hour."

I began to bestir myself. I ran to the kitchen and brought food and the ingredients for mulled wine, for the boy was soaked to the skin. Then I went to his room and picked out the plainest and shabbiest of the clothes he had left behind at the beginning of that Cambridge term which now seemed like a lifetime ago. Old as they were they were too fine to fit the rôle he had chosen, so while he sat by the fire, eating with the voracity of a wolf, talking all the while, and Rawley mulled the wine, I busied myself by cutting off the bits of fur and velvet and the fancy buttons as I listened to his talk.

The King, he said, had men in plenty, for the reverse at Newbury had brought forward many formerly lukewarm; but he was tragically short of arms. However, arrangements had been made; the King of France had no wish to see his brother king defeated and was sending weapons of war.

"To get them in . . . that is the trouble. The Cropheads hold all the ports, and places like Plymouth and Poole where we hold the land inward are too well watched and guarded. So we thought of the east, where they hold both port and land and so feel secure and are less careful. And we hope to land arms at Hull, and Yarmouth . . . and Bywater!" He broke off and eyed us over the bread and bacon which he was stuffing into his mouth.

"A bold scheme," said Rawley thoughtfully. "Under their very bows as it were."

"I'm glad you're in favour of it," Charles said quickly, "because this is what you must do . . ."

It all sounded wildly fantastic, as unreal and unlikely as the games children play or the dramas that unfold themselves on a stage, and when Charles finally stood up, looked at the hat from which I had removed band and buckle, and said, "Still far too jaunty," and pulled on the sodden woollen cap again, I stared at him, feeling that it was all—his visit, his talk, his disguise—part of a dream from which I must surely soon wake.

"There," he said, "now don't I look like Jeremiah Oh-Lord-Arise-Scatter-Thy-Enemies Jones? And now, can you get me a horse? You'll find the one I came on in the Low Meadow. It's foundered but it was a good horse and could be again."

A few minutes later, out in the windy dark, he kissed us and mounted. We said, "Be careful of yourself" and "God keep you."

"And you. And speed you in all you do." Then, raising the old cap, he cried, "God save the King!" softly but as though it were a battle cry. He touched the horse with his heel and in a second the double dark of the night and the avenue's shade had engulfed him.

We never saw him again, but I know he is alive, somewhere.

He left us wholly committed to the King's cause.

IX

It would be tedious to describe in detail the campaign of subterfuges, shifts, and lies upon which we then embarked. What we had to do sounded simple enough. We had only to provide transport for the arms between Bywater and Merravay and warn the innkeeper of The Red Lion at Colchester who would then make the next link in the chain. (Almost without exception the innkeepers were Royalist because they feared that the Puritans, once in power, would close their houses.) Had Rawley and I been a simple farmer and his wife, used to driving our own teams, it would have been easy enough; as it was it demanded great cunning. We had decided not to involve any one of our servants, not so much because we did not trust them as to avoid the slightest risk of an indiscreet word, an ill-timed significant glance; consequently we were obliged to behave as though these old faithful friends were all enemies. To me fell the task of carrying the warning to the men at The Red Lion and many were the devices to which I was driven to shake off, even for a few minutes, the servant who had for years attended me whenever I rode so far. Twice, I remember, I went so far as to have a tooth drawn by a man who had lately set up as a tooth-dragger in a room behind the inn. Sometimes, too, I chose to ride the Barbary and saw to it that the servant was mounted on a slow-moving horse and I pretended that it was past my power to hold the great black horse to the pace of the plodder.

We tried never to repeat a story or to play the same game twice; and as the weeks mounted into months we had the satisfaction of knowing that the arms had at least reached Colchester safely and been sped on their way. Now and then when the King scored one of his spectacular—but, alas, indecisive—little victories we could look at one another and think that perhaps, with our scheming, hard riding, and sacrifice of sleep, we had contributed a trifle towards it.

One day in May we were notified in the usual manner that a load waited at Bywater. This time we were providing the team and wagon in the least troublesome, though most expensive, way. Rawley was going to Bywater, where he meant to buy the best that the market offered. After nightfall he would drive it to the place where the Colchester men with their vehicle always waited—a lonely place where a tongue of Layer

Wood ran down to meet the road to Bywater. There he would stay with it until later next day and then drive it home. Such a procedure would be easily explained in view of the approaching haysel and harvest.

I had decided to use the tooth-dragging again as my excuse for a visit to Colchester, though this time I had decided that I would not carry the pretence quite so far. Rawley and I rode out together as far as the cross-roads and there in the sunshine, under trees where crinkled young leaves were unfolding, we said good-bye to one another.

Colchester, which was a completely Puritan town, was very dull that day and full of soldiers; as soon as my errand was done I started for home, not even bothering to look into the shops, which, if they had anything gay and pretty—which I doubt—kept it well hidden. I decided to ride round and visit Thomasina, who was expecting another child at the time. Truth to tell I always found the day before one of these night ventures intolerably long and trying; I was not cut out for a life of risk and excitement; I could too easily imagine the number of things which might go wrong. I should find Thomasina's company soothing and diverting.

She was, as always, delighted to see me, but I thought that the be-haviour of the other members of the family was strikingly cool and formal. The King's cause was no longer flourishing as it had been at the time of the christening of Robert Rawley Blackwood, and Thomasina's mother-in-law, with whom I never had been much of a favourite because long ago she had hoped to marry one of her many daughters to Rawley, said with a dark look that if things went on as they were doing the war would soon be over and there were those who would be sorry for the attitude they had taken. The Blackwoods had recently had soldiers billeted on them and spoke highly of their behaviour. These soldiers of the New Model Army were models indeed; they neither drank nor swore; they did not steal; they left the maids alone. And think of it! When some went to billet on the Hattons at Mortiboys and Mrs. Hatton said, quite untruthfully, that she thought they should move on as they suspected a case of plague in the house, the sergeant in charge had said, "God will take care of His own!" and moved in, uncaring.

Still, even the barbed chatter served its purpose in keeping my mind off the journey which Rawley must soon make with the wagon so heavily loaded that even the best team he might buy could only move slowly through the night. So I stayed on until the shadows were long across the lawn in which Mr. Blackwood took such pride, and it was dusk when I reached Merravay.

The day had been very warm and my sticky clothes were turning chill on me, so I went to my room to wash and change. I was taking my time over it, thinking that in a few minutes Rawley would be setting out; then I could linger over supper, walk in the garden for awhile . . . anything rather than go to bed and lie there thinking about that slow progress through the dark. There was no doubt about it, Rawley was dearer to me than any cause, even though, through Charles I owed it my allegiance.

I was putting on my dress when a servant came to tell me that some soldiers had arrived, seeking accommodation for their horses and themselves. That had happened before, not often because Merravay lay far back from the road, but often enough for us to be used to it and for me to know that all that Mrs. Blackwood had said about Puritan soldiers was quite true. In fact, as I ran down, hastily fastening my dress, I thought it was a pity that soldiers of the New Model Army were so very abstemious. Otherwise I would have opened a cask of good brown ale and made sure that when they lay down they slept soundly. Although the place of rendezvous which we had chosen for our transactions with the Colchester men was at a safe distance from the house, its very existence made me nervous and vulnerable to thoughts of danger.

It was only a small contingent, a captain, a sergeant, and eight troopers; they asked civilly for what they might have demanded or taken without a word. They looked tired, so did their horses, but when I suggested that the animals should be turned loose in the pasture the captain thanked me and said he would make his own arrangements. As I turned away, leaving him to do so, Sir Walter Fennel rode into the yard.

It was months since I had seen him face to face, for since the decline in the social relationship between our families the strictly "farmyard" business which he had had to do with Rawley had been conducted out of doors. He greeted me with surprising cordiality and then, looking towards the open cart-shed where the soldiers were installing themselves, he said,

"Ah, I see you have company. Is Rawley home yet?"

"No. I do not expect him until tomorrow morning."

"But he has only . . . I called this morning and your servants said that he had gone to Bywater. I hoped he'd be back."

I was heartily glad that *this* time there had been no secrecy, no subterfuge, no juggling with means of transport or even with time.

"He could have been, of course. But Rawley is an old sailor, remember, and once he gets to Bywater, where there are ships to look at and sailors to talk to, he likes to take his time." I smiled. "In the meantime, is there anything I could do? I know a little about most things."

"Thank you, Alice; no there is nothing. . . . Unless you cared to invite me to supper. I have been in the saddle all day and it would be late before I reached home."

I managed, with difficulty, to conceal my enormous surprise.

"It would be a pleasure," I said. "It is a long time since you honoured our table."

Fear, or fear's beginning, began to move, cold and slippery, in my stomach. Across the yard the soldiers were watering their horses . . . but they had not unsaddled!

"Since you will stay I think I will invite the captain to join us," I said. I would have him under my eye.

Sir Walter strolled across with me and I thought—I could not be sure, for I distrusted my knowledge-engendered suspicion—that a significant glance, a look of recognition and confirmation, passed between the two men.

The captain accepted my invitation and I led the way into the Ship Chamber, where I excused myself, saying that I must go to the kitchen to speak about extra places at table. I did not close the door and, having gone with a tapping of heels and a rustle of silk across the hall towards the kitchen quarters, I stole back along the wall.

". . . a bigger force," I heard Sir Walter say.

"Others are posted and patrolling. No loophole this time," said the soldier.

Before I had reached the kitchen I had known—and thrust aside—the impulse to do the obvious and dangerous thing. My first thought had been to run straight out, leap on the black horse, and make a dash for Bywater. But the soldiers were in the yard and before I could get the horse out of the stable they would have ringed me round. Besides such an act would be a confession of complicity. Then I thought of making an excuse to ride out openly—to say, for instance, that I was anxious about Thomasina Blackwood and must go to see how she was faring. But that— even if they accepted it—would accord ill with my having invited them to supper and most certainly Sir Walter would have insisted on accompanying me. No, I must think of something more crafty.

X

The meal lasted a thousand years. I sat there, noting the thickening darkness outside the windows. In May the nights are short, and Rawley, if he had not already set out, would be about to do so. Slowly, creakingly, he was moving towards the trap.

I was very gay. I gave, I think, a good impersonation of a woman with nothing on her mind save the entertainment of her guests; and that fitted in well with what I had to do.

When the meal was over I rose and moved to a side table where a silver dish held the last wizened apples of the autumn's crop.

"Now," I said, "I must ask you to excuse me for a few moments. Every night, without fail, I give my black horse his apples and he is more of a stickler for ritual than Archbishop Laud ever was!"

Laughter greeted that sally; but in the glass above the side table I saw them look at one another and make ready to move. Forestalling them, I said,

"You, Sir Walter, know my Barbary and his antics, but perhaps the captain might be entertained to see his performance."

They followed me out. In the yard the creak of leather and rattle of chains informed me that the troopers' horses were still ready.

"We should be fair," I said. "I expect your horses like apples, too."

"They're not accustomed to pampering, ma'am."

"Just this once," I said. I held apples to the questing velvet muzzles; I spoke into the long twitching ears. Then I opened the door of Barbary's loose box, called to him, and he came. He danced as I told him, rearing and pivoting on his back legs; he held up one hoof, then another; he whinnied to order. I handed the dish to Sir Walter at last and said,

"His best trick, for some reason, he will only do when I am on his back. Captain Allbright . . . please."

He helped me to mount.

"Kneel!" I said to the great black horse; and he buckled his knees and lowered himself. "Give him his reward," I cried, and as Sir Walter held out the apple I leaned over, saying, "Good boy, *good* boy!" Then I spoke into his ear. And at once he was up, a great mad thunderbolt of power, striking out back and front, gathering himself for the great leaping bounds which carried him out of the yard, not towards Bywater but in the other direction. I clung to his mane and screamed for help.

We thundered out of the yard and were halfway up the avenue before I spoke to him again and began to steer him across the fields into the marshes—safe now, thank God, for the spring had been early and dry. Headed for Bywater by the shortest way, I got myself astride him and, lying low on his neck, said, "Run now; run as you never ran."

I reckoned that Rawley would still be on that part of the road where it ran alongside the river. It would be the action of a moment to back the team, unhitch and let the incriminating load roll of its own momentum into the water. Rawley could go back to his bed at The Ship, and the horse and I would finally come to a standstill somewhere quite incredibly far from Bywater. I might even stage a minor accident. . . .

Nobody, I thought, could blame me for overestimating my control over a horse which most people already regarded as a dangerous demon and certainly no one would believe that the refusal of the troop horses to budge an inch could be in any way due to me! Later I learned that they did stand fast, even when prodded with pikes; and I learned too that nobody had any difficulty in believing that I had bewitched them.

I found the wagon just where I had reckoned. It was blazing fiercely, and of the four or five dead men around it one was Rawley.

So now I do not care what they say about me, or what happens to me. My spirit is already dead in me. My flesh shrinks from the thought of death by burning. Yes, that appalls me and I can only hope that what Thomasina said on her visit to me is true—that the smoke chokes the victim before the flesh chars and the boiling blood bursts the veins.

There, I have set it all down, honestly. And what does it all amount to? Five times in my lifetime—is it five?—there was Robin's whistle, Rawley's letter, the petticoat, Charles' letter, and Cromwell's manifesto; yes, five times something which I have held in my hand has communicated something to my mind. Twice—once over the matter of Robin's innocence and once in the matter of Rawley's affection—I have imposed my will on my circumstances. And always I have been able to make animals obey me implicitly. Does this amount to witchcraft? Am I damned not only in this life but in the life to come? I cannot remember ever wishing, or working, ill to anyone. I cannot, even now, wish positive ill even to those who tell those twisted, lying stories about the transparent black dog in the harvest field.

No, if I could wish anything it would be that I might die, quickly, easily, before the faggots are lighted.

Interlude

Lady Alice Rowhedge was found guilty of witchcraft and condemned to be burned. In the brief interval between the delivery and carrying-out of her sentence, she was taken back to the cell in the old Bridewell in the Friargate at Baildon. She must have gone and stood by the narrow window, unglazed and rendered still more narrow by a rusty iron bar. What happened, happened so swiftly that people going home from the trial and arguing about her guilt, or her innocence, actually *saw* and stepped aside to avoid a small black dog which was proceeding along the Friargate in peculiar circular fashion, seeming to wish to bite his own tail and crying as he went.

Alice Rowhedge—with what was almost her last breath—said that she saw the dog and imagined that he had a thorn in his flank. She called him and he came and she put out her arm, not without difficulty. The dog bit her, sinking his teeth into her hand, not once or twice but many times, for on account of the narrowness of the window and the angle at which her arm was held she could not easily withdraw it. The dog ran on as far as the corner, where a blacksmith, recognising the nature of its ailment, clubbed it to death with his hammer.

Inside the cell Lady Alice told the gaoler what she had done and what had happened and added, in what he called a wondering voice, "No dog ever bit me before!" Then in almost no time at all she fell into frenzy, and from frenzy to coma, and died.

Only the most stubbornly rational people—and they were rare at the time—reminded themselves and their hearers that the dog was real enough to have been killed by a blow from the blacksmith's hammer and that its wretched little carcass had lain on his dunghill for days, plain for all to see. The vast majority believed that a dog of quite another kind, the dog of the harvest field, had come to save the witch from her just deserts.

An abbreviated version of the story which she had written while she was awaiting trial was printed under the title of "A Witch's Confession," and a copy of it found its way into every household where one literate person lived, and even the least superstitious people were forced to admit that she *had* after all, died before the faggots were piled. Her story, with many variations, many embellishments, was told by the winter fires and under the summer trees, told so often that it became part of the folklore of the region.

After the King had been executed—another thing to argue about; for even in Suffolk, where most men had been against him, there were those who thought that such an extreme action boded no good—Merravay was taken in hand by the Commissioners and divided into three portions. The two that consisted of land only found a ready market, but the third, consisting of the house and gardens and about thirty acres of land, was hard to dispose of. Merravay itself had become a place to avoid, for dark and sinister stories were creeping around. And the house staring there blank-eyed across the fields, deep in its grounds where the nettles and brambles encroached upon the pinks and lilies and roses of Lady Alice's garden, grew daily more like a place where ghosts would walk than a place where people should live. Only little boys, inspired by greed and bold in company, would venture there on sunny afternoons to snatch nuts from the shrubbery and pears from the sheltered walls; then, retreating with their loot, they would tell tales of strange things seen and heard and resolutely braved.

One such party, early in a new season of nuts and pears, did receive a genuine fright; for Phyl Whymark, the woman from the tavern, suddenly appeared from the house and ordered them to be off and not come back. Merravay was her property, she said.

From a safe distance the boys mocked her, mocked her claim to ownership. But it was valid enough. And the older people, with longer memories, said, "Ah, so she got it, after all!"

The Matriarch

THERE'S no doubt about it, I ain't as spry as I was!

It's as much as I can do to stagger out here into the sun and drop down in this chair like a sack of meal.

But then, I reckon I must be close on ninety. Nobody can know for sure; they kept no count of birthdays when I was young. I got meself born, and I've kept meself alive, and when I come to take stock I can't help thinking that I ain't done so badly. A mite of luck, but in the main hard work and mother wit hev got me where I am today.

And where am I today? I'm sitting in the garden at Merravay, and I can look to right and left and straight ahead, and, for all I'm so long-sighted, as far as I can see belongs to me, my own, my very own.

Maybe I was meant to hev it; for there was a time long ago, though to me that fare like yesterday, when Sir Rawley Rowhedge was minded to marry me. He would hev done, too, but for the spells put on him by that whey-faced cousin of his—her that would hev burned for witch-craft if the Devil hadn't snatched her away. Nowadays folks make mock of witches and such-like, more fools they! I could tell 'em something; but I don't. What happened betwixt Rawley and me was our business then, and I've kept the secret all my life.

Till I took up with Rawley I'd kept meself to meself, and that weren't so easy. For one thing my mother was a byword for loose living; for an-other I went up to London every year, driving geese. We lived rough, sleeping in stacks and ditches along the road, and I was reckoned to be pretty. . . .

When Rawley took up with me and spoke serious about marriage I reckoned that was the reward of virtue—the virtue I'd often fought tooth and nail for; and when he fell under the spell and jilted me and give me fifty pounds, I reckoned that was the wages of sin. Between the two there was a bit of my life I never cared to think on. He was a right proper man, Rawley was; and I could never bear him much grudge; it wasn't his fault.

I was heartsick, but people like me don't brood over their feelings, leastways not their softish ones, and I plucked meself up and reckoned meself lucky to hev the money. And nobody was scornful to me. People reckoned he'd just hung about our place time he was drinking to drown his sorrow, and the one he was thought to hev jilted was Miss Headway.

I looked round for a way to put the money to good use. I did think about heving a pastry-cook's shop, for I was a fair hand at cooking; but there'd be no customers much in a village and I hated all towns. Moreover, by this time, my mother was dead and there was only one of my brothers—if you can call 'em that—living at home, and the way he was going on he didn't look like making owd bones. So I thought I'd wait a bit, and if he drunk hisself to death in good time, I'd spend my money making the tavern a better sort of place, the sort travellers would pull in at.

I found out a lawyer man that everybody spoke well of and went and arst him about putting money somewhere safe where it could breed a bit. I laugh to myself even now when I think about that first little business betwixt Mr. Turnbull and me and where it all led to in the end.

I'd no sooner laid the money away safe than I found I was in the family way. Christ in glory! I was so savage I could hev kilt myself. I'd allust set myself to be a cut above my mother, who'd had a bastard most years, and here I was, going the same road.

There was a chap or two would hev married me if I'd played my cards right, but I was still sore for Rawley and couldn't fancy any of 'em. So I told meself I'd get out of this fix same as I'd got into it, secret-wise.

First of all I tried every old-wives' cure I ever had heard of, mainly through hearing my mother say she wouldn't touch 'em. I jumped off ladders and heaved the heaviest things I could find, and one night went and stood in cold water up to my neck. But my John was a sight stubborner then than he ever was in later days. In the end I knew I'd either got to stand and brazen it out or get away. I towd my brother I was off to London to try to pick up a little money and threatened him well what I'd do if he burnt the place down or anything else silly time I was away, and off I went.

I knew where to make for—the Poultry Market, where hundreds of geese waddled in and were killed and dressed every day and where anybody that could see and had two hands could hev a job.

I wasn't exactly a stranger, and my home was nothing to be homesick for, but, God, I was miserable that time. I hated London, and the Poultry was a stinking place even for London, and the people I worked and lived with were low, scum of the earth. Still, it was good place to hide in.

I worked hard and laid by a shilling or two, and when my time came near I bargained with the woman at the house where I'd been sleeping to let me hev a room to meself for a bit. She towd me about a place started up by some kind ladies, a laying-in place for poor women, but I didn't want nothing like that. Nor I didn't want her messing about. I towd her so. The night I went back, feeling a bit queer, I give her two shillings.

"Thass rent till I get about again," I said, "and you keep outa my way."

She laughed. "You don't know whass coming," she said. "You may be hollering for me afore you've done."

"I may holler, but you keep out. I paid for this room and if you bust in, I'll claw you," I said.

I shoved a brukken chair under the knob of the door and settled to wait. I'd helped my mother more times than I could remember; I knew just what to do . . . and what not to do.

Next day, or the one after, I meant to go out of that room with my waist in the right place and nothing to show that any man'd made free with me.

I was my mother's second or third, and by the time I was of an age to help her she'd hev a baby as easy as she could wring out a cloth, so I'd no idea what heving a first baby meant. By noon next day, when the baby was born, I was that wore out with the pain and the struggle that what I had planned should happen damned nearly did happen, willy-nilly. But I roused myself enough just to take a look at the thing that had caused me such a lot of trouble . . . and with that one look I was undone. John and me hev been through a lot of things together, but I never loved him more than I did at that minute.

II

I could hev stayed in London, where one bastard more or less didn't matter; but I wanted my child to grow up in a healthier place; so regardless of shame and jibing, back to Nettleton I went as soon as I could face the trudge. And once there I cast round in my mind for some way of making a little money at the same time as I tended the baby and looked after what trade there was at the tavern.

I hit on pork pies.

I've worked hard all my days, but never harder than in the next few years. I reared, killed, and cleaned my own pigs, sold the choicest joints and made the rest—down to the shreds of meat that I could scrape from the toes and the jaws—into pies. There was the tavern, too; and a baby that I tried to bring up clean and healthy, and my brother well-nigh as helpless and a sight more nuisance. But I managed.

All this time the Witch, Alice Rowhedge, was living smooth and soft up at Merravay. She'd had a baby, too; a boy, a fine handsome little chap, but not a patch on mine, or so I thought. Hers was more like Rawley, with the same chestnut-coloured hair; my John took after me and that was lucky. I could see Rawley in him though.

I had kind of cherished the notion of getting him a bit of schooling and give him a push up in the world that way; but he never took kindly to learning. Any other sort of work he was a wonder at, very willing and very strong.

The years went by, my brother died, John grew, the war broke out, and the tavern trade dwindled, but the pie business flourished, and John and me had laid penny to penny till we'd got another fifty pounds to set aside with that that Rawley had give me; and we was looking about for a bit of land to rear more pigs and geese on, when Captain Samuel Fletcher came into our lives.

Him and half a dozen troopers arrived one afternoon and billeted theirselves on us. The men went into the bar-room, what was hardly ever used for its proper purpose; for, what with the rules and the scowlings, you could hardly sell a drink them days. Captain Fletcher follered me into the kitchen and after beating about the bush for a bit arst me if I could let him hev a sup of something. I was wary and said no at first, but then I see he wasn't trying to trap me, he was a proper drinker and he wanted something badly. So I went down the cellar and brung up some good owd October ale and a little brandy that I'd been howding on to. He was as happy as a yard dog let off the chain for a bit.

He got to telling me what he suffered in Colchester, where the taverns were shut down, and I towd him how I was planning to get out of the trade and get some land and he said, "Ma'am, take my advice and wait. There'll be land going begging when this is over."

"How so?" I asked.

"Once Cromwell is safe in the saddle," he said, "he'll take the land off all them that fought for the King. And once they get to breaking up the big estates, mark my words, land'll be mighty cheap."

"Not about these parts. Them with land about here are all for Parliament."

"I know one who isn't," he said, making a knowing sort of face. I arst who, but he was a man who could keep his own counsel even in his cups, which is a thing I respect.

Then he suggested that he should give me a regular order for pork pies.

"Delivered to me, at Colchester barracks. And to my mind, ma'am, all a good pork pie needs is a drop of something to wash it down."

"And to *my* mind," I said, "there's nothing easier to carry in and out than a nice bit of washing. You send me your dirty linen. . . . For send bare pies amongst a lot of soldiers," I said, "I just dare not."

We understood each other.

Thass funny to think that about this same time the Witch up at Merravay was setting about her bit of smuggling.

I've never been much of a thinking woman, I been too busy; but now and then thoughts'll go through your head time your hands are busy, and one thing I thought once is this. Loving a person and hating one are alike in this—you take note of what they do, where they go, and what happen to them. I *hated* Alice Rowhedge so much that if somebody'd stood at the crossroads and said her name in a whisper I'd hev heard it.

Well, things went wrong with her and she was carted off to gaol. At first we thought it was for helping to get arms to the King and, of course, there was nothing I could say; but when it come to witchcraft that was different. I knew she'd put a spell on Rawley; men don't suddenly, overnight, fall in love with their ugly cousins that hev been living under the same roof with them for years. Alice Rowhedge was there when Rawley's wife died, but he hadn't turned to her then, he'd turned to me. So though I wasn't going to say ought about the one spell I *knew* she'd worked, I could and did say about the time when I was stooking at Merravay. . . .

III

After a bit the thing what Captain Fletcher said would happen, did happen. They put Merravay up for sale; but I could hev cried with vexation because of the way they did it. No separate fields and pastures the same as I'd been counting on. Three big lots they cut it into; the New Holding land and the Merravay land next to it was one—and Sir Walter Fennel bought it; the Slipwell land and the other part of Merravay on that side was another—bought by Mr. Blackwood of Muchanger; the house and two fields and meadows made the third. It was as plain as the nose on your face that Sir Walter and Mr. Headway had had a say in the dividing; not that I minded their getting what they wanted; what raised my gall was the thought of the two fields and meadows near the house, any one of which would have suited my purpose, all going back to wild while the house went to rack and ruin. Nobody wanted that lot, for people who looked to live in a great house wanted more land, and people who wanted a little land didn't want a great house. So there it stood, shorn of its acres, useless as a ship gone aground.

I was still smarting when one day Captain Fletcher came grinning into my place and I rounded on him pretty sharp.

"That was rotten bad advice you give me," I said. "But for you and your land going begging I'd hev bought Croop's meadow time that was for sale. I went and let that go; and now I shan't never get the bit of land I hanker after."

He grinned and I went on: "And I should like to clout the head of the fool that divided that place."

"Clout away," he said, and stuck his close-cropped skull towards me. "You!"

"The same, ma'am. I'm one of the Commissioners. The army is in command now. Bless you, I thought I'd done you a good return for favours received. I knew that neither of the bespoke customers needed a house . . . so I tucked away a nice little thirty-acre bit *under* the house, so to speak . . . and then you go for me like a vixen!"

"If you did that you're more of a fool than I thought you! Thirty acres and a mansion; what use is that to a poor woman like me? All I've managed to scratch together in twenty years' hard grind is a hundred and fifteen pounds."

"Well, offer me that!"

"For Merravay and thirty acres. Man, you're mad."

"Maybe. Go on, make a firm offer and its yours. Not today; not to-morrow . . . but before the year's out. 'In default of better offer,' see? We must do things orderly."

"But suppose you have a better offer," I said, very dry in the mouth.

"Well," he said, dragging out the word. "I'm only one of four, and there're strict eyes everywhere; but there are ways and means. For one thing it's a very bad-reputed house. They say the Witch walks there. Of course . . . that wouldn't bother a sensible woman like you; but, being an honest man, I should be bound to warn any prospective buyer. Shouldn't I?"

"You ain't mocking me?"

"I'm dealing with you, ma'am, as you dealt with me, fair and square and underhand. And now, have you anything to wet the bargain?"

I never said nothing to nobody, not even my John, in case things should go wrong. The best part of a year went by and sometimes the impatience in me was like a pain; another season wasted and me getting older and the land going back to wild. They say in our parts, 'Fallow hath no fellow,' but they only mean for a year.

However, the day came when Captain Fletcher visited me again, this time with another man, and all very strict and stiff. They had come to tell me, they said, that since no better offer had been made for Merravay, they would take mine, ridiculous as it was.

"I don't know about ridiculous," I said. "There ain't so many people want a house where queer things are to be seen and heard, nor land so weeded over that you can't tell ploughland from pasture. I made my offer afore the weeds had got such a howd!"

That changed his tune for him!

Knowing what I knew about Alice Rowhedge's power, and hearing all the stories that were springing up and spreading about the house, it is a wonder that I didn't feel a bit funny about going to live there, especially as I'd been one to speak against her; but to tell the truth I never give the haunting a thought. I went up alone to look at the place for the first time as soon as I'd handed over my money and got the keys. There'd been a red climbing rose over the porch and part of it had come loose and grown right over the door, so I had to fight my way in, scratching myself something cruel. I'd expected it to be musty, and dampish and darkish inside, but it wasn't; it was warm and dry and sweet-smelling and there was nothing but the silence to show that nobody'd been there for a long time. I walked all through, thinking about the uses I could put some of the rooms to, and if I thought of anybody it was Rawley; which room had he slept in, where had he taken his food? And what would it have felt like, I wondered, to hev come in, married to him, with the place all furnished? I'd hev been shy and awkward, and scared of the old grandmother; now I was bold and certain of myself, and knew I'd got the best bargain in the world. Maybe that suited me better, after all.

I was in the kitchen then, looking round and planning how John and me'd live there and how he'd come in when the day's work was done and how I'd be getting the meal ready time he washed. It'd suit us fine, I thought. And then I heard the laughing. High and shrill and merry, as though somebody'd heard my thoughts and laughed with a—Ah, so you may think! Alice Rowhedge had always been a one for laughing when she was little, given half a chance. For just a minute I went cold, and caught my breath. . . . Then I realised that the laughing came from the garden, and out I went and found six or seven little urchins getting pears off the trees by the wall. I towd them to be off and not come back, and they ran a little way and then stood and mocked me, "Owd Phyl Whymark, t'ain't your place."

"Oh yes it is!" I said. And that was the first time I said it. And somehow after that it seemed true. And—So much for ghosts! I said to myself. Let that be a lesson to you.

I'd been to Mr. Turnbull, of course, to get back my money and the interest it had gathered, and I'd asked him, this time, to lend me fifty pounds to buy stock with. He said something about security.

"You write yourself a paper," I said, "to say that do I die or come to ruin, you're to hev fifty pound worth of stock."

"But if you were ruined, Mistress Whymark, there might be no stock."

"Well, the house and land can't get away. Write it so."

He coughed and fidgeted about with the things on his table; then he said,

"I think it would be bad to burden a property with a mortgage so soon. Tell me—you hold your tavern freehold, do you not?"

"I did; but I just fixed to swop it with Matt Bowyer for his owd mare and wagon."

"Has that transaction taken place?"

"We talked about it last night."

"The licence to brew and sell ale is in order, I take it?"

"Oh yes; but that ain't worth much these days."

"Slightly more than a mare and wagon, I think. I believe I could get you fifty pounds."

He did, and six months later they made a loop of good hard road that just reached the old tavern, and the coaches came. But I didn't grudge it; I'd been prepared to take an owd horse and wagon for the place, so I hadn't been wronged; and the new road made it easier for me to get my stuff to London. I began on that right away, heving no truck with the little towns what could get more stuff when they needed. My time in the Poultry Market had taught me what a hungry place London was. Whereas geese might open at two shilling apiece in Baildon or Colchester and drop to eightpence when folks'd sell at a loss rather than trail 'em home again, in London there was always a hundred daft people rushing about to find a goose after nightfall, even on Christmas Eve itself.

At first, heving set everybody plenty of work to do, I'd go up with John to show him where to go and how to do his deals, but he took to that the same as he always took to anything real and in the way of work; so then I could stay at home. I had broody hens sitting and fatting hens penned all over the ground floor of the house. I had geese in the orchard, and sheep under the trees in the avenue, pigs in the yard, and calves in the meadows. Sometimes it fared to me that I was feeding half London, I poured food out at such a rate; cheese and butter, bacon, meat and table fowls, eggs and cream. I used to work till I was past speech, wellnigh deaf and blind. I never did stop except to throw a bit of food into meself and John when he was home; and at night I used to drop onto my bed, in my clothes as though I'd been stunned. And I know that old Noah packing his Ark never got so many living creatures into a square yard as I did at Merravay. Every penny I made I put straight back into the place and in ten years I never bought myself nothing but footwear and a herring now and then. I couldn't grow herrings and I was inordinate fond of them.

V

One morning—a lovely June morning it was—I noticed my hands while I was milking; and they was the hands of an owd woman, all gnarled and twisted like tree roots. And I did a bit of reckoning and knew I must be fifty, maybe a bit more. Getting along; soon be going down-hill . . .

That day I said to John, sudden-like,

"Did you ever think about getting married?"

He gaped at me. "I been thinking," I said. "I'm getting on. I should like to see my own grandchildren."

"You ain't sick, are you?"

"You know I'm never sick—ain't got time. But I reckon that if you're going to marry you should do it soon. You're thirty!"

He didn't say anything, or seem to think any more about it, and I reckoned that that'd be another thing for me to handle. So I looked around for a good strong girl, a farmer's daughter, likely to be a good help to us, but at the same time bright and lively. And I picked just the one, a girl named Hester Fulger that made beautiful lace in her spare time. I thought I'd ask her to dinner one Sunday, for though I'd never had no advantages I knew how things should be done. Any girl bidden to Sunday dinner to a house where there was an unmarried man knew which way the wind was blowing. But afore I got so far with my plans John went off to London on his next trip, was away two days more than I'd counted on, and got back just as the late summer dusk was coming down, bringing a girl with him. He walked into the kitchen, howding her by the hand, and before I could speak for the surprise at seeing her he said, "Mother, this is Alison, my wife."

I never see, in all my days, a poorer, more dwindling, more scared looking creature. She was clean, and had a sort of prettiness with her great tangle of curls and huge eyes, but she was about the size of a twelve-year child that has never had a square meal in all its life and expected everybody it met to give it a clout.

"Married?" I said; and the word went on ringing through the kitchen.

"Two days ago," said John.

"I'm afraid this has given you a shock," said the girl. Her voice surprised me; it was sweet and clear and very sure.

"I am a bit took aback," I admitted. "Hev you and my boy been long acquaint?"

"Two years," she said. I wanted to ask where he had found her. I tried to take comfort in the fact that she was too shabby to be a street whore. I turned back to the stove to hide my mortification.

John said, "Whass for supper?"

"A bit of gammon and peas."

"That'll do. Only Alison can't eat fat, so give her my lean and me her fat, will you."

It was only a little thing, but I do believe it was the first time in all his thirty years that he'd handed me an order. While I dished up he took her cotton bonnet and hung it on the peg over his working clothes and set her in a chair by the table, as if she was the Queen, and she turned her great eyes about, taking it all in, missing nowt and saying nowt. I took my place, feeling ill at ease, but trying not to let the upset put me off my food, trying to think of the next job waiting for me. It was no good, there across the table she set, my daughter-in-law . . . where I'd meant to make a bid for Hester Fulger. Oh, it was hard!

She ate very dainty, taking her time, and now and agin wiping her lips on a bit of a handkerchief. And for all her eyes looked so scared, she wasn't as nervous as I was; for though I couldn't find a word to say and could only look at her and then away agin, quick, she looked me full in the face as if she was taking my measure, and once she smiled, a right sweet, friendly smile, but not as if she was asking me to like her, more as though *she* was minded to like me. In one of my sharp glances I noticed her hands, thin and small they were, like a little bird's claws, but red and rough with hard work. Taking them into account and the smallness and the frightened look, I guessed that John had picked her up out of pity, same as he might a stray kitten. There was a very gentle streak in my boy. Nice for her, but what about me, counting on a good strong girl to take on when I got older; and what about the healthy great boys I'd pictured in my mind's eye?

Next morning when John took his place aside me at the early milking, I said to him sharp and sudden,

"What come over you, boy? And where did you find such a dolly?"

At The Shepherd and Dog, just behind the Poultry, where he lodged in London, he said. He'd had his eye on her for a long time, feeling sorry for her doing menial, ill-suited work. "She looked like a flower on a muck heap," he said.

I nearly said that we hadn't much use for flowers at Merravay; but I held my tongue. He was my boy; we'd stuck together through thick and thin; and if he wasn't as bright and sharp as I could hev wished at times, maybe he wasn't to blame for that. I wasn't going to quarrel with him on account of that little bit of thread!

Then presently we went in to our breakfast, and there she was, with it all ready and neatly set out. She'd found, somehow, the one tablecloth I owned, the one I'd washed and got ready against the day I arst Hester Fulger to Sunday dinner! And she'd put a few rosebuds in a mug in the middle of the table, and got water hot so we could wash our hands. Something new had come to Merravay . . . and I suppose you couldn't say that it wasn't wanted.

So in time we shook down together; though there were odd minutes when I was minded of the Bywater man what caught a mermaid in his net and brung her home and married her, minutes when I would think— What a tool for a busy woman to hev to put up with! She couldn't push, she couldn't pull, she couldn't lift. She wasn't unwilling, she just hadn't no strength. She'd wash—she was a great one to wash—but by the time she'd got the things soaked they was too heavy for her to lift and wring out; and though she took to the dairy work very kindly, when she churned I had to heave the cream in and then listen till she called, so I could tip the butter out; else she'd turn the churn over, trying. There was things she could do that I couldn't, read and write and reckon in her head, and she sewed beautiful; she mended us up very tidy; I never was much good with a needle and I never had time.

She quickened sooner than I'd thought for, but she carried the baby so ill that I often wondered whether it'd come to anything. I used to look at her and think of myself in like case and think maybe, in a rough and ready way, the burden is fashioned to the back. What she'd hev done wringing geese's necks and taking their insides out up to the very day, God alone knows. Then her time came and for a bit we reckoned we'd lose her, and it was then that I knew I had a fondness for her. My best Dutch cow calved the very same day . . . but I stayed by Alison, though John had fetched the doctor and I wasn't needed all that much.

The baby wasn't the poor pingling little thing I'd expected, and in a way braced myself to take and add to my load. A great lumping girl it was, and Alison said it must be named Phyllis for me.

Less than a year later Alison was in the family way again and this time we all had hopes of a boy. Young Phyllis was doing well; the place was prospering. Things looked fair and pleasant for us, and then the blow fell. And what a blow it was!

VI

Along come Mr. Turnbull one afternoon, when I was just laying the oak logs to my smoke oven to cure a couple of pigs, and say he's sorry to bring me such tidings but the fact is that Merravay, and all the land to it, do now by rights belong back to Sir Charles Rowhedge what fought for his lawful king.

We'd known, of course, that the King was back in London; good for trade that was, too. We knew owd Oliver—the tavern-shutter—had been dug up and hung in chains . . . just like the Witch in her writings said she had seen him. A rare stir in Nettleton that caused. But apart from the men what had signed the order for the owd King's killing they said nobody was to be punished . . . but I could see in the blink of an eye that Mr. Turnbull, what had been a good business friend to me, thought it right and fair that I should be cast out of Merravay . . . and if that wasn't punishing!

"But I paid for the place. All legal and above board."

"Ma'am," he said, "you made a token payment to them as had no right to sell. Count yourself fortunate," he said, "that so small a sum was involved. There are those in England today, thousands of them, especially in the West country, who are going to lose property for which they paid the full market price."

"Lose it? You mean just go away and leave it . . . have nothing?"

"Not perhaps so precipitately as that. Sir Charles, who has been engaged in the nutmeg trade in the Dutch East Indies, has arrived in Amsterdam, from whence he has written to me. I have written to inform him of the . . . er . . . position and he will probably come to see about things for himself. But I thought it only fair to warn you that Merravay is no longer yours."

I set the logs right and closed the door of the fireplace, opened the oven and saw the smoke flowing smoothly through. I took up one half carcass and hung it carefully on the hooks. Two pigs . . . four sides of bacon . . . mustn't waste or fumble . . . they at least were *mine*. But I felt sick.

"You have done well out of your venture, taking it all in all," said Mr. Turnbull, as though he was chiding a child for sulking when a treat was over.

It was true; I'd made profits; but they was all out there, walking about, eating their heads off, past profits carefully bred back to make future ones . . . it'd have been better if I'd bought meself diamond rings, or stuffed money into a mattress. Cut the ground from under me, and my stock was nothing but a liability—or so much dead meat!

I shut the door of the smoke oven very carefully so as not to check the flow.

"I sincerely hope," said Mr. Turnbull, "that you will be successful in finding alternative accommodation. You are lucky in having had a little warning. . . . I have heard of others less fortunate."

But what comfort was that to me?

There followed another bit of my life that I don't ever want to think about.

One thing that made me mad was that when those who'd sided with the King had held on and been fined and sold some land to pay the fines the people who bought that land weren't to be turned out. Not far from us the Hattons had been fined and sold a bit of the Mortiboys estate, and the man who bought that was reckoned legal owner still. I'd bought Merravay at bargain price, that I'd never deny . . . but it was the best price Fletcher and his friend could get. I'd bought it, bought it . . . worked and slaved over it, put my money back into it, and I had less rights than a squatter. It didn't seem fair. They talk about angels in disguise; Captain Fletcher was the Devil got up to look like an angel, so far as I was concerned.

Still . . . I plucked meself together again; it was no use setting down and crying. I took a sharp look at my stock and I knew there was two things I must, at all costs, save out of the wreck—my brood mares and my Dutches. The mares had a story of their own. Lady Alice Rowhedge had done her riding on a famous black stallion; and after she was tried there was talk about killing him, but Mrs. Blackwood, who was Rawley's daughter by his first wife, took the animal away to Muchanger. There she was the only one with a good word for him; he behaved like the Devil, savaging stable boys and always trying to break out and get back to Merravay. Maybe he started the stories of Lady Alice riding that bit of road.

When I first went to Merravay, I bought, cheap as I could, a work mare that was owd, had had a hard life, and was past all foolery you'd have said. My John, who was good to dumb beasts, fed her up and fussed her, and she got right frisky and one fine morning we found her and the Witch's stallion in the meadow together. In due time she dropped a foal—a mare—that was a rare freak; because put to a work horse, she'd give you one twice her own size, heavy and solid out of the ordinary, and put to a riding horse, she'd drop something lighter and swifter and more shapely than was ever seen in our parts. Whatever went into her came out *more*; if you'd put her to a jackass she'd have handed you something with ears a yard long. I'd reared two of her mare foals, one heavy and one light, and they'd dropped some extraordinary young 'uns, the heavies heavier and the light 'uns lighter than any ever known. I meant to howd on to them two mares come what might.

Then there was my Dutches. They had a story too. While owd Oliver was still fighting the Dutch, one of their ships was brought into Bywater. The captain had had his wife and child on board, and he'd got a cow and her calf, too. They was for sale—by orders of the Mayor of Bywater—one day when I happened to be there; and lots of folks had gathered round the pen to see them, they being curiously marked, pied, black and white. I noticed that when the calf—a heifer—had suckled its fill the cow's bag wasn't half empty and I thought—Thass a good yielder. I made up my mind that if the bidding wasn't too sharp I'd try for the pair myself. And though folks had come to stare few made bids for animals they didn't reckon to be a canny colour, so I got them cheap; and then, keeping a sharp look out, I heard of a man called Stebbing, in the Yarmouth trade, that had brought a cow and a bull of the same kind back from one of his voyages; and I swopped his bull's service for my heifer calf and for a year or two we went hither and thither till I had a herd. He never got one because most of his animals died, eating yew. Dutches give more milk, and more cream to it, than any kind known and I could ask almost any price I fancied for a heifer calf.

So the first, the least, thing I must do, knowing I was to be chucked out of Merravay, was to find pasture and shelter for my Dutches. And till I began to try that I never knew how much people was against me. No! No! No! Nobody'd rent me house room.

In the end I was so desperate that I thought of Strawless Common. So I went out there and tried; but there wasn't a cottage to let and the grazing rights went with the cottages and the rough lot that lived there said if I put my beasts on it they'd stone 'em.

It was coming home from Strawless that I heard the Witch laughing.

I ain't a fanciful woman, as I'd proved; but I hadn't ate for days, nor slept for many nights, and I was ill with worry. For many a long year I hadn't given the Witch a thought, except that now and again, with my broody hens setting in her big hall, and my motherless calves sucking gruel in her withdrawing room I'd now and then thought—Ha! And it's me and my boy and my creatures that hev Merravay now!

And now she was laughing at me. Her boy was coming to drive me out and I couldn't find a corner for my mares and my Dutches. Them that laugh last laugh loudest . . . and she was laughing last. And I heard her, just like she used to laugh when she was little and could get away from her Granny and come out where I was getting the geese ready.

Hearing the laugh, it struck me I was going crazy, and small wonder. John was gone to London, all ignorant of what was toward; and Alison I couldn't bring myself to tell, her being in the state she was; there wasn't anybody that I could talk to.

I got back to Merravay and there was Phyllis tied into a chair, and Alison, wearing a pretty apron, with a meal that I had no taste for, waiting. And she said,

"There's a letter for you, Mother Whymark," and she took it from behind the salt jar on the dresser.

I took it and turned it about in my hands. I knew Mr. Turnbull's seal. The fool, I thought, writing to me, when he knew I couldn't read. I laid it on the table and made a show of eating, feeling sick and sicker . . . I knew what was in it . . . the date by which we must be gone.

Alison lugged Phyllis off to bed, and as soon as I was alone I broke the seal and looked at my letter. A date, I reckoned, might be set down in figures. But it was just a mass of words. I set there staring. Alison came back and began to gather the crocks.

"Leave them," I said. "Look, you'd best come and read this to me. But I don't want you to fret. I've known about this . . ." I tapped the letter ". . . for a week or so now, and I ain't yet worrited my way out. But I shall, my dear, don't you fret. Just read out what it say and let's know the worst."

So she read it out. It was all a mass of long, learned words, but the gist of it was plain enough. Sir Charles Rowhedge had decided that he never wanted to see Merravay again, since he had heard from Mr. Turnbull the details about his father's and mother's deaths. So he'd given the lawyer the office to sell the estate, either in whole or in parts. For the house and thirty acres now in my "temporary possession" Mr. Turnbull thought a thousand pounds a fair price and was giving me the benefit of the first refusal.

"There you are, my girl," I said, when she'd done. "That's what I've been living with these last weeks. We're homeless. And whass worse I can't find a place for the Dutches!" Then I remembered the state she was in and that we was hoping for a lusty boy, so I pulled up short and patted her shoulder and told her again not to worry. I'd think of something, I'd manage.

And as I said that I heard the Witch laugh again; and suddenly something went snap in my head. I knew I was walking up and down, up and down the length of the kitchen, beating my hands together and talking, talking, telling her everything that I had tried, the rebuffs I'd met with, the hatred I'd uncovered. I knew I was doing wrong, for Alison started to cry, and I turned on her and said, "Cry. Go on. Be glad you *can* cry! I wish to God I could."

Then she was taking me by the arm and pushing me into a chair. "You must be calm, Mother Whymark," she said. "You'll wake the baby and drive yourself to distraction. We'll think of something. We're not ruined yet. . . . Look, I'll get you something to drink. Something to put heart into you." She walked towards the dresser and I thought she was going to get a mug and fill it with milk, and I said, "It's kind of you, Alison, but milk wouldn't settle in me now. I feel right sick. But I'm all right. I'll steady meself."

She stood by the dresser and laid her hand on the side of it and looked at me very odd.

"I couldn't help finding out," she said. "There was such a mass of cobwebs behind it that one day I got a man from the yard to shift it for me. You needn't have bothered to hide it from me. Working in an inn set me rather against it. . . ."

I didn't understand; and when I see her, what never could heave anything, take and try to shove the great dresser aside, I was afraid she'd took leave of her wits.

"What are you doing?" I asked, sharp-like, "and what are you talking about? You come and set and calm yourself."

She gave the thing another piteous little push and said, half crying, "I can't budge it. You ought to have had more foresight and kept at least a little brandy where one could get at it."

"What brandy?" I got up and went over to her quickly, calm and sensible again now that she'd gone distraught.

"The brandy that's in the cellar."

"What cellar?"

"Down behind here. . . ."

"I never knew," I said. I took and give the dresser a mighty heave and there, sure enough, was a door, matted with cobwebs again. "Christ in Glory!" I said.

"I thought you'd put it there on purpose. I'm sorry . . . I've wronged you in my mind."

"This dresser . . ." I gave it another bit of a shove ". . . was here when I come; I thought it was a fixture. Mrs. Blackwood took the movable stuff. You say you been down there, Alison?"

"I peeped. I wanted to know what you were hiding from me."

"Git a candle," I said. I pushed the door and it give way, it wasn't locked though there was a great keyhole. A short flight of steps, made of red brick like the house, led down into the dark. Alison come along with the candle, and, bidding her be careful, I led the way down.

It was a great cellar, and as far as the light of the candle reached we could see the casks alaying on the brick stillions and the bottles on the racks. I was dumb-struck. But I could see what had happened. Rawley had been fond of his liquor, and had had some connection with ships and foreign parts; when the war started he'd laid in stuff to last him a lifetime; and when the end come, somebody, some faithful servant maybe, failing to lay hand on the key had done the next best thing and shoved the great dresser in front of the door. And but for Alison's craze to root out spiders nobody'd ever hev known what was hid. So here it all was, French brandy enough to float a ship, in a manner of speaking, and other things as well; wines from France and Spain and Madeiry and the clear fiery stuff that the Dutch drink. It was like some poor toper's dream. In one little bin there was even a lot of homemade stuff, cherry and damson and sloe brandy in pretty little flasks sealed with pig's gut; they gleamed red and purple like jewels in the candlelight as I hauled them out.

Rawley's gift to me, made all unbeknownst. That was the thought that went through my head. And there was a picture, too; Rawley laying dead in his blood, the Witch gone on her last wild gallop, the soldiers prowling through the house, and some foresighted creature shoving that dresser in front of the door!

And then it come to me what all this stuff was worth. With the King back and everybody wishful to make merry there was a great dearth of real good liquor in the land. Put with the mite I'd saved, what I could raise selling off stock, the price I could get for this wondrous store might just save us. And with that thought I came over all weak and wobbly.

"Ally, we're saved," I said, and I leaned myself up against a cask and began to cry like a baby.

Alison turned and scuttled up the stairs, leaving me in the dark. And I thought of the Witch laughing at me, just a minute since, and Rawley saving me. I'd allust known it wasn't just a lustful passing fancy he'd had for me . . . he'd meant me to be mistress of Merravay, and spite of all, spite of the spells and everything, it had come about.

Alison come back with a couple of mugs. She took up a bottle at random and very expert knocked off its neck against the wall. She splashed some of the liquor into the mugs. It was Dutch snaps, and snap it did. It fair took my head off. "Oh Ally," I said, when I got my breath back, "if you hadn't been such a spider-chaser!" And I started to laugh.

So the time come when we began to see the fruits of our labours. London kept growing and prices went up and we was all ready to make the best of 'em. I was still working from dawn till dark—and beyond—but in such good heart that the work came easy. In the year 1670—the year when Alison bore her son at last, her second child had been a girl, called for *her* mother, Maud—I had enough money and enough pluck to buy back the New Holding land from the Fennels. They'd put a lot of money into some wild-cat scheme for starting a company to trade against the big East India Company, and they'd come to grief and had to sell acres to get clear. And after that nothing went wrong for us; we was proper farmers at last, not just dealers and hucksters.

There was one more baby, another girl, named Agnes, who turned out just like me to look at but feather-brained. The owdest, young Phyllis, hadn't my looks but she was most like me inside. Right a dangerous little girl she was when young, for you had but to say, "No, my dear, you can't manage that yet!" and next thing you knew she'd managed it and stood there looking at you, a bit sneering. Long before she could reach the table she'd stand on a stool and make bread, grunting and clenching her little teeth and kneading away at the dough as if it was her enemy. Maud, the next one, I hadn't much use for, a whining child and very jealous of Phyllis, who was two years owder in age and twenty in all that mattered. The boy, called John like his father, came just right— when things was going well; he hadn't Phyllis' fighting spirit; very easy going he was, happy and idle. Just the stuff to make a gentleman of.

Alison often said I spoiled John, and maybe I did. *My* John took and died the year after Agnes was born. He wasn't much more than forty and there should hev been long years ahead of him; he'd never ailed to my knowledge, and the day he died he ate his dinner as usual. It got dusk and then dark and in the end I went to call him to supper and there he was, dead on the stable floor with a bucket of water overset beside him. That was a sore blow to me; and it changed something inside me. All the scraping and striving didn't seem much good when folks could take off and die young like that. He'd never had much out of life except hard work and hope for the future, and just as the good times was coming . . . So maybe I did pander to the boy, giving him what I'd hev liked to give his father.

And the money kept pouring into Merravay. There'd been two laws passed that did me a power of good. One kept out the cheap foreign corn and the other kept out the cheap Irish cattle. In Ireland, I was towd, there's rain every day and the grass is knee-high; the Irish put a bull and some cows in a field and then lay down on their beds and wait till 'tis time to drive the young down to the cattle boats. Costing nowt to rear, they sold very cheap and was a thorn in the flesh to such as us. Owd

Oliver was allust fighting the Irish, but he never had the sense to deal 'em a blow that way. King Charles did, and I blessed him for it.

I was able to lay money by now, as well as set the house to rights and send Johnny to a right good school that Alison knew about.

Alison came into her own at that time. Never in all my days had I touched a curtain, nor trod on carpet, nor seen any eating tools except a knife, a two-pronged metal fork, and a horn spoon; I was more ignorant even than girls what had gone into service. But Alison knew all about such things.

I liked everything she bought, it was all good solid handsome stuff and I paid for it gladly. Johnny had to hev a proper home to come back to and not be shamed; but feel at home in the rooms that Alison furnished I just could *not*. I felt I must walk on tiptoe and speak in a whisper. All them lovely shining things was mine, but they didn't know that, and there was no way of letting 'em know. They just shone at me, scornful.

And then there was clothes. All my days I'd worn a short skirt, well clear of the mud and dust, and a bodice with sleeves that'd roll up out of the way; on my legs I had knitted hose and on my feet what was called in our parts "high-lows"—higher than shoes to keep out the mud, and lower than boots to be easy to get in and out of. A good pair, well nailed, would last ten or twelve year and they shape to your feet; they get wet and fold in the right place and though they seem as hard as wood they're a lot more comfortable than any soft shoe. But, of course, in my rig I looked what I was, an owd workwoman.

That didn't suit Alison; so she bought a roll of plum-coloured silk and she made a dress. Lovely she made it, with lace ruffles and everything . . . Lord, if I could hev had that when I was a wench! But I was too owd. The waist of it nipped me so I had to breathe careful, and the skirt was so long and full that I tripped over it and nigh fell flat on my face.

The girls laughed and Alison got cross with 'em, fearing I'd mind. I just said, "Unhook me, then I can laugh too!" For there is something good and comical in sparrers got up in pheasants' feathers. But I said, "I'll wear it, Ally; I promise you. 'Tis a beautiful gown and I thank you for sewing it. I'll lay it by and keep it for the weddings."

And then Ally said, in a bitter sort of voice that she didn't often use, "Weddings! Where're they going to find husbands I'd like to know."

That was what we call a "lickser," meaning anything, a question, or a job, or a situation that hev you licked. There was Phyllis, on the plain side, mighty proud and masterful, handy and smart, she'd hev made any man a good wife. But what man? The poor was scared of us, the better sort scorned us. There we was, so far as marrying was concerned, neither fish, fowl, nor good red herring. No decent sort of farming man would hang round a plain girl, however good, for fear of being thought after her money. And I doubt whether Phyllis would hev taken a poor chap.

And there was Maud, a bit better looking, but a misery and given to good works. Cracked on the parson, she was . . . but he was married well and truly, with six little 'uns.

And there was that good-looking young scatterbrain Agnes, without a thought in her head except horses—but it was early days to worry about *her*.

But the days mounted up; same as the pence that turned into pounds. And it come to the time when Johnny was finished at Cambridge and was coming home for good. Alison said, "I just hope that he'll take an interest in the land and the stock. That is his only hope. . . ." She'd been ailing for a bit, so I was gentle with her and just said,

"Hope of what?"

"A happy full life," she said. "He'll have no friends here, will he? Nobody to talk to . . . to associate with. And I'm so afraid that he'll turn to London, where any young man with money to spend is welcome and fussed over. . . . It's such a pity . . . because, given half a chance, he could fit in here so well."

And I groaned to myself. I could send Johnny away and buy him an education and give him everything that was needed to make a gentleman of him. But there was no denying that once back at Merravay he'd be just the grandson of owd Phyl Whymark, who'd come from the tavern with her bastard, got Merravay for a song, and made a fortune.

I said, a bit harshly, "Ally, when I was his age I was hard put to it to keep myself and my child with food to eat. And I still reckon that two meals a day and roof overhead is the main thing to strive for. The rest is just trimmings! Either they come of their own accord or they ain't worth worrying about."

But for all that I was as glad as anybody when it turned out that Johnny wouldn't lack company, for a while at least; for when he come home that summer he brought his own with him. And what company, too! Young Lord Thrapston, no less, that was son to the Marquess of Whardale—lucky for him to be born in the purple for he was a nitwit if ever I see one. So far as I know he never did but one sensible thing in his life, and that was taking up with our Agnes.

Just at this minute he was in trouble. He'd got into debt and gone gambling, and his father, a very furious owd man by all accounts, had said he'd have his hide when next he set eyes on him, so he dussn't go home, and had to go what he called "to ground" till such time as his aunt, as was away drinking some special waters at a place called Bath, could get up to Leicestershire and talk the owd man round. So without a roof to his head or a penny in his pocket he was glad to accept Johnny's invitation to ride home with him and stay with us for a bit.

He wasn't like anybody we'd ever seen before. Since he'd gone to school and all that, Johnny had allust seemed sort of frisky and non-sensical to me, but set aside his friend Toby, Johnny looked as sober and solemn as a Baptist minister. Still, daft as he was, allust larking about and laughing, he had a way with him, though not much to look at, too much nose and not enough chin; and I reckon that Johnny had warned him to look out for *me*, for he did seem to go out of his way to be civil.

He'd been with us three weeks when he had a letter from his aunt that set him whooping and halloing as though he'd started a fox. She'd talked his father round, as he had said she would, and he was free to go home; and I was looking forward to the day when he did for Alison would keep me rigged out in the silk gown and in place of my comfortable high-lows a pair of thin shoes, no more than slippers, in which my feet seemed to hit the ground cruel at every step. But he didn't shift and he didn't shift and there was Agnes looking as mischievous as a monkey . . . and next thing I knew they was talking about being in love and going to get married.

Oh-ho, I said to myself, so the wind is blowing from that quarter again, is it? Well, it ain't going to blow Agnes what it blowed me! Maybe there's a body in Leicestershire clever with spells too! Though that weren't really what I feared, more the father and the argumentating and maybe auntie shedding a tear or two. So I took Agnes by the scruff of her neck and shut her in her bedroom and I took his lordship and I talked to him like he'd never been talked to before. But he held that he was serious; he'd never seen a girl like Agnes, he said, nor never would again and he was ready to marry her tomorrow.

"Then you'd best go down and fix things with Parson," I said, "for next time you see Agnes will be at the altar at church!"

He said so long as I was willing for him to see her there that was all he arst, and he grinned at me cheeky and went and got on his horse and rode off hell for leather.

But he didn't come back, and he didn't come back. And Alison cried and scolded me as if I was a babe, using all the long words she knew. She said that but for my interference all *might* have come right; I'd scared him off and ruined Agnes' chances. Johnny remembered hearing of somebody up in Norfolk that had a hunter to sell, and took hisself off to get free of the unpleasantness. Phyllis and Maud went about looking smug and self-righteous.

After a bit I let Agnes out, and she was no mite concerned.

"He'll come back," she said. "And if he don't, there's other fish in the sea!"

But he didn't come back and I was priding myself that at least, thanks to me, there was no harm done, and trying to make Alison see a bit of sense and make the other girls keep a civil tongue in their heads to Agnes, for the whole of that week and the best part of the next.

And then he did come, bringing the aunt he set such store by with him. She was a widow, a Lady Pernherrick, very rich and as odd as they're made. The main thing that I remember out of the confusion she chucked us all into is her looking Agnes over as if she was a horse she half meant to buy and saying,

"Hmmm, not bad, not bad at all. Time we had some new blood in our family. Getting very parrot-jawed."

Agnes bore the scrutiny just right, looking neither shy, nor saucy, nor put about; she'd been in the dairy when the owd dame arrived, and was wearing her print dress open at the neck and rolled at the sleeves and she did look pretty as a picture. Alison behaved very comely, too, though fussed inside I know. She got busy with refreshments and Agnes said,

"Now, if you'll excuse me, I'll go back to my butter; it was on the turn."

And his young lordship looked at me and said, "With your permission, Granny Whymark, I'll go with her."

VII

After that, little by little, I began to loosen my grip on the family, though I kept howd of Merravay. It was partly the company that made me fall into the background. There was no lack of company once the news of the wedding got noised abroad. I fitted out Agnes in the proper manner and I give her six hundred pounds for a dowry; and you could see people think, as if their heads was glass, that what was good enough for the Whardale family might just about do for *them*. If it'd happened sooner I reckon Phyllis and Maud would hev got husbands too, but they was a mite owd and not much for looks, and there was allust a shortage of young men in our parts—among the gentry, I mean; and of course after Agnes' catch the others wouldn't look at nothing less. So the comings and the goings and the matchmakings all fixed upon Johnny. I'd hev been the last to grudge his company but 'twas no use pretending that I took to the Fennels and the Headways and the Blackwoods, neighbours though they were and try as they did to suck up to me late in life and say I was "a character." When I was trying to hire a bit of land for my mares and my Dutches, and willing to pay whatever might be asked, they'd had no doings with me. So I never mixed with 'em, and kept meself to meself when there was parties.

There was a time when it looked as though Johnny might marry Miss Caroline Blackwood, and that give me a bit of worry. For they were cousins of a sort. Mrs. Thomasina Blackwood was Rawley's daughter by his first, foreign wife; she'd had a lot of children and Miss Caroline was the last of 'em. With animals I'd bred cousin to cousin, and closer relations too, many a time; but now and again I'd wake in the night and picture to myself Johnny marrying Miss Blackwood and bringing forth something not quite as it should be, a kind of punishment for me keeping my secret all these years. But there was nowt I could do except hope for the best and things worked out all right. Johnny went off merrymaking with Agnes and Toby and came back engaged to marry a young cousin of theirs. Poor as a church mouse she was, for her father'd been one of the King's men that had stayed and been fined heavy and sold land that had to stay sold; but she was a lady in her own right, which was one in the eye for the neighbours. I was mighty well pleased.

And oddly enough it was over Johnny's getting engaged that me and Phyllis had the nighest thing to a set-to that we ever had.

"I suppose you're *pleased* about this," she said in a tight, sour voice.

"I ain't sorry," I said. "Somebody young and well bred is what I allust hoped for for Johnny."

"For Johnny!" she said in a wild way, "for Johnny! That's all you ever think of, you and Mother. Maud and me could work like black slaves and feed in the kitchen like labourers but the house must be set out for Johnny! Maud and me could work without wages and be grateful for a new pair of shoes so the money can pile up to make our brother a gentleman and he can marry a lady who'll despise us, and treat us like dirt!"

"Howd on, now," I said. "I look to live long enough to learn her her place if she come treating anybody like dirt. While there's breath in my body I'm mistress here, and master too, and don't you forget it!"

"But even you can't live forever. What's going to happen then? Johnny'll have Merravay, of course; he's the boy, he's the heir! No matter that he can't tell a bull from a bullock, and is wasteful and careless and brainless. Oh, I can see him, with his lady wife to help him, going through what we've sweated to store up, like a knife through butter . . ."

"Do we start measuring sweat, Phyl, I reckon I'm still a bit ahead of you. Naturally property go to the man that carry on the name and the family, so it allust was, so it allust will be. Granted you've worked, good and hard, and been careful and managing and saving, and I been pleased to see you so. But 'twould be no manner of use you having the place, for you're another that can't live forever and you're a bare branch. . . ."

With that she bruk out crying, a thing she hadn't done since she was a toddler, and then only with rage. Cried and carried on, saying how unfair everything was and that she'd give her whole life to Merravay and now was to be chucked out, and how I was taunting her with not being married. Finally I spoke to her right sharp.

"Here, that'll do, my girl!" I said. "D'you take me for a fool? Thass right bad luck to talk of death and willing, but I'll tell you this for your comfort. Nobody but yourself'll ever chuck you outa Merravay. D'you think I'm one to forget how when you was a little mawther you'd help me with anything you could set hand to? You should know me better. Moreover I ain't blind to what Johnny is, but he is as I made him, as I planned he should be. So I've made my will, all right and legal, and there 'tis, set down by Mr. Turnbull, that you and Maud are to hev a home here at Merravay and one quarter of the profits between you—and thass fair, for Johnny will hev a wife to keep and a family to rear, God willing."

I'd made that will after a lot of thought and turmoil. And Phyllis' share had been part justice and part craft. I knew my Johnny and I knew my Phyllis, too. She'd see her share didn't dwindle, and, looking after part, she'd be bound to look after the whole.

But was she grateful?

"I'd rather you left me something of my own, Gran. A bit I could make something of. Leave me New Holding; the house is half down, but it'd do and it's good land . . ."

"But I've been scraping and striving all my life, Phyl, to get the land *together*; I can't go mincing it up. The more acres together the cheaper to work and the bigger profits. Why, girl dear, I mean to buy back the Slipwell land if ever 'tis for sale; I might live to see that day."

"Buy back!" she spat at me. "As though it had once been yours! Land and money, land and money, that's all you ever think of. I'm trying to talk to you about *my life*. If Merravay had been mine I'd have given my life to it; but it isn't and never can be! And I'm not a brick of the wall or an acre of land that you should treat me as part of it." She stood and breathed hard. "Go on then," she said, "buy your land, get it together, keep it together! And in the end you'll lay under it. Under six foot of graveyard clay, like the rest of us."

The funny thing was I'd allust thought Phyllis was fond of me.

"Aye, so I shall. And I shall lie quiet and with nothing on my conscience about the way I've treated you, you young hussy!" I said.

But I wasn't really angry with her. She got her temper from me, and her land hunger. She was the most like me of the lot. But that was all the more reason for chaining her down.

However, as it happened, two things got together to make me think things over. One was that I couldn't take, try as I would, to Johnny's wife. She was pretty, with eyes the colour of bluebells and hair the colour of primroses, and she was small and sweet-mannered, but I distrusted her from the start. I could do with some gentry—Lady Pernherrick I'd truly liked and one or two more that came to the wedding. It was the woman in Lady Rosemary roused my gall; I'd have felt the same about her whoever she was, wherever she'd come from. Sly, a worker-round, and spiteful.

The other thing was that when Caroline Blackwood married somebody in the West Country her owd father and mother decided to sell Muchanger and go and live near her. An owd admiral wanted Muchanger but not all the land, so I seized my chance to buy Slipwell; and that brought me close to Mr. Turnbull again and one day I opened my heart to him.

"You know how I've left the main part of my property," I said. "But I don't feel right easy in my mind about Phyllis. I want her to stay here so long as is possible, but I can see trouble that might brew. If it so happened that her temper was too much tried . . . I'd like her to hev something to fall back on. But it mustn't be open . . . do she wouldn't try at all. And I want her to try."

So he set his wits to work and in the end I altered my will entirely. She was to stay at Merravay and hev her share as arranged so long as she wished. But if she married—I put that in for cover—or at any time decided to leave Merravay and break with Johnny she was to consult Mr. Turnbull. And I left the New Holding land not to Johnny, but to a trust until otherwise claimed, Johnny to pay a peppercorn rent which was to provide a harvest horkey for the workmen. It was all wrapped up in whereases and aforesaids and renewable tenures and conditional something elses, but he'd got it clear. If ever Phyllis and Johnny parted company New Holding would be hers. But she wouldn't know that till the break was made. So she'd stand till the end and howd her own . . . I hoped for all their sakes.

With that done, there wasn't much for me to bother about. So now I take things easy. When the sun shine I creep along to a sunny place, between the porch and the jut of the house and just sit there. The garden hev come on wonderful; the stone-pot things that once made handy feeding troughs for my beasts are set back on the wall and they're full of flowers, stiff tall things called tulips that come from Holland, like my Dutches. And over the wall there's a field of corn, doing well; thick and green with hardly a weed in it. And beyond that and to both sides 'tis all mine, gathered together with hard work and a bit of luck.

But I ain't as spry as I was . . . and often, time I've got meself out here and looked around and done a bit of thinking, I'm right glad to shut my eyes and hev a bit of a doze. . . .

Interlude

The death of old Mistress Whymark—as she had come to be called in her later years—caused hardly a ripple. She was immensely old and had been, for some time past, feeble of body and inclined to wander in her mind. Her last will and testament gave pretty proof of her senility.

She was not forgotten. Her achievement took its place in the folklore of the neighbourhood and was often mentioned as an example of what sheer hard work and tenacity of purpose could do. Her name was generally mentioned with respect; money was money, after all; and in that period of wild and often fatal investments, when so many fortunes vanished overnight, the possession of solid money and untrammelled acres attained an enhanced importance.

The old woman's shrewdness and driving energy appeared to have passed in greatest measure to her eldest granddaughter. Mr. John Whymark was careless, good-natured, open-handed, and convivial, and much—particularly in the early days of the marriage—under the thumb of his pretty wife. Miss Phyllis Whymark took up, was driven into, and finally unable to desist from, an attitude of permanent opposition.

In any dispute about management and husbandry she had one strong ally, her dead grandmother; and she could always say,

"But I can't allow that. That would jeopardize Maud's share and mine. I must guard our interests." Also it became increasingly plain that when Phyl's judgement was respected things prospered; when she was crossed they tended to go wrong.

Accepting her authority in most things, Mr. Whymark, nagged by his wife, sometimes defied her over matters of personal expenditure. "God knows what you do with your money, Phyl; surely I can do what I like with my own!" The most contrary thing he did was to plant an avenue of lime trees and turn two good fields into park land. Miss Whymark, having invoked Granny's name in vain with a monotonous mention of turning in graves, actually wept over the waste of good ploughland. She avoided the avenue and on the rare occasions when she went to the village, would plod on foot across the fields and emerge near a miserable little holding called Church Farm, from whose few acres a man named Fulger wrested a poor living for himself and his family.

There she would sometimes see a thin lanky boy and a thin small girl immensely busy at tasks only just within their capacity to tackle. The sight gave her peculiar pleasure. So young, so hard-working, they would get on in the only way which Miss Whymark valued—Granny's way.

Then one day, on skirting the yard of the small holding, she heard sounds of merriment. The erstwhile admirable Fulger children appeared to have acquired a very beautiful little pony with a fine saddle and harness.

More spoiling, thought Miss Whymark quite sadly; and she walked on, wondering, as she so often did these days, what the world was coming to.

The Governess

THE first actual money that Luke and I ever earned was sixpence a week for enjoying ourselves.

Luke was twelve then and I was ten, and we'd both been hard at work for as long as we could remember but we'd had no wages—nor looked for any—until the day when Father came home and said,

"Old Mrs. Maybrook called me across the road today as I came home from the smithy. That child is to have a pony and it is to be stabled here, there being no room for it at their place. She'll pay two shilling a week for its feed and grooming and you two'll tend it. You'll have sixpence a week—to save."

"How'll she buy a pony? Through the parlour window?" Mother asked.

Years and years of being married to Father hadn't quite got Mother out of the way of making little jokes. I could see the point of that one, and if Father hadn't been there I should have laughed and Mother and I would have gone on wringing the last bit of fun out of it. The point was that in the whole three years that the Maybrooks had lived in Nettleton nobody had ever seen Mrs. Maybrook out of doors. She'd moved into Ivy Cottage, a very gloomy little house near the church, and there she lived with a surly old maidservant and a little girl—about my age—who was reckoned to be her granddaughter. Anything to be done out of doors the servant did, but now and again when she was ill Mrs. Maybrook would rap on the parlour window and attract somebody's attention, then stand back in the shadow and give her orders and presently put the money on the window sill. The old man who sometimes did a day's work in their little back garden said she acted the same way when she gave him his directions; he said it was because she was so pocked she didn't look human.

Everybody was sorry for the child. Even Luke and I who worked hard and were often scolded and punished wouldn't have changed with her, cooped up in that dull house with two old women. It was nice to think she was to have a pony.

I don't know how Mrs. Maybrook managed to buy the pony, but it came within a week, and it was as pretty and dainty as a lady. Luke and I fell in love with it at first sight and gave its toilet far more attention than we gave our own, which was apt to be scanty, especially on cold mornings. We harnessed it up and tried it; we'd never ridden a proper saddled pony before. It was just my size, but when Luke, who was very big for his age, was on it, he looked like a duck's egg in an ordinary eggcup. I told him so and we both laughed and Father put his head out of the barn and said, "Stop that foolery." He always feared that if you were laughing you were wasting time.

"And," I said softly, when Father had taken his head into the barn again, "you look a bit like Jesus on the ass's foal on Palm Sunday."

Luke said, "Shush," very shocked. But it was true. In those days he had a sweet, patient, long-suffering kind of look, and that, with his clear grey eyes and mass of light brown curly hair, gave him a saintly air, as if he didn't quite belong to this world. He was a proper Fulger; Father must have been very handsome before hard work and bad temper scored the lines on his face. I took after Mother, small and brown-coloured, and lively and merry—when we were let to be.

The afternoon came when the old maid from Ivy Cottage hobbled along to our place, holding Luella by the hand. I'd seen her before, of course, but never close to, and never dressed up as she was that day. She had proper riding clothes, made to her measure, dark green velvet they were, and a little hat with a feather. In her hand she carried a small crop with an ivory handle.

Luke and I always kept the pony fit to go into a parlour, and in a moment we had it saddled and led it out, very proud.

"There you are, love. There's your pony," said the maid.

Luella did not move forward; she stood there looking timid and reluctant.

The old woman turned to us and said, "Now don't you let her fall off, or the creature run away. And bring her back at four, up to the house. I can't come out again."

Luke looked at me; so, though I was a girl and the younger, I had to speak up.

"We were told to look after the pony. We can't take her out on it. We both have jobs to do."

"Your father about?"

"He's ploughing. If you want to ask him you must go to him and don't speak till he turns at the furrow's end."

"You're sharp!" she said with disfavour. "Mind you don't cut yourself!"

She stumped off and I looked at Luella.

"Most likely he'll say no, so you'd better let us help you on now."

She looked at me and at the pony and at Luke and then back at me again; then she said,

"To tell you the truth I'm rather scared of it. This wasn't my idea at all."

That was the first time I had heard her speak, and for a moment I could only stand and go on hearing her voice after it was silent; she spoke so clearly, with such sweetness, the words coming out so gently and yet so firmly. I could hardly bear to use my own voice after that. I said, as coaxingly as I could, but sounding gruff and rough all the same,

"There's nothing to be scared of. It's easy! Look, shall I show you?"

I scrambled onto the pony and rode round the yard.

"He's as gentle as a lamb," I said.

I brought him to a standstill near her and hopped off.

"Now you try."

"But I can't get on."

Luke spoke for the first time.

"I'll set you up," he said, and came forward.

I held the pony's head and Luke went to lift Luella. Immediately the pony pivotted sharply, so that Luella almost fell with Luke atop of her.

"Now no fooling about. That ain't what you're paid for!" said the old servant, hobbling back. "Yes, thass all right; your dad was sensible. So just be careful. There's no need for her to be venturesome; she ain't going to be a jockey."

With that she departed. Later on, when I knew the Maybrook household better, I realised that this incident was very typical. There was the care and the carelessness side by side; the pretty pony, the elegant clothes, the escort to our yard; but whether the pony were gentle or vicious, Luke and I fitted or unfitted for responsibility, nobody bothered to ask.

II

That was the beginning of happy times for us. Over the plough handle Father had bargained sixpence an hour for our time. ("I never reckoned Father rated us that high, boy," I said to Luke, "just think what we earn in a week!")

It was a mercy we weren't paid by results, for Luella never did master the riding; to the end it took both our efforts to get her on and less than nothing to topple her off. And the pony was no help. He was an angel with Luke and me, and a devil with her. But once she got over her first fright of him she didn't mind; she'd laugh and say, "You ride him," to whichever one of us was due for a turn, and then, with the other she'd play tag or Granny Grumble, or just saunter along and pick flowers.

She'd never had any young company before and seemed to cling to us; when we parted she'd watch us out of sight and keep waving and calling.

Towards the end of September that year there came a day which we, being hardy, called "fresh," but Luella soon had a blue-white face and chattering teeth; so we took her off the pony and all had a good game of tag to warm her up; however she caught cold and didn't come out for several days. Then one day the old maid came stumping along to ask if I could go and keep her company. Highly elated, I put on my Sunday gown and shoes and went to Ivy Cottage and spent the afternoon in a paradise of dolls and draughts and dominos and musical boxes. That day I didn't see Mrs. Maybrook; the servant brought tea and cakes to the room we played in, and we drank the tea from the dolls' cups and cut the cakes into tiny pieces to fit the little plates. I'd never spent such an afternoon in all my days and went home dazzled.

Soon after that there was another message from Ivy Cottage. I saw the servant arrive and leave, looking utterly disgusted; and I waited, with my heart in my mouth, to know what she had come for. Nothing was said that day, but when Luke and I were in bed I could hear Father and Mother threshing something out in the kitchen below, Mother's voice quick and eager, Father's slow and grumbling.

In the morning Father said to me, "Tuesdays and Thursdays you get up early and do all your jobs and then go along to Ivy Cottage; and mind how you behave."

It was not to play, this time; it was to have lessons with Luella's governess, Miss Pelham. They thought Luella would learn better if she had company.

Luke, seeing me off, said, "Dog's nails! I wish I could come too!" (In the old days people used to say "God's nails" when they wished to be emphatic and "Damnation" when they were annoyed; now, because of chapel and the text "Swear not at all," they said "Dog's nails" and "Tarnation" instead.)

Although Luella had chattered freely while we were out together she'd never said anything about her home, and we'd never asked any questions; and it was quite a surprise to me to discover that Mrs. Maybrook was not her granny, but her mother. Mrs. Maybrook was very little older than my mother; it was the scarred face and widowed way she dressed that made her seem so elderly. But the mystery remained, even when one was close to, almost part of the family. It took me a long time to gather, bit by bit, that Luella's father and brother—a good deal older than she— had both died of the smallpox, which had ruined Mrs. Maybrook's looks; and that Luella had only escaped because she was put out to nurse. Even then I knew enough about things to know that only rich, fashionable people put their children out in that way, and the idea didn't go along- side the dull little house, the one servant, and Mrs. Maybrook's clothes, and other evidences of very modest means. At the same time, everything in the house was on the rich side, velvet curtains and silver things and such, and once when Luella and I were playing "dressing up" and she was a princess, Mrs. Maybrook let us have things out of her jewel box. I can believe now that they were neither so many nor so wonderful as they seemed to me at the time, but it did seem strange to me that she should have rings and brooches that she never wore, and only one cross old servant and a man odd times for the garden.

She had a voice exactly like Luella's, but with sad notes in it; she was a sad creature. There were times, though, when she was different. Now and then, on those winter afternoons when Miss Pelham was ready to go and catch the coach back to Baildon—it touched Nettleton on Tuesdays and Thursdays, that is why the lessons were on those days —Mrs. Maybrook would drift in, carrying a square bottle with a gold pattern on its sides and two little glasses that matched.

"You must have something to keep out the cold, Miss Pelham," she would say. Miss Pelham would say, "That is very kind of you," and take her glass and sip daintily. Then she would go . . . and times, if the road was slippery or there was anything to carry, she would take me with her, which Luella and I hated . . . other times I could stay for a little while; and then Mrs. Maybrook would fill her glass again, and again, and grow merry, telling us funny stories and making jokes and imitating everybody, even Miss Pelham, not unkindly but in the funniest way. Then her voice lost its dreary sound and was like music. She could say my name, Deborah, so that it didn't sound plain at all. I used to sit there, listening to her and thinking what a shame it was about her face, and how she was paying me to play and to learn, which I'd always wanted to do. (Father had asked a shilling an afternoon for me, though I still did my work at home!) And for Christmas that year she gave me a red woolsey dress.

Then the spring came and the outings started again. I was glad for Luke's sake, because although I always told him every single thing that had been done or said at Ivy Cottage he had felt cut off.

One morning, late in April and lovely weather, Luella said, as we heaved her onto the pony,

"Let's go to Merravay."

That suited me, because Merravay lay near to the woods which, I'd heard tell from children with more time for idling, was a famous place for flowers. I ran to get a basket and when I came back I found that Luke had turned the pony's head towards the fields.

"It'll still be a bit miry at Vinefields Bottom, Luke," I said. "Wouldn't it be best to go through the village and up at the front?"

"You couldn't get near. They've built a great wall round and put a gate with lodges. And two fields gone to waste planted with trees. Dint you know?"

"Oh, I want to go *near*. I want to see the house," Luella said.

"Why?" I asked.

"Oh . . . I've just heard a lot about it."

"So have we—and nothing in its favour, eh, Luke?"

We had heard enough about Merravay. Within the living memory of people like our old great-aunt Hester who lived with us, the Whymarks had made a fortune at Merravay, all out of sheer hard work; and the old woman who had done most of the work had lived to be ninety, so in holding her up as an example to the young the old people could very truthfully say, "Hard work never killed anybody!" Sometimes when Aunt Hester droned on about it I used to think to myself, Maybe not, but hearing about it is killing me! Of course I daren't say it, and of course nobody ever did die of boredom or great-aunt Hester would have been knee-deep in corpses.

From our little field the ground sloped down to the swampy bit where the kingcups grew and then up and up. We reached the top of the rise and were at the edge of a field of young corn. On its farther side was Layer Wood, and to our left, slightly downhill, stood the house. Luella turned the pony and sat there staring while Luke and I took a good look at the place about which we had heard so much.

It was a big house, with many windows and clumps of chimneys; the bricks of the walls and the tiles of the roof were a pretty colour, an orangy pink, like hawthorn berries when they first start to ripen. The colour showed up pleasantly against the dark green-black of two huge trees and the shining green of the lawns. But . . . it was just a big house.

"Oh," said Luella on an outgoing breath. "Oh. Yes it is beautiful. Better even than I expected."

She seemed quite overcome. So I looked again. The field at whose edge we stood was divided from the garden by a deep ditch that was like a long narrow horsepond drained dry in a drought. On the house side the dip was topped by a low wall, the same colour as the house, and along its edge there were some things like fir cones made of grey stone, and between each pair of cones there was a big grey vase full of yellow flowers—daffodils maybe. Back of the wall there were yew trees, like those in the church yard but cut into shapes. All very pretty, neat, well cared for, but it didn't rouse in me the kind of excitement that came on me when our lilac tree bloomed, or when I thought of that distant wood full of primroses.

"Isn't it beautiful? Luke . . ." Luella turned to him.

"Lookit the stacks!" he said, craning his head. "Eight, ten, and I can only see a corner of the stackyard. Dog's nails! And lookit the far side, out towards Slipwell. Beasts without number!"

"All got together with the sweat of the brow, lad," I said, imitating as best I could Aunt Hester's voice. "Do you work as hard, you may do as well. Hard work never killed anybody."

But the joke fell flat. They just went on staring. So I looked towards Layer Wood. Except for a few hawthorn trees that were freckled with green and some firs which stood here and there along the edge, the whole wood seemed to swim in a purple-pink haze as the swollen buds shone in the sunlight. I could just imagine how the pale tide of primroses shimmered under the trees.

"Oh, come on!" I said. "You've seen the house. Let's go to Layer."

Luella ignored me, but Luke shook himself free of his trance, and said, "Aye, come on. Our time'll be up!"

"You go," said Luella, "I'll stay here."

"And the pony'll run away with you as soon as we've gone," I said petulantly.

"Oh, take the pony!" She dismounted in a way which, but for her smallness and lightness, would have been comically clumsy.

With me on the pony and Luke loping alongside we soon reached the wood; and it was just as flowery as I had heard it was. The primroses were huge, the biggest I had ever seen, and the most fragrant. Every stem was four inches long, and I made up my mind to borrow one of Mother's precious glasses, so that the pink tips would show, blushing and beaded in the water. In those days flowers meant a great deal to me, and while I gathered the primroses greedily I saw with delight that the bluebells and foxgloves and windflowers were coming on. It was like Heaven, only there the flowers, they said, never died, so how, if the primroses lasted the year round, the later ones would find room was a mystery. But I remembered that once when I had voiced a similar perplexity about something I had heard in chapel, Father had sternly bid me to bear in mind that with God all things were possible.

As we went back—Luke riding this time—we could see Luella standing just where we had left her.

"Can *you* see anything to stare at like that about that house?" I asked.

"Only the stacks. Thass a rare pity, Deb, that we ain't got more corn-land. Still, I reckon I'll make my fortune out of beasts!"

As we pelted down towards Luella we called, but she only waved a hand and went on staring.

"She's daft," I said.

"Daft as a hen with its head off," Luke agreed; but his tone was tolerant rather than critical.

It took all our persuasions and finally mention of the scoldings and beatings that awaited us if we outstayed our time to get her to move, and when she did she looked back and said,

"I wish I lived there."

"Why? It's so lonely," I said. "I'd rather live in *any* house in Nettleton. What d'you say, Luke?"

"Not *any* house, Deb," he said cautiously. "Say Squirrels, or Curlew, or Monks." He named the three best farms in the parish.

"But that is a beautiful *house*," Luella said dreamily. "I shall come here again."

"So shall I," I said, thinking of the bluebells and foxgloves.

Yet, for one reason or another, we never did, though all through that spring and summer we had many pleasant outings, mainly without Luke, who, to his disgust, was kept at home to do "real" work, though, so far as I know, Mrs. Maybrook still paid for his time. Not that it mattered, except to Luke, for I was quite capable of managing the pony.

III

Then came the winter day when both Luke and I fell victims of the sweating sickness, which carried off more than a few that year.

Mother, who had great skill with herbs and simples, set about brewing one of her noxious remedies. It was market day and Father went off to Baildon, promising to bring back a lemon if he could find one not too dear. And then, through my whirling, throbbing head shot the remembrance that this was the day when I should go to Ivy Cottage for my lesson.

"You must let them know," I moaned.

Mother said that with all this illness about they would guess, but my muddled mind had fixed on that and I kept on till at last she said,

"Well, I daresay Aunt Hester could make her way there at a pinch. It's a straight road and everybody's gone to market now."

Aunt Hester took kindly to the idea.

"Aye, I'll go. And I shall take some of my lace to show the lady."

I was vaguely against that for no reason I could exactly name, but I was too grateful that she should go at all to say anything. In her youth she'd been a great maker of lace. I always thought that was what had ruined her eyesight. She'd made so much that she still had furlongs of it laid away in well-chalked linen to keep it from turning yellow. It was sixty pounds, saved from years of lacemaking and lent to my father, that ensured her a home with us. Even after her eyesight failed she had gone on peddling lace until some knave in Baildon paid her with a bad shilling. Now and again one of her regular old customers would come and buy a length out of the chest and that was always a great day, but such days came seldom.

Mother said, "Yes, do," and went on pounding away at the rosemary and nettle leaves with the rolling-pin.

Aunt Hester was so long on her errand that we had drunk the brew and were so muddled in our heads that I was never quite certain whether this happened or whether I dreamed it——

It seemed to me that she came back, blundering as usual over the threshold, clinking some money in her hand and saying that Mrs. May-brook had bought a dozen yards of her best three point, and adding,

"I know something."

"Say it then, say it. Can't you hear my calves blaring?"

"I know who old Mrs. Maybrook is."

"Well, we all know that!"

"Ah, but thass just what you don't know! She's Miss Blackwood, my Miss Caroline that used to live at Muchanger."

It seemed to me that Mother began to pay attention.

"How d'you know? Did she make herself known to you?"

"No, but I heard her voice. And I've told you a dozen times that the strength of my eyes have gone elsewhere, nobody hear like I do, and I'd know her voice anywhere."

"You hear well, I will say. But if 'twas so, surely we'd know. The gentry, the Fennels, and the Headways would all be around her for the sake of old times."

"Ah, but they don't know. 'Tis only my ears know. She's come down in the world and lost her looks, but she crept home at the end, same as I should have done if I'd moved with the family that time. She never wanted to go, Miss Caroline didn't. . . ."

"Well," said Mother, "well, fancy . . . oh them calves! All right, all right, I'm coming."

It seemed to me that after she had gone Aunt Hester pottered about, muttering to herself about somebody who'd been treated badly, played fast and loose with, been homesick for years, and now come home to die. And it seemed to me that presently she turned to me and said that this was a secret, not to be mentioned.

I may have dreamed it all, for presently I was riding wildly on a seesaw, putting a wreath of buttercups round our sow's neck, quarrelling with Luke about who should lick the honey spoon and a thousand other things which I can't remember at all.

Then I was clearly myself again, and Luke and I both had quinsies in our throats. And one day when Luke could speak, he asked who was looking after the pony.

"The pony's gone," Mother said.

"Gone where?"

"How should I know, child? A man came and took it away. Now you know as much as I do, so don't ask any more questions."

It wasn't until we were almost well again that we learned that both Mrs. Maybrook and the old servant had caught the sickness and—as Mother said, not having anybody to make them a good brew—had died.

"Then who sent for the pony?"

"The man mentioned Mr. Turnbull. But it was your father he talked to, not me."

"And what happened to Luella?"

"Mr. Turnbull is looking after her."

So that was the end of being paid to be idle and to have lessons. And most likely we'd never see Luella again. What a hateful world we had struggled back to.

One day I said to Aunt Hester, "You were right about her coming back to die."

"Who?"

"Mrs. Maybrook." But she pretended not to know what I meant; and then I could not be sure what I had remembered and what I had dreamed.

IV

Father worked harder than anyone I ever knew, and had the worst luck. Nothing he ever did turned out right. When I was almost thirteen we were so poor that it was decided to put me to service, a fate which, being the only girl in the family and always with a job in my hand, I had hoped to escape. I'd heard some horrid tales about the way servants were treated, and Aunt Hester's admonitions to me—and she should know, she had been in service all her life till her eyes failed—did nothing to reassure me. They were so much concerned with humility, and truth to tell, I was, at that time, rather a proud little girl. I'd always been quick and handy and good at contriving, and sometimes even Father who was quicker with blame than praise would say, "Let Deb try," when there was anything particularly tricky to do. Also I'd done very well with the lessons at Ivy Cottage; Miss Pelham knew who paid her, of course, and so refrained from comparisons, but Mrs. Maybrook herself said my writing put Luella's to shame. I could sew neatly too, and I had once cherished hopes of being apprenticed to the dressmaker in Baildon; but for that one had to pay a premium and then earn nothing for four years at least. So it was service for me; and because Lady Rosemary Whymark happened to come—on Lady Fennel's recommendation—to buy some of Aunt Hester's lace for edging handkerchiefs and Aunt Hester happened to mention that I was in need of a place, it was to Merravay that I went as a kind of maid-of-all-work when I was just one month short of thirteen years old.

I'd been there six years and worked my way up to be Miss Sophie's personal maid and even to do most of her ladyship's sewing, when I heard that the three young Whymarks were to have a new governess and that her name was Maybrook. I began at once to think about Luella.

In all that time we'd had but one bit of news of her. One day Luke had done a thing quite unlike himself, he'd gone to Mr. Turnbull's office and asked about her. Mr. Turnbull, Luke said, was very civil and kind and told him that she was at school in Epping, quite well and happy, and that he saw her regularly and would, on his next visit, say that someone who remembered her had inquired after her. "But for all that he never asked my name," Luke said. Sometimes, before I left home, he and I would occasionally say, "Do you remember?" and Luella would come to mind. But for six years I had only seen Luke on my free day, the last Saturday of each month except December, and he was always busy and growing up so swiftly that our childhood, our shared memories, had fallen into limbo.

Now, hearing the name Maybrook, I could only hope that Luella hadn't been reduced by circumstances to become a governess . . . or that if she had she was not the one doomed to come to Merravay. I'd lost count of the governesses who had been there in my time, but I could say for certain that they had all been miserable. It was, without any obvious reason, a most unhappy household, full of undercurrents, changing allegiances, conflicting loyalties.

At first sight, and afterwards, down on my knees scrubbing and polishing, I thought Merravay a large house, but the whole of Suffolk would hardly have been wide enough to contain its inmates peaceably.

The master, Mr. Whymark, was a very easy-going, good-natured man for nine tenths of the time. He would shut his eyes and ears to the perpetual squabbles about him and often let them develop when a word from him could have quelled them. Then he would suddenly lose his temper with everybody, just and unjust alike, and stamp and shout and either fling out of the house or shut himself in his library and get drunk. Every time he did that the disputants would drop the original quarrel and begin blaming one another for upsetting poor John.

Lady Rosemary was that sad thing—a pretty woman who was growing old and resenting it. She still had eyes like frozen forget-me-nots and a great sheaf of honey-coloured hair in which the white ones hardly showed at all, but the skin round her eyes and under her chin was crinkled like young beech leaves, and she was too stout. Provided that she believed you were devoted to her personally, she was pleasant to work for, though tyrannical in her demands. She seldom lost her temper, and could say the most waspish things in a cool, controlled voice. Once, they said, she had been extremely poor, but an uncle who had gone to Virginia at the end of the war had left her a good deal of money and a tobacco plantation, so she could afford to indulge her whims. Yet most of the rows in the house were concerned, directly or indirectly, with money. For, living at Merravay, were two Miss Whymarks, and the elder was parsimonious past all belief. Even my poor mother who never had a penny to spare, was not so mean, so watchful, so worried over candles, logs, wasted crusts. Most people think of ruin as something which might, if they are not careful, come upon them some day; Miss Whymark faced ruin, and spoke about it, every day of her life. She also made constant reference to her Granny—the old tavern-keeper whom Aunt Hester so much admired; Miss Whymark evidently admired her too and kept her memory green by acid remarks about "the old days" and "Granny's time" and the probability of Granny turning in her grave. For some reason which I never understood Miss Whymark wielded enormous power, both within doors and without, and everybody went in dread of her. But there was this to be said in her favour; she was the same every day, and if you worked yourself silly, never answered back, never wasted a grain of salt or a half inch of candle you did at least know where you were with her.

With Miss Maud it was entirely different. She was just as queer, not with meanness, for she could be extravagantly generous, but with imagining that she was being slighted and insulted. Even over food; whatever was carved she would cast sharp little glances at all the portions and unless hers was ostentatiously the best she'd push it away, burst into tears, and run off to her own room, where she kept great stores of sweets and cakes and a little outfit for making drinking chocolate. She was as susceptible to gross flattery as she was to imaginary insult, and was forever taking sides, having favourites, carrying tales. Nothing was real to her, and for that reason she was very dangerous. Still, she did a lot for the church and for the poor, of whom there were plenty, especially after Strawless Common was enclosed and the cottagers were turned off.

Of the eight children born to Lady Rosemary five had survived; the deaths had occurred to the middle ones of the family, so now two were fully grown and three still in the schoolroom.

Mr. Roger was old enough to be soldiering abroad when I first went to Merravay. He came home during my third year there, invalided out of the army, looking very sickly and much older than his twenty-seven years. After staying at home for eight or nine months he went off to Virginia to see to some business in connection with the tobacco plantation, and he had stayed away. I had seen little of him; he was very quiet, though restless in the house, and well liked by those who came into contact with him.

Miss Sophie had grown to young womanhood during my time; she was two years older than I. When she was older and more settled she would probably be considered handsome, for she had inherited her father's brilliant colouring and height, but she was too thin and awkward to be a pretty girl. She was clever in a way which was no help to a young lady of her kind; she read everything she could lay hands on and could talk about what she had read. Lady Rosemary checked and chided and snubbed her at every turn, and did her best to prevent her from reading; consequently Miss Whymark encouraged her and frequently snatched up the London papers as soon as they arrived and carried them off to her room, where Miss Sophie could read them undisturbed. This action was purely perverse upon Miss Whymark's part, for the whole world might have sunk under the sea or gone up in flames without rousing in her one flicker of interest, provided Merravay remained untouched.

The three young children, Miss Julia, Miss Arabella, and Master Billy, were, despite their material comforts, more pitiable than enviable, for around their innocent heads unpredictable disputes of ancient origins were likely to break out at any moment. They were pampered, scolded, admonished, and cossetted by the four adult women according to mood or arbitary situation. So they were growing up secretive and defensive, prepared to regard all grown-ups as potential enemies. Very often in the lapses between governesses it fell to my lot to take them for walks, while Miss Sophie took charge of their lessons, which she did very happily and efficiently. She had offered to take on the work permanently but her ladyship scoffed at the notion, "You don't need anything else to round your shoulders and screw up your eyes, my dear," she said. When they were without a governess they took their midday meal with the family and the sessions at table were very trying.

One of them might leave a little scrap of fat on the side of the plate. "We were told to eat what we were given," Miss Whymark would say. "If we had wasted good food things would be very different here at this moment."

"Poor Julia is like me. I never could eat fat. Leave it, darling!" The indulgence in her ladyship's voice could not disguise its challenging quality.

"Well, let us hope these good times will continue, so that we can afford such fastidiousness. We should be ill prepared for a setback now, what with the waste of good food within and the waste of good land without."

The grass had grown smooth over the fields that had been turned into park land, and the young trees were branchy, but no resignation had grown over Miss Whymark's resentment at the loss of the arable land.

"Surely, Phyllis, the reason why most gentlemen's residences stand in parks and not in fields is to show that they can afford to spare a little ground. And for the same reason there is no need for the children to lick their plates as though they were starving dogs."

At this point the master would get up and go. Then Miss Maud, if she were at odds with Lady Rosemary, would make her contribution, "Every time I go into the village I see *many* poor little children who would be only too glad to eat that meat. Julia dear, clear your plate in gratitude to God who has provided so well for you." But if she had fallen out with her sister, Miss Maud would take a different tone, "Really, Phyl, what a fuss to make about a little bit of fat! All the scraps go into the swill pail!"

Her ladyship was then quite likely to say, with marked ingratitude, that the swill pail was not a subject to mention at table.

With slight variations of subject and side-taking this kind of scene would be repeated more frequently than anyone could believe possible.

The new governess—Luella or another Miss Maybrook—had the house by the ears some days before she arrived.

On a late January morning I was seated by the big window in Lady Rosemary's room, the one known as the Queen's Chamber. Her ladyship had attended a ball at Baildon on the previous evening, had risen late, and was sitting by the fire, drinking her morning chocolate. I was mending a lace flounce which had been trodden on and torn. At the moment Lady Rosemary and Miss Whymark were allied against Miss Maud, who was vehemently supporting the rector over the tithes; and as a sign of the brief, uneasy allegiance Miss Whymark came into her sister-in-law's room and accepted a cup of chocolate.

"Johnny has a new bee in his bonnet now," said her ladyship conversationally. "He thinks that governesses don't stay because we are so unpleasant to them. He read me a lecture on kindness to poor creatures. For what it is worth I pass it on . . ."

"If you have Miss Runackles in mind, Rose, I can only say that to me waste is waste and the hussy who wastes in this house gets short shrift whether she is governess or scullery slut."

"Johnny also thinks," the cool voice went on, "that the room we give the governess is dreary."

"Perhaps he would like her to have my room," said Miss Whymark very tartly.

"Well . . . of course, he is very muddle-minded," said her ladyship, not denying or confirming the possibility of such an audacious suggestion. "But, naturally, I should never entertain such an idea. No, actually I intend to give Miss Maybrook Sophie's room."

"But Sophie won't like that!" said Miss Whymark.

"No. But the move might serve to draw her attention to the fact that at Ockley there are eighteen bedrooms of which she could take her choice. I haven't told you about last evening! I was so infuriated. There we stood, having just arrived, and Sir Frederick came across to us, making it quite plain that he had been waiting for her. She said, 'Oh!' And what do you think Johnny did? Whisked her off into the dance, under the poor boy's nose. A father dancing the first dance with his daughter. There I stood, not knowing where to look or what to say. I was never more mortified!"

"Johnny isn't in favour of forced marriages," said Miss Whymark in a voice that indicated that she, too, thought them obnoxious.

"What a strange term! *Forced!* It just happens that that poor infatuated boy sees something in Sophie that eludes everyone else. That he is the most eligible young man within fifty miles has hardly any bearing on the matter, he is the *only* man not entirely senile who ever looks at her. But I could see how dashed he was. A few more incidents like that and she won't have a partner at all."

"She's still very young."

"She's twenty-one. That may seem young to you, Phyl. To me it seems dangerously old. I've seen too many girls go right through the wood, picking and choosing, and come out with a crooked stick at last—or no stick at all."

That was a direct challenge to Miss Whymark; for there was a legend in the house that both the old ladies had been very choosy in their youth.

"Well," said Miss Whymark, very slowly and clearly, "I should be sorry if you hoped, by putting Sophie in a poky room, to influence her attitude. For *I* have seen what happens when people marry for the sake of a comfortable home."

That was a frank production of the old well-gnawed bone. To my astonishment her ladyship ignored it.

"The one good thing about this idea of pampering governesses," she said in a ruminative voice, "is that it made Johnny see sense about the alterations. A house where the simple business of allotting everyone a habitable room causes such a commotion is obviously too small or badly planned. And when you think that one day Roger will bring a wife home, and that there are still two girls in the schoolroom . . . well, something must be done. Anyway Johnny at last sees the necessity and I am going to write to that man Kent this very day, before he has time to change his mind again."

That put spark to tinder and started a row of quite extraordinary violence. The idea of altering Merravay came into direct conflict not only with Miss Whymark's parsimony but with her sentiment as well. Merravay had been good enough for Granny, it should be good enough for anybody.

They wrangled, entirely forgetful of my presence, for several minutes.

"For two pins I'd persuade Johnny to build an entirely new house, fit for civilised people to live in, and leave this Merravay barn to you."

"Nothing would please me more," said Miss Whymark, stomping off to take counsel with Miss Maud.

I had finished my work, but was wise enough to stay with my head bent and my hands apparently busy for a moment. Suddenly her ladyship became aware of me,

"Deborah," she said, "I am planning some changes. Daisy can do what is needed for Miss Sophie, and I want you to take charge of the schoolroom. I seem to remember Miss Runackles complaining that the food there was always cold and the fire unsatisfactory. We want Miss Maybrook to be comfortable, so that will be your main duty in future. Of course, you will still have time to do things for me. Yes, that is a very neat piece of work, hardly detectable. Hang it away carefully."

Her ladyship was going to keep her bargain; the new governess was to be comfortable. And poor Miss Sophie was going to lose her bedroom and her maid . . . Daisy was a heavy-fisted, hard-breathing half-wit.

The quarrel about altering the house went on, making itself felt in many strange ways. With Miss Whymark more violently economical than ever; with Miss Maud rushing out the drawing-room one evening in tears, wailing, "Little did I think when I used to get up in the dark on winter mornings that I should live to see . . ." And finally with Mr. Whymark standing in the hall and shouting at the top of his voice,

"For God's sake, Phyl, stop dragging Granny in. Bless her heart, *she* spent money on Merravay as soon as she could afford it. Why shouldn't I? And let me tell you that if she is turning in her grave it's because you're trying to make her out as damned mean as you are. She wasn't, by God, she was a riotous old girl! Though why the hell she fixed up such a punishment for me I shall never know . . ."

VI

The day of Miss Maybrook's arrival came; it was a day when the coach did not run into Nettleton, so it was arranged that the cart from Merravay should go to fetch her from Baildon. But it turned out a pouring wet day and at midmorning Lady Rosemary decided to send the carriage instead. She had forgotten that this was one of the days when Miss Maud, carrying her own little locked tea caddy, was to go and favour the rector's wife with her company, her criticism, and advice, all washed down with the best Suchong.

At two o'clock, from the window of her room where she was changing her dress, Miss Maud saw Jack Lantern putting the horses to the carriage and screamed down that he was early, the fire wouldn't be lighted in the Rectory parlour. Lantern shouted back that he was off to Baildon and would drop her on the way.

"That you will not do," said Miss Maud, and still wearing her shabby dress, with her hair in disarray and the tea caddy clutched to her breast, she scampered downstairs, muttering that fifty years ago when she had sat up all night dressing fowls for market she'd imagined that she was laying up comfort for her old age. Was some chit of a governess to be considered before her now?

Her ladyship, appealed to by the coachman, said laconically that if she had said once she had said a hundred times that a place like Merravay should have three carriages and it was entirely Miss Whymark's fault that there was but one.

Miss Whymark said of course the two errands could be combined; Miss Maud got into the carriage and said she should scream if it moved an inch before three o'clock. In the end it was decided to send the slow cart to Baildon after all; and the governess was expected to arrive, no doubt soaked to the skin, some time between six and seven o'clock. So soon after five I made a handsome fire in the schoolroom and the children settled down by it to roast chestnuts, gloomily speculating upon the nature and appearance of their new governess.

I was drawing the curtains when I heard my name called and ran down. Her ladyship was standing in the doorway of the drawing-room, with Miss Whymark close beside her. Halfway across the hall Miss Maud, just back from the Rectory, was rubbing a few rain spots from the tea caddy. Briggs the footman was just behind the screen, slowly closing the door and lingering to see and hear as much as possible. And just inside the screen stood Miss Maybrook—Luella—explaining in the voice that took me straight back to childhood that having decided that she was not to be met, she had hired the post chaise!

I have seen a flock of sheep with young lambs, all at variance with one another, turn, as one animal, to face a strange dog, then draw together, heads outward, and present a united, defiant front. It was just like that. A governess . . . hiring a post chaise . . . seven shillings . . . What was the world coming to?

Having told me to take Miss Maybrook to her room and then show her the way to the schoolroom, her ladyship backed into the drawing-room, followed by the Miss Whymarks. Briggs stuck his nose in the air and stalked into the kitchen to make his report. Luella and I stood face to face.

She was much altered; but for the voice—and of course the name—I doubt if I should have recognised her. I had always thought of her as a pretty little girl. Even making allowances for the effect that her clothes and her cleanliness, her smooth hair and skin had had upon me I still think that as a child she was pretty. But all the prettiness had vanished. She looked at least thirty years old, pale and thin, hollow-cheeked and sharp-nosed. Her eyes were enormous, slightly prominent in their hollows, with thin, veined lids edged with long lashes and set under thin dark brows which ran from a little frown mark over the nose, upwards and outwards to her hair. Her mouth was enormous too, deeply curved, with the lower lip turned out in a wistful, discontented, yet very sweet way. I stood and stared at her, thinking that if I had met her in a street and she had asked the way I should have told her, unknowing, and then gone on wondering why I was suddenly thinking of Mrs. Maybrook and Ivy Cottage.

"But you're Deb . . . Deborah Fulger, surely. Do you remember me . . . Luella Maybrook?"

"Of course," I said.

"How lovely," she said, and stretched out the hand she had ungloved. I had taken care of my hands, making excuses to myself about the impossibility of doing fine needlework with rough fingers, but as I put mine out to meet Luella's it looked and felt, for all my care with the goose grease and witch-hazel, as big and coarse as a ploughboy's. Her's was nothing at all. There was just nothing of her except those great eyes, that mouth, and the voice.

"Oh, I am glad to see you again," she said as I lifted the shabby little valise. "I've thought of you and Luke so often. Those happy days we had. And then I didn't even say good-bye to you; you were so ill. I always meant to write to you; but I was so miserable . . . whenever I started to think about those days I just cried, so the letter never got written."

"Luke once asked Mr. Turnbull for news of you. He said you were well and happy."

"He may have thought so. He wanted to, I expect. Men can believe anything they want to. Well and happy . . ." she said with surpassing bitterness. "Still, I survived. And here I am. I owe that to Mr. Turnbull at least. Deborah, what are they like? The children?"

By that time we had reached the bedroom door, and I said apologetically, "I meant to light the fire, but I didn't think you could be here for at least an hour."

She told me about the taking of the post chaise.

"They all seemed *shocked*. Are they poor, Deb?"

"Heavens no! The old one who stood in the doorway is fanatically *mean*." I set the valise on a chair and went across to open the door of the clothes closet, which in this panelled room wasn't easy to see, and as I did so I told her a few things about the characters of Merravay's inmates and what to be careful of . . . "that is if you *want* to stay here," I ended.

"But I do. Of course I do. It did seem the greatest good fortune . . . when I heard from Mr. Turnbull I could hardly believe . . . I always so wanted to live here." She made a funny wry face, "In my innocent childish dreams, Deb, I used to plan that someone left me a fortune and I bought it; or I married a very rich man who bought it for me. I never saw myself coming here as a governess. . . . Still, here I am, and I must make the best of it. But that's enough about me. Tell about you. Have you been here long, and are you happy?"

"Six years; and I'm *settled*."

"And Luke?"

"He has the farm now. He's doing quite well. My father died, very suddenly two years ago." For some strange reason I heard myself saying aloud something that had been in my mind ever since Father died, something I never had said, or dreamed of saying to anyone. "We all thought he was vilely bad-tempered, but the truth was that he'd been ill for a long time and nobody knew."

Luella had been bent over the valise. She straightened and turned to me.

"Poor Deb. Does that worry you? You mustn't let it. How could you know? Perhaps he was proud of not complaining. And anyway, as far as I can remember he *was* a cross man, well or ill. I used to shake in my shoes if he looked at me. And think how he used to shout at Luke who was always trying so hard."

That speech soothed a sore place in my mind. Father had grown more and more cantankerous and had made Mother and Luke most miserable. He'd sent me to service and took my wages every quarter without saying so much as thank you. When Aunt Hester died and left her sixty-pounds share in the farm equally between Luke and me he never even told us, and there were times when I felt I positively hated him. Then one morning he'd walked into the kitchen and said, "I feel queer," and fell on the floor. Mother could see that he was past her help, so she sent Luke full pelt for the doctor. Father was dead when he arrived, but he was young and curious, and there had been two cases in our neighbourhood where women were suspected of poisoning their husbands; so he stripped the body. He found a lump the size of a bladder of lard in Father's groin and said it was a wonder he'd kept on his feet, leave alone done so much work, because he must have suffered agonies.

After that I had felt very badly about the way I had felt towards him. I'd wake sometimes in the night and think of him, mad with pain and taking it out on Luke and Mother; and working on and then dying, like a sick horse. And I'd think how he'd never known any success, and never had a drink or any fun, not even a really good meal. It seemed pitiable and heartbreaking.

"I know just how you feel," said Luella. "One of my pupils died suddenly after being peevish all day and I'd chided him. Oh dear . . . I think of it still sometimes; though Heaven knows I paid for that! My next place was quite unbearable. So bad that I left without giving notice or waiting for my wages. *That* was why I wrote to Mr. Turnbull; I knew he still had a little money left over, and I just asked him to send me some. When he sent it he said he'd heard about this job."

We had not closed the door behind us and now, far off along the gallery, I could hear Miss Whymark's stumping tread.

"I mustn't stand here talking," I said, "I'll show you the schoolroom. Then I'll light this fire and afterwards you can unpack in comfort." As I spoke I thought how delightful it was to have someone to talk to at last; and how very remarkable it was that Luella should be prepared to take up our friendship where it left off, not a bit conscious, apparently, of the difference in our positions.

We met Miss Whymark just where a lamp hung on the wall, and as she was carrying a candle, and I was too, we could see one another clearly. I stepped back, and she stood and regarded Luella with cold curiosity. I felt that she had come up to see what prodigal act this extravagant taker-of-post-chaises had committed within ten minutes of her arrival.

"You look very young for a responsible post," said Miss Whymark—surprising me. "How old are you?"

"Twenty, ma'am; and I have had three years' experience."

"You look delicate, too."

"Apart from a cold I have ailed nothing since leaving school, where I had all the childish complaints—an advantage to a governess."

"That is a highly unsuitable dress you are wearing."

I had been a little surprised when Luella took off her shabby hooded cloak and revealed the dress. It was sombre in colour, a deep lavender grey banded with purple velvet; it was not over-extravagant in style, but it looked costly.

"I'm sorry you should think that, ma'am," said Luella in a voice which held interest, a trace of surprise, but no embarrassment. "Lady Hereford gave me this gown, since I had no mourning of my own."

"Mourning?"

"For little Lord Henry who had been my pupil, poor child."

Oh dear, I thought, this is a bad beginning; two titles mentioned so soon; and Miss Whymark had scant respect for the aristocracy. I waited for some scathing words. But when she spoke, after another long assessing look, Miss Whymark said civilly,

"Well, I have no doubt you are hungry after your journey. Schoolroom supper could be early this once. Deborah will see to it. Good evening."

Unperturbed by the encounter and quite unconscious of her luck, Luella followed me to the schoolroom, where the children, counting upon a later arrival, were in the middle of their chestnut-roasting. They looked up guiltily.

"Hullo," said Luella. "You do look cosy. And what a lovely smell. Oh, chestnuts! Now how could you guess that I should be hungry?"

She knelt down on the hearth, holding her hands to the fire and turning her gaze almost gravely from one flushed young face to another. Some kind of trust was established immediately, for before I had finished drawing the curtains and making the table clear for the untimely meal they were peeling nuts for her and saying, "Have this, it's bigger." "No, this, it's cooked all through," "No, this one, Miss Maybrook, I did it specially for you."

Downstairs in the kitchen I found that Briggs had reported that the new governess looked harmless enough.

VII

Her ladyship had lost no time in sending for Mr. Kent, and before my February Saturday was due (a day to which I looked forward most eagerly, because I could tell Mother and Luke about Luella) he arrived to look over Merravay and work out the best way to make it larger and more up-to-date. Such improvements had been in her ladyship's mind ever since she and Mr. Whymark had visited the house in Leicestershire where the Miss Whymark who had made the fashionable marriage lived. Moreover at Muchanger, a nearby house, a beam that was said to have smouldered for six months, which might be true for it was solid oak and measured two and a half feet each way, burst into flame in the middle of a windy night and half the house was burned down. Muchanger had been rebuilt in the new style, and after that her ladyship had nagged and cajoled and finally bargained to get Merravay altered.

I saw Mr. Kent arrive on a mild blue and white February morning. He was shabby; he looked awkward and surly; and he rode on what was plainly a hired hack. But I was interested in him, because, secretly practising my reading at every opportunity, I had saved old papers from the lighting of fires, and seen in one a brief account of a quarrel he had had with someone who employed him. And I thought him lucky to have been chosen by Lady Rosemary to work on Merravay, because she was a lady who was very much copied, and if he pleased her it was more than likely that he would be altering houses in Suffolk for years.

He alighted and then walked all round the house, staring, before he rang the bell. Then he went in and was closeted with her ladyship and plied with refreshments for almost an hour. The master, like Pilate washing his hands, had left the house early and gone to shoot at Mortiboys.

Presently her ladyship went out with the architect, and they paced up and down for a while and then crossed the dip and stood in the field. Mr. Kent waved his arms about and looked like a scarecrow in a high wind. And then he was back in the yard, wrenching the hired horse from the first good meal it had had in its whole life, poor thing, by the look of it, and off he rode, with his head sunk between his shoulders, and with a dour, defeated look on his face. I guessed that he had failed to satisfy her ladyship and I felt sorry for him.

But it wasn't that at all. From the conversation which Briggs overheard that night at table, the truth drifted down to us. Mr. Kent had refused to touch Merravay. He said that he had never before seen a house, particularly an old house, which his fingers hadn't itched to improve; but Merravay as it stood was perfect. He wouldn't touch it himself and he hoped God would strike dead anyone who attempted it.

Here Briggs had the exact words to report.

"So I said to him, 'Mr. Kent, houses are made to be lived in, not looked at!' and he said, 'Aye, and paper is made for wrapping things; and there are shops in London now where they'll slap a pennorth of brawn in paper for you. But if some lout went to wrap my pennorth in a page of Shakespeare's sonnets I'd cry shame on him . . . as I do on you.' Then he asked me who designed this house and said whoever did it was an artist. And then he went off."

That was the first, I might say the only, time that I ever heard of a man sacrificing a chance of winning bread and butter, not to mention fame and fortune, for the sake of an idea. I still could not see exactly what was so special about Merravay, though I went to the top of the field and looked again, hard, earnestly. Nevertheless I could never think of Mr. Kent, obviously poor and in need of a job, riding away from a promising, sizable one because he didn't wish to spoil something he thought beautiful, without feeling respect and a kind of awe.

Soon after that came the last Saturday in February and according to my habit I left the house just before the midday meal. Since Father's death I had gone home more gladly, for Mother's merry spirit, never entirely subdued, had bobbed up again; and Luke regarded me as a shareholder in the farm. Mother thought, or pretended to think, that part of Father's trouble had been due to bad feeding, so nowadays she kept a good table; and curiously enough the extra outlay was not noticed, for in the very things where Father had failed, try as he might, Luke was succeeding.

I was hurrying home, thinking of the welcome and the toothsome dishes that awaited me, and of all the things I had to relate, when I met Luella and the children coming in from their morning walk. She asked me where I was going and said she would like to come with me.

"I'd like it, too . . . but . . ."

"Oh, they have plenty to do," said Luella. And they all three began saying what they should do: work on a sampler, mount and label a collection of winter berries, read. No other governess had succeeded in teaching Billy to read, but Luella had made him a book of his own, called "William Whymark's Book." It had pictures of familiar objects, with short sentences printed under them. The first picture was a little boy, lopsided of face; under it it said, "My name is William Whymark. I am a nice little boy and I will learn to read."

"Run along then. Don't make a noise, and have lots to show me when I come back," said Luella. Falling into step beside me, she said, "After all, teaching them to be self-reliant is part of the job."

"You're very clever with them," I said. "Their other governesses seemed to hate the sight of them and yet were afraid to take their eyes off them. And always complaining. Not entirely without cause. They once put a frog in Miss Runackles' bed!"

"How detestable. I should retaliate with three hedgehogs if I could find them!" She linked her arm in mine. "Will your mother mind my suddenly appearing like this? Oh, I do so want to see her, and Luke, and the place again. I always longed to be asked into your house. Oh, what a long time ago it all seems."

We walked along briskly, talking of this and that. She said what a good thing it was that Merravay wasn't to be altered.

"It would just have been too ironic if they'd started to tear it down the moment I came back."

"I confess," I said, "that I don't understand it all. What is it that attracts you so much?"

"Why do *you* love flowers so much?"

"I've never asked myself. I just love them. They're beautiful and . . ."

I groped for a word which would express the inexpressible, handicapped by the fact that I was never called upon to converse about ideas . . . "well, silly as it sounds, they seem to *promise* me something. Don't ask what, Luella, I couldn't tell you to save my life . . . but it is true, just one flower can seem to promise something that hasn't to do with hard work, meals, making ends meet, being down to earth . . ."

"That is it, exactly. All things that are just beautiful carry that promise . . . in different languages to different people."

"Promise of what?" I asked, half fearful.

"I should think . . . Heaven. Tell me quickly, Deb, when you think of Heaven what is it?"

"Layer Wood in every season at once," I said without hesitation.

"Yes. And I think, 'In my Father's house are many mansions' . . . and all like Merravay. And the idea of many mansions in a *house* has precisely the same magic . . . other-worldly . . . preposterous touch as your every season at once. D'you see?"

We went on, walking and talking so fast that we made ourselves breathless. Presently Luella said,

"Do you still read a lot?"

Despite all effort at control the red colour flared into my face. My reading at Merravay was a guilty secret. I felt that the purloined key of the bookcase and the most lately "borrowed" book, both safe under my bolster, must be imaged in my eyes—I saw them so clearly—as I asked, uneasily,

"What makes you ask that?"

"The words you use, the way you put them together . . . that's all"; she was sharing my embarrassment. I realised that during this walk with its delightful resumption of good fellowship I had forgotten to keep my usual check on my tongue. Guilt and secretiveness had now such a hold on me that I was careful never to use, in ordinary circumstances, any word that Daisy might not.

"Well . . ." I said, deciding to tell a half-truth, "yes, I do. After you went away I was at home for a year and I didn't see a written word of any kind. When I went to Merravay I was surprised to find that I *could* still read. So for practice I read the papers when they are weeks old and used for lighting the fires. And I write too. I copy pieces out of the paper sometimes, and I write what the weather is like and what flowers are blooming. *But* nobody up there knows, Luella, and I don't want them to."

"Why ever not?"

"I might find myself in the schoolroom!" It was a stupid reason, but all I could think of at the moment. Fortunately at that moment we reached our yard gate and she had no chance to ask why I feared that fate.

Mother and Luke were astonished to the point of incredulity to see

Luella, but delighted too, and when the exclamations ended we settled down to what, I think, must have been the merriest meal ever to be eaten in that house. Since Father's death Mother had resumed her making of homemade wines, elderberry, cowslip, and blackberry, and now, with many apologies for their lack of maturity, she produced samples of all kinds and we grew very lively. Luella seemed to slip into place with unbelievable ease; even the silk dress did not strike an incongruous note. Only her voice, her clear laugh, did that.

We lingered over the meal and then Mother and I went into the scullery to do the dishes. Luella offered to help but Mother would not allow that, so we left her with Luke by the fire. After a few minutes Luke put his head and one arm round the door and picked up the wooden pattens which Mother used when walking in the yard.

"I'm going to rack up now," he said, "and Miss Maybrook wants to come with me. I'll take these."

From the unglazed hole in the wall that served our scullery for a window, I watched them crossing the yard, Luella walking clumsily in the pattens, and laughing at her clumsiness. At the miry part by the pigs' pen she stumbled, and Luke took her elbow to steady her. Luke was laughing too, and I realised suddenly that I had never seen him really merry before. In Father's time he had been suppressed and subdued, and then at a stride he had passed to responsibility and the deadly seriousness that goes with ambition. But he was laughing now.

"She've turned out a lot better than I should've expected," said Mother, dropping a pinch of wood ash on a greasy plate and scrubbing vigorously. "To tell the truth I allust thought she was a mite dim-witted."

"Ah, that was because she couldn't manage the pony," I said, thinking that even then she had managed *us* and we had managed the pony for her. I looked back over the month she had been at Merravay—a whole month—and nobody, not even Miss Whymark, had yet found a word to say against her.

That evening Luke drove us back to Merravay in the cart. He and I were the best of friends; he had, at Father's death, told me that a third of the farm was mine. I had always returned to Merravay on foot, feeling very cherished and privileged if he strolled with me, in winter, until the lights of the house were visible across the fields. It had never occurred to him to drive me, and in justice to him I must say that the idea of being driven had never occurred to me either.

VIII

Quite early in March another architect, of whom her ladyship had heard a good report, came to make a visit of inspection. He was young and good-looking, well dressed, and full of confidence. He measured and tapped, walked about the house, and stared at it from various angles, and then retreated to the library to draw some preliminary sketches. When they were complete Miss Sophie borrowed them and brought them to the schoolroom to show Luella. I was there and she invited me to see them too; because she was well disposed to me just then since, though it was no longer part of my duty, I helped her with her hair and her clothes. I had, one evening, almost been caught doing her hair when her ladyship suddenly came in to tell her daughter which dress to wear; luckily I heard her voice and hopped into the clothes closet and hid myself. Afterwards Miss Sophie and I laughed almost hysterically together, and some sort of barrier fell and never went up again. Luella also helped with the constant titivation of the wardrobe—even her ladyship would ask her advice; for, with Lady Hereford, Luella had lived in London and had had opportunities to see the ladies of fashion.

So now we all three bent over the sketches as though they were dress patterns. I could see at a glance that Mr. Armitage's alterations were to be fundamental; the house's new face was to be flat, with many windows set in rows, and instead of the deep old porch the new door was to have a pillared portico.

"I tried not to like it," Miss Sophie said. "Poor Aunt Phyl is so upset because what she calls 'Granny's garden' will now be built upon; and the window tax will be calamitous. But now I have *seen* it. . . . Don't you think it is impressive—and so well designed?"

"It would be fine on any other house," said Luella. "I shall go on hoping to the very last minute that something occurs to baulk these plans."

"Well nothing will," said Miss Sophie in a pleased way. "Mamma is delighted with them, and with Mr. Armitage."

Two evenings later, after the architect had ridden away, Mr. Whymark came to a belated realisation of the extent of the alterations planned, and once again there was no need for us to wait for Briggs or Parker to bring news from the front of the house to us in the kitchen. The master, really angry and a little flown with wine, could make himself heard at Slipwell.

Where, he demanded to be told, was it proposed that they should live while the whole of the front of the house was pulled down? Yes, he knew he had promised, though how the devil he'd been such a fool he didn't know; but he'd only meant a couple of extra bedrooms and new doors and windows if she set such store by them. Live in a house with no front he would not!

There was then a babble of female voices, the words indistinguishable, and then the master's voice again.

"You keep out of this, Phyl," he roared. "All right; you agree with me; I don't want your blasted agreement. It's this everlasting pull devil pull baker that's been the ruin of this house. Am I never to have any peace? It's a bit late in the day to point this out to you all, but this is *my* house and you'd do well to remember it. All of you. Parker! Bring a fresh bottle to the library!"

And it was then, according to Parker, that the door opened and Mr. Roger walked in, saying,

"This sounds just like home!"

He had always looked old for his years and he had aged considerably in the two and a half years he had been away. A wig was now more to him than a sign of rank or mark of fashion; it was a necessity. The yellow sallowness of his skin had darkened and his face had fallen into grooves and lines—all melancholy; he looked rather like a hound. But he had a smile of singular sweetness; it was not merely a stretching of the lips and a brightening of the eyes, it was a lighting up, a rearrangement of his whole face. My work, of course, did not bring me near him; and Merravay, despite her ladyship's complaints, was big enough to allow two people under its roof to meet by accident very rarely, but on the few occasions when I did see him I found myself waiting for that smile, the sudden flash of sunshine in a sombre sky; it reminded me irresistibly of Mother's wryly merry looks behind Father's back in the old days.

Mr. Roger's arrival did a good deal to console her ladyship for the blow dealt her over the alterations. For four or five days everything was pleasant and lively and excited; parties to celebrate Mr. Roger's safe return, and reciprocal parties in other houses. And then everything changed.

For all this part of the story I had to rely upon what Luella, coming home with me in March and April, could report.

Mr. Roger had gone out to Virginia, it seemed, because the overseer of the plantation—sometimes called the agent, too—had died, and it was necessary to appoint another person, completely trustworthy and knowledgeable. That was soon done, but by the time it was arranged Mr. Roger had become deeply involved in the business of slaves and slavery. When he had learned all there was to learn about the slaves on the plantation, which would one day be his own, he had set out and visited dozens of others, places where rice was grown, and cane sugar and cotton.

What he had seen and heard appalled him. He had all the facts set down in a number of little black notebooks: the numbers of slaves on various plantations; how many died, were bought, sold, born each year; their weights, their rations, hours of work, diseases and punishments. He had come back to England with all this carefully gathered and meticulously recorded information, with the avowed intent to try to have the whole system abolished. He began by offering her ladyship a paper upon which she had only to write her signature and the two hundred slaves on her Virginian property would be free. That must be the first step, he said, because it would be a hopeless handicap to his campaign if people could turn round and say that his mother was a slaveowner.

Legally—as Luella pointed out to me—her ladyship, being a married woman, owned nothing; but in point of fact Mr. Whymark had always refused to have anything to do with the American property. I imagine that he resented it because it had made his wife independent, able to follow her whims. He now pursued his established course. To Mr. Roger, when appealed to, he said, "It is for your mother to decide"; and to his wife, "You must do as you think best. In your place I'd sign."

Two days later he said he didn't intend to have his life made miserable by the discussion of the woes of a lot of black fellows he'd never set eyes on, and forbade the mention of the subject in his presence.

The sense of conflict made itself felt throughout the house. We all, willy-nilly, began to take sides. I had no particular love for her ladyship; she had treated me fairly but had never done anything to endear herself to me, and I knew very well that if, one evening, lacing her into her gown I had dropped dead, she would have minded the resultant confusion and loss of time far more than my demise; but I could see her predicament. Mr. Roger was her eldest son, her best beloved child; he had been absent for overlong, she was delighted to see him home; she was mildly shocked by a few carefully selected incidents which he related to her and she wished to please him. But he admitted that by freeing her slaves she would, temporarily at least, reduce her income; and since she was now going pig-headedly towards a modified alteration of Merravay she needed the money because it bolstered her authority.

Miss Whymark, because anything likely to reduce her ladyship's power seemed most desirable, was an abolitionist; Miss Maud said that if the slaves could be sure of enough fat pork and meal to keep life in their bodies they were better off than many poor people in Nettleton. Miss Sophie, anxious to do anything, short of marrying Sir Frederick, to please her mother, said, not without truth, that a careful investigation of the ordinary farm labourer's conditions of life and labour would expose some shocking facts. Luella, partly because she was very tender-hearted, and also—I think—because loss of money would restrain her ladyship's rebuilding, was firmly on Mr. Roger's side; and when she found that he needed several copies of his charts and facts and abstracts written out, offered her services.

I was, I think I can say with truth, an entirely disinterested abolitionist. And it was not Mr. Roger who had converted me. It was somebody called Thomas Rowhedge who had been dead for almost a hundred years.

Soon after I first went to Merravay a brick in the breast of the chimney in the Ship Chamber became porous and a great dark patch came through the plaster. During the process of taking out the faulty brick it was discovered that the panelling on one side of the chimney was not solid; it was the front of a cupboard, and the cupboard was full of ancient books. When they had been cleaned and their leather bindings polished, they were housed in a special glass-fronted bookcase in the library, and during my time as maid-of-all-work it was one of my tasks to dust them occasionally. It was then that I discovered, to my delight, that I remembered how to read. For a week or two I contented myself by peeping into the books and reading a page at random while I was supposed to be dusting, and then one day I came across a thick, leather-bound book, written by hand, and noticed the name "Alice" recurring. A Lady Alice Rowhedge who had lived at Merravay many years before, and who had been—they said—a witch, had become a part and parcel of the folklore of our district, and many a winter night I had sat by the fire at home and listened to Aunt Hester's tales about her. A dark, shuddering curiosity seized me as I handled this book, and presently, when I left the library, it was hidden under my apron. Five minutes later it was under my pillow. I was fortunate in having been put to sleep in a little room directly under the rafters, reached by an almost perpendicular ladder which even Miss Whymark in her visits of inspection never climbed, a room cruelly cold in winter and roastingly hot in summer, a lonely, unenviable eyrie of which I remained in undisputed possession.

That book was, from my point of view, disappointing, but it had given me a taste for reading in bed, and for several weeks after that I "borrowed" books from that case. Then her ladyship caught Miss Sophie reading something which she said was most unsuitable and she locked that case and carried off the keys. The case left open contained books of surpassing dullness; most of them were ones which Mr. Whymark had had when he was a young man at Cambridge; some of them weren't even in English. But by that time the reading habit was strong in me; and when I had been reduced to carrying *A Mirror For Magistrates* to bed with me, I realised that I had only to ask her ladyship for the key under pretence that the locked books needed dusting. I never gave it back to her.

Amongst the books with which I was thus guiltily free to indulge was a slim, handwritten one containing a play called *The Middle Passage*. Under the title Thomas Rowhedge had written,

> "This Drama is rooted in a True Story, told me many years
> since by my Father, who was himself the Sea Captain."

It was all about slaves and the things they endured on their journey from Africa to America. It made terrible reading, but there was poetry in it too. In the end the Captain, to the detriment of his pocket and the extreme fury of his partner, turned them all loose on a desert island, saying,

> "It may be that you die here. Even so,
> Die as free men whose hands, too late unbound,
> Have failed to wring a sustenance from this soil,
> That shall be my blame too, an added guilt

> To that I bear already. But from hence
> It shall not be my profit. Not for me
> The Judas coin with blood upon its rim."

I didn't believe, of course, that a rough sea captain would talk that way to black men, or that they would understand him if he did; but it was good to read; and it set me against the slave trade and everything connected with it. So when Luella offered to make the copies for Mr. Roger, I volunteered to help her. We used to work in the schoolroom at night, after Miss Whymark had made her last round and the house was quiet. Despite the fact that Luella had had years of schooling and much more practice, I still wrote the better hand; but if Mr. Roger ever noticed the difference he never said anything. He himself sat in the library all through the lovely month of April, sorting the papers and scribbling away like a clerk. With every passing day her ladyship regarded him with more disfavour, and when he began sending letters to Sir George Fenstanton, who was our Member of Parliament, and trying to enlist his interest in the business, she went about with a tragic face, burst into angry tears frequently, and said, not caring who overheard her, that to have thankless, unloving children was the hardest fate a woman could have. She said that Mr. Roger was trying deliberately to ruin her, to take the roof from over her head, the bread from her mouth.

During this same month of April a rumour began to creep about the kitchen that Sir Frederick Fennel had proposed to Miss Sophie and been refused. This remained rumour until, during the Easter week when the balls began again after the Lenten lapse, I received first-hand proof of it.

Her ladyship's own maid—Kate, Luella, and I were helping to dress her and do her hair, and I was watching for an opportunity to slip away and see what sort of mess Daisy had made of Miss Sophie's hair, when the young lady herself, wearing a wrapper, came in.

"Mamma, do you wish me to wear the yellow or the blue?"

Without turning her head, upon which Luella was erecting one of the new high fashionable coiffures, her ladyship said quite sweetly,

"Neither, my dear. I do not intend that you should accompany us this evening. Since you have decided to emulate your aunts you may as well stay at home with them. Miss Maybrook! That last pin pierced my scalp!"

Not altogether by accident, I thought, catching sight of Luella's face. Even the fanatically devoted Kate looked troubled. The cold venom, the unkind timing of the announcement, had not been pleasant to see.

"As you wish, Mamma," said Miss Sophie.

"She'll learn," said her ladyship pleasantly. "I can see that I have been overindulgent with my children and the result is a headstrong wilfulness. Still . . . it may not be too late to rectify matters."

Rectifying the results of almost thirty years of what she called indulgence towards Mr. Roger took the form, a few days later, of refusing

155

to entertain Sir George Fenstanton and the Bishop of Bywater. He asked her at table, in Briggs' presence, so we all had a first-hand account of it.

"If those two, lately at daggers drawn, propose to visit you together, Roger, we know why! All right, Johnny, I am not mentioning the subject! I may not be clever, but I have sense enough to see that when a politician and a churchman get together some third person is about to be robbed. I do not intend to receive them under the roof that they and you are trying to rip from over my head."

"Don't talk such nonsense, Rose," said Miss Whymark. "This house stood here years before any of those black men were born and will stand long after they're all set free or dead. I do resent the way you talk as though Merravay depended upon a few poor slaves."

"Did I or did I not say that I wouldn't have this thing discussed in my presence?" Mr. Whymark shouted.

"Roger brought it up. That's all he thinks about," put in Miss Maud. "I tried to make him interested in the poor Thackers, turned out in the road with eight children, but no, they ain't black enough to . . ."

Then, Briggs said, they all began to talk together. Mr. Roger accused his mother of trying to build a fine new house out of dead Negroes' bones; Miss Whymark accused Miss Maud of spoiling the Thackers, who should shift for themselves. "It was a regular bear garden," said Briggs.

That evening Luella said that we must work extra hard over the copies; she had seen Mr. Roger sometime during the day and he had told her he was off to London in the morning and wanted the papers to take with him.

We worked late, thinking the house asleep, and when Mr. Roger came in I was caught unawares. There was no time for me to lay down my quill and pretend to be busy with some much belated domestic task as I usually held myself ready to do.

He had been working too; there was ink on his fingers and a blob of it on the end of his nose. He had discarded his wig, and the few remaining strands of his rust-coloured hair were all on end. His neckcloth was loosened, and he looked more like an over-driven scrivener than the heir to a fine estate.

He took in the situation at a glance.

"Ah! So that's how it's done. I often wondered. Bless you, child. I thank you from my heart. As for you," he turned to Luella who was ruling a line to frame a column, "but for your help I should have been another month. I truly cannot express my gratitude . . ."

She laid down the ruler, stood up and stretched and yawned, as gracefully and unself-consciously as a cat. He stood smiling, the lines in his face softening out and changing as a dark furrowed field changes under the touch of the sunshine. And then, as he looked at Luella, the smile died out, and for a moment, or less, for a mere second, before his face resumed its everyday expression, there was something else. . . .

"You know, I take this as a symbol . . . that two young people should sit up o'nights, spoiling their pretty eyes to help the cause. It proves to me that, once the facts are known, all right-minded people . . ."

He broke off at a sound beyond the door.

"Miss Whymark," said Luella in a horrified voice.

"It's all right . . . she's with us . . . I'll explain."

The door opened after a knob-fumbling pause and there was Mr. Whymark.

"Thought I heard voices," he said in the staccato voice which came upon him when he was drunk. He stared at us all. "Wanted to see you before you go. Off tomorrow? That right? Wanted to say . . . all a great pity, very great pity. Mustn't mind your Mother, y'know, very excitable, always was, always will be. 'Nother thing too, wanted to say. Ah, yes. Mustn't get carried away. Take little chaps that climb chimneys. Know what? They all die before they're twelve. On paper, my boy, on paper. 'S'fact. Read about it 'tother day. Die before they're twelve. But you go 'long Goose Lane, old Sweeper Armstrong, claims to be ninety, put's son to the trade. Young Sweeper as old as I am, lot healthier; regiment of youngsters, all climbing chimneys and lively 'scrickets. See what I mean? Mustn't get carried away; make crass fool of y'self."

"I see exactly," said Mr. Roger. "I won't do that. Everything I say is soundly based on fact."

"So you reckon to set Thames on fire with all that paper, eh?"

"I hope to convince somebody who can. Sooner or later."

"Well," said Mr. Whymark, staring round aimlessly for a moment. "Well, wish you luck, m'boy. Ha . . . 'nother thing. Money. Can't do without it, y'know. More pull in a good dinner and a bottle of the right stuff 'nin all the talk in the world. And even if you do turn the black chaps loose, don't mean we shall go on the parish. Plenny money here, trust old Phyl for that."

"I have all I need at the moment, sir," Mr. Roger said, the smile lighting his face again. "But I thank you for the thought; and even more for your good wishes."

" 'Snothing," said the master, waving his hand in the air. "Just heard voices and came along, say a friendly word. G'night."

He wheeled round with a lurch and then, arrested by something, turned again and peered at Luella.

"You . . ." he drew back, shaking his head. "Just f'r a moment, mistook you. Very peculiar thing. . . ." Muttering, he took himself off.

"If they were *his,* he'd free them tomorrow," said Mr. Roger, gathering his papers together.

"Because it would—for him—be the easiest thing," said Luella.

Mr. Roger looked up sharply. "All too true! Do you see through everybody as clearly as that, Miss Maybrook? Let's hope not, eh—er—Deborah? Still, that sort mustn't be discounted, you know; they have the will to good; in mass they form a power called public opinion. Well, thank you again, both of you, more than I can say. Good night."

"Well, that's over and done with, thank God," said Luella, yawning again as she dropped the lid on the ink bottle. "And tomorrow is your free day, Deb. Your mother did say . . . but would it be more change for you to go alone?"

"Of course not. And I'm sure they'd both be horribly horribly disappointed," I said.

IX

She came home with me in April, and we gathered primroses together again; and in May when the cowslips were in flower and the lilacs shyly showing their colour. My days at home had always been very cheerful since Father—poor man—had died, but Luella's coming contributed something else, something special. Both then and later, I gave hours of thought to the problem of Luella—and not without cause. I never put my finger exactly on what it was she did to people and for people, but I think I was near it when I concluded that she was a little like a flattering looking-glass. She was always herself and allowed you to be yourself, but in her presence, under her response to you, you were a little more how you would like to be. That, and her boundless capacity to enjoy herself . . . and, of course, the other thing which still eludes me, the thing there is no word for. It wasn't that I was charmed with her and therefore imagined her to be charming; there was the way in which the children had taken to her, the fact that in strife-ridden Merravay she had no enemy.

On our April day she asked again to be allowed to help with the dishes and my mother laughed and said, "All right then, love, come along," and taking one of her own print aprons she wrapped Luella in it, greatly amused because it was so much too wide. "The scullery is a hovel," said Mother. "My bowl is cracked and the dishcloth is the tail of one of Luke's owd shirts, but you'll hev to excuse all that," and plainly she knew that Luella would, otherwise she would never have let her cross the threshold.

In May that year the weather turned gloriously warm and on my free Saturday I decided to wear my summer "tidy" gown, but it had rotted while laid away and it split when I put it on. So I donned one of my clean working prints and rather morosely set out side by side with Luella, who was wearing a sprigged muslin, light and airy and very pretty. I grumbled a bit and she said,

"Ask Luke to buy some stuff for you next market day, and I'll make you a dress just like this. You need six yards, and three yards of ribbon. You should have a cherry colour. We could sew in the evenings and have it ready for the next outing."

"We shouldn't be able to collect the stuff till then," I said, still depressed over the split dress.

"Don't be so silly. Luke could bring it up, couldn't he? Or you could walk down to fetch it. It's light till nine."

The gulf between us, so often firmly bridged by her friendliness, by the memory of old days, by the hospitality of my home, suddenly yawned. Miss Whymark—I think because she was afraid that servants would *feed* their visitors—had made a rule forbidding relatives and friends to call upon them except in cases of emergency, in which she must first receive the caller and hear the business. As for running home to fetch a parcel. . .

Embarrassed, and more cross than ever, I explained this.

"She really is . . ." said Luella, as always instantly understanding. "Well, all right. I'll fetch it for you. After all in my last post I had a free day each week."

Luke, of course, willingly accepted the errand, but when we explained about Luella coming to fetch it, alone, on the evening of market day, I saw something happen to his face. And I thought to myself, Yes . . . like everybody else he has fallen in love with her, or maybe he has been all along. It was natural, perhaps inevitable. But I was filled with foreboding.

That deepened when, about ten days later, as we were putting the final stitches to the new dress in the last light of a lovely, lingering summer evening, Luella said,

"There, Deb, it's lovely and you'll look lovely in it. And I promised Luke that you'd ask for permission and we'd go to the Fair with him."

"The Midsummer Fair!" I said aghast. If there was one person in our district more averse, more opposed to the two fairs that took place, one at midsummer and one at the end of harvest, than Miss Whymark herself was, it was my brother Luke.

"Yes, the Midsummer Fair," said Luella, biting off her cotton.

"But Luke . . ." I began and stopped. No point in letting her know how completely off his head she had driven him. It must be that; nothing else would explain this sudden change of front. "Luke doesn't realise," I said. "Miss Whymark never allows anyone to go to the fairs."

"But I promised. I never have seen a real old country fair. But I've heard about them. Deborah, they still have *mummers,* simple little plays done in mime, just like the mediaeval days . . . now, in the eighteenth century. Did you know *that?* And climbing greasy poles to win a pig, and prizes for making the ugliest face through a horse collar. . . . All the old things that have amused people for hundreds of years; and all dying out except in remote places like this. Deborah, I would love to see it."

"Well *you* can. I can't. That is one of Miss Whymark's rules. No fair-going. You see, there is another side to it. People go wild and get drunk and very mediaeval indeed. They reckon that two thirds of the bastards in the villages around . . ."

"Deborah, there are people who go blind because they read too much, people who die of over-eating and over-drinking. The world is full of fools."

"I am just trying to explain how Miss Whymark sees it."

"And I am trying to explain how *I* see it. Look, I'll ask her for us both. I did promise Luke."

"But it isn't a thing that decent people . . . Oh, Luella, how can I explain. It's all so outdated. Poor, rough people stick to the old things, they don't know any better . . . but the others move on." Was Luke, my dear brother, so serious, so ambitious, really one of the "poor rough people," or had Luella's desire to see the mummers persuaded him?

Suddenly it came to me that I was worrying myself unduly. Six years under Miss Whymark's inflexible rule now enabled me to say, quite light-heartedly,

"This isn't for us to decide, Luella. You ask Miss Whymark." Stupid old woman, she betrayed me! She couldn't, she said, permit me to go, because that would create a precedent of which the other servants would take advantage. But she was sympathetic . . . mark that . . . sympathetic with Luella's desire to see the mummers, and if she was *sure* of a reliable escort . . .

"I wouldn't have credited it," I said when Luella told me.

"She even asked me, since I *was* going, to take note of the prices of cheesecloth and knitting needles. She wrote the Baildon prices down and if the Fair ones . . . Deb, what is the matter? Why are you looking at me like that?"

"I've just thought of something else, Luella. You see . . ."

The thing I had to say seemed to choke me.

"Well?"

"You see . . . when a girl goes, by herself, to this particular fair, with a man, it's supposed to be a sign . . ."

I still couldn't say it. Luke so simple, unable to read or write, dear to me, oh, very dear to me, a good man, but for all that, with his muddy boots, sweaty shirt, hard hands, not to be thought of . . . a cat may *look* at a king but . . .

"A sign of what?" asked Luella crisply.

"Special favour," I gulped out. "You see . . . lots of country men are shy, they can't say things. So to make it easy for them there are these old customs. And the Midsummer Fair . . . it's easier for them to say, 'Come to the Fair' than 'Will you marry me?' But it means the same."

"Deborah, really. I never heard anything so entirely old-fashioned! It's just a spectacle, something to look at. And Luke didn't ask me alone . . . we were both supposed to go. Practically his last words to me when we parted were joking ones about minding to have this dress ready for you. And it is; and you shall go. I shall ask her ladyship . . ."

"Luella, please! If you did that Miss Whymark would make my life a misery for months. She'd take it as a direct insult and never rest till she'd . . . why, she might even give me the sack. Even if you did ask and got permission, I simply dare not go."

"This really is a very difficult household," said Luella. "I had set my heart on going, and I promised Luke."

"I'm not preventing you. I'm just pointing out what it means."

"Luke has more sense. Still . . ." She broke off and brooded for a moment, winding a strand of hair about her finger. "You may be right. But there's so little time now. If we could catch Lantern we could send Luke a note."

"Luella, you know he can't read!"

"Well, he said he would wait for us at the end of the avenue at ten o'clock. One of us must run down and explain. I don't trust Lantern to deliver a verbal message."

"There again," I said, "I can't go galloping off at ten . . ."

"Very well, then, I will."

She set off next morning just before ten, wearing her working dress and no hat. I lingered over my work in the schoolroom, wishful to hear how Luke had taken the disappointment. She didn't come back. Presently the children had finished the tasks she had set them and I took them out for a long walk, starting off along the avenue. There was no sign of her. It was a perfect day for the Fair, warm and sunny with a little brushing breeze.

She came back at dusk. Her peculiarly white skin was powdered with freckles across the nose and brow, her hair was a tangled froth of curls, and out of their hollows, deepened and darkened by fatigue, her green eyes shone like water. She was laden with fairings; a pair of fine white stockings for me to wear with my new dress, wooden dolls with painted faces for Miss Julia and Miss Arabella, a monkey on a stick for Master Billy. She had even remembered Miss Whymark's needles and a great roll of cheesecloth. And she had a wonderful time—a perfect day, she called it.

I had saved some oatcake and a glass of milk from the schoolroom supper and she settled down to it, talking all the time. "I really shouldn't need any food at all. Luke and I have been eating and drinking most of the day. But I am hungry. Oh, I must tell you about the plays. Deborah, you would have loved them; they were enchanting . . ." She rattled on while I lighted the candles. Then, as she tilted her head to drink her milk, the heavy tangled hair swung backwards and I saw something glitter in her ears.

"Did you get a fairing, too?" I asked.

"Oh, yes, these . . ." She loosened the earbobs and laid them in my hand; little daisies with petals made of silver and a scrap of yellow stone

161

for centres. "Aren't they *pretty*? The prettiest on the booth. Luke gave me them. And I gave him a wonderful pocketknife. . . ."

So now, by all the traditions of our countryside, the wordless proposal had been made and accepted, and Luke had every right to regard her as his pledged sweetheart.

But that was too absurd even for me to say aloud.

X

Nevertheless, on our June free day, which came round soon after, I could detect a subtle change both in Mother and Luke. That was not really so surprising. To people of leisure and education it might seem strange to build any permanent plans upon the foundation of four or five visits and an outing; but for working folk that was the way. With free time so scanty and distances—on foot—so great, the business of courtship must be reduced to the minimum, and rely largely on symbols. I'd known many girls get married on the strength of an invitation to Sunday dinner and two or three subsequent walks.

It was not that Luke made any open display of feeling, he was not the kind to do that; but his eye dwelt upon Luella with a possessiveness that was new; and when, in the evening, I remembered that it was time to call for the new shoes which Farrow the cobbler was making for me, he was not slow to say, "Then if you start out a bit afore us and Luella and me walk the field way and take it easy, you'll just about get there together."

"We'll wait for you, Deb," said Luella. "At Vinefields Bottom, you know, where the pony once threw me off into the mud."

Such references to our childhood days were often on her tongue and, hearing this one, I wondered whether she realised that those days had gone, that we were not children any more, that walking with a young man through the fields, on a June evening, might have some significance. I pondered the matter all the way to Goose Lane. I told myself reasonably that there would be nothing so startlingly strange, so fundamentally incongruous in her falling in love with Luke. He was very handsome then; the long-suffering, saintly look had disappeared, his face had hardened and now wore an expression of resolute intent which, if it were baulked, as Father's had been, might deteriorate into the same surliness. He was ambitious, too, and seemed, so far, to be lucky in all his dealings. He would make a good husband . . . for some girl. . . . But, perhaps because I had so chancily attained the state myself, and had been so hard put to it to maintain my hold, I did set a disproportionate value on being able to read and write, on the wider interests, the ability to take impersonal views, to converse as opposed to making flat statements. I knew that for myself I could never contemplate marriage with an ignorant man, and therefore it was highly unlikely that I should ever find a husband, and I knew that compared with Luella I was ignorant indeed.

But then I had never been in love. Was Luella?

July and August passed all too quickly, as they always did, as May and June had done. Soon winter, with the mud and the biting wind and the early dark, would be upon us again.

In July Mr. Roger came home, for the Parliament gentlemen had all gone to their country homes to overlook their harvests. He told Luella, who told me, that he had gained a hearing from one or two influential people and "planted a seed here and there." Her ladyship seemed pleased to see him again, and had evidently decided to treat his activities as a form of unimportant sickness from which he was almost recovered and which need not be mentioned any more.

The corn ripened and harvest began and soon everyone was thinking about the horkey, the high light of the Merravay year.

As was their custom her ladyship and Mr. Whymark went to stay with his sister, Lady Whardale, in Leicestershire, leaving home a week or ten days before the Feast. They had made a point of being absent just then ever since the two fields were turned into parkland, for at the horkey Miss Whymark always made a speech at the table and that year she had been tactlessly blunt in her remarks about how the founder of the feast would have felt about the innovation. Her ladyship, younger then, and more impetuous, had jumped up and protested and there had been a scene.

This particular horkey was entirely a Whymark festival, Miss Whymark's festival. Some money had been left by the old lady and just for once in the year Miss Whymark spent lavishly; she had even been known to contribute a little of her own money in a year when prices were high. In fact any careful observer—as I, in my necessarily limited way, was—might observe a change come over Miss Whymark the moment that the master and mistress drove away. During the fortnight of her undisputed reign she was less carping, more genial; partly it was excitement over the feast and partly, I think, a kind of endeavour to cast blame for the unpleasant atmosphere usual in the house upon the absent Lady Rosemary. And relief may have had something to do with it, too.

Two days before the event, when we were already beginning to bake and boil, and clear the centre of the great barn where the long table was set out, Mr. Armitage arrived.

Her ladyship had written to him earlier in the year, cancelling the ambitious plans for the new front in a mood of angry despair. Later her spirit had revived and suggestions for the extra rooms and some modification of the frontage had been made, and she had written again, asking the architect to pay another visit. Perhaps he was annoyed, or wished to assert his independence, for since then nothing more had been said or done. Now here he was and her ladyship was in Leicestershire.

Miss Whymark was not so busy with her plans as to forget that she was opposed to any alterations to the house. But she did not make the obvious move of sending away the young man who had come to make plans for its alterations. On the contrary she set herself to woo him. She insisted that he stay, she lodged him and fed him well, and several times during the next day or two she dragged herself away from her delightful preparations to walk about and talk to him. Once when I went to find her and ask something I heard her telling him what Mr. Kent had said about the house. There was no doubt that she was a wily and forceful old woman . . . probably not above a little bribery; it was quite possible that her ladyship might return to find that Mr. Armitage had deserted the cause.

There came the day when the last load of corn, decorated with ribbons and boughs and flowers and topped by "The Maiden," was dragged into the stackyard; and another year's harvest was safely in. The first cask of ale was broached and then the labourers went to their homes, whence they would return, washed and reclad, accompanied by their womenfolk, to sit down at six o'clock to partake of the hospitality of a woman long dead.

The meal lasted for a long time, for these were guests who did not, every day eat their fill and Miss Whymark had provided nobly, with succulent cold roast sirloin, hams, pork pies, and pasties, with pickles and sauces, tarts and jellies, cakes, biscuits and sweetmeats, all washed down with ale in plenty, and tea and homemade lemonade. This year as usual she made her little speech, glorifying her grandmother's memory. She could say, "Those of you are old enough to remember with me . . ." in a very moving way which set the older people nodding their heads and thinking sentimentally of days which seemed golden in retrospect, not because of old Mistress Whymark's goodness and kindness but because they themselves were young then, and more vigorous, more hopeful. This year Miss Whymark struck what was, for those of us who understood the situation, a very topical note.

"We meet here, every year, to remember, to look back. It is a custom, an *old* custom, and none the worse for that. There are those in this world"—she looked directly at Mr. Armitage—"who do not fully realise the value of the old, the tried, the proved. There are those who cannot see that there are some things so old that they are nearly holy. . . ." She went on at some length, and a great gloom descended upon the company, who, hearing the trend of the speech and missing, perforce, its point, began to wonder what it boded. Later on I heard speculations voiced; was this the last horkey? Was everybody over fifty going to be sacked? Was Miss Whymark going to retire?

When she ended her speech and the applause had died down, Mr. Armitage, quite uninvited, rose to his feet.

"Madam," he said, "you have entertained me royally, and your speech has given me a great deal to think about. May I, in return, attempt to entertain you? I cannot, alas, sing for my supper like the boy in the nursery rhyme, but I can . . . Ah, I'll start with Master William Whymark. He looks a nice little boy, doesn't he; I believe his book says that he is a nice little boy; I am astonished to find him so greedy! What can he be doing with this and this and this."

Quick as light, from Master Billy's ear, from the back of his collar, from his curly topknot of hair, he produced an orange, a mince pie, and four sugar plums.

Before the laughter had died down, and while the children still stared, wide-eyed, he turned to Miss Whymark.

"I'm practically a stranger here, but I have seen, in a short time, that yours is a hard task, madam," he said dolefully. "You have all these rapacious, wasteful creatures to look after. Let me see if I can help you a little. Is that of use?" He took a candle out of her cap, another from her fichu, an egg from her elbow, two sausages from between her shoulder blades. The slight edge on his words delighted the company, everyone of whom had, at some time, suffered under Miss Whymark's parsimony. She was flustered, and astonished, but true to her character; as he juggled with the egg she called out, "Be careful; be careful." And then the mirth was unrestrained.

Through it, he said to Parker, "We know you are careful of the silver, but must you carry it on your person?" From Parker's pocket he drew four silver spoons.

When he had finished he sat down, not in his old place but next to Luella, near enough for me to hear him say,

"That went well didn't it? Was I word perfect?"

"You were *wonderful*," she said, "you remembered every tiny thing. And how you could, and do the juggling as well . . ." So she had pointed out the idiosyncrasies upon whose frank, but not unkindly, mention so much of the success had depended. Mr. Armitage looked at her approvingly, and settled down with a smoothed, pleased look; he evidently liked being told that he was wonderful. Luella had done it again.

Then there was the dancing, with old Mortlock and Young Lantern playing their fiddles and Miss Whymark stepping stiffly out, first with Parker, and then with the bailiff and two or three more in strict order of seniority. A few old people stood, or sat aside remembering with discomfort the implied threat of possible changes to come, and picking their teeth. The young ones romped through the ancient dances and the presence of Mr. Roger, Mr. Armitage, and Luella added to the extra merry mood which the juggling display had begun.

Luella romped like a child, completely unself-conscious, utterly given over to the process of enjoying herself. Once, and not so long ago, I should have done the same; now I derived more pleasure from watching. And amongst the things I saw that evening, and marked and remembered, was the expression on Miss Sophie's face as Luella, one arm linked in Mr. Armitage's, the other in the clean-smocked shepherd's, rollicked through the movements of "Three Meet." Envy, admiration, wistfulness, wonderment, they were all there.

A fortnight later, when Mr. Armitage had gone his way and the master and mistress were home again and the chestnuts—always the first to hope or despair—were showing some lemon-yellow leaves, everyone was surprised that Miss Sophie, returning from one of her solitary rides, announced that she was going to marry Sir Frederick Fennel "very soon." I was not surprised. I knew the exact moment when she had made that decision. For I also, in moments when my lack of certain things has been borne in me, have thought—Ah, but this, and this, I have and may be sure of!

The engagement—Miss Sophie's grasping at the one thing she could be sure of—pleased everyone; and several people, recovering from their surprise, claimed credit for bringing it about. Her ladyship held that it had been her stern treatment which had resulted in the change of mind—the thought of the dull home-keeping winter had brought the silly child to her senses. Mr. Whymark said that he had always been of the opinion that so long as the girl wasn't pressed or bullied nature would take its course. Miss Maud said frankly,

"Well, I gave her some advice, based on my own experience. I said, 'Roger will bring a wife home one of these days, and you'll find that living in your brother's house isn't all honey, however kind *he* may be!' That made her think."

The wedding had been arranged for the second week in October. How many people, I wondered, saw the significance of that? Miss Sophie's birthday fell in the following week; she would be twenty-two. She would be married before she was twenty-two. In her present mood that mattered.

It mattered to me, too; for I lost my September Saturday because there was so much to do, cleaning the house and making ready for the Whardales, who must, of course, come to the wedding and must stay at Merravay. And if I had ever yearned and longed to go home for any reason but sheer homesickness, it was just then.

For when I went home with Luella on the August Saturday, Mother had said, "You girls must fend for yourselves today. Mr. Loveridge, across at Squirrels, stuck a fork through his foot day afore yesterday, and I'm seeing to the brews and plasters." She was very busy and important, and sure of her skill in cures; she said he would mend.

But in little more than a week Jack Lantern, who brought us the village news, told us that Mr. Loveridge was dead. I felt, on the verge of my mind, sorry for his wife, a town-bred woman and helpless, and his six-year-old son; but they would be all right, in a way; for Squirrels was their freehold and known as a splendid farm. It would sell easily. Another week passed and Jack Lantern, not without a trace of awe in his voice, said to me one morning, "So that brother of yours has took over Squirrels! Well, to be sure, some people get on in this world!"

My curiosity swelled like a boil, and one day when Luella told me that she was going into Baildon with Miss Sophie to buy materials and engage the services of the best local sempstress to help with the dresses, I said, "Luella, please make some excuse and stop at the farm and ask what this is all about."

She came home with quite a story. Mrs. Loveridge hadn't had complete faith in Mother's remedies and had called in the doctor, who had made mock, in a pleasant way, of the plaster of dock leaves and iris roots which she had applied, and he had taken it off and put on his own. According to Mother, Mr. Loveridge's foot had started to rot from that moment and he died. The widow immediately veered round and was full of remorse and kept saying that if only she had trusted Mother. . . . Then Luke had looked after the business of getting her harvest in, as he would have done, as a matter of course, for any neighbour in similar plight and so she felt kindly towards him. And she didn't want to stay on the farm herself; nor did she want to sell it, because there had been Loveridges at Squirrels since the beginning of time. And the upshot of it all was that she had agreed to let the farm to Luke on a ten-year lease, on condition that when her boy was fourteen Luke would take and teach him to run it, and that he would not cut down the rose that sprawled over the house front, or the lilacs which Mr. Loveridge had planted to screen the privy.

Squirrels had always been well handled and the land was in good heart; such a farm was very rarely for hire, and in getting a lease on it Luke had had a piece of luck that fell to no more than one in a thousand.

Luella had had no time to gather details, and I did not know then that Mrs. Loveridge, despite her distress and her sentiment, had fixed a rent which, if Luke worked twenty-four hours a day, kept his health, and met with nothing but good fortune, might still leave him a small margin of profit.

During the next week—the one before the wedding—I heard from Jack Lantern that Luke had already found a tenant for our old house, but was going to keep the land. The tenant was a cousin of Farrow the bootmaker, a Kersey weaver whose lungs had weakened; he wanted the house, the orchard, and a shed or two where he could keep a goat and a few chickens to eke out what he could earn by field labour in good weather when he felt able.

To hear all this in bits and pieces was very irksome, and as soon as the wedding was over and the house guests gone I asked Miss Whymark if I might run home for an hour one evening.

Luke was out and Mother was alone in the middle of her packing and sorting, muddled, distracted, but happier than I'd ever seen her in my life. Despite the fact that the light was failing and I had but a short time to stay, she loaded me with bundles and baskets and hurried me off, across our orchard, through a gap in the hedge, and over the meadow that divided the two houses. A well-defined track showed me how often she had come and gone that way during the last few weeks. She talked incessantly, breathlessly, as we scampered along.

Squirrels was a good big solid old house, with one or two panelled rooms and a multitude of cupboards.

"Now this is what I call a farmhouse!" said Mother with deep satisfaction. "It's like the one I was born in. Ah, I give up a bit when I married your poor father! But then I thought and hoped he'd get on; and why he never did is a mystery; he worked hard enough. Still . . . And to think that I can get out my bits of brass and copper that my granny give me that've been in a box under my bed all these years and never had room to set out. Oh, I'll hev a nice kitchen again! Now come and see what'll be the parlour."

We stood in the thickening twilight in the big square room. It had two windows and the red rose, which must not be cut, grew all about them, with a belated bud or two close to the panes.

"You know, Deb," said Mother in a less excited voice, "I never said a word, but I hev worrited myself of late. I could remember how *I* felt once the first glow had wore off and there I was, with that place in the passage where you knock your head twenty times a day, and nothing but pegs on the doors for your clothes. Well, that just show, no sense in worriting. Things kind of work round, if you wait. And Luella'll hardly know she ain't at Merravay, once this is set out. . . ."

The chilly little wind of the autumn night moved in the rosebush and set the buds tapping against the window.

"You seem . . ." I began, and stopped. "Isn't a bit soon to take for granted that Luella——? Or do you know something that I don't?"

"Well, bless my soul! Nought's been *said*, at least to me, but surely we all know. Why, she went with him to the Midsummer and everything. And look how they carry on, laughing and skylarking about. What could be plainer? And him talking about buying a *carpet!*"

What could be plainer?

The wind was in the big chimney now, making a plaintive sound; and the buds, the last, too-late buds tapped at the glass, as though asking for shelter.

"I don't know," I said. "Sometimes . . ." But what could I say?

Mother suddenly laughed with just a hint of mischief.

"I know what ails you, my girl. You're just a thought jealous. You marnt be that, now. Your turn'll come."

I was spared having to answer that because she suddenly clapped her hand to her mouth.

"Dog's nails! I left a beef pudding in the copper. It'll hev boiled dry and that boy ain't had a proper meal since the day afore yesterday. We must get back. You can see the bedrooms another time."

Luke was swilling himself under the pump when we trotted into the yard. He seemed surprised to see me.

"I been wanting to hev a word with you, Deb."

"I mustn't stop now. I'll see you on my day," I said.

"No, I'll come a step with you."

"But you're hungry and the pudding's spoiling."

"That can wait." He picked up his jacket and shrugged himself into it and then called to Mother that he'd be back in ten minutes. I was terrified that he was going to talk about Luella; but he began with a half-shamefaced apology.

"I ought to hev talked it over with you, Deb; but time was short and I knew I'd never get a chance like that again. Now I've got to spend what is yours by rights, as well as my own, stocking the new place; and if you should want to get married I couldn't give you your portion straight out like I allust meant to, see? But you'll be better off in the end. In two or three years' time, if my beasts go ahead like they are doing now, and corn keeps its price, we'll be well-to-do, Deb. Only just now we must sow before we reap, see?"

"That's all right, Luke. I'm not thinking of getting married. You're welcome to use my share for as long as you like. I'm glad you've had the chance. I hope everything goes well with you."

And now don't say anything else; let me go back with my doubts; let me not have to say anything about what is too formless, too uncertain, to be put into words.

I mentioned the meal waiting.

"Just a minute," he said. "That ain't all. I been wanting to talk to you about . . . Luella and me."

Exactly what I had dreaded.

"You see, like I said just now, putting money in afore we can take it out I'm going to be short of *spending* money. It was in my mind to ask her at Christmas. Back in the old place I could've spared a guinea or two to hev things nice. Now that look to me as though we've got the parlour and nothing to put in it. But I don't want her to think I'm shilly-shallying. What d'you think I oughta do, eh, Deb?"

Despite his quietness he was usually so sure, of himself, his plans, his rightness, that this clumsy, hesitating bid for help and direction struck me as horribly pitiful.

"You should talk to her," I said at last.

"Well, I hev tried. But you know, I ain't handy with words and she sort of head me off and go rattling on about something else. She on't be serious."

Deadly serious himself, of course, he was attracted by her apparent lack of seriousness—just as, no doubt, long ago that dour man our father had been attracted by Mother's lightness of heart. Strange how things fell into pattern.

But I knew that Luella could be serious enough when she chose to, and my foreboding deepened with the thought that when she headed him off she did it deliberately.

"I ain't asking she should scrub floors and feed calves. Time we're married I mean to hev hired labour, and if I can't, damn-all-to-Hell, I'll sit up o'nights and do things with these hands. You tell her that, Deb, and tell her thass up to her to say whether we do it Christmas, or wait a bit."

"Damn-all-to-Hell, Luke, d'you know what you're asking? I can't go telling her things like that before we even know whether she wants to marry you or not. Have you ever even made it plain to her that *you* want to marry her?"

"I been more or less courting her since the first day she come back, ain't I? You never see me so much as look at any other female, did you? I took her to the Fair . . ."

"That's just it," I said angrily. "All these silly old customs. A man has a tongue in his head, hasn't he, and could ask a plain question without making such a morris dance."

"Well, a word in season wouldn't cost you nothing, Deb; and it'd clear the way for me a bit," he said, unruffled by my sharpness. "Thass all right for folks that are handy with words; I ain't. I start and get all tied up and then off she go on another tack and I'm lost. You just edge a word in for me, sometime when you're heving a chat. Eh, Deb?"

"I'll see. I think the best thing for you to do is to show her the house and everything next time we come, and then ask her. Then you'll know where you are. And Luke . . ."

"Yes, Deb."

"You mustn't . . . I mean, don't count too much, or be too much disappointed. You see . . . nowadays everybody doesn't attach such importance to things like going to a fair."

He laid a heavy hand on my shoulder.

"Hev you got any reason to say that? Any reason to think . . ."

"No. Truthfully, Luke, none at all."

No reason for anything I said, or thought; no reason for feeling cold and empty and sad and sorry for everybody. . . .

Let him ask her and have done; the thing had been on my mind, a vague disquietude ever since the February evening when he had driven us home.

XI

That last Saturday of October was one of those rare lovely autumn days; it began with a mist like a bloom on a grape and opened out to a noon of marigold yellow and closed with an evening of hyacinth blue, full of the scent of apples and burning leaves. Luke wasn't home when we arrived; he had gone to one of the farm sales, of which there were always plenty round about at that time of year. Mother, Luella, and I spent the afternoon moving the last few things across from our little old house into the new one. I was glad to be so busy, for I was as nervous as though I were the one who was to make the proposal, or to receive it. For one thing I was terrified lest Mother should say something tactless and premature to Luella; but I wronged her there. Luella of course, threw herself into the moving, the rearranging, the admiration of the rooms, with exactly the enthusiasm which she would have shown over a dolls' house which two children had just acquired.

At dusk Luke came home, pleased with his purchases. He was wearing his market clothes, buff breeches and a bright blue coat with brass buttons. He looked extremely handsome, solid, reliable, and genial.

We sat down and ate the first meal that Mother had cooked in that kitchen. When it was over I saw Luke look at me and tighten his mouth. "I reckon you've seen the house, Luella. I want you to see the barn. Mrs. Loveridge said 'twas a thousand years owd and used to be the main house. 'Sbig as a church." He lighted two lanterns and led Luella away.

Mother and I washed the dishes. Then we polished and set out the cherished pieces of brass and copper ware.

"And there's another thing," said Mother suddenly. "There's room for *me* here. I allust wondered whether the time'd come when Luella might feel about me the way I did about your great-aunt Hester. Not that I *grutched* her houseroom, poor soul, but she did fare to be allust underfoot. That on't be so here. So long as I'm useful I can busy myself, and when I'm useless there's room for me to be out of sight and out of mind."

"I hope that time is a long way ahead," I said. I wondered what was happening in the barn.

After what seemed a long time they came in. My first thought was that Luke had baulked his fence, for he did not look like a man whose suit had been accepted, or rejected; and Luella, very white and small-faced, looked even less like a girl who had been proposed to. For one demented moment I thought that she had expected Luke to speak and been disappointed when he didn't.

They admired our handiwork, and we all ate plum cake and drank a glass of elderberry wine. Then Luella said,

"It's a nice night, Luke, and the horse has been out today, so we'll walk home."

"Right you are," he said. "I'll walk with you to the avenue at least."

"But you're tired, too."

"A bit of a walk on't hurt me," he said. Voice, manner, everything, just as usual. Just as usual his leave-taking with his mention of seeing us next month "or maybe afore."

We began to walk through the deeper darkness of the avenue, through the light brittle fallen leaves, which gave off a dry autumnal scent. Luella walked in silence and I was just about to say some trivial thing when she said,

"Luke just asked me to marry him."

"I'm not exactly surprised," I said; though I was surprised to know that he had done it after all. "Well?"

"I didn't know what to say." Her voice sounded far away, lost. "It's very difficult, Deborah. Marriage is such a *final* thing . . ."

"That, I should imagine, is what people in love like about it."

"In love . . . when you're all dazed and dazzled, when you're not yourself at all. In that state you have to make a decision that affects your whole life, everything you do, and have, and are, from that moment on. It's a frightening thought, Deb."

"Yes; I suppose it must be." But what did you say to him? Tell me, without my having to ask.

"You look round," she went on in that remote voice, "and what do you see? Most people would say they married for love . . . and they end like the Whymarks. I'm inclined to think that the more you follow your heart the worse you feel when you wake up one morning and find that it misled you."

"I think you're unduly cynical, Luella. Is that bound to happen?"

"I think that love—not the kind part, the friendliness and the working together; they last—but this thinking that the sun rises and sets with the one person, and the . . . the physical part, that *is* bound to wear off. Time alone would . . ."

"What did you say to Luke?"

"Almost exactly what any well-reared young woman is told to say in the circumstances." She gave a sudden laugh, harsh, almost hysterical. "That I wasn't sure—and that, God knows, is true—that I must have time to think. Straight out of the book, Deb, word for word."

Well, that suited Luke exactly; no wonder he'd looked so calm. My spirits rose a little. This seemed an apt moment to say my few words. And since he had come into the open himself it would do no harm to mention my certainty that he would make her a good husband, and was utterly devoted to her.

"I know. I know. Anyway, if I do marry him, I shouldn't mind the work. I should delight in it. And I could help in other ways—read the papers for him, and do accounts, for he'll end with a bigger business than he can keep in his head, smart as he is in his quiet way . . ."

"Luella, you *are* in love with him!"

"Yes. Oh yes, I am. At least I have this. . . . Oh, Deb, you'd never understand. In some ways you're still such a child; you have never . . . I mean all your ideas are out of a storybook. Fall in love and live happily ever after. Dear Deb, I hope *you* will. You might. You *are* single-minded!"

"You're not." It was half question, half statement. "Luke is," I added, as she did not answer.

"I know. And they're the ones who get their way in the end."

"In this case, I truly hope so."

"Thank you, Deb. That was a pretty speech!" She laughed in the old light-hearted fashion, thrust her arm through mine, and, saying that it was turning cold, hurried me towards the house at such a pace that further speech was impossible.

I felt quite gay too. I believed that she was being a little coy and shy and girlish.

Early in November somebody got up and made a speech in Parliament about the slave trade and its iniquities; and then the papers took up the subject and printed some articles and dozens of letters. Mr. Roger's name was mentioned several times. My turn to study the papers would not arrive for two or three weeks, but I heard all about it from Luella. Her ladyship, faced with the fact that what she had determined to regard as a foible, a bit of child's play, was being seriously discussed in London, reverted to her earlier attitude, and tears and angry recriminations became an everyday occurrence. At the end of the week Mr. Roger went to stay at Ockley with Miss Sophie, who, as soon as the wedding ring was on her finger, had proceeded to take a subtle revenge on her mother. It was a simple one, too; it consisted of charming, affectionate behaviour to everyone else and cold, flat, formal behaviour to her ladyship. A typical example was one morning when she arrived, carrying an enormous bunch of lilies, the like of which I—or indeed many people in England— had never seen before. They were shaped like the white ones which fill cottage gardens in June, but they were pale rose-pink in colour and splashed with purple at the heart. And this was November. At Ockley they had hothouses.

"Sophie, how beautiful!" said her ladyship.

"They are pretty," said Lady Fennel coolly. "They're for Aunt Maud, for the church."

"I'm afraid the cold will kill them," said her ladyship after just a second's recoil.

"If they can survive here. . . ." Lady Fennel shivered inside her furs. "This room is like an icehouse. How poor Deborah can sew at all! No wonder she has chilblains. Have they started this year yet, Deborah?"

"Ockley is too warm," said her ladyship. "And that is why, in my opinion, Freddie takes cold so easily. Such a pity! I always think a man with a heavy cold . . ." she made a grimace of disgust.

With things on such a footing between them it was natural enough that Lady Fennel should now take sympathetic interest in her brother's cause.

On the last Saturday of November I had to go home alone. Luella and the children had gone to Ockley for four days. The rector at Ockley was a very old man and fond of old customs; he had revived a winter merrymaking known as a "church ale," a thing which few villages had had since Cromwell's time. There were mummers there, too; and if her ladyship resented the fact that now every member of the family except herself had been invited to Ockley for some special occasion, she gave no sign, merely saying that it was instructive for the children to see things which would be done away with by the time they grew up.

From that visit Luella returned in rather low spirits which I attributed to the cold which she had caught. Ockley was splendid, she said, and Lady Fennel had been more than kind, and the church ale had been most entertaining. But all this I gathered by questioning; the usual rippling enthusiasm was absent.

I passed on to her the invitation which Mother had sent, for her to go home for Christmas, any day, all days, when she was free. I, of course, did not go home at all in December.

"I don't like to go to your home to be merry, Deb, while you have to stay and work," she said. "Anyway I can't begin to think about Christmas yet. This cold and everything . . ."

"Poor Luella," I said. "I believe you should be in bed. You look feverish." I put out my hand to touch her forehead and see. She shrugged away from me.

"You shouldn't hang about me. You'll catch it. I'm all right. I'm better. It's just . . ."

The days moved on and it was the seventeenth of December. The day of the Christmas Market, when they judged the fat bullocks and gave the prizes. After the judging the beast was sold, with butchers competing heartily for it; then it was paraded round the town with the crier going ahead, ringing his bell, calling out the weight of the bullock, the name of the man who had reared it and of the butcher who had bought it. Everybody then ran hotfoot to the butcher's to bespeak a joint of that beef for Christmas, and it was a standing joke that whatever the bullock weighed alive, it weighed two tons dead, since no one was ever disappointed of his order. Joke or no joke, it was a fact that the winner of the first prize put ten pounds into his pocket, sold his animal in a competitive market, and gained himself a reputation as a breeder.

It was one of those days with a hard dry wind when fires burn fiercely, consuming solid logs as though they were paper. Midway through the morning I carried a fresh basket of logs to the schoolroom and just as I reached the door it opened and Mr. Roger, whom I thought to be at Ockley, stepped out.

"Ha . . ." he said, in a manner quite unlike his own. "I hoped I'd see you—er—Deborah. Wanted to wish you a happy Christmas and . . ." he pressed a guinea into my hand and laughed. "To buy a new pen with, bless you!" He patted me on the shoulder and went running downstairs.

The children were not in the schoolroom; Luella was alone, looking so small-faced, so pale and shaken, that I dropped the log basket and ran to her, asking,

"What's the matter? What happened?"

"Nothing. Nothing, Deb." She linked those little white birds' claws hands and moved them up and down in a distracted gesture. "I must get the children in. He told them to run away for a minute and they did so without their coats, in this wind. They'll catch their . . ."

She moved towards the door. I reached out and grabbed a handful of her skirt. I heard my voice, thin and strangling, say,

"What did he want? What did he say to you?"

"Deb . . . I can't. I've hardly . . . later on . . . Deb, please." She put out one hand and pushed mine away with them, then lifted it to her cheek, driving her knuckles against the flesh. Then she was suddenly calm. There was a rustle of silk, a waft of perfume from behind me.

"So you came too," Luella said. I turned.

"I thought it best. Nobody knows better than I how nasty Mamma can be," said Lady Fennel. "Good morning, Deborah."

It was both greeting and dismissal, delivered in the way that gentry are born with. But I didn't move.

"Look, Lu, I think this may be very unpleasant. You'd better come back with me, now."

"I must get the children in."

"Deborah can do that. You come and get some things together. I know, my dear, I saw every sign of storm. Let Roger face it. . . . There, what did I tell you?"

From downstairs there came a wailing scream, and then the sound of commotion; voices, doors slamming.

"I've had enough scenes to last me the rest of my life," said Lady Fennel coldly. "I'm having no part in this one. I came to spare you. Come along." She took Luella quite roughly by the elbow and begun to hustle her out of the schoolroom. I caught her by the other arm,

"He asked you . . . and you . . . ?" I knew, of course, but I wanted her to tell me. To my surprise she gripped my hand and used it to steady herself against the impetus of Lady Fennel's pull.

"Wait a moment, Sophie. I can't just run away like this. I haven't committed a crime! Yes, Deb. Mr. Roger Whymark has asked me to marry him and I have said I will do so."

"That is all I wanted to know," I said. "I hope you'll be as happy as you deserve."

"And Mamma," said Lady Fennel, "is going to call you ugly names and derive great pleasure in ordering you from the house. You're a fool, Lu."

"I know."

"And you're shaking with fright. Mamma will come screaming at you and you'll fall in a fit, that's what you'll do."

"I am not frightened. Why should I be? I am worried about those children. If you, Deborah, would be so good as to go and look for them, I could stay here in case her ladyship should wish to speak to me; otherwise I must go myself."

"I'll go," I said, and went to push past them as they stood in the doorway.

"I still think . . ." Lady Fennel began again.

The children when I found them were wearing their coats and hoods, and because I wanted a little time to think, and thought that they would be as well out of the house for a while, I took them for a long walk along the edge of Layer Wood where we were sheltered from the wind. So I missed what was, by all accounts, the most spectacular and noisy scene ever to take place in Merravay.

When we got back the house had the air of having been battered into silence. Her ladyship had taken to her bed; Miss Whymark had taken refuge in her accounts; Miss Maud had gone to the Rectory with her story, and since Luella was nowhere about and her brush and comb and a few other things were gone from her room I gathered that she had, after all, gone to Ockley. Mr. Roger was still in the house, waiting for Mr. Whymark's return from the Fat Stock judging. And of course rumour and counter-rumour had the house by the ears. They even said that her ladyship at one point had thrown a vase at Miss Whymark, who was taking Luella's part . . .

I should have found it all very interesting and very amusing—if it hadn't been for Luke.

I should have thought it very right and proper, highly suitable—if it hadn't been for Luke.

I should have regarded it as highly romantic, especially as Luella had such strong feelings about Merravay—if it hadn't been for Luke.

But there it was. My dear, serious-minded, single-minded Luke had been jilted—there was no other word for it—and I honestly felt worse than if I had been jilted myself.

At intervals all through the afternoon I had thought about how he would take the news and every time I felt as though someone had kicked me in the stomach.

And there was Jack Lantern, about to go home, carrying the news; and Miss Maud even now telling the story at the Rectory. I couldn't leave Luke to hear it from the lips of a casual gossip.

At seven o'clock I put the puzzled children to bed and then I did what I had never done before, walked away on a working day without asking leave. Whom could I ask, anyway—go to Mr. Roger, reading in the library, and say, "I must go and tell my brother that you're going to marry the woman who for the last seven weeks has been making up her mind to marry him"? Look him in the eye and say, "You be careful! She's in love with Luke Fulger; she's marrying you for another reason; she doesn't believe in love because it wears out." All so true, so reasonable . . . and too fantastic to consider for more than a moment.

I battled against the wind all the way home; and there was Mother alone.

"Luke meant to go to Baildon, but he heard of a sale—a man died over at Minsham and he thought he might pick up a few things cheap. And what brought you, my dear?"

As she asked the question she opened the door of the oven and took out a loaf of currant bread, whose readiness for withdrawal from the oven she tested by turning it over and rapping its bottom with her knuckles and then holding it to her ear to listen to its response.

"It's done," she said, and busied herself. The scent of hot bread was for once not appetising to me.

Presently we heard the creak and rumble of wheels.

"Ah, so he got a wagon. He took just the horse, in case."

He'd got the wagon. He was pleased. He came in. He ate great helpings of the mutton and apple pie—ordinarily almost my favourite dish. Tonight I couldn't look at it, though I had had nothing to eat since breakfast. I felt like a hangman watching a condemned man take his last meal. And then I felt I was exaggerating; and I wished I'd been in love myself and had some other standard than books to judge by; and I wished that Mr. Roger had died in Virginia, or on the high seas; and I wished that Luella had never come back. And I wished, almost most of all, that it hadn't fallen to me to break this bit of news.

Most of the time we were talking about Christmas and finally, when Luke had eaten his fill, he got to his feet, took a candle in hand, and said to me,

"You come here a minnit, Deb."

He led the way into the cold, almost unfurnished parlour. On the old table that used to be Aunt Hester's there were two parcels.

"Thass for you, with my best wishes," he said, pointing to one of them. It was a cloak, grey and smooth and fine, a lovely cloak, lined with red. Choking, sick, I thanked him and did what he was obviously yearning for me to do, looked at the other, smaller parcel.

A little fur tippet. Small, but so smooth and light and silky that I could see that it was the best of its kind . . . even her ladyship, though she had bigger and more, had no better.

He took it up in his great brown work-scarred hands.

"She'll like that. I did what you said, Deb, and asked her straight out like and she ain't in no hurry; so, seeing's I got time to get carpets and such like, I reckoned I could get her a pretty present. . . . And that is pretty, ain't it?"

And if I cry now, just cry and run away without saying a word as I long to do . . . he'll be like Mother and think I'm jealous! Oh God, what did I ever do that You should bring me to such a pass?

"It's lovely, Luke. Lovely. Fit for a queen. You have the best of taste. But my cloak is even better. It'll last me a lifetime. Oh Luke . . ." I leaned against him. "I am grateful . . . and I do love you. . . ."

"Why, Deb," he said, "there ain't no need to carry on that way about a little owd Christmas present. Tell you what, you put it on now. I'd'a kept the horse hitched if I'd known you was here. S'nasty owd night."

"The wind was against me coming. It'll blow me home. I will wear the cloak, Luke, and I'll be proof against anything. Will you come a step or two with me?"

We stepped out into the tearing wind, turned the corner of the house into a sudden calm, and stopped to gather our breath. And then, like a surgeon who must inflict agony and can best show mercy by being swift, I laid hold of his arm and said,

"Luke, I came to tell you. Luella is going to marry Mr. Roger."

He said nothing. His arm went stiff under my hand and I heard the breath go out of him. Presently I heard my own desperate voice explaining, consoling; and then we were at our yard gate, across the road in the teeth of the wind again, under the lighted window of The Evening Star, in by the way that the coach passengers used, into a warm, blazingly bright room; still with my hand stiff on his stiff arm; and still he said no word.

In the bright room, loud with voices, confusingly full of men, I turned and looked at Luke. The wind-whipped red was still in his cheeks, but all round his mouth and the root of his nose there was a white shadow as though a chalky finger had brushed him. And his eyes were blank, stunned.

A man . . . landlord? . . . wearing an apron, bald, holding a ladle, came bustling about.

"Well, if it isn't Mr. Fulger himself. Just talking about you. Congratulations, I'm sure. Mr. Everton, sir . . ."

Another man, red-faced, beefy, thumping Luke's wooden shoulder, shaking his wooden hand. Congratulations indeed. Thirty years in the cattle trade, never seen, never hoped to see, a better beast than the one which had just won Luke the Fat Stock Christmas Prize.

"And what shall it be, sir? On the house, I insist. This is a great day for Nettleton. We're pleased and proud indeed."

Ha, I thought . . . Luke is an up and coming man who has just taken over a big farm and never set foot in this place before. But it was possible that they were pleased . . .

"Brandy," Luke said, breaking the silence at last.

"And the young lady. Will she partake on this great occasion?"

"Brandy," Luke said again.

I put on a false, gay, rallying voice. "Luke, you forget. The news must have stunned you. I will take a small glass of Madeira, if you please."

I might have been thrust into a place where no lady should be, but I would show them I knew what a lady might drink. And though to mention being stunned by news was so cruel that I flinched as I said it, it was sensible, too. It offered some excuse for the way he was behaving.

"But you must have known there wasn't a beast to touch it," said Mr. Everton. "Why, alongside yours the rest all looked like Pharaoh's lean kine. . . ." Somebody asked facetiously what breed that was; somebody else said well, be fair, the second-prize winner had beef on him too; somebody took Luke's glass away and gave another, full. When he had drunk that he drew a long deep breath.

"I clean forgot the bullock, Deb. Little owd Weaver took it in for me and I got thinking about the sale; then my supper and then . . . Clean forgot."

"You've got that sort of a mind, Luke. And if you'll think steady about the next thing and never look back, you'll be all right."

Then they were surging about him again, asking him questions, refilling his glass. Every minute took us one pace away from the dreadful thing; so I waited, patiently, though I would not let anyone fill my glass again.

The wag-on-the-wall clock over the fire jerked along to nine.

"I must go," I said. "I shall be locked out."

"It isn't every day you have a thing like this to celebrate," said the landlord.

"She's right though. Must be getting along."

"We'll hope to see you again, Mr. Fulger."

"Aye, and afore long," Luke said.

The moon had risen and rose high, with wind-driven clouds scudding across her face, so that moments of pitch darkness were followed by moments of brilliant, unreal light. Once the lights of The Evening Star were behind us we might have been in the middle of the desert; it was not a night to tempt anyone abroad and in winter the village people went to bed early to save fuel.

Luke and I walked in silence; that and the rushing wind, the fact that the one glass of wine in my empty stomach had seemed to affect my weight, and the confusing alternations of light and dark made everything seem unreal and dreamlike. Wake up and think—What a hateful dream, thank God it isn't true!

Then all at once I heard the sound of a horse's hoofbeats. We were then on the stretch of road which led only to Merravay and then on to the Lower Road, which nobody used in winter because of the mud.

The wind made it difficult to be sure of direction and for a moment

I thought the sound came from behind us; that would be Mr. Whymark coming home, very late from the Fat Stock Show. But next time I caught the sound I was sure that it came from the road ahead of us, and it was coming towards us, fast.

And suddenly I thought of Lady Alice. It was on just such nights as this that she was said to ride abroad. Ordinarily I regarded the legend with some scepticism, but tonight I was in a state to believe everything. I grabbed Luke's arm and said,

"Can you hear a horse?"

He listened. "No."

That increased my cold panic; for it confirmed the stories of how two people could be walking, arm-linked through the night, and one would see and hear the phantom while the other declared that nothing but the wind went by.

"I can. And it's coming from Merravay and the Lower Road. *Her* ride. Oh Luke. It's Lady Alice!"

"Don't be so sawney," he said and listened again. "I hear it now. 'Tain't galloping."

I too had heard the pace slow down; but then, sometimes, passing people, she did slow down and lean from the saddle the better to cast the evil eye on them. Every story I had ever heard came back into my mind. I cast about for somewhere to hide, but the hawthorn hedges on either side the road were as high and solid as walls.

"At least stand back," I whispered; and I pulled him close to the hedge.

The horse, moving at a steady trit-trot, was close to us when the cloud moved and the whole road sprang into light. Luke and I, in the shadow of the high hedge, were partly hidden. I cringed and closed my eyes. But at the last moment some strange compulsion came upon me. I *had* to look. And there was Mr. Roger on his brown horse with the white blaze.

Fright had driven every bit of sense out of me. With relief as sharp as pain, I said, "It's Mr. Roger."

In the next half second I was alone under the hedge. Tattered by the wind there was borne back to me the sound of hooves, of pounding feet, of Luke's voice calling.

The moon went in again. In the sudden blinding darkness I dragged myself from the hedge in which I had been half embedded and set out towards them on legs that seemed to be made of flannel. Two dozen yards of road stretched on and on, an endless journey.

Then it was light again and I had reached them. The horse stood broadside on, and Luke and Mr. Roger were grappling together. Urgent in my mind was the thought of Mr. Roger, so light and thin and brittle-seeming, Luke so heavy, thick-muscled, and strong; two such ill-matched men mustn't fight. I shouted to them through a mouth stuffed with chaff, and put out my flannel hands and seized Luke by the coattails. Something, elbow or fist, came up and hit me under the chin. Sparks of light burst out from the top of my head. My teeth had gone into my tongue and my mouth was filled with blood. I tried to scream again but nothing came but a blubbing sound. I spat, and just managed to call Luke's name.

Another cloud moved. There was a thump, a grunt and the slither of feet in the mud. Then quietness. The next burst of light showed Luke on his feet, Mr. Roger spread-eagled on the ground. His wig and hat, still wedged together, lay between him and the horse.

I wavered forward and knelt down and set my hands on him. I'd handled enough dead fowls and rabbits in my time to know the "dead" feel. It wasn't there. Immediately my mind began to work again, smoothly and sensibly.

"He's only stunned," I said. "Take his hat, ditch that side, get some water."

Running home as I had done, I had gone in my apron. I took it off and used it to dribble the cold water over his face. Then I remembered that most gentlemen carried flasks when they rode abroad. Luke found it and handed it to me, but Mr. Roger's flask had not been unstoppered lately; I had to hand it to Luke to unscrew. There was no more than a teaspoonful of brandy in it, and, careful as I was, it seemed to run out from his mouth uselessly.

"I never meant to kill him," Luke said. I went on dripping the cold water.

"Perhaps . . . the doctor . . ." I said at last, thinking sickly of all the miles between us and Baildon.

Luke turned towards the horse. Stopped and stripped off his coat and the fisherman's jersey which Mother had knitted.

"Keep him warm," he said, handing the garments to me. As I was wrapping them I saw Mr. Roger's face begin to twitch. His eyelids flickered, opened, closed again.

"It's all right . . . he's come round," I said.

His eyes opened again, looked at me, recognised me.

"Deb," he said, in a puzzled way.

"Yes. It's all right. We'll look after you."

"Shouldn't speak with your mouth full," he said in an inconsequent way, giving me that singularly sweet smile. After a moment he said, "I'm all right. Was I thrown? Belle'd never . . ." He began to struggle up. Luke leaned down and lifted him as though he'd been a child who had tumbled.

"Fulger," said Mr. Roger. "No coat. Cold night, too."

"We're quite near the Lodge, sir," I said. "Could you sit on the horse if Luke lifted you? Or shall he carry you?"

"I can walk. I haven't broken anything. My wig . . . where is it? Feel the cold, you know." I set his wig, muddy as it was, on his head.

"All this is very odd," he said in the same bewildered way.

"I hit you," Luke said in a humble, broken voice. "I'm main sorry now. I was out of my . . ."

"Don't bother him now," I said. "Let's get to the Lodge."

"Ockley," said Mr. Roger clearly. As he said it he sagged, bowed forward with a stream of blood and vomit gushing from his mouth. And once more my hands knew; live weight and dead weight are not mere butcher's terms.

It was Luke who broke the immeasurable silence.

"I'll carry him to the Lodge. You get back to Mother and warn Tad Thatcher on the way."

Tad was constable that year.

"I can't do that. They'll hang you." My bitten tongue had swollen, every word cost me agony, but I must talk now if I never did again.

"I kilt him."

"You did not. You hit him. It was an accident. You had cause; and drink in you too. But they wouldn't . . . no, Luke, if I can manage . . . this must be between us two forever."

"A man should take his punishment."

"You'll be punished . . . your conscience . . . all your life," I said cruelly. "But there's Mother . . . worked so hard, helped you, d'you want her to end in the poorhouse and me be branded murderer's sister all my days? Don't ruin us all for one unlucky blow. Let me look at you!"

I inspected his face.

"He hit me more about the body like," he said simply, and I found that heartbreaking—summing up as it did in so few words the dead man's lack of viciousness even when attacked.

"Hands," I said sternly. One knuckle was barked a bit.

"Suck it." I ran my eye over his clothes. If he'd gone to the Fat Stock Show he would have worn his best, and the mud on his breeches' knees where he had knelt would have shown. On his stained workaday ones it was unnoticeable.

"Put on your other things. Now listen. You must do exactly what I say. Back to The Evening Star. You set me on my way . . . went back to celebrate. Buy drinks for everybody. Go home. Don't say a word . . . ever. Do that and I can save you."

"But Deb . . . I'd as lief hang as live now . . ."

"So you think now. You wouldn't when you found yourself in the lockup. For Mother's sake, Luke. Hurry. Be too late soon." Oh, if I could only get him moving. What could I say?

"Most likely they'd hang me too, Luke, for helping you. I can't hide my mouth."

That did it.

"But what'll you do, Deb? Alone here with *that*. Murder can't be hid."

"Never you mind . . . less you know . . . better. For God's sake, move!"

The moment he turned and began to walk woodenly away I set the horse's head towards Merravay and dealt it a blow which set it galloping off. With any luck it might go rushing past its own gate, and even if it failed to do so the people in the Lodge would have heard galloping and be unlikely to be able to say positively whether they had heard one horse or two.

Then I waited for a little while. I was not frightened. I stood there in the dark, alone with a man just murdered, and worked everything out as though I were doing a sum. Afterwards, as long as I lived, I was to go through the whole thing in my dreams, starkly terrified, and wake screaming; but then, when it mattered, I was calm.

I ran to the Lodge and shouted and threw things at the window until Bert Baxter put his head out. Presently I was mumbling out my story—so exact in many details; how I had just left Luke, and turning the bend in the road had seen Mr. Roger struggling with a man. How I had been hit myself. The man—a stranger—I said, had thrown himself on his horse and galloped away. The Baxters had heard a horse . . .

At some point of my story somebody whipped round and asked what I was doing out that night, and even for that I had an answer. I had so wanted to know whether Luke had won the Fat Stock Prize.

Interlude

Deborah Fulger's story was accepted without question. People found it easy to believe that the assailant was a highwayman lying in wait for some market-merry farmer jogging home from the Fat Stock Show. Only a stranger to the district would have gone into ambush on a road that in winter led nowhere except to Merravay.

Sir George Fenstanton, who had been extremely fond of Roger Whymark as well as interested in his schemes, had another theory. He believed that the anti-slavery campaign had alarmed someone with vested interests, someone powerful and unscrupulous enough to hire an assassin. Occasionally in his cups he was heard to say that he could make a shrewd guess and that if only he had a shadow of proof . . . but that was never forthcoming.

In the early days of his grief Sir George swore that he would continue Roger's work; but he was not the stuff of which reformers are made, and in the end his contribution to the cause was accidental and posthumous.

During his lifetime he had gathered together, and had had printed and bound in fine Morocco leather, every word which Roger Whymark had ever written on the subject of slavery. Decades after his death a friend of his grandson's, a man named Clarkson, rode over from Bury St. Edmund's and was shown into the library to wait because Sir Philip was down at the stables to overlook the dosing of a favourite hunter. The monograph lay, as it had lain for years, on the writing table, side by side with a silver inkstand, arid as the Sahara—Sir Philip was no scholar. Mr. Clarkson, a hopeless print addict, picked it up and began to read and never noticed that the ten minutes he had been asked to wait had stretched to fifty. When his friend, soiled, sweating, and apologetic, did arrive, Mr. Clarkson raised a face upon which horror and excitement conflicted.

"This," he said, holding out the monograph, "is the best prepared and correlated mass of evidence on any subject that I have ever seen. Years old, of course, but nothing's ever been done. Conditions are worse now, if anything. Would you mind if I borrowed it? I'd like Wilberforce to see it."

Sir Philip, who could read if he had to, just as he could bear toothache, said that Clarky could have the whole damn library for all he cared.

"Who exactly was this Roger Whymark?"

Sir Philip knew all about that. He described the tragedy and went on to say how after it the family had split up; they'd built a fine new house at New Holding and only an old aunt and the family governess had gone on living at Merravay. They'd sealed themselves in by planting a shrubbery across the top of the avenue.

"Like in the story 'Sleeping Beauty.' Only they weren't. At least, I never saw the old aunt, the other I did, once. Enough to frighten the French. She's dead now and she left the house back to the Whymarks. I hear old Bill's trying to sell it."

Sir Philip naturally knew about the Whymarks whose eccentricities and bargains and quarrels had been the subject of dinner-table chat. He was not familiar with the story of Luke Fulger, who at the opposite end of the social scale had become a legendary figure. Humble people still spoke of him as proof of what could happen when a man let success go to his head. Sober, hard-working, sensible chap that he seemed, he'd won the Fat Stock Prize and that had ruined him, for he went on drinking to his victory till the day he died. There never was, there never would be again, such a drunkard as Luke Fulger was. From the night of the Show onwards nobody ever saw him sober.

And when he died his sister Deborah, the best sister ever a man had—she'd stuck to him through thick and thin and even found him a wife, hoping to reform him—had put a stone over the grave. A plain stone with just his name, the dates of his birth and death, and the words, "He will be long remembered." And those words were truer than most such cut in stone over graves; for people were still saying—as naturally as they said, "Hard as iron"—"Drunk as Luke Fulger." Not that anybody ever was, of course.

The Nabob

THIS evening, entering the house, I had for the first time a sense of ownership; that inner confidence of possession which says, "Mine! My house! My hearth!" Why that feeling should strike with such poignancy at this late hour I cannot imagine. It has always been fairly plain that I had only to outlive Father to inherit Merravay; and he has been dead for almost a month. Moreover for six years, ever since his stroke, I have been master here; but it wasn't until today when I made my will, naming as my heir a young man for whom I care very little, that I felt the place to be really mine.

In the room which I invariably use when alone, a comparatively small and cosy apartment with a little ship forever sailing across the chimney-breast, all the papers relative to Merravay were still lying about. I say "papers," though this is so old a house that some of the deeds are written upon leathery parchment in script that is, to me, almost illegible. A name, a date here and there, stand out.

Unlike Ockley, where the Fennels have lived, father and son, for three hundred years, or Mortiboys, which the Hattons claim to have been in the family from Saxon times to within living memory—when Chris Hatton staked it on a gambling game—Merravay has changed hands several times; good business for the lawyers, for even when, as happened in 1729, it passed from Whymark to Whymark, it was the subject of formal and complicated transfer. One Whymark received it in exchange for some land at New Holding, where their present family house stands. Earlier, in the middle of the previous century a Phyllis Whymark appears to have bought Merravay twice! She could not sign her name; instead there is, in each case a large, firmly inscribed cross, and written below it, "Phyllis Whymark, her mark."

I sat for an hour looking through the deeds and thinking. In these dry and dusty documents with their formal phrases one aspect of Merravay's history is told. What of the human stories behind? For wherever living people meet there is a story. I, for instance, have inherited Merravay in the most normal way; I take my place in the company of its owners as "George Frederick Sandell, my beloved son." Neat, dull, ordinary. But behind that there is a story too. The story of what I paid for my heritage. But the paying has been so protracted and so subtle that I am at a loss to say exactly what I gave. The self-dramatising devil that lurks in us all, prompts me to say, "My soul"; but that would surely be an exaggeration. A scrap of integrity here, a bit of self-esteem there, a little cowardice, a little cynicism, a larger amount of what sometimes seems to be a ridiculous obsession.

It began in the November following my sixteenth birthday, when Father came home from India, unexpected, unannounced, and took me away from my school at Withernsea. I had spent ten years all but a term there, and been dully miserable all the time. There are, I believe, worse schools, places where boys are starved, savagely beaten, and taught nothing. Ecclestone House was not like that. Mr. Ogilvy loved to teach and was, on the whole, sparing with punishment, though he could lay on at times; and nobody *starved*, though a constant diet of bread, potatoes, and porridge induced in us a perpetual, nagging residue of hunger for something else, so that we nibbled hips and haws out of the hedges, chewed leaves of wild mint, and avidly devoured apples no larger than marbles. Our way of life, our surroundings, were of unrelieved dreariness, all cold and grey and dull. Most of the boys had begun life, as I had, in warm sunny places overseas, pampered, perhaps spoiled, by native servants; Ecclestone House specialised in caring for boys whose parents were abroad. Only a few of us could look forward to a holiday or to a visit from a relative. In ten years I had only left Withernsea once. Time, thus unbroken by things to look forward to or back upon, stretched endlessly. As a forcing place for scholars Ecclestone House was unsurpassed. With every other outlet for interest closed, all but the most congenitally stupid boys sought what relief mental effort could offer, and Mr. Ogilvy could point proudly to many old boys who had done very well in after life.

I was just a dull, average kind of boy; without, I think, much imagination; and to this day I believe that if Father had removed me one year earlier we should have got on well together. That I should have been much happier, I know for certain.

But during my last year, a new parson came to Withernsea, and very soon evinced interest in the school. Ecclestone House being run on what was known as "sound Church of England principles," the clergyman was naturally persona grata within its walls. He liked boys; he saw that our lives were dreary and pitied us; he also, I suspect, saw us as potential raw recruits to the cause he served. He used to ask us, two or three at a time, to his house, where, having regaled us with strong, sweet tea, inch-thick slices of sparsely buttered toast and very solid seedcake—all of which, unluxurious as it was, seemed to us like heavenly manna—he drummed into us, bluntly and openly, the principles of his Methodist-flavoured faith. His religion had little to do with dogma or ritual; it was not highly coloured and perhaps not very spiritual; it was vigorous, earthy, and militant; and it boiled down, really, to the simple order, "Put yourself in his place." He told us that it was good for us to be cold and hungry because when we got out into the world we could then sympathise, in the real sense of the word, with those countless people who were doomed *always* to be cold and hungry. By example as well as precept he bore home to us that "Put yourself in his place" did not mean just another man's place; it applied equally to women, and to animals. Christ's words, "These my little ones," he said, meant every living thing on earth except one's self.

To this day I can never think of the Reverend James Carter without thinking of the parable of the Sower and the Seed. So much that he said must have fallen on the stony ground, or in the weed-choked place; but there may be many men in the world who stop for a moment now and again, and think, and measure, as I have done, their conduct against the standard that he set. And I hope that to bolder, more positive characters than mine, he has been an inspiration. To me he has been little more than a hair shirt, worn secretly.

The first person to whom I began applying the principle of justice to all, was Mrs. Ogilvy. In school she was known as "the old hag," and was credited with every meanness, every furtive shift, known to woman. Our parents—those who were abroad—were charged five pounds a year for our clothing; yet everybody knew that only when a boy was about to leave, or go home for the holidays, was he given a new garment. Mended, patched, let out, taken in, clothes were passed from boy to boy in endless line. We held that against her; as we held the dull food, the thin blankets. It was easy to think of her as a harpy, battening upon our privations. Then one day I looked at her and saw her with Mr. Carter's eyes, and I saw her as a fellow victim—either of Mr. Ogilvy's greed and mismanagement, or of a system which compelled them both to make the lowest possible charges in a competitive market. Anyway I saw Mrs. Ogilvy as a woman, past her first youth, continually harassed, running Ecclestone House with such poor help as could be obtained, since nobody with any choice would work there. She always wore a kind of linen cap in the house and her face sagged heavily, like a hound's, but one day a strand of hair broke loose and fell along her cheek, and mingled with the grey of it there was a glint of yellow, and I found myself thinking that once upon a time she had been young and her face hadn't sagged and her hair must have been pretty. And perhaps Mr. Ogilvy—young then, too, though that was unimaginable, even to me—had loved her and told her how pretty she was!

And, oh dear! I thought to myself, how sad everything seems when you start putting yourself into another person's place; and now I can't bring myself to say that my Sunday jacket is inches too small.

So I was wearing it, and the breeches that must be hitched dangerously low if they were to meet my hose, and the shoes with the patches-upon-patches, on the day when Father arrived and Mrs. Ogilvy came and told me to make myself tidy and go to the parlour because he had come.

The man in the parlour, standing by the too-recently lighted fire and sipping, with an air of distaste, a glass of that Marsala known to the school as "parent-juice," was a stranger to me despite the fact that I had prided myself on my exceptional memory. They say that white children who start their lives in tropical countries mature early; that may be true. Or it might be that for ten years I had been in the same dull place, with very little to overlay the vivid memories of childhood. I believed that I remembered my father, my mother, my ayah. I am certain that I remembered my ayah's earrings; three strands of copper wire threaded through a blue bead, and the left-hand bead chipped in two places. But the man in the parlour bore no resemblance to the parent I had remembered, who was red-faced, fleshy, blue-eyed, and cheerful-looking. This man was tall, stooping, and very yellow; even the whites of his eyes were yellow. His face was heavily lined and his mouth was a thin, greyish-purple gash. Nothing familiar and nothing pleasant.

I recovered myself quickly, bringing Mr. Carter's principle into play and I thought—Well, he saw me last, a fat, curly-headed six-year-old, all in white, fresh from the ayah's hands; and what does he find! A lanky scarecrow, overdue for the barber, with legs and arms sticking out in all directions. I mustered a sheepish grin. Father came over to meet me, set his hands on my shoulders, and kissed me.

"I'd have known you, anywhere," he said. "The hair alone! Not to mention the nose. . . ." He stood back, looking at me with, for a moment, undisguised satisfaction. Mr. Ogilvy, not much interested, for he had grown used to men coming from the ends of the earth to claim boys they had not seen since infancy, muttered something about there being a remarkable resemblance, and went on to say that I had been a good, untroublesome pupil. As he spoke Father's look of satisfaction changed to one of deep disgust.

"They aren't your best clothes, are they?" he snapped.

With a nervous, side-sliding glance at Mr. Ogilvy, I nodded.

Father said, "Well, I'm damned. . . ."

He swung round and began to rate Mr. Ogilvy who said,

"I'm afraid that is not my business, Mr. Sandell. All what I call the domestic side . . ." At that moment Mrs. Ogilvy, who had hastily changed her gown and put on a clean cap, came sidling in. "Ah, my dear, how timely," Mr. Ogilvy said. "Sandell's father was asking about his clothes. They do look a trifle small. Perhaps you should explain that Sandell has grown, rather phenomenally, in the last week or two."

There followed a thoroughly nasty little scene. Mrs. Ogilvy said—which was not true—that the tailor was making me some clothes. Father pointed to a mend, a patch, a place where the jacket I was wearing had been let out, and expressed his doubt that this had been made for me, had fitted me, so lately as last year. He did not lose his temper; he did not raise his voice; coldly, relentlessly he stated his grievance. Mr. Ogilvy glared at his wife and her face, after going dark red with angry confusion, began to quiver. Seeing that, I said, "It is, Father, entirely my fault. Two Sundays ago, when I put on these clothes I realised that I had grown out of them. But I knew Mrs. Ogilvy was planning for the tailor to come . . . and I didn't expect to grow quite so much in just a fortnight. . . ."

"Quiet a minute, my boy. Let me speak," said Father. And speak he did, to such point and purpose that Mrs. Ogilvy began to cry and Mr. Ogilvy offered, with injured dignity, to return Father five pounds if he wasn't satisfied.

"Never mind that, now," Father said, a little mollified by the offer nonetheless. "The boy is alive and looks well, that's all I care about. D'you own a topcoat, George? Get it then, and we'll go."

"You mean now? Am I leaving today?"

He nodded, and I went bounding away, so full of joyful excitement that I thought I might burst.

At Hull, where we stayed for a few nights in an inn which seemed unbelievably luxurious to me, though Father had many faults to find with it, I was fitted out with clothes and had my hair dressed; then we drove, by post chaise, to Peterborough, where my sister Olivia was at school. I asked Father whether he intended to remove her as precipitately as he had done me, and he replied that he wasn't sure, a great deal depended upon Olivia and upon the school. Olivia was almost two years older than I, but we had come to England together in charge of a woman friend of my mother's who was bringing her own children home. Once during our ten years of exile that same woman, kind soul that she was, had invited us both to spend Christmas with her family. I had not seen Olivia since then though we wrote to one another two or three times a year. I tried to tell Father what she was like, but apart from the fact that she was amiable and pretty I could find little to say. I could inform him that she liked her school, for during that brief holiday I had listened with astonishment, incredulity, and envy to her account of it. And when we arrived the homelike, easy-going atmosphere of the place made itself felt in a moment.

Olivia had quite grown up, though she was not now as tall as I; she was dressed in a way becoming to a young lady and bore far more resemblance to the mother I just remembered than to the sister I had seen five years before. She was very pretty, with a face like a kitten's and extremely black hair which grew off her forehead in a point.

She came into the room where we were waiting, a little shy, but demure and with a smile ready. I thought that Father would be delighted with her. But his manner was strange, stiff, and quite unaffectionate. I put that down to shyness, and to her looking so like Mother, which probably waked sad memories in him. Having shaken her by the hand and asked her abruptly how she did, he stood back and stared while Olivia turned to me and put her arms about my neck and kissed me and rubbed her cheek against mine and said how lovely it was to see me. Then she said,

"And dear Papa! After all these years. Oh, isn't it exciting? Oh, I could cry for joy!" And she did begin to cry.

"Now, now, there's no need to be silly," Father said.

At that moment one of the Miss Rossiters, followed by a maid with a tea tray, came bustling in. She was a very animated and garrulous old lady and passed over the awkward moment by asking Father a series of questions that needed no answers. Then she said, "Come now, Olivia dear, dry those happy tears and pour tea. Exhibit to your Papa those pretty manners which we have tried to inculcate."

Olivia's dimples peeped, her cheeks went pinker as she sat down behind the tray. She asked in the prettiest possible manner,

"How do you like your tea, Papa. With cream? Sugar?"

"I never drink it," he said.

"Well," said Miss Rossiter gaily, "we know what to say in that case, don't we, Olivia?"

Olivia was obviously disconcerted; but she said,

"I say, perhaps you prefer sherry or Madeira. Many gentlemen do."

"But not to *me*, dear. To your guest."

More confused than ever, Olivia repeated her words to Father.

"That is right, child," said Miss Rossiter. "And *then* you ring the bell."

Father said later that it was at that moment that he decided to remove Olivia from school. "Damn play-acting. Time she learned sense!"

II

We spent the next few weeks moving about, looking at properties that were for sale in the east of England, the part which Father preferred because it was driest; and so, in early February, we came to Merravay.

A handsome old man, mounted on a large grey horse, met us at the lodge gates.

"The house is rather difficult of access, I fear," he said when he had greeted us. "So I came to show the way." He led us along an avenue of limes to a point where the trees went on but the road was blocked by a mass of shrubs, dark laurels and lilacs just pricked with green buds. On our left several trees of the avenue had been removed to make a gap, and beyond this another avenue of younger trees led away and ended in a great white-pillared house in the Palladian style.

"Of all the stupid things they ever did," said the old gentleman in a confidential, conversational voice, "blocking this avenue was the silliest. That is my house," he pointed to the big white one. "Merravay lies there." We could see, at the end of the closed avenue, a cluster of tall, rose-coloured chimneys. "And now we must take the cart track," he said, and led the way between two trees on the right-hand side to a beaten path only just wide enough to allow passage for the carriage. It skirted the closed avenue for a while and then curved to end in the stable yard at the back of the house.

It struck me that Father was well disposed towards Merravay from the first. In other places which we had inspected his first words had usually been of a critical nature. Here, as soon as he alighted, he stared round and said, "I like that. I've seen several places where what they called the 'home farm' was a mile or more away. Difficult to keep an eye on."

"We could go in at the back, I found both keys," said Mr. Whymark with almost childish pride. "But I think you should see the front first." He opened with some little difficulty an elegantly patterned gate of wrought iron, set in a length of red wall, and ushered us into a moderately well kept garden. But he sighed as he looked round.

"Dear me! What an air of neglect. I send over fairly regularly and have it tidied, but it's painfully obvious that nobody has *loved* it lately. Do you like gardening, Miss Sandell?"

"I've never tried. I think I should," said Olivia.

"Now we'll take this little path and come out at the end of the garden. Of course the best view is from the top of the field. Still, this gives some idea . . ."

We emerged by a low red wall, set with grey urns filled with daffodil spears, and there we turned to face the house. I thought it very beautiful; and evidently Mr. Whymark had some feeling for it too. He looked at it for a long moment and then gave another gentle sigh.

"Isn't it *grim?*" Olivia whispered to me, catching my arm as we followed Father and Mr. Whymark up to the house.

"I rather like it," I said. And a moment later, when the great door was opened and we stepped into the hall, I suffered that emotion which, in other circumstances, is known as love at first sight.

I was so fascinated by the place, so anxious to look in every nook and cranny, literally feasting my eyes, that I could not wait for Father and Mr. Whymark to make their more systematic and leisurely progress. Dragging Olivia by the hand, I went from room to room, upstairs and downstairs, delighting in all I saw. The two men were still upstairs when

Olivia and I came back into the great hall, and there I knew the full measure of my enchantment when Olivia said,

"Oh I do hope and trust Father doesn't buy *this* house! It's *much* the worst we've seen."

In the past weeks Father had so often checked and snubbed and chided her and told her not to be silly that she had developed a meek, almost mute manner in his company, and when she was alone with me, indulged in a compensating exuberance. So I ignored a good deal of the emphasis in her words.

"Why don't you like it? I think it's beautiful!" I looked round as I spoke. The hall was as long and wide and high as a small church. Just inside the door was a fixed oaken screen, most delicately and exquisitely carved. At the farther end a magnificent staircase led up to an open gallery. At the foot of the stairs the banister rails ended in a great solid post carved into the figure of a man, so lifelike that one could see the ripples in the hair of his head and beard. He leaned on a staff, and the set of his shoulder, the bracing of his hands on the staff, gave one the impression that he was holding up the staircase.

"Look at *him!*" cried Olivia, following the direction of my stare. "Imagine taking a candle and going up to bed past him! Oh, I should be terrified. Dear George, George darling, I do beseech you, try to persuade Father not to live here."

"But he's a benevolent old fellow," I said, going nearer to the figure. "He'd wish you pleasant dreams as you passed." But that wasn't true! There was a sternness about the carved face.

"Oh, but look," I said, "it's Moses with his stick turning into a snake. Why, Olivia if this were in a church or anywhere except a private house people would go to see it. It's a wonderful piece of carving—it's a work of art!"

I put my hand over the knotted, gnarled wooden ones that clenched the stick, and felt what I can only call a satisfaction. At the same time, through the great window I saw a view of the garden, the green of the grass, the warm rose of the wall, the dark field, the wood beyond.

"And what a view!" I said.

"What of? A ploughed field and a wet wood. Oh George, no! Truly it frightens me; there's something terribly unfriendly about it. Hateful."

"Now that is silly," I said. "Considering that it's empty, and has been for five years I believe, it seems to me extremely welcoming. Think of that one we saw at Kelvedon. This doesn't seem like an empty house at all."

"No; it doesn't. It's haunted, George; that's what it is. And the ghosts hate us for disturbing them."

I knew enough by this time to realise that her opinion would not influence Father in the slightest; I had no fear of that; what I minded was that she should say such things about the house I liked so much. So I said peevishly,

"Oh, for Heaven's sake, Olivia. Don't talk such absolute nonsense."

She saw that I had lost patience and began in her pathetic, eager-to-please, frivolous little way to try to make me laugh.

"It was nonsense. I was joking. But, George dear, can't you just imagine . . ." and she started to rattle off an account of just what ghosts Merravay might harbour, headless ladies and men dragging chains.

Charm, particularly charm of speech, is difficult to define and impossible to describe. Odd little turns of phrase, the timing, the glance that accompanies the words, all mean so much. But whatever it is, Olivia had it in full measure, and soon I was laughing and protesting that now she was frightening me.

In the midst of this a sound on the stairs made me look up and there was Father, followed by Mr. Whymark, coming down. Father was looking at Olivia with such cold distaste that the laughter died on my lips. It was a look of physical revulsion, such as a man might turn upon a dish which had once badly disagreed with him.

Mr. Whymark said genially,

"I can't tell you how it delights me to hear young voices in Merravay again. I spent my early childhood here, you know. I had two sisters, not much older, and after Miss Maybrook became our governess we had very merry times. She was so kind to us . . . and so gay. Poor girl." And again there came that gentle little sigh.

Father said briskly that he had still to see the buildings and wanted to get back to Baildon before dark.

On the way home he said that if the question of access could be settled to his satisfaction—meaning that if Mr. Whymark knocked the cost of making a new avenue off the purchase price—he was prepared to buy Merravay.

"Did he happen to tell you why the old one was blocked?" I asked. I was in that state of mind towards the place, which, in the case of people, leads one to ask where they were born, what games they played as children, what is their favourite book.

"Oh, some long-winded story about a row between his mamma and an aunt. So far as I could make out, the aunt liked the house and his mamma loathed it—his elder brother came to a tragic end, or something. The aunt owned the land where the New House stands, so they swopped. And they couldn't share the avenue—which by the way I don't wish to do either—so she had it blocked. And then some jumble about the aunt leaving it to, why yes, that governess he mentioned, who lived there all alone apparently, like a hermit, until five years ago, when she died and left it to him. He's been trying to sell it ever since. I should say he's hard-pressed for money. Small wonder! He told me he'd been married three times and had eleven children in all. Talkative old fool; but if we mean to settle here it'll pay us to humour him . . . up to a point."

I was so delighted that Father liked Merravay that I could overlook his attitude towards a charming old gentleman.

III

One of the things I had said to Olivia in an endeavour to cheer her, once we knew that Merravay was to be our home, was that no house should be judged in its empty state. Imagine, I said, the difference which carpets and curtains and pictures and furniture would make. That remark was both prescient and an understatement. I had no idea then of what Father intended to do. Lodged in a warehouse at Hull were five or six enormous crates containing things he had brought from India. Their freightage must have cost a fortune, for each of them displaced its own bulk in tea, or pepper or cloves or nutmegs—all very valuable commodities. Father had brought rugs and carpets, so silkily smooth, so brightly coloured, that it seemed wrong to lay them on the floor and walk over them; he had brought yards and yards of the thin embroidered silk which at that time, I learned was being hung upon walls in rich houses and imitated in paper for the decoration of homes less wealthy; he had brought cabinets and chests in red or black lacquer heavily gilded; and there were dozens of ornaments too, some beautiful, some grotesque, made of ivory and ebony, of silver and mother-of-pearl, of jade and soapstone.

Even the ordinary household furniture which we bought during visits to London—visits which included my introduction to theatres and tea gardens and coffeehouses—was all beautiful and all costly; elegant ribband-back chairs, sideboards and tables and chests of drawers in satinsmooth walnut wood.

Father paid me the intoxicating compliment of inviting my opinion about everything he bought. My taste, like any other hobbledehoy's, was unformed and dubious, but I knew what was elegant and pleasing even then. Sometimes the expense worried me, especially as Father often grumbled about it and tried to haggle with the shopkeepers. Once I mentioned the matter and he laughed,

"Bless you, boy, I could buy the shop and the man who owns it and never notice. But it doesn't do to let them know; they'd fleece you!"

Sometimes, when the burden of choice between two things weighed heavily on me, I would say, "But which do *you* prefer, sir? After all you have to live with it."

"You have which you like. It'll all be yours one day."

Perhaps I dwell unduly on those days, when everything seemed wonderful and exciting, rich, pleasant, colourful and comfortable. But even then . . . there were moments. One I particularly remember. On a miry day, on a bit of bad road, going uphill, the horse in our hired carriage, a poor thin old beast, made heavy going. I said I would get out and walk to the top.

"Damn silly idea, get yourself muddy," said Father. He leaned and called to the driver.

"Get along! Use your whip, man! What's a whip for?"

Settling back, he went on to talk pleasantly on the subject which I had interrupted.

I should, of course, have known then.

We moved into Merravay around midsummer, and with the sunshine without and the splendour within there was little to remind us of the day of our first visit. The drawing-room walls had been hung with the silk, a deep maize-yellow embroidered with flowery boughs and bright birds. In other rooms where the surface of the panelling did not lend itself to hangings the oak had been painted, white and gold, or pale bluish-green. The great open hearths in most of the rooms had been enclosed with slabs and pillars of marble, and provided with basket grates, graceful as Grecian urns. But the hall—the place which at that time I liked best— was almost untouched. Father had decided that the stair posts and the fine screen would be ruined by being painted, so he had left them and the walls in their natural state, and he had retained the open hearth there, too. But to compensate for the lack of colour he had gathered against the dark background all the brightest of his Eastern treasures; the most glowing rugs, the red laquered cabinet and chest, great bowls and vases of painted porcelain. Just to look at the colour, so lavishly spread, was to know a lifting of the spirit.

It may be because I had left a place of bright sun and gaudy colours and lived so long in grey Withernsea, where the schoolroom floor, the sea outside, and the sky above were all the same dull neutral hue, that I was, and shall always be, susceptible to brightness, even to the extent of loving a dirty gypsy woman because of her scarlet neckcloth, even to the extent of liking to see poppies in a cornfield, indicative of bad husbandry as they be.

I know that when I entered Merravay for the first time after everything was in place I thought—I shall feel pleasure every time I come in here, no matter what happens.

I should, in fact, have been perfectly happy during our first months at Merravay if only Father would have been nicer to Olivia.

Nothing she did, nothing she said, could please him, that was the truth of it. I'd been long enough with him now to realise that he didn't care for women at all; he always spoke contemptuously of them, but he could be, and often was, perfectly civil when face to face with a woman of his own class. To Olivia he seemed unable to be civil; and at the same time he seemed unable to let her alone and allow her to avoid him, as she tried to do. Like a man with a sore thumb, he must keep picking.

"Where's your sister? What's she up to?" he would say. He would enter the house, "Olivia! Olivia! Oh, there you are . . ." and launch into some complaint, nothing too trivial, nothing too absurd. He had a curious theory that women must be kept busy, otherwise they got into mischief, grew fanciful, took to tea-drinking and gossip. In this belief he assiduously invented little jobs for Olivia. His linen was badly laundered, Olivia must do it; yet to judge from the resultant, never-failing complaints she was worse than any laundress could be and keep a job. The maid who cleaned the silver dropped and dented one of the branching candelabra, Olivia must polish it in future; and it is a fact that from the moment she took on the task he never touched or saw a piece of silver without giving it the closest scrutiny, and nine times out of ten he would find something to rebuke. It was like a sickness. He had bought, in London, one of the new pianos, and Olivia, who had learned to play a little and had a good ear and clever fingers, liked to play. The music she made was always wrong, too loud, not loud enough, miserable belly-aching stuff, a silly tinkle. But when in despair she ceased to play, except when he was out of the house, that wasn't right either. Why had he given all that good money for a silly toy if it were never to be used?

It all sounds petty and trivial, almost laughable, and sometimes indeed Olivia and I did laugh together—a little hysterically—about it, but it was hateful to watch, a continual jarring of the nerves. In the beginning I had occasionally put in a politely worded, mild, reasonable protest: "That's hardly Olivia's fault, sir," I would say. He would retort, "It's none of your concern, my boy!" or, "I know what I'm about, George," and I soon learned that by speaking I did more harm than good, for always later on he would be more actively disagreeable to her. I should, of course, have hated it had he taken a similar attitude to me, but at the same time I did not enjoy the pointed contrast. Sometimes Olivia would say, half laughing and half crying, "Oh you're all right; you're *George, my dear boy,* the fortunate fellow who can do no wrong!" And to that I could only reply, "I believe he's a woman-hater."

"Then why did he ever bring me here? He could have left me at Peterborough. I was much happier there, George, truly. If this goes on I shall write to Miss Rossiter and ask if I can go back and teach the small girls. I shouldn't want any wages."

"You'd do better to stay here and get married," I said.

And indeed as time went on the idea of Olivia's finding a husband and having a home of her own became to me as delectable an idea as ever it could have appeared to any girl herself or to the most scheming matchmaking mamma. I grew more and more inclined to shuffle off a feeling of guilt and responsibility where she was concerned by thinking that this state of affairs couldn't last forever; Olivia would soon find a husband and be out of Father's clutches.

Nor was it by any means a far-fetched idea; for one of the fears which Olivia had voiced, the fear that life would be very lonely at Merravay, proved to be entirely unfounded. We had no sooner settled than Mr. Whymark invited us all to dinner "to meet a few neighbours," and soon we were entertaining and being entertained at least once a week and sometimes more often. Perhaps it is the ever-present danger of life becoming dull in the country which makes country people really cultivate and bother about their social activities; I know that all around us were people who seemed to enjoy the company of their fellows and to be extremely tolerant of one another's little peculiarities, and to be willing, though with a certain understandable caution, to welcome newcomers into their circle. Very soon Father gave a special Indian dinner, with curries and strange pickles and fruits and sweetmeats, and with Candy our Negro servant in his finest clothes moving round like a shadow; and that was a great success. It was plain that the new state of Merravay's interior impressed everyone very much. And Father, without making any particular effort to be agreeable or ingratiating, seemed to strike just the right note, particularly when he confessed that he knew absolutely nothing about English agriculture and expected that for a year or two he would lose money. At that the English countryman's desire to be helpful with dictatorial-flavoured advice came uppermost. Almost every man at the table immediately offered to ride over and just cast an eye on this and that. Then Sir Evelyn Fennel, who lived at Ockley Manor and was related to the Whymarks in some degree, said,

"You'd do better, Sandell, to get a good steward. Otherwise you'll have civil war. Great-uncle William here on my left will tell you to plant seeds in the dark of the moon, he is so old-fashioned, while Hodge here on my right is so much day-after-tomorrow that he's taken to marling his land." Everyone laughed.

Father said, "As a matter of fact I have engaged a foreman who seems to know his job; a fellow called Tom Fulger."

There was a tiny silence.

"He's knowledgeable enough," said Mr. Hodge at last, a little grudgingly. "Worked one time for Coke at Holkham. Yes . . . he knows his job."

"Well . . . what don't you like about him?" asked Father, going in his direct way to the heart of the matter.

"Damned revolutionary," said Sir Evelyn. "You keep your eye on him. He had the nerve to say—and in a public place—that any labourer that was worth his salt was worth ten shillings a week! That's where the rot starts. *They* don't want it; they haven't got wit enough to think up such nonsense; but you get one or two big-mouthed malcontents like Tom Fulger rip-ranting about and then there's trouble."

I came to know Tom Fulger very well during the next year or so. During the September after our move to Merravay I had my seventeenth birthday, and shortly afterwards Father asked me in a kindly casual way whether I had any ideas about my future. I had none; I was enjoying my present way of life and asked nothing but that it could continue. I hesitated to confess this lack of ambition and enterprise to a man who so often spoke about "making opportunities" and "taking time by the forelock" and so on; therefore I said,

"I haven't given the matter much thought, sir. Have you anything particular in mind?"

"I'm asking you."

"Well . . ." I said.

"Surely to God, boy, you know what you *want*; or what you *don't* want. The world's open to you. Would you like to go to the University, travel a bit . . . ?"

"If it were merely a question of what I should *like*, I should say that I should like to go on living as I am at the moment but to have more to do with the land, the farming side. That does interest me and if I learned about it, properly, one day I could run it for you."

"Nothing would please me more. But why be so timid about it? It's the thing I should have suggested myself, but I wanted you to choose."

"Well, I thought perhaps you might think that it was . . . unenterprising. That perhaps you thought I ought to go out and tackle the world, like you did, Father."

"I had to, my boy; if I hadn't it'd have damned soon tackled me. But you're different; you can have what you want, do what you like. And you don't have to thank me," he said with a note in his voice that I had never heard before. "You're part of the prize I wrung out of the struggle. When I was your age I was sweating over ledgers in an airless hole in a dirty stinking place called Kumalpore; and God help me if I made a blot. Yes sir, no sir, let me kiss your arse sir, to clods and clowns that hadn't half my brains or my breeding if it comes to that. And when I see you at the same age, George . . . I'd see you off on the Grand Tour, or to Cambridge, or if you wanted to go and make a young ass of yourself in London, it'd all be one to me, because it would be like having it myself."

I heard those words then and I felt warmly, gratefully, towards him for saying them, for lifting the burden of gratitude from my heart, for making so free with all that he had. But later on I saw what lay behind them. I was nothing really, just a peg upon which he could hang another self. That was why I could have a fine new saddle horse in the same week as he had grudgingly handed Olivia the price of the cheapest possible muslin dress, and told her to buy the stuff and sew it herself. But that, as I say, came later. At the moment I was delighted because he was pleased with my choice of occupation, and delighted that I was to stay at Merravay, to know it better, to serve it.

IV

In that way I became, to an extent, Tom Fulger's pupil. He was a tall lean fellow with a face like a saint in a stained-glass window and a remarkable repertoire of swearwords. His family had lived in Nettleton since the beginning of time, and his grandfather had been, by all accounts, a substantial farmer. One day when we were driving into Baildon market he pointed out to me the house in which his grandfather had lived and where his own father had been born. It looked a big, solid, prosperous place.

"That's why I never touch a —— drop of the —— stuff, not even home-brewed," Tom said, leaving me to guess the connection. "I had an old great-aunt, my granfer's sister, wonderful old woman too she was and kept things together longer than they'd have held otherwise, and I've heard her say that he was all right, doing wonderful well, taking prizes with his beasts, and God knows what, and then one day something upset the old sod and he went and downed a glass of —— brandy. And never stopped. Drunk hisself out of Squirrels, drunk hisself out of Church Farm, drunk hisself out of two or three jobs old Deborah got him. They still say around these parts, "drunk as Luke Fulger." And all on account of once being upset in his belly, or maybe it was toothache. Soaking old sod, I hate even to think about him!"

I thought, but I did not say, that probably it was a Fulger trait never to do anything by halves. Tom was the most thorough man I ever knew. And just a little demented. He thought every man, irrespective of whether he owned property or not, should have a vote; he thought every labourer should have ten shillings a week; he thought every child should go to school; he thought all foxes should be shot, all race-horses put to work, and only big, healthy bulls allowed to run with the cows. There was hardly a thing which had come under his notice about which he had not had some thought, and most generally his thought was in direct opposition to everyone else's. He afforded me a great deal of entertainment and presently, when I had come to realise how sound and right all his ideas about agriculture were, I sometimes asked myself whether a man could be so sensible in one direction and wrong in all others. And that, of course, was a dangerous line of thought.

When I look back on that year and the next one I feel like a very old man. I suppose that if one is ever to have boundless enthusiasm and endless energy one has them at seventeen, eighteen. And perhaps the change of diet had an effect on me. I could rise at first light and be out with Tom, who had no nonsensical ideas about "gentleman farmers" or lily-white hands. Later in the day I could shoot or hunt or ride with Father, spend another couple of hours with Tom, play cards or dance all evening. I've ridden home from a ball at the Baildon Assembly Rooms, changed my clothes, and spent the rest of the night in the lambing pen and not felt a penny the worse.

Olivia and I had no lack of friends of our own age. Of Mr. Whymark's third family two girls and one boy were still under twenty, a gay, high-spirited trio; the girls particularly were allowed more freedom, both of speech and movement, than was common. It was young Phyllis Whymark's hoydenish ways which precipitated a scene in our family.

Father, although thinking little of Mr. Whymark's capacity for business, was well aware of his social value and did nothing to discourage friendship between the two houses. Olivia was always at liberty to accept the frequent invitations to the New House, to ride, to picnic, to go shopping with Phyllis, who had developed for her one of those doting friendships in which girls delight. One bright April morning Phyllis came galloping over to know whether Olivia would ride to Ockley with her. Olivia came out to find me in the yard. "Do you think I might go? Father isn't here so I can't ask *him!*"

I said that naturally she could go. I had not noticed that before each previous outing she had had to seek permission.

"Oh yes," she said, when I commented on this. "Always. Cap in hand, 'Please, Papa, may I go?' Just like school. Well, have I your permission then, George?"

"Oh, don't be silly," I said, a little embarrassed; and then to cover the brusqueness, added, "Enjoy yourself."

She came in just before dinner; I had spent the day on the farm and come in and cleaned myself early; Father, who had been to Muchanger, was still upstairs, changing. Finding me alone, Olivia lingered for a moment, abandoning the quiet, repressed manner which she now as a matter of habit assumed upon entering the house. There was a new baby at Ockley and Phyllis was to be its godmother; there were hothouses at Ockley and in them the strawberries were already almost ripe. The simple, innocent excitements of the day were held out for my sharing.

"Well, miss, and where have you been all day?" asked Father from midway down the stairs. He looked quite savage.

"At Ockley, with Phyllis, Papa," said Olivia, instantly deflated. She moved to the stairs and stood aside to let him pass her and then began, quickly, to mount them. Father walked to the centre of the hall and said, "Come here!" He raved at her for several minutes, going on after he had reduced her to tears.

Once I said, "Look here, sir, she did consult me and I . . ."

"Keep out of this, George," he said and raved on. Olivia, crying, said, "But you weren't at home, Papa; so I asked George . . ."

"Will you leave George out of this?" he said furiously, and raved on. Finally he dismissed her to her room, saying that he did not wish to see her at dinner.

I made a cub's move.

"If Olivia has no dinner I don't want any either," I said.

"Now for God's sake don't you start!" he said; and taking me by the arm, hustled me without ado into the dining room just as Candy padded in with the soup tureen.

I sat down in my place, realising that I had put myself into a ridiculous position. Whatever I did now, whether I ate or refused to eat, I should look silly. And at the same time—so lacking in dignity is crude nature—I realised that I was extremely hungry. The plate of soup which Candy placed before me both looked and smelt painfully appetising. But I did not take up my spoon. I folded my arms and sat there, feeling a fool and looking like one.

After a moment Father cocked an eyebrow at me and said,

"George, you look exactly like a dog 'On Trust!' Eat your dinner, boy, and don't be so ridiculous."

"I know it's ridiculous," I said, "because it makes no difference to the situation whether I eat or not! All the same I think you were very unjust and unkind to Olivia just now and it isn't the first time either."

"Well, suppose we discuss that afterwards. Argument at table leads to indigestion. Richard Whymark was at Muchanger today and gave me a message for you. The pups are ready to leave their mother and he'd like you to have first choice. Young Stephen Fennel is going over there on Thursday, so if you want the really first choice you'd better try to get there tomorrow."

"Thank you for telling me," I said in a voice I tried to make cold.

He was too wily to repeat the friendly overture. The rest of the meal-time passed in silence, giving me ample opportunity to think "I am right. I am right," and then to wonder whether the need to think so repeatedly wasn't in itself a sign of weakness.

We went back to the hall, where a fire was burning. Father took his usual chair and stretched his thin yellow hands to the blaze, then, rubbing them together, leaned back and said in a conversational tone,

"So you think I'm unjust and unkind, eh?"

"To Olivia, sir; not to me. And that makes it rather hard for me to say . . ."

"Go on. State your case."

"Well, just before dinner, for instance. You shouted at her that you would not have her careering about the countryside, her whereabouts unknown, her company unapproved, and her behaviour uncontrolled. But if you had been here and asked for your permission you would have given it, I think. Well then, I fail to see how an exchange of words between you could make all that difference to her whereabouts, or her company, or her behaviour."

"Very lucid, George. Very true, too. Up to a point. The point being that in leaving the house without my permission she was flagrantly disobedient. It was no crime to go, with Phyllis Whymark, to Ockley, to see a new baby, I agree with you there. But the trouble with females is that given an inch they immediately take a mile and if, on this occasion, she escaped without reprimand, next week she would be off without leave on some less innocent errand."

I almost said, "That is silly!" but checked the words just in time.

"Well, are you satisfied?"

"I don't want to offend you," I said, "but it isn't just today's occurrence. You are, to my mind, very hard on Olivia always. She does her best to please you, but you never are pleased. She's young and inexperienced in housekeeping, but in that matter you behave to her as though she were forty and judge her harshly; and then in other matters you treat her as though she were a child; so she is never right. And it makes me unhappy to watch."

Remembered, that speech sounds mild and reasonable; but then it seemed bold and challenging, and I waited with lively apprehension for the wrath that must surely follow. But Father said nothing. He got up and went to the red lacquer cabinet and took out the brandy. He poured some into a glass and drank it in a manner contrary to his habit. He was—at least by Suffolk standards which were all I knew—fairly abstemious, and would sit for a whole evening with a similar measure of liquor, sipping and toying with his glass.

Filling the glass again, he closed the cabinet and returned to his chair.

"It's a pretty good rule, you know, George, not to bother about what can't be helped."

It was difficult to find an answer to such a pontifical statement, so I sat still and waited.

"And if a . . . well," he looked up and smiled, "let's say a yellow dog with very floppy ears bites you, it's understandable that in future you don't care for yellow dogs with very floppy ears. You agree?"

Father's speech, though often pungent and succinct, seldom tended towards the metaphorical. That it did so now showed, like that gulping of brandy, that this was a critical moment.

"Well, sir . . . that would rather depend. Quite a different yellow dog . . ."

"Bitch, bred of the bitch that bit you?" he asked, raising his heavy eyebrows. "Have I said enough, George?"

I could have left it there, I suppose. But I said,

"Either too much or too little. You seem to be implying . . ."

"Telling you, my boy, telling. I can't like her, George. That's something you'll have to accept if you and I are to remain on friendly terms. Every single thing about her, her size and shape and colouring, the sound of her voice, the very way her hair grows . . . and that laugh! You may not believe it, but I have *tried!* And it's useless. Simply by existing she sets my teeth on edge."

"Because she is so like Mother?"

"That stumps you. Well, there you are, you forced it on me, George. You started it. So you'd better know. Your mother isn't dead. So far as I know she's still living in a dirty little bungalow at Kumalpore with a down-at-heel scrivener with the lung rot. And, by God, I hope she's hungry!"

I'd remembered her, pretty, kind, and gay; and dead, preserved from change and age, static, enshrined.

"I was busy," Father said in a flat harsh voice, "busy trying to make money. I'd always given her everything I could; I wanted to give her everything that there *was*. But women are like that, George. You might as well know it now. Offer them a daisy and they want the moon; climb the sky and drag down the moon by sheer force and nothing will please but the daisy. While I was sweating my guts out *he* was playing his damned little tinkles; putting Hindu songs into English and setting them to music. Hindu love songs . . . out of a country where women are less valued than cows. My God! The top of my skull still lifts when I think of it."

I said the only thing I could think of. "I'm terribly sorry."

"Why should you be? Sorry for yourself, perhaps. I offered . . . when you and Olivia came home—I could have afforded it then—I offered that she should come with you. But the rot had set in; she couldn't leave then. So tuck this away in your mind, George; never let a woman get the upper hand of you; they're all as false as Hell. And now let's forget it. We've survived, and that is the main thing. Have some brandy . . . you look a bit white about the gills. Mustn't take it to heart, you know."

It was only later on that I realised that my protest, the revelation it had provoked, and the understanding of Father's attitude which the facts had engendered in me had done nothing to help Olivia or to soften her lot.

And whenever I think of Olivia I think of Candy too, because all my memories and all my remorses are inextricably tangled.

Candy was an African Negro whom Father had bought in Zanzibar; he was often referred to as "my man, Candy," and it would have been as true to have said, "my slave, Candy." He had been bought for money; he received no wages; Father regarded him, and Candy regarded himself, as a chattel.

Coming through the Bay on the voyage home Candy had met with an accident and had broken a leg, so Father had left him in Hull in a hospital for the sick poor, and I only learned of his existence after Father had decided to buy Merravay and was, one evening, discussing the staff we should need in the house.

"A cook and three maids will be plenty," he said. "Your sister will make herself useful and my man Candy will be both footman and but-ler."

"Who is Candy?" I asked. Father explained, and I with some muddled recollection of Mr. Ogilvy's dissertations about socmen and serfs said, "But I thought one couldn't have slaves or be a slave in England."

"That's as may be," said Father. "When you go to London you'll see every other fashionable lady attended by a little black boy. They buy them young, give them plenty of gin, and make them sleep in cupboards to keep 'em small. They put collars on 'em, too, like dogs. I once saw one with a collar studded with garnets and turquoises; very pretty." He smiled, "I shan't put a collar on Candy, he's an ugly old devil, but you'll like him; I never saw his equal for getting a shine on boots. You look incredulous, George! See here." He reached for the paper, turned it about, and held it to me pointing to a column. And there, sure enough, were several advertisements for black boys, wanted, for sale, or lost. The lost ones, I noticed, were all pock-marked and bow-legged; the ones for sale all handsome and very accomplished.

"Well," I said, "I never knew that!"

"If you will forgive my mentioning it, George, there were one or two things omitted from Mr. Ogilvy's curriculum!" He smiled as he said it and I smiled back.

"Can he speak—and understand—English?" I asked.

"Well enough. His last master was Portuguese, but I've had him nearly two years. I'd made up my mind to retire and that was my last visit to Zanzibar and I'd heard such accounts of English servants from people fresh out from home, I thought I must make sure of one good servant. And Africans are much stronger than Indians. . . ."

Candy came down from Hull in the wagon with the crates of furnishings, and my first thought about him was that he was very ill clad for the English climate. It was a day of bitter March wind and he was wearing a pair of thin cotton trousers and a short jacket of the same stuff. His huge feet were thrust, hoseless, into a pair of shabby shoes. He was a good deal older than I had expected him to be; his close-curled black hair looked as though it had been lightly powdered; and he was less black than I had imagined, for at that moment he was the curious pinky-grey colour which Negroes go when they are ill, or cold, or frightened.

"Poor thing," I said, "he's frozen. He must have some warmer clothes."

"He's all right; he'll warm up when he starts moving about. What he certainly is, is damned filthy." Father turned to Candy and said, as one says to a child, "Dirty! dirty!"

Candy's eyes rolled like loose marbles in their sockets.

"Four days, no water, no wash. All ize, ize. No water."

"Plenty of water here," Father said. "Help with this stuff and then wash!"

That was a day when we were only at Merravay in order to see the furniture safely in, and just before dusk we drove back to Baildon to the inn where we were staying. When we went towards the carriage and

Candy climbed up beside the driver I was horrified to see that he had taken literally Father's orders to wash. His coat and trousers were now clean, but quite wet and already plastered to him by the wind.

"He's wet, the fool," I said, "he'll catch his death. Shall I give him my coat."

"George, please," said Father, putting one hand on my arm and pulling me into place beside him, while with the other hand he drew up the rug. "He's all right. He'll take no more harm than a dog would. You must get that into your head. You might just as well go and give your coat to one of the horses."

If Candy had sneezed or snuffled next day I could have said, "There, I told you!", but he did not. He took no apparent harm at all.

The next time—or at least the next time I remember—that I spoke up on Candy's behalf was, oddly enough, the time when I thought he would be too hot. It was when we finally moved into Merravay and I discovered that Candy was to sleep in the chimney room, which was just a space partitioned off around the main chimney stack of the house. The whole of one side of it was made of the red brick chimney; there was floor space about six feet long and four wide, and it had no window. Three little round holes bored in the top of the door which divided it from the passage admitted the only air.

"He'll stifle," I said.

"You'll see," said Father.

But, just as Candy had not frozen, so he did not stifle. I used to remind myself of that, trying to believe that Negroes were different, less sensitive. I had to take comfort in that thought if I could, for Father was hard on Candy; just as he was hard on dogs and horses, hard on Olivia, hard on everybody except me. I really must have been the world's worst simpleton, always to think myself exempt; never to guess that he knew all about the hair shirt Mr. Carter had slipped over my head; never to guess that I was as much his slave as Candy.

I didn't. I went on my gay, happy way, thinking how lovely everything was and how much I should enjoy myself if only . . . if only . . . if only . . . thinking that Olivia would one day marry and get away . . . thinking that Candy after all must be made differently . . . thinking all the coward's thoughts.

V

Time slipped away. I found myself devoting more and more attention to the farm. Father took singularly little interest in it though he would walk around the yard every now and then and make a great fuss if a bucket or a wisp of hay were out of place; he liked it all spic and span and he liked to show visitors round. But the ordinary routine bored him, and I came, almost unconsciously, to look upon my work as my refuge.

Olivia had her twenty-first birthday. Father gave her a pear-shaped ruby on a gold chain and then cut into her timid expressions of gratitude and pleasure with the remark that she was now an established old maid. Long before this, towards the end of our first year at Merravay, Olivia had put into action her threat of writing to Miss Rossiter to ask if she could go back to Peterborough as an unsalaried teacher. Miss Rossiter had written her a long letter, rich, I suppose, in sorry wisdom. Any girl, she said, who had a home and a father who was willing and able to provide for her, should thank God every morning and evening for such blessed security in a world where so many unfortunate females had none. Dozens of women, some as young as fifteen, some as old as fifty, had applied for the last post they had advertised and almost had said that they were willing to work for no salary; some had even offered small sums of money as well as their services in return for bed and board. So would dear Olivia—the letter ended—please cultivate a meek and cheerful spirit even when things were a little difficult, and remember always to count her blessings. . . .

When I read the letter, I said,

"Well, I never did think it a very good idea. You stay here and get married."

And steadily, over the next three years, whenever I thought of Olivia I assured myself that she would get married; she was so pretty. But though at parties and picnics men paid her plenty of attention and she never lacked partners at the balls we attended, somehow no young man, to my knowledge, ever sought for Father's permission to marry her; and all too soon she was twenty-one and Father, when at a loss for other taunt or gibe, could always remark that she was becoming an old maid.

Just before my birthday, my nineteenth, Father surprised me by announcing that he had invited an old acquaintance, a Mr. Douglas Booth, to come and stay. My surprise arose from the fact that Father seemed to have severed all connection with his past; and although he spoke freely and authoritatively about India and Indian affairs—then much to the fore on account of the trial of Warren Hastings—I do not remember hearing him mention any one of his former associates by name. I evinced some interest in Mr. Booth, but Father had nothing much to say about him, save that he had known him years ago but had not seen him since his return to England. I was left to judge for myself that he was a man for whom Father had some regard. It was arranged that he should occupy the master bedroom, the one which local legend, confirmed by Mr. Whymark, said had once been slept in by Queen Elizabeth. And Olivia, whose wardrobe was, for a girl in her position, very modest, was given permission to buy two new dresses.

Mr. Booth arrived on the afternoon before my birthday. He was considerably Father's senior, small, very dried and brittle looking. To begin with he seemed painfully nervous and shy, but later on his manner showed traces of aggressiveness and self-importance. His carriage, his horseflesh, his clothes, and appurtenances were evidence of his wealth, and he irritated me on the first day because when he was looking over Merravay he followed each favourable comment by another which showed that, compared with his own place in Berkshire, Merravay was very small beer indeed. I remarked upon this to Father who said,

"Well, I believe Gore Park is quite palatial. He inherited it from his grandfather, who made a great fortune before the public conscience became quite so tender about such things."

"Oh," I said. "I thought he'd been in India with you."

"So he was. He held an official post. But he's regarded as the only man who ever went to India and came away with nothing but his pay in his pocket. A phoenix!"

"Is he married?"

"Not that I know of," Father said carelessly.

That evening Mr. Booth regained the ground he had lost in my opinion over Merravay by being very pleasant in a nervous, unobtrusive way to Olivia. He asked her if she played the piano and she said she did but had not practised lately.

"If it wouldn't trouble you, I wish you would play a little for me. I am exceptionally fond of music and used to play myself . . . before . . . well, my handicap . . . you know." We had all noticed that the first and second fingers of his right hand were missing; he referred to the loss as though it were something to be ashamed of.

Olivia glanced at Father, he nodded. She went to the piano and played with nervous clumsiness at first and then with more assurance. Mr. Booth named several of his favourite tunes, some of which she knew and some of which she had never heard, and he listened with unassumed interest and pleasure. When she had finished he thanked her and said she had a very pleasing touch. Father stayed silent; Olivia blushed.

Next morning, learning that it was my birthday, Mr. Booth apologised, too effusively, for not having known and come provided. He insisted that I should accept a very fine seal from his own fob. In the evening, when several neighbours came in to dine, and to dance later on in the hall, he apologised again for his inability to dance—perfectly understandable on account of his age—and instead of retiring to play cards with the other old gentlemen, he hovered about, looking like a little grasshopper, on the verge of the gay crowd. I thought him pathetic and once stayed out from the dance to talk to him; but he said he was enjoying himself, the music gave him pleasure, and he liked to see people making merry. At Gore Park, he added, there was an enormous ballroom with mirrored walls. "But seldom used; all too seldom used."

Next day we went to Ockley to shoot partridges, returning for late supper in the evening. The principal dish was a large game pie which Mr. Booth praised quite fulsomely.

"Yes," said Father, "Olivia has turned out to be quite a skilful little housekeeper."

Even then no breath of suspicion stirred in my mind. I was simply glad that someone for whom Father seemed to have regard should say the things which I often wished to say about Olivia but knew would be ineffectual coming from me. Old, ugly, fidgety, and annoying as he was, I felt my heart warming to Mr. Booth for pointing Father the way to a better appreciation of Olivia.

A very pleasant week followed. Mr. Booth had arranged to leave on market day, so, knowing that I should be up early and breakfast alone, I said good-bye to him overnight. When I shook, with an inward shudder, his cold, scaly, mutilated hand, and uttered the conventional hope that we should soon meet again, he said shyly,

"Indeed I hope so. I hope to see you all at Gore Park. I particularly want to show you my home farm. And the whole estate, of course; eighteen thousand acres in all."

"I shall look forward to that, sir," I said; and took my leave.

Next day, coming back from market, about to enter the house from the rear, I heard a little tapping sound from over my head, and I looked up and saw Olivia signing to me from her window. As soon as I had divested myself of my boots I went along to her room. Pressed against the glass her face had looked very white and distorted, but that, I told myself, might have been a trick of the light.

She must have been crying for hours; her eyes and her nose were puffed out of shape, and at sight of me she began to cry again so violently that it was some time before I could understand the reason for her distress. Then it came out.

"Oh, George. Father says I am to marry Mr. Booth!"

I said—I shall always remember the words—"I wouldn't let you."

At that she flung herself into my arms. "I thought you'd be on my side."

"Of course I am. I never heard anything so ridiculous. Why, he's older than Father! Father must be stark staring mad."

"With rage, now he is. I said I'd rather die."

I could understand that. This bit of news had scraped from my mind all pretence that I liked the man because he had been pleasant to Olivia and civil to me. I knew that all along I had seized on the small bearable things about him because I hated the sight of him and felt guilty for taking such a dislike to any human creature. Now I could admit to myself that I loathed him, everything about him; the dark, reptilian, leathery skin, the pale, bright, reptilian eyes, the scanty, scurfy hair and the bad teeth. And that sly, creepy manner. And his age! How could he dare to think of marrying any pretty, fresh young girl, leave alone my sister?

"I'll go and talk to Father now," I said.

Father was dressed for the evening; Candy on his knees was easing on the light, buckled shoes.

"Ah, George. I was coming along to talk to you while you changed. I've something to tell you. You're late, aren't you? Run along, I'll be with you in a minute." Candy rose and went to the chest, sprinkled a fine linen handkerchief with lavender essence, and presented it humbly to Father, who accepted it without a glance and tucked it into his cuff. "Come along," he said, "I'm damned hungry, but you must change; you smell, George. What is it, pigs or yokels?"

"I'd better say what I have to say now."

"Oh. I see. Five minutes, Candy. Well, George, I take it you've been treated to a display of hysteria. I was coming to warn you. I expect Olivia cried on your shoulder and said that she would rather die, eh? Women use these expressions so lightly, you know; many would rather die—by their own evidence—than pass a spider in the open road. You mustn't take that to heart, George."

He said all this in a light, flippant way which was somehow more deadly than anger would have been.

"I'm not going to stand by and see Olivia married to that little toad," I said hotly. "He's old enough to be her father and as ugly as sin. The whole idea is so revolting I wonder you entertained it long enough to tell her about it."

"Well, I agree that it is rather a striking example of Beauty and the Beast, so far as appearances go; but it's the right way about, you know. Now if you contemplated marrying an ugly old woman, George, I should take a very different view. As it is, I am delighted."

I could see that. My fury mounted.

"Yes; but then you've never had any natural feeling for Olivia, have you? I happen to be very fond of her and I won't stand by . . ."

"Don't repeat yourself, George. Time's short. As for that accusation . . . if I were as doting a father as old Whymark I could hardly hope to arrange a better match for my daughter. Mr. Booth admires her very much; he is in a position to give her every comfort; I'm sure he will be kind to her, and once she has forgotten about the handsome young man that every girl expects to find round the next corner, she'll be very h——"

At that moment the great gold-and-silver inlaid, pearl-and-coral encrusted elephant bell which Father had brought from India, and which served as a gong, rang out.

"I shall begin," said Father, moving away from me.

I tried to hold on to my bold, angry mood, while I hastily washed and threw off my market-day clothes; but when I rushed down to the dining room, ready to take up the cudgels again, Father, with a sidelong glance at Candy, began at once to talk upon some trivial subject. He put himself out to be pleasant, and since I knew that to anger him would be of no help, I contrived to be pleasant, too. Imperceptibly the atmosphere warmed.

Candy put the port wine, the fruit dishes, and a bowl of walnuts—the first of the year—on the table and withdrew.

"Now," said Father, "we can continue. Bawling her head off and talking about dying, she upset you, I know. She was just being girlish; they always behave that way when they're first proposed to."

"Olivia was genuinely distressed. And so should I be. God! In her place I should be thoroughly sick at the thought."

"That is one of the troubles with you, you know. I've often noticed it. You will always go putting yourself into somebody else's shoes—Candy's, Olivia's, even a horse's. That is such a waste. You can't understand how they feel, you only judge by how *you* would feel in their place. Naturally the idea of yourself in bed with old Douglas hugging and kissing you makes *you* feel sick. If it didn't there'd be something seriously wrong with you! Where it's a matter between man and woman it's entirely different. Damn it, George, have you never seen a fine lady give a hearty kiss to a filthy sweep who had crossed her path and brought her, she thought, luck? Make a little allowance for sex, boy. And for God's sake don't go and encourage her whimsies. It is a pity she got her word in first."

"That makes no difference. Even if she wanted to marry him, Father, I should hate the idea. He's too old, and ugly, and creepy. I want Olivia to marry somebody nice; somebody she *could* be fond of."

His thick eyebrows arched quizzically.

"Have you a candidate in mind, George? Take your time," he said, as I hesitated. "All these avid suitors take some counting, don't they?"

"Well," I said, "I know that just at the moment . . ."

"Come, come," he said with testy good humour, "face facts, George. She's twenty-one and there's a dearth of young men. Of old Whymark's eleven, only three were boys and it's the same wherever you look. Also, much as this will shock your tender susceptibilities, there's this to remember. Love fizzles out and the lucky people are those who have something left when the kissing is done. Can't you see that she's damned lucky to get such an offer? And believe me, once the first coyness wears off she'll realise it. Poor old Douglas, he was too shy to speak; he asked me to prepare the way and then he'd write her a nice little letter. By the time that arrives she'll have come round and be as pleased as a dog with two tails. You'll see. So don't you worry, George; and don't encourage her to keep up this play-acting. And now, since we're alone for once, how about a game of chess?"

In the next few days he ignored the subject.

Olivia and I talked of the matter when we were alone and she certainly didn't seem to be affecting the deep revulsion she professed; and whenever I was with her I shared her feeling and repeated that of course the idea was absurd, untenable, that of course I was on her side and would support her in her refusal.

Then one afternoon two letters arrived, one for Father, which I didn't see, and one for Olivia. It was a stilted, pompous little letter, and it said that the proposal it conveyed was made with Father's full knowledge and approval.

"You see, they settled it between them," said Olivia.

Father was out that evening. Next morning, having been out for a couple of hours, I came in to breakfast to find him literally forcing Olivia into a seat at the table.

"You will sit there and eat your breakfast properly. Pretty, eh? You look like an old woman who's lived through a famine! You'll eat your breakfast and then you'll write that letter."

Olivia dared not refuse the food he kept thrusting at her, but she cried all the time, and there is something about a person who is eating and weeping that is, well, unendearing to say the least of it. I was shocked to find that my pity was giving way to irritation, as pity so often does in the end. After the nasty meal was over, Father tried to force her into the library to write and she refused and he started to shake her and I said,

"Stop that," in a high shrill voice quite unlike mine.

"Yes. That was a mistake," said Father as Olivia wriggled out of his hands and ran loudly crying upstairs. For the first time since the affair had been mooted he seemed to lose a little of his composure.

"Look here, George. That letter must be answered. More hangs on this than you know. She's carrying coy reluctance just a little too far. Go and see if you can talk sense into her."

I went up. Olivia turned and said, "Oh, poor dear George, I've made you fall out with Father."

I remembered all the things he had said about women being different, and being coy and being hysterical and being silly about spiders and kissing sweeps.

"Now for God's sake, Olivia dear," I said, "be quite honest with me. Is it just . . ." She looked at me and I was ashamed. But as though she had sensed my Father-instilled doubt, she jumped from the bed upon which she had flung herself and went to her dressing table.

"He thinks I'm pretty, does he?" she said. She took up the scissors and with three sharp snaps of the blades cut off all the little curls which clustered about her forehead. Then she dragged the points of the scissors down her face from just below the eye to the jaw. The parallel furrows leaped up, beaded with little drops of blood.

"All right," I said, answering something that hadn't been put into words. "I'll tell him. Don't worry any more."

Father was waiting.

"It's useless," I said. "She just can't do it; and I don't want her to."

"Let's go for a ride," he said.

It was one of those mellow autumn mornings when the thin mist shreds away and the sky is harebell blue, and everything wears a gentle, wistful look. Father led the way along the narrow headland that divided the front field from Layer Wood, which was blazing with copper and gold and sharp yellow. Single damp bright leaves fell slowly down, spinning.

Speech was impossible while we rode one behind the other; but at the top of the field Father halted and I drew up beside him. From this point one had the best view of Merravay, for the field ran down towards it and the trees rose behind it so that it seemed to be cupped in the loving hand of the earth. This morning the worn old walls, the slightly uneven roof, were drinking in the sunshine and giving it back again in a glow of apricot and rose and tawny. A thin column of smoke from one of the chimneys went spiralling up, blue against blue. In the garden the flower-beds were fragile patchwork against the solidity of the lawns, the carved yews.

I had meant to speak as soon as we halted, but, having looked at Merravay, I was compelled to sit and stare for a moment, thinking that I had never seen it so lovely.

It was Father who spoke first, breaking the silence by saying in a rapid, staccato, strangely distinct voice, as though addressing someone slightly deaf or stupid,

"Look here, George; this has gone far enough. I gave you several perfectly good reasons for my approval of this match; there is another which I wasn't particularly anxious to talk about. But since you are so stubborn and will insist on encouraging her, I must tell you. You've read all this ridiculous nonsense about Hastings, I suppose. All right! Now when they drop the net for big fish they take small ones, too. An inquiry of that nature turns up a lot of things one believed to be done with and forgotten. And I've realised in the last month or so that at one point I am vulnerable. It would be very useful for me to have Douglas Booth on my side."

"You mean that you did something . . . and now he's blackmailing you!"

Father laughed.

"Really, George, you do so tend to melodrama. If there is blackmail in it, the boot surely is on the other leg. I'm the blackmailer. I've got what poor old Douglas wants; and whether he would ever be called upon to repay me is very much a matter of chance. I just want to make sure that, in the event, he would stand by me. You're not the only one who likes Merravay, you know. I'm fond of the place, too."

"What has Merravay to do with it?"

"I should not, if it came to the point, sit there waiting for Messrs. Fox and Burke to slap *me*, George. My gains, ill gotten as they may seem to such sentimentalists, cost me dear, and I shall hang on to them. At the first breath of trouble, unless I can be sure of Douglas, I shall sell out and go abroad again."

He paused to let that sink in.

"And I still think," he continued, "that Olivia would be better off in her own home, with a rich and doting husband and a pack of children—she's the sort who would breed once a year—than she will be as governess or companion to a lady! For I tell you frankly, George, and you can tell her, that if she doesn't go to Gore Park she doesn't stay at Merravay. As it is, the effort to be fair and just to her is just a little too much for me and after *this* . . . if she defeats my neat little scheme for self-preservation by sheer pig-headedness . . . I doubt if I could keep my hands off her. You saw what happened this morning. If she won't go my way, she must go her own, and discover just how much fairness and justice there is in this world."

I said the only thing possible for me.

"The day Olivia goes out to earn her living, sir, I shall go with her."

What effect I expected that speech to produce I find difficult to say. I knew, or thought I knew, that his affection for me, though rooted in his self-love, was firm and strong. But he was evidently one of the "if thy eye offend thee, cast it out" manner of men. He turned and gave me a long assessing look and then said in a reasonable way, far more chilling than any sneer,

"Well, if that is the way you feel, George, there's no more to be said. You're a nice-looking boy, you write a clear hand and have pleasing manners when you choose. You'd be worth every penny of eight shillings a week as a clerk; I started with less. In that case Mr. Booth can hang himself for all I care. I always had a nagging desire to be a country gentleman and I thought you liked Merravay. I was prepared to settle and found a family. But without you it would be pointless to stay. So if you've had your fill of it we'll say good-bye to Merravay as soon as possible."

With that he swung his horse round, set it to the low fence between field and meadow and went galloping off, leaving me with his last words ringing in my ears.

I often wondered whether he used the phrase "Good-bye to Merravay" deliberately or not.

The next four or five days were as wretched as any I remember. Olivia kept to her room. Father and I met at table after the first evening when I absented myself and he sent Candy to fetch me. "I see no reason why we should avoid one another, George," he said. "You're young and romantic, I'm old and practical, and we take different views, as men are entitled to do; but let us behave in civilised fashion."

My interviews with Olivia were just as trying in another way; she cried and cried and kept begging me to make it up with Father. I had told her, so far, only that Father had threatened to turn her out and I had said that I should go, too; I hadn't mentioned Merravay. She had written another letter to Miss Rossiter, explaining that now she was about to be homeless, and begging her to employ her or find her employment of any kind.

"She'll help me now that my circumstances have changed, George; I am positive of that; and truly I should be happy, glad, pleased to go from here if only you hadn't said that you'd come too. It's so much worse for a man to be poor. Nobody expects a woman to have anything, anyway. And I shall have a place to go. It was a kind, noble gesture, George dear, and I do appreciate it, but you're making everything so much more difficult for me."

Constant crying and misery had marred what looks the scissors had left; and, looking at the bristly hair and deeply scratched face, I kept thinking—Yes, that was a gesture too; and whom did it hurt?

"Do please say that you'll stay with Father."

My jangled nerves gave way,

"God damn it all, Olivia, why should I? He's kind enough to me, but the way he treats Tom Fulger and Candy and you sets my teeth on edge. There are times when I hate him, and I won't go trailing about the face of the earth in his company just for the sake of his filthy money!"

"What d'you mean by trailing about, George?" she asked, suddenly quiet and intent.

"Well," I said, confused, "nothing really. But there is some sort of threat; he may have to leave Merravay. It's some sort of inquiry or something which Mr. Booth could ward off if he was so minded. That's one reason why Father is so . . . oh for God's sake, Olivia, don't *cry!* I didn't mean to tell you that. I was just trying to show you that I might as well go with you of my own free will as wait and be chucked out."

"And now I've lost Merravay for you," she cried, and threw herself face downwards on her bed.

"Well, if you can't discuss the thing reasonably . . ." I said, and went away.

On the fourth or fifth morning, at breakfast, Father said to me, "Has Olivia written at all?"

"Not to my knowledge."

"Well, tell her to do it today. A civil, decent proposal demands some answer and there's no point in being more offensive than necessary. Tell her, too, that she'd better start looking about for a post. *I* meant what I said, George."

The slightest possible emphasis on the first pronoun fired my temper.

"So did I," I said.

"Then you'd both better start looking!"

He ate some food rather more quickly than usual; then, emptying his mouth, said,

"This is all your doing. If you hadn't backed her up she'd have given in within twenty-four hours and written Dear-Mr.-Booth-you-do-me-too-much-honour-and-what-kind-of-ring-can-I-have? As it is, she thinks you'll bring me round. If George is for me, who can be against me? They're all as crafty as foxes, and she thinks she's on a safe bet because I'm fond of you. I *am* fond of you, when you're amenable, but I'm damned if I'll be blackmailed, even by you. You've turned against me and I'm one of those who do not love their enemies."

"A few days ago," I retorted, "we were civilised people taking a different view—or so you said. Now you call me your enemy."

"A few days ago I was counting on your fondness—not for me—for Merravay, George. So we're all wrong. And why God Almighty ever took into his head to make women I shall never understand. Surely his infinite wisdom could have devised some less troublesome way of propagating the human race. Everything ruined by one cock-snitched little bitch's whim . . . encouraged by *you*. You'll remember that to your sorrow!"

He was going to spend the day at Muchanger, and shortly after breakfast rode off.

I had arranged to work with Tom that day, but suddenly I had no heart for it. My future at Merravay, learning about and then managing the land, the crops, and the flocks, was like a path seeming to lead on and then stopping suddenly. I had no future here.

I wandered idly into the garden. There was a slight autumnal chill in the air that morning, but the sun was shining on the dew that lay like silver on the lawns and sparkled on the thousands of cobwebs which stretched from leaf to leaf. A brilliant cock pheasant rose from a bed of marigolds and flew to the red wall, where he rested for a moment between two of the grey urns and then flew on to the field. The furrows lay striped in dark chocolate and faint purple. The wood blazed with a last desperate fire.

"I saw Father leave," said Olivia, coming up softly behind me.

"Yes, he's gone to Muchanger."

"Did he say anything?"

"Yes; he said you must write to Mr. Booth today. And he said we must both begin to look about for jobs. And he said everything was my fault." I tried to speak lightly but failed to keep the inward dreariness from sounding in my voice.

Olivia plucked a marigold and stood staring at it as though counting its petals.

"George dear, do please give in. I'll tell you something . . . I didn't think either of you would hold out so long."

I laughed. "That's exactly what Father said. We must be a very stubborn family."

"I'm being stubborn for my own benefit, George. You're doing no good at all. I do with my whole heart beg you to make it up with Father."

"I tell you I don't care about Father."

"But you do about this place."

"I shall survive."

She turned and stared at the house.

"Isn't it strange," she said musingly, "I hated it from the first; you loved it; but it was inimical to me from the beginning. Like a person. Quite apart from any other reason I shall be glad to leave the house. If it belonged to me absolutely I shouldn't want it, shouldn't want to live in it."

"If it belonged to me absolutely . . . Look, Olivia, we're wasting time again. We must make plans, think what we're going to do."

"I think I should write that letter first."

"It would be as well," I said. She turned and went into the house.

In less time than I expected she came to the door, the letter folded and sealed in her hand. "I've done it," she called brightly.

We walked towards one another, and when we met she held out the letter, address uppermost, very clearly written.

"Doesn't that do Miss Rossiter credit?" she asked.

Something cold and gall-bitter rose from the pit of my stomach to choke my throat. Oh yes, I thought, you may well be gay, now. You're leaving a critical parent and a home you hate . . . anything to you will seem an improvement.

Just at that moment Phyllis Whymark arrived; she wanted Olivia to go with her to Baildon to match some ribbon.

"Of course," said Olivia, "I was going to take this to post anyway."

"What on earth have you been doing to yourself?" Phyllis asked.

"A series of accidents. I burned my hair with the curling iron and scratched my face on a rosebush."

"I've been in the wars, too. Look, young Billy hit me in the mouth with a ball; took one tooth out, clean as a whistle. I shall never get married now!"

"Married!" said Olivia. They went off laughing.

A day at Muchanger seemed to have restored Father's good humour too. Olivia had not returned when we sat down to dinner, but since she was no longer expected at table her absence was not remarked upon, and he seemed to go out of his way to be entertaining, giving me a lively account of his day's doings. It was impossible to avoid the thought that with Olivia out of sight and mind, with Olivia safely away, we two got along pretty well. A self-pitying consciousness that I had made a fool of myself to no purpose came inevitably upon that thought's heels.

We were halfway through the meal when the door slammed, and before I could do more than hope that Father would not connect the sound with Olivia, she had reached the dining-room door and stood there, looking pretty and in some way different. Her riding clothes were worn and shabby, but they had been made for her and fitted better than some of the clothes she had made for herself, and the little cocked hat hid her spoiled hair; the flush of a day in the open did something to conceal the marks on her cheek; but the difference lay deeper than mere appearance. She moved and looked like a free woman at last; as though the shy, demure schoolgirl had spent three happy, successful years somewhere and now looked in to visit us.

Father looked at her, his ordinary expression of cold distaste shot through with positive venom. For the first time in years she met his look without flinching and stared back, her eyes as hard as his own. My heart began to beat with a nervous flutter.

"This is an unexpected honour," said Father with heavy irony. "But I trust that you do not expect to dine here. You are both late and unwelcome."

"I dined at the New House," said Olivia. I caught her glance and signed to her to go away, but she stood her ground and it occurred to me that she might be a little flown with wine. The females at New House were very free in such matters and often stayed at the table with the menfolk, sharing the port wine.

"It's all right, George," she said, answering my sign, "I have something to say to Father."

"Nothing that you have to say would interest me, now, miss. Get out!"

"All the same, you should know," said Olivia hardily. "I wrote to Mr. Booth this morning and accepted his proposal."

Astonishment held us both speechless for a moment. Then Father said, "Well, I'm damned!" and began to laugh.

I said, "Olivia, you didn't!"

"I hope that pleases you both," she said, and her glance flicked, like the very tip of a whiplash, from Father's face to mine; then she turned and walked, very straight-backed, to the door.

"There you are. What did I tell you? That's women for you, George. Unpredictable as the wind. All that fuss, and she meant to have him from the start."

"She did not! She changed her mind this morning. And I know when . . . and why . . ." I was almost crying, so sharp and terrible was my remorse, my knowledge of my secret disloyalty, my recognition of a flashing relief.

"You must have been remarkably eloquent, George," said Father.

"It's nothing to laugh at," I said savagely, jumping up from my chair.

"And she shan't do it. I shan't let her. I'd sooner see the place burned. . . ."

I went blundering towards the door, but Father, from his end of the table, was quicker, and he stood there with his back against it.

"Don't be in such a hurry," he said quietly. "Such militant chivalry will keep for a minute. Sit down and hear what I have to say."

"You won't talk me round," I said. But I let him push me back into my chair.

At that moment Candy returned and I realised that all this shattering little incident had happened in the time it took to change plates between courses.

"Oh, take it away, and yourself with it," snapped Father, motioning the dish away. "Put the decanter on the table and get out."

As soon as we were alone again he poured wine for us both and then, for just a second, sat silent, twirling the stem of his glass between his fingers.

"It would be most unkind of you, George, to withdraw now whatever it was that you said, or did, this morning! I mean that. You see, you'd be taking away her excuse for doing what she wants to do, what she has wanted all along to do."

"I don't believe that."

"You can test the truth of it presently; but I won't have you for the second time go blundering in blindfold. On that first evening, if I'd caught you before she did, I could have explained, warned you, and none of this fantastic muddle would ever have arisen. You see, George, he is ugly, and he is rich, a most damning combination where women are concerned. A woman could marry an ugly poor man and still feel noble, or a rich handsome one and feel romantic. D'you follow? What Olivia was waiting for was some reason that would be acceptable to that vanity which women carry about with them like a set of scales—and you gave it to her. Her warped female sense of values would seize with delight on the notion that she was saving you from exiling yourself. I'll bet that she was writing that letter before whatever it was you so fortunately said was out of your mouth."

To myself I admitted the truth of that—the apparent truth; but his whole premise I could not accept.

"I will take back what I said if she will take back what she wrote." I tried to remember exactly what I had said; so little; so vague; it must have been my manner rather than my words which had provoked that impulse of self-sacrifice.

"Well, you can try," said Father calmly. "It would, as I say, be unkind; and I think it would be useless too. She knows that such offers don't come every day. Also, if she hasn't whispered it as the most deadly secret to Miss Whymark, who by this time has told everyone within reach, I'm a Dutchman." He paused while I thought about that.

"I'd rather have her silly then, than sell herself in a loveless marriage to that little toad on my account."

"You know, George, you are most devastatingly like a woman in some ways—the way you talk. Sell herself! Loveless marriage! Old maid's twaddling stock phrases! And the way you shift ground. This morning apparently you conveyed in some way your wish for a match to take place; the moment it's settled you're all against it. It's time you grew up, you know. Men know what they want and take it by hook or by crook if they can, and are glad. If you feel impelled to pity *some*body," he said, a malicious grin beginning to slide over his face, "pity poor old Douglas. He'll have to line up with me now; and then start at his inflexible age to accommodate himself to Olivia's whims and fancies."

"Not if I can prevent it," I said.

"Run along and try," said Father settling back and lifting his glass.

Olivia listened politely to all I had to say, but she would not budge an inch. At one point, made cruel by exasperation, I cried,

"I believe Father is right. I believe you want to marry the man after all. And you're the girl who would rather die!"

"I'm not," said Olivia, giving me a strange look. "That girl did die, writing the letter. I'm a different girl, George."

"Oh, don't talk rot," I said, and my voice sounded like Father's.

"It's true. I am different. Why, I actually heard myself boasting to Phyllis about the glories of Gore Park!"

I gaped at her. So Father had been right about the whispered confidences. Probably right about the secret wish to marry. . . . Despite that creeping doubt, however, I continued to argue and plead until at last Olivia said, "Really, George, I did think that now I should be left in peace."

V

I suppose that the final, the fatal, defeats never come to a man from the outside; they are inflicted from within. And I suppose that those inner defeats are never the result of one great battle; ground is lost inch by inch. What Father stood for as opposed to what I tried to stand for was not triumphant until I began to believe that he was right; but the struggle had begun long ago. Perhaps as long ago as the day when we met in the Ogilvys' parlour. I could look back and think, if I hadn't been so easily silenced when I tried to speak up for Mrs. Ogilvy . . . if I had got out on that hill and walked in the mud . . . if I had stood up more resolutely for Candy . . . I should have altered not Father's nature or behaviour but my own; I should be a stronger character. It was the dreadful weakness of my own character that distressed me most when I thought about Olivia; the weak hysterical support, the weak self-pitying withdrawal of it; the weak tardy effort to replace it.

Outwardly all went very well. The wedding, by Olivia's express wish, took place before Christmas. Father, pleased with her at last, did everything in fine style and gave her a generous marriage settlement. Two of his casual prophecies were fulfilled; she bore her first son within a year and within six years had five, all healthy and surprisingly handsome. And, given her inch she took her mile; Mr. Booth certainly had to accommodate himself to her whims and fancies. It would be difficult to find a more masterful and exacting wife, a milder, more tolerant husband. Sometimes it is easy for me to believe that Olivia Sandell did die that sunny autumn morning, and went, a wistful little crop-haired ghost, to join the ones she always said haunted Merravay.

I lived on, most enviable young man; but something in me had been damaged. For one thing I could never marry, never again feel at ease with any woman; Father's cynicisms and Olivia's transformation combined to put that out of the question. And with men I became conscious of a feeling of inadequacy. I could still work and do business with them but I could not share their pleasures. With the passage of time I became misanthropic as well as misogynous, quite against my will.

I never opposed or openly criticised Father again. The impulse would arise sometimes, especially when, during the troubled time six years ago, wages became a matter of hot dispute, but as soon as I had convinced myself that he was wrong I would remember the number of times when he had been proved right. I never even argued with him again. And he seemed to lose interest in me. Our relationship settled down to a placid coolness to which his illness and long immobility hardly made any difference at all. Six years ago Tom Fulger—long since gone from Merravay, which I was capable of running on my own—came as the representative of the farm labourers to see Father about raising the winter rate of wages to match the rising price of goods. Father, who had never liked Tom, lost his temper and had a stroke. A few days later, without telling him about it, I raised all the wages. After six years, during which I visited his room every morning and evening and saw to it that everything was done to alleviate him, he died. And after the funeral I moved into the great bedroom, where I had always wanted to sleep.

Romantic, defeated, impulsive warm heart turned cold, unfriended—for that raising of the wages set every neighbour against me—a self-hater, a weak, poor-spirited fellow, I sit here tonight and know that I am happier and more fortunate in the final issue than anyone else I know. For I love, with an unchanging love, something that cannot change. And today, with the willing of Merravay to Olivia's third and favourite son I have shaken off an old nagging sense of indebtedness. If I liked the boy better my sense of repayment would be that much less complete; willing it to him, as Olivia asked me to do, hurt so much that now I feel I owe her nothing. Tonight Merravay really belongs to me.

Interlude

George Frederick Sandell Esq., of Merravay, died as he had lived, an eccentric.

Even before his father died he had gained himself a reputation for sloppy sentimentality, and during his term of office as a Justice of the Peace he caused scandals and made many bad neighbours by his lenient sentences to poachers. In the end sentiment killed the miserable, puling fellow.

A hot-headed agitator called Tom Fulger, who had once been manager at Merravay, sided with the labourers during the riots and stack-burnings which broke out during the demand for higher wages or cheaper food which followed the end of the Bonaparte wars. In Suffolk the Yeomanry was called out one November and Fulger was shot through the head.

What must Mr. Sandell do but order a stone to be put over his grave?

Several people thought that the rector of Nettleton failed in his duty in allowing the erection of the stone at all. The rector, however, perceived a golden opportunity. Mr. Sandell was far less regular at church than a gentleman in his position—for the sake of setting a good example—should be. The rector said that when the stone was set up there must be a proper dedication service. He planned to speak very frankly at that ceremony.

Mr. Sandell protested that there was no need for a commotion; he only wanted Tom's grave marked so that in years to come, when the workers had got a fair bargain, there'd be something to show whom they had to thank for it.

The day of the dedication dawned clear and bright, a typically English April day. The rector, warned by his wife who was weatherwise, put on his hunting boots and wore a number of warm garments under his cassock. When the driving sleet came down he stood his ground without marked discomfort. Most of those who had come to watch and listen had understood from the rector's opening sentences that the rector's views were as sound as their own; they retreated to the shelter of the church. Mr. Sandell, bareheaded, stood as though in a dream, staring at the ornate stone, over which the sleet was sliding, blurring the words:

TO THE MEMORY OF THOMAS FULGER

WHO IN HIS DEVOTED ENDEAVOUR

TO ATTAIN

BETTER CONDITIONS

FOR

HIS FELLOW MEN

LAID DOWN HIS LIFE.

Even when the rector's sonorous phrases had come to an end Mr. Sandell stood there. He was seen to shiver as he at last walked to his carriage; and ten days later he was dead of inflammation of the lungs.

His heir was a nephew, who upon taking up his heritage, added the name of Sandell to his own of Booth, and, largely on that account, he was regarded with considerable suspicion for a time. But he, thank God, had no nonsense about him; he took after his grandfather, the old Nabob. He was entirely sound over matters like poachers, wages, and trespassers.

He became extremely popular. He married one of the Fennels of Ockley and slipped into place in the county like a hand into a glove. Once again the great hall at Merravay became the scene of gay gatherings. All was well.

The Poacher

WHEN I was seventeen I was sent to Merravay in disgrace. I had committed the heinous crime of falling in love with the wrong young man; then, forbidden to see or speak to him ever again, I had proceeded to fall—in conventional fashion—into a decline.

My papa, who was very angry with me, approved of Merravay as a place of exile because it was one hundred and fifty miles away from Archie; my mamma, in whom rage had given way to exasperated concern for my health, thought that the good country air and a change of scene would be beneficial. So a letter explaining the circumstances was sent to Uncle Alan, and back came an invitation rendered lukewarm by the accompanying apologies. He was afraid, he said, that I should be lonely in his womanless household; and he was afraid that I should find life at Merravay dull in this season; and he was afraid that if they were hoping for some young man in Suffolk to prove a counter-attraction they would be disappointed—there was a great dearth of young men.

The fact that winter was approaching was one reason for Mamma's desire to get me away; for in the garrison town where my papa was stationed at that time the winter was the gay, social season; and since I could not be left at home without arousing comment, or be taken out without the risk of seeing Archie, it would have been a very awkward situation indeed. And nobody cared, I least of all, how dull life at Merravay would be. I felt that every place where Archie was not, was hateful; and besides, was I not going to die very soon?

Of course I can look back on it now and laugh, and feel a little sorry for my parents, and put all the blame on *The Posy,* that apparently innocuous little magazine. Until I was fourteen and my mamma for reasons of economy dismissed my governess, I had nothing but contempt for *The Posy,* for at that time I was interested in everything under the sun except clothes and love stories; but once Miss Tibbenham had gone I seemed to be stranded in a mental desert, and *The Posy,* which Mamma took regularly because it had fashion pages, was the only oasis in that desert. It seemed harmless enough and was highly thought of by all parents. Its fashion pages told us what was being worn just then, and how to reconstruct an old garment to look like new; it had a "Household Management" page, mainly hints on how to be mean with food and strict with servants; it had a "Pretty" page telling us how to deal with freckles and such things; and it had a serial which invariably lasted just six months. Twice a year for three years we were regaled by a new version of the same story; there was always a girl, crossed in love, who fell into a decline and died. She lay, pale, "beautiful in death," with her long hair streaming, and covered with roses in each one of the six stories.

So, of course, when I was seventeen I fell in love, was crossed, and fell into a decline. I had mistimed things somewhat, for unless I lasted out until the summer, which seemed unlikely, there would be no roses for me.

However, I went to Merravay, as to death, and made no protest.

It was a place often mentioned in family circles, generally with an accompanying comment about Uncle Alan's luck and Grandmamma's unashamed favouritism for him. My grandmamma, whom I could just remember as a strict, intimidating old lady, had spent her girlhood at Merravay. Her brother, who never married, had made Uncle Alan, her third son, his heir, and everyone believed that Grandmamma had ordered him to do so. They said also that my oldest uncle, who inherited Gore Park, had greatly hoped that when Alan went to Merravay Grandmamma would go to end her days there; but she did not. She stayed at Gore Park and retained her martinet sway until the end.

A young male cousin of mine had once stayed with Uncle Alan and reported that the shooting in East Anglia was superb but that Merravay itself was a dull hole: and an elderly female cousin, who had for a short time kept house for Uncle Alan after the death of his wife many years ago, still spoke of Merravay as the most beautiful place in the world; but she was given to easy enthusiasms, as spinsters so often are.

II

Complicated arrangements for my safe escort across country were made, and I arrived safely one fine September afternoon and went straight to bed. Self-inflicted as my woes were—or as, looking back, I see them to be—they were real enough then and I was genuinely ill. Uncle Alan's first comment, when he met me at the coach stop, was that I looked more ill than he had expected and that he hadn't realised that I was "a doctor's case."

He was a tall, stout, handsome, self-indulgent and, up to a point, genial man; his wife, of whom he was reputed to have been very fond, and his six-year-old daughter had both died during an outbreak of cholera which had swept through the country like a plague. His son was, according to family parlance, "damn odd"; he was scholarly and spent most of his time abroad, brooding over the ruins of old cities, Jericho, Babylon, Thebes. Papa and my two uncles whose inheritance had been small professed to pity Uncle Alan for having so odd a son, just as they professed to pity Uncle Frederick, who had inherited Gore Park, for his gout. It consoled them for their envy.

Uncle Alan was obviously ill at ease with a strange young female, and an ailing one at that; but he had made meticulous arrangements for my comfort. I was installed in a vast, beautifully furnished bedroom and given a maid, Susan, to attend me. One of the symptoms of decline, as laid down by the stories in *The Posy*, was that the subject should eat nothing, or almost nothing; and I hadn't been in Merravay for twenty-four hours before I realised that Uncle Alan's food was far more difficult to resist than Mamma's "invalid diet" had been. Mamma's idea had been to offer gruel, steamed fish, and blancmange; Uncle Alan appeared to think that if one couldn't eat a roast partridge one might be tempted by oysters, a smoky-hot puffy omelette, breast of chicken in cream sauce, or peaches in brandy.

But it was not, I must contend, the food which brought me round. I was still miserable enough to be resistant to that. It was Uncle Alan's embarrassed, clumsy, almost boyish concern which brought me downstairs on the evening of my third day in his house. And after that I had something new to think about.

I went down, making what I thought of then as a valiant effort, thinking that if I were going to die, I might as well die on my feet. We dined together and afterwards sat in the drawing-room, an immense apartment, beautifully furnished. He asked me if I played chess—I didn't—or the piano, which I did a little. I played for quite a long time, sometimes with tears in my eyes because music is of all things the most conducive to emotion. At nine o'clock Clayton, the manservant, brought in the tea tray, ordered specially for me; and when the tea was drunk Uncle Alan said, "Maybe you should get back to bed now."

I rose obediently and bade him good night and he uttered some of his awkward, kindly intentioned words, so that I almost cried again. Then I walked to the door, opened it, closed it behind me, and was immediately seized by what was perhaps the first genuine emotion I had known since Miss Tibbenham had read me some of Macaulay's poems.

It was a highly unpleasant emotion too. Sheer stark terror. And utterly reasonless.

The hall at Merravay is very large, not like the hall of a house at all, more like a church or a barn. But everything that could be done to soften its austere appearance had been done. The stone floor was almost completely hidden by lovely rugs; the furniture was beautiful. On a bed of ash in the huge hearth three enormous logs were blazing, lending their light to supplement that of the two lamps and many candles. There was no reason at all why I should be frightened, should stand there by the closed door of the drawing-room, paralysed by terror, with cold sweat breaking out all over me. Nothing to see, save the big gracious apartment; nothing to hear.

To be frightened was an entirely new experience for me; I was far from being a nervous creature. My sheltered life had prevented me from ever being very greatly tested, but the common everyday accidents of life had never found me wanting. An unruly hired horse had run away with me and finally thrown me, but I rode again next day; and once when Miss Tibbenham and I had been left alone, with only a daily woman, she had gone out to the chemist's one evening, slipped on an icy path, broken her ankle, and been taken in by some kind people near by; I'd slept alone in the house for ten days then—which every girl of twelve wouldn't do! The daily woman had made quite a fuss about it, making me go round and lock every door and shutter the windows before she left at dusk, and predicting the most shocking possibilities.

Now here I was, utterly unable to cross a room because I was frightened. Of nothing!

I stood there, shivering and sweating and waiting for whatever it was to pass over. But it didn't. The terrible fear—fear of nothing—mounted and mounted. I wanted to scream, but though I opened my mouth and tried to, no sound emerged. How long I stood there I don't know; or how long I should have stood there. I knew that Uncle Alan was in the drawing-room, I had only to take a step backward and turn the handle and I should be with him. I longed to take that step, but I couldn't move.

It was he who moved. He was a pipe-smoker; but he was too polite—just then—to smoke a pipe in his own drawing-room in the presence of a female. After I had gone—and how avidly he must have been waiting for that moment—he came to fetch his pipe from the library, where, I discovered, he usually sat when alone. He opened the drawing-room door and walked straight into me.

The terror, whatever it was, receded at once with the opening of the door, with his first step into the hall.

"Good God!" he said, as his stout warm body hit my cold shaking one. "I thought you'd gone to bed."

My first impulse was to gasp out that I had been frightened. But something that was half common sense and half good manners rose up in me and took charge. Poor Uncle Alan . . . a sick girl thrust on him was surely bad enough . . . spare him the mad fancies.

I said in what struck my own ears as an amazingly ordinary voice,

"I just wanted your arm . . . on the stairs."

"Poor girl, poor girl," he said, "I didn't think of it. Very remiss of me. Well, here we go. Lean on me."

He scooped me across the hall and up the stairs and into the warm lighted room where Susan was busy with the bed-warmer and the hot milk of the bedtime ritual.

I was too near the edge of sleep to come back and start worrying when I realised that from the moment when I had said good night to Uncle Alan I hadn't thought about Archie at all. For the first time in months I slept without crying myself to sleep.

III

I have heard old ladies say tartly that a sharp smack of the face is the best remedy for hysterics; it may be that a sharp shock of fear is the best remedy for decline; certainly I woke next morning with something other than my love-sickness on my mind.

The memory of the terror was still vivid, and as soon as I was fully awake I began to dread a similar experience. Unless I stayed in my room—a thing I felt less inclined to do now than at any time since my arrival—sooner or later I should be obliged to face that walk across the hall alone.

Yet, now that I was capable of thinking about it, and of taking courage in the bright morning sunshine, the place drew me. I felt I must look at it, investigate, search for some explanation. I was up and dressed by eleven o'clock.

The hall faced south and had two enormous windows through which the sun spilled slantingly; on the bed of grey ash two logs burned; the place felt warm and looked gay. I stood at the bottom of the stairs and stared for a long time; nothing sinister met my eyes. With a feeling of daring mingled with scepticism, rather like that with which children play Old Man, I went and stood by the drawing-room door, exactly where I had stood last evening. Then I walked slowly round, looking at everything and touching some things and finding nothing frightening at all. I didn't know what I was looking for, but if I had come upon a suit of old armour, or a skull made into an inkstand, or a hideous foreign idol such as I had seen at Gore Park and other places, I should have regarded that as the focus of evil, probably made up some story about it, attributed my susceptibility to my low state of health, and been, if not comforted, satisfied. But there was nothing; and finally, having walked all round the hall, I sat down on the window seat farthest from the stairs, full in the sunshine.

I was on my feet again in a minute. Absurd and ridiculous and impossible as it seemed, even to me who was on the search for the absurd, the ridiculous, the impossible, to sit down there in the full sunshine was like lowering oneself into a well of icy water. It wasn't just the deathly cold; it was the awful feeling of misery and despair.

I had bounded away from the window seat and now stood two feet away from it in a place where the sun lay on the floor. Warm sun.

After a while I walked to the other window, touched the smooth, age-polished wood of the seat there; it was almost hot. I went back and timidly, but with dogged curiosity, felt about the other window. There was no detectable draught but there was the chill, a chill which not only affected one's flesh but seemed to pierce one's very soul, so that the light went out of the day and there was nothing but utter desolation.

I was familiar, of course, as who is not, with a ghost story or two, "The Flying Skull at Francoy Abbots"; "Maria Marten"; "The Nun at Borley"; but in all of them something was seen or heard. No story that I knew had ever mentioned cold as a sign of haunting; yet as I stood there I was perfectly certain, as—with very little else to go upon—I am sure to this day that the far window seat in the hall at Merravay is a haunted place.

IV

Apart from exercising craft and guile to ascertain that I never had to cross the hall alone after dark, there was nothing that I could do. I daren't mention the subject to anyone; I daren't ask a question. Now that I had been jerked back into life and found myself capable of taking an interest—however morbid—in something outside my own affairs I realised how idiotic my recent behaviour had been. Doubtless to other people it had seemed so all along, and if I now started to talk about a haunted window seat they would be justified in thinking me quite demented. And I must admit that now and again the thought that I might be going out of my mind did occur to me! Obviously I was not a very steady-minded girl. I could now go for increasingly long periods without thinking of Archie at all, and when I did think it was with hardly a pang—yet the past week I was prepared to die for love of him. Had I merely fallen into a fresh state of delusion; changed an imaginary grief for an imaginary terror?

All this went on below the surface. Poor Uncle Alan was delighted by the outward change in me; and attributed it to the air and the food. He began to take trouble over my social life. He had several friendly neighbours; the Fennels, to whom he was related by marriage, were within easy visiting distance, and the Whymarks, though their house was hidden by the trees, were practically next door.

I particularly remember a visit which Uncle Alan and I made to the Whymarks early in October. For one thing it was the first time that I had been on horseback since early summer when the storm broke over me and Archie. For another there was at New Holding a very old lady, Miss Phyllis Whymark, who said that she remembered my grandmother and that I was very like her to look at. That pleased me, because my grandmother had been accounted very handsome in her day. Miss Whymark opened her mouth and pointed to a gap in a set of otherwise remarkably sound if yellowed teeth.

"I do so well remember," she croaked, "the day after I lost this tooth I went over to Merravay and there was your grandmother, my dear, in worse case. She'd burnt her hair off curling it, and torn her face on a bush. We laughed and said that now we'd never get married. And believe it or not, as soon as we were alone she told me that she was going to be married before Christmas. I was so jealous I could have clawed her eyes out! Ah, but that's a long time ago."

We had lunch at New Holding, and after the meal some of the young ones led me off to see their puppies. As a consequence my boots were caked with mud, and being town-bred and used to my mamma's house-proud ways, I didn't enter Merravay on my return. I went to the back door, sent Susan up to fetch my house shoes, and called to a boy in the yard to come and pull off my boots as I leaned against the wall.

The main back door at Merravay had a porch, one side of which, at that hour of the afternoon, caught the westering sun. I moved into the sunny place, braced my back against the wall and lifted my foot, and stood there trapped within another circle of the same icy cold, the same deadly misery, as lay about that window seat. It struck with the same impact as a pailful of cold water, strongly thrown. I gasped and gave a violent shudder. The girl Susan, standing by with my shoes in her hand, said,

"You didn't ought to stand there, miss. Thass the one sunny place in the yard and thass allust cold."

I put my hand on the red, warm-looking wall.

"Yes," I said carefully. "It looks warm but it strikes cold."

The boy tested it and said shyly,

"That fare warm to me like, miss."

"You got so much muck on your hands, Sam, you couldn't feel nothing," said the girl sharply. "You didn't ought to handle miss's boots even with them hands."

He went very red about the ears and as soon as he had dragged off the second boot, went hastily away. Susan was still stooped over my shoe, and I said in as casual a way as I could manage,

"There's the same cold current of air, or whatever it is, in another place, I've noticed. I wonder if you have ever . . ."

"Ah," she said, with a wealth of meaning in her voice, "that winder in the great hall."

I could have kissed her.

"Set to clean it, I was soon arter I come here, miss. Never again. No, not if I was sacked for refusing."

"Because of the cold?" I asked lightly.

"No, miss. Because of the badness. It's there, too," she said, looking towards the side of the porch which we had instinctively left as soon as my shoe was on. "Thass all very well for folks to mock, but this was the Witch's house when all is said and done."

"What witch?"

"Oh, thass a long way back, miss; hundreds of years ago. But there's them that hev seen her tearing past like the wind on a great black horse; honest, steady folks, miss." Susan's face had gone very white and stiff-looking. I shivered, this time from a cold that came from within me. I told myself that this was all nonsense, ignorant country superstition; but after all I had used the word "haunted" in my thoughts about the cold place in the hall; and if one were credulous enough to think of a window seat as being haunted, why boggle at talk of witches? And why also, with a most practical view of the nonsensical, proceed to point out to oneself that the ghost of the witch, riding a ghostly horse, would surely confine its activities to the out-of-doors?

I had no sooner thought of that than Susan said,

"I allust reckon, myself, miss, that Lady Alice used to sit by that winder and make her spells and such; and there by the porch I reckon she used to keep her nasty beasts."

Thinking it over, I came to the conclusion that Susan's explanation was as likely a one as any I should ever think of. And though it left me far from satisfied, it was the only one that I was ever likely to get. I had to adjust myself to it. But, perhaps because I had never taken witches very seriously, the atmosphere which lay about that window seat had seemed to me much more dreadful than any one would have expected to be left there by a maker of spells.

Lady Alice Rowhedge, I discovered, however, had left a mark on more than the atmosphere of her old home. I never mentioned her—both from caution and delicacy—to my uncle; but a chance word, intentionally dropped here and there, brought me a good deal of information. In the country memories are long, and so are lives. One day, over at New Holding, I dragged the conversation round to the subject and learned to my astonishment that there before my eyes was someone who had known someone who had known someone who had actually seen the witch. This old Miss Phyllis Whymark had had the story from her father, who had it from his aunt, another Phyllis Whymark, who had it from her grandmother, another of the same name, who had been present at the trial when Lady Alice was found guilty and condemned to be burned. It had happened in the days of the Civil War . . . but it seemed suddenly as near as yesterday as I sat and listened to the old woman's croaking voice.

And yet even then I was not content. This something, this palpable evil, which haunted the hall at Merravay and haunted me, so that I was driven to the most shameful devices to avoid going into the place alone after dark, never *really* in my mind, seemed to be linked with the Witch; and when old Miss Whymark ended her story with the ritual words "All nonsense of course," and popped a strong peppermint in her mouth I said,

"That is really very interesting! Are there any other phantoms at Merravay?"

She laughed and choked on the peppermint. "You're just like your grandmother, my dear! Ah, she was a one for ghosts! She once told me something she daren't even tell to her brother George that she was so fond of. She once *saw* something."

"What? Where?"

"A boy, just about to be taken with a fit. In the hall. She said he looked so real that she went to help him and found that he wasn't there at all. Very upset she was at the time, I recall, and I had difficulty in persuading her that it was all imagination."

"Do you believe that?"

"Dear child, what else could it be? Bodies are shovelled into the ground and spirits go off to God or Satan according to their deserts."

"I wonder," I said. "I wonder whether a very strong feeling mightn't leave a mark, stay there and go on and on . . . still being felt . . . like weather. I mean . . . if you woke up just after a thunderstorm, you'd know . . . by the atmosphere . . ."

"Heaven save us," said the old lady. "If people's feelings lasted like that the world would be so full of them we should all go about with no room for our own. Isn't that so?"

And that so exactly, though unwittingly, described what had happened to me in the hall at Merravay that I could only say:

"Yes, of course, that is quite true."

V

Well, now I come to the really incredible part of this story.

My Uncle Alan's bugbear was poachers. Quite a large portion of the Merravay estate was taken up by a wood, called Layer Wood. Up to the time when he inherited the property there had been what was called a "right of way" through it; it was the shortest path between the villages of Nettleton and Clevely. Little girls went there for flowers, little boys for nuts, and all too often, according to my uncle, men went there and "knocked off one for the pot." For poor people the times I look back upon were hungry times.

Uncle Alan, who set great store by his pheasants, closed the path at both ends and put up notices. Then he engaged a number of keepers.

And finally he set mantraps. By his account—and I must confess that I never heard the other side—he was within his rights, but he met with a good deal of opposition, especially over the closing of the path, which was a right of way by ancient custom that even the rector recognised and supported. However, Uncle Alan had won in the end; Layer Wood was "preserved," and anyone who trespassed there risked falling into a mantrap, while anyone who poached risked the utmost rigour of the law.

Midway through November, on a very foggy evening, Uncle Alan and I were playing chess, the rudiments of which he had managed to teach me, when there came a noise and a stamping and the sound of men's voices approaching the front of the house from the garden.

Uncle Alan cocked his head and said, "That's Palmer, by God!" and jumped up and was across the hall and had the front door open before I could catch the table and steady the chessmen which his precipitate departure had disturbed. He had left the door open and I could look through it, across the hall, and see, as though in a theatre, the scene that was taking place there. Palmer, my uncle's head keeper, whom I knew by sight, and one of his underlings held between them a wretched-looking boy of about my own age. I couldn't see much of his face, for he sagged between the two men, but his very black shaggy hair and something about him made me think of gypsies. Presently, after a good deal of talking in the thick, slurred Suffolk voice, which at that distance I could not understand, Palmer pushed the boy forward. Then I was almost certain that he was a gypsy. He had one of those big-nosed, high-cheekboned faces which at the best of times have a hungry, haggard look, and for the boy this was not one of the best of times.

It may be weak in me, but I never like to see dogs with their ribs showing, or horses with thin drooping necks, or people who look miserable. This, I know, is no virtue in me; I just hate the feeling of discomfort that they rouse in me. Once when I was quite small I was so affected by the blue fingers of a flower-girl that I wanted to give her my little muff. Mamma explained that the girl didn't mind cold hands, she was used to them, and would instantly have sold the muff and bought gin with the money, and that I must try not to be a silly little girl.

I was no longer little and had—I thought—become rather less silly lately, but my heart went out to this boy who looked so cold, and hungry and thin and captured. The other three looked very well pleased with themselves, and presently Uncle Alan rang the bell and Clayton came, and went, and returned with two big mugs on a tray. I thought— Oh dear, nothing for *him*; and he looks as though he could do with it.

Then they all four went out by the door that led to the kitchen quarters and for a few minutes I had something else to think about. The door between the drawing-room and the hall was open and I was alone: was that the same as being alone in the hall? Would the terror come stalking in? The obvious thing to do was to get up and shut the door; but that I could not do. I could only sit there and wait.

I was pathetically pleased to see Uncle Alan when he came back, and he was pleased to have someone to whom he could tell his tale. At last the expense of the mantraps had been justified. In the fog last night that little devil of a poacher would have got away if he hadn't stepped on one of them and been nipped by the ankle.

"*Last* night?"

"So Bowyer says. Anyway he was there at six this morning, but Bowyer knew he was snug enough; and Palmer was having his day off, so he left him there till they made their night's rounds."

"In a trap. Is he much hurt?"

"Of course not. Just nipped."

"He must have been very cold . . . and hungry."

My nice kind uncle, who had pressed all those tasty dishes on me and taken such pleasure in my better appetite, laughed jovially and said,

"He'll be hungrier by the time he gets to Baildon gaol!"

"Is he on his way there now?"

"Dear child! In this fog? It's worse than last night's. He's in the old buttery. When I first became a J.P. they would insist on hauling offenders up here at unearthly hours—so much nearer, in many cases, than the lockup in Nettleton—I just had to find somewhere to put them. Now let me see . . . my dear, I'm quite sure you've been cheating. Never in a thousand years would I allow my queen to be. . . ."

"You got up so hurriedly that you knocked the table. I just gathered them up anyhow."

"Then there's no point in going on, is there? And I apologise, my dear, for the suggestion that you cheated. Your Aunt Mary," he broke off, horrified. I realised that never before had he mentioned his dead wife by name. In a flatter voice, but with obvious, calm resolution, he continued, "She would cheat me, but so prettily. Draw my attention to something, you know. And then move a piece. And I never let her know I knew!"

That was somehow so pathetic, so revealing, that the distaste I had been feeling for him because he had laughed about the poacher being hungry melted away, or was overlaid. As soon as I had dismantled the board and was ready he lent me, as was his habit now, his arm to the top of the stairs.

In my room Susan was busy with the warming pan; the hot milk which I was supposed to drink last thing at night stood in the hearth, and a plate of cheesecakes, a comestible which I had once been edged into admitting to liking, stood on my bed table.

Conversation, as Susan helped me to undress, turned inevitably upon the poacher. Susan, from whom, because she had been sensitive to the cold spots, I hoped for something else, was full of glee because he had been caught. She was Nettleton born and bred and all against gypsies.

"Thass been them all along, miss. Mr. George was real soft about them, I've heard my father say again and again. Said they was colourful! Thass on their account Layer was closed and set with traps. But for them and their thieving ways honest folks could still go there for primroses. They come, they take what they fancy, and off they go, leaving us to bear the blame. Now they've got one. And I'm glad!"

She said much the same thing in several different ways; then she said good night and left me.

For what I did next I take no credit for kindness, but for boldness . . . yes. It was not kind of me to wish to feed the boy; it was simple self-defence. I couldn't lay my head on the pillow and sleep, knowing that he was hungry; the jug of milk, the dish of cheesecakes, kept yelping at me reproachfully. But it was—considering the circumstances—very brave of me to step outside my bedroom door. Brave because, from the first night of the terror, my own room had possessed a compensating quality of sanctuary. All terrors bring their own cures. If you are frightened of the dark the first dawn glimmer can scatter them; if you fear spiders the mere removal of one can bring peace . . . and from that, so small a thing, up and up to the very fear of death with its mitigation through the hope of life everlasting, every dread is balanced in the human mind by the compensating factor of dread removed. To me, once night had fallen, there was the terror in the hall . . . and, had I ever been called upon to face it, the similar terror of the back porch. I could take temporary refuge in the drawing-room, the dining room, or the library; my bedroom was my absolute sanctuary. To leave it once I had gained it called for an effort more violent and more sustained than any I had ever made. To any rational person my dilemma must seem incomprehensible; but to me it was real and painful; either I must get into my bed and lie all night worrying about the hungry young poacher in the old buttery, or I must open the door and go down—not through the hall, for I could take the backstairs—but through the open dark, where the terror, apparently confined to one place, might possibly be at large.

Oddly enough what the poacher might do to me never once entered my mind.

I had a little blue silk bag with a pattern worked on it in beads. I set the jug of milk in the centre of it and wedged the cheesecakes all round. I could hang that on my arm, carry a candle in the same hand, and still have one free for opening doors.

The first one I opened timidly. I was out on the gallery which ran along above the hall, which was the haunted place; and before I took a step out I waited. If I felt the cold, if I sensed the terror, back I meant to bolt like a rabbit. But there was nothing. I took the few necessary steps along the gallery and then turned sharply to the right, into the passage that led to the top of the backstairs. Halfway along it was the room which one of the Whymarks, who knew Merravay well, had said was the schoolroom when their family lived there; and at its far end was a ladder which led to the space under the rafters. Compared with the front part of the house this was all ugly and grim and outwardly far more frightening . . . but I felt no fear there. It's all right, I thought to myself. Truly if, just in the passage, I had been joined by two or three friendly and quite unfrightened people I could not have felt more reassured. The knowledge that the terror was limited, that so long as I did not go to meet it in the hall it could not come to me, did a great deal to restore me to my natural confidence.

Except for the setting in of a great iron stove at one of its open hearths, the kitchen at Merravay has been unaltered for generations. I found what they called the old buttery by sheer accident, recognising its new purpose from the heavy padlock on the door and the opening in its upper panel. The aperture was no bigger than an ordinary book and was divided into halves by an iron bar. Having found what I had set out to find, I hesitated. The boy might be sleeping the sleep of exhaustion, and if so it would be small kindness to wake him back to his woes. I stood and listened, and I heard the straw rustle as he moved. Stepping up to the door, I held my candle high so that he could see me, though I could not see him, and I said,

"It's all right. I've brought you something to eat."

For a moment there was no answer; then the straw rustled more noisily and there was a dragging, shuffling sound; and into the faint radiance of the candlelight, just behind the bar his face emerged. A hoarse, choking voice said,

" 'Sthat true? You ain't making game of me?"

"Oh no." I set the candle down and began to fumble in my little bag. I handed him a cheesecake. I expected him to snatch it and start eating, but he held it in his hand, looking at it as though he doubted whether it were really food. Then he said,

"God bless yer! But if yer could . . . miss, I'm perishing for a drink of water . . ."

"I have some milk. . . ." But the milk was in the jug and the aperture was too small to allow of its passing. The boy had his face close to the bar now, and I could see the avidity in his eyes, the cracked dryness of his mouth. "Just a minute," I said, "I'll have to get a little mug." I hurried back to the kitchen and snatched a pewter pipkin from a hook. I filled it and passed it in carefully. The boy drank, passed it back to me to be refilled, and emptied it again. And again, until the last drop had gone.

"God bless yer," he said again, more clearly. "You saved me life, I reckon." He ate a cheesecake then, cramming it into his mouth so fiercely that the good crisp pastry broke and he lost some crumbs.

"Take your time," I said. "There are three more." I handed them in one by one. He licked the last crumb from the palm of his hand and asked,

"What made yer do it?"

"I thought you looked hungry."

"For a minnit I thought you wus a angel." I saw his face change. Its open pathos gave way to craftiness.

"Miss, lemme out," he said, and as he spoke he put his face to the opening and stared at me with such urgency, such pleading, and such wiliness that I stepped back a pace.

"I couldn't. Even if I wanted to. You're padlocked in."

"I know that. But this here winder is on'y boarded over. I on'y want a bit of a tool. Knife'd do. They took me knife. Hand us in a knife, miss."

I just stood and stared at him, and, encouraged by my silence, he began to talk so quickly and so brokenly that I only caught a phrase here and there. He spoke about being transported for seven years at least, being loaded with irons, starved, and beaten; he said he hadn't touched a pheasant, that there was enough gypsy in him to prevent his having a fair trial.

One had, of course, heard stories about convict ships and settlements which, even if exaggerated. . . . And he was young, and so thin.

Also, just at that moment I was feeling a strong dislike for my kind uncle, by whose orders a boy who had lain for a night and a day in a trap had been locked up without being given so much as a cup of cold water. And, not being country-bred, I was insufficiently convinced of the sacredness of pheasants.

At that moment my candle flickered; looking at it, I realised that very shortly I should be in the dark. The effort to think clearly and quickly, the excitement of making a sudden and unconventional decision, fluttered my heart and dried my throat. I turned without speaking and hurried to the kitchen, where I first found a new candle and then looked round for a tool. I looked with a certain wistfulness at a heavy, sharp-edged wedge rather like a big chisel, which was used for jointing carcasses; but I was cautious. If the boy failed to get out . . . So I chose an anonymous-looking knife with a short stout blade.

When I got back to the door the boy had retreated to his straw and was crying in harsh gasping sobs which stopped when he saw the light. He came to the opening with tears making little runnels of cleanliness on his dirty face.

"If you don't succeed in getting out you must account for the knife," I said, and handed it in. He put his mouth to my fingers and slobbered at them like an affectionate dog. "I hope you do get out and then keep out of trouble," I said. I was backing away while he blessed and thanked me, and then he said with another abrupt change of manner, "Wait, lady. Look I got sumpin for yer." He fumbled about in his clothes. "They dint find this when they went over me. Got it in me mouth, see! Hold yer hand, miss. I mean it. Buy yerself sumpin pretty. Thass all right, I never stole it. I come by it honest, give yer me word."

His thin dirty hand had come up to the lower edge of the opening, and between its finger and thumb was what looked like a golden guinea.

I gasped. Not with the surprise which the boy evidently expected—for he said slyly, "There now! Go on, take it. S'real!"—but with some other feeling for which I have no name. To say that I knew makes at once too great and too small a claim, but there is no other word. I *knew*, instantly and surely, that the gold coin between the gypsy's finger and thumb was connected in some way with the hatred and misery and despair which lay over the cold spot in Merravay hall and by the back porch.

"Where . . . did . . . you . . . get . . . that?" I asked.

"Up in the wood," he said without a second's hesitation. "Time I was in the trap, scratching about. Under a lotta leaves that was."

"*Is* it a guinea?"

"Course it is. Here, see for yerself." He stretched his hand past the bar. "I ain't never handled one afore, but I know a guinea when I see one. Take it. It's yours."

"I don't want it . . . I mean . . . thank you very much for wanting to give it to me. I couldn't take it. I would just like to know . . ."

"Look at it; see for yerself. All right then, hold the candle and I'll tell you. This side there's a old woman on a stool, and some words writ. This side there's a flower, rose outa the hedge. That got the right edge, too, ridgy. Thass a guinea all right. And I come by it honest, like I told yer. And I'd like you to have it . . . Whass the matter? D'you hear sumpin?"

The more he thrust the coin towards me the worse I felt, for the little shining coin seemed to hold the very essence of whatever it was that affected me with such terror. I knew, just as people know the first onset of a familiar pain, that unless I went quickly I should be too frightened to move.

"Good-bye," I gasped out. "Good luck."

"Just a minnit, lady," he said. "I wanta get on but I gotta say this first. I ain't Gyptian proper, I don't know the words, but I give yer the blessing. May yer marry a rich man that'll be good to yer and have plenty of strong healthy children and live to be old with yer own teeth and when yer . . ." But I had started to walk away, to scuttle like a scared rabbit making for its burrow.

In the morning when it was found that the boy had gone there was a considerable fuss, which would doubtless have lasted longer and caused me more secret embarrassment had not my cousin Rupert arrived home suddenly. At first I was a little frightened of him; he had an odd, abrupt manner and a way of saying things which would suddenly make you see them in a new way. He had no trace of Uncle Alan's geniality of manner, but now and then when they argued about things like wages, corn laws and pheasant preserves he would say, in his offhand, dry way, a word or two which led me to think that he might be, at heart, the kinder person of the two. We didn't get to know one another very well until he had been home for about a fortnight. Then there came an evening when Uncle Alan was out and we were alone together. It drew on towards bedtime and I began making my wretched little plans. When my uncle was at home the matter of going upstairs presented no problem. Once he had got the idea of helping me upstairs at night it had become a habit with him, and though I was now quite able-bodied he helped me and would have gone on doing so, I suspect, if I had lived with him for twenty years.

Suddenly Rupert looked up from his book and said,

"What is it that you're so scared of?"

Questions rapped out like that often receive a truthful answer, and this one did.

"There's something in the hall that I don't *like* by day and just can't face at night."

"Show me," he said, and stood up and reached out his hand to me.

"It's nothing you can see. It's just a feeling . . . it's . . ."

"A miasma?"

"I don't know." I didn't like to say that I didn't know what the word meant.

"Show me where."

I went out into the hall with him and pointed.

"Do you feel it now?"

"Oh no. Only when I am alone. And it isn't just my fancy . . . one of the maids . . ."

"Now who started this? You or the maid? You see, I've often noticed about maids; they come from crowded little hovels and the mere *space* frightens them."

"Oh, I felt it before I ever spoke to her about it."

"It's strange," he said, musingly, and—I was glad to see—quite seriously, "how eclectic these things are. Hit and miss. I only once knew a case when everybody was affected. We were digging just south of El Khasan and a workman turned up a bit of a bowl—he was about to pick it up, but didn't; instead he turned and ran, and so did we all, fifteen of us, including a stout old German professor who hadn't run for thirty years. Sheer, reasonless terror. Now, tell me more about this."

I told him from the beginning; and at the end I said, "And there was the coin too . . ."

"What coin?"

"I can't tell you. It is a secret."

"Describe the coin." I did so as well as I could. "That would be Elizabethan or Marian . . . about the same period as the house, you know."

"I wish I could tell you about the coin. All about it. You could go and look. There might be something that would explain . . ."

"Then why not tell me?"

"I'm not sure about . . . well, at least I know that you aren't quite as strict and fierce as Uncle Alan is about it . . . but I don't quite know how you feel about pheasants."

"I like to eat them roasted." He smiled at me, suddenly young and friendly. "Tell you a secret, I always come back to Merravay when my appetite gets the upper hand. Like a bird migrating. I sit down one day, wherever I am, to the usual makeshift meal and think—They're roasting pheasants at Merravay! And home I come. There now, your coin-secret could hardly be more self-revealing and shameful than *that*. Tell me. Did you find it in a pheasant's gizzard?"

When he smiled like that I felt that I could tell him anything. I said, "Promise not to tell Uncle Alan. He has been so very kind to me. And he'd be so upset and angry."

"So he would if you went and told him that I came home for the sake of the food! All right, I promise."

So I told him. And he laughed and said, "You did absolutely right. And this is all very interesting. I'll ask Palmer in the morning where that trap lay, and I'll go and pry about. Like to come with me?"

"I would! I longed to go by myself, but I didn't dare. I did find out exactly where the trap was. You needn't ask Palmer. But I might get scared."

"With me to hold your hand—or to run with you as the case might be?"

"No," I said, after I had thought for a little. "I think that, with you, it would be all right."

And it was. The trap was still in the same place and Rupert looked at it and said, "Most likely he'd scratch about, as he called it, in this direction, trying to pull himself up by these hazel twigs. And it slopes a little. One should always allow for the force of gravity. We'll try in this direction first."

The trap had been set with cruel cunning on the old path, so that anybody who blindly persisted in using the right of way would fall into it. On the inner side of the path there was a little clump of hazels standing in the piled-up drift of the leaves of many autumns.

As soon as I arrived at this spot I began to wish that I had not come. It was a crisp, bright morning, and I had company, but I felt uneasy, depressed in my spirits, and afflicted with a curious physical feeling, as though my clothes or my skin did not fit. I looked at the trap and thought of the boy lying there all night and all day, and that was a bad thought too; but below and beyond that there was more. At the same time my morbid curiosity was lively; I knew that we were on the right track; this place, the back porch, and the hall at Merravay had some dark connection.

Rupert pushed in amongst the hazels. I started to follow and then drew back.

"I think I shall stay here," I said.

"Wise," he said, "these leaves are soaking wet."

I looked up and down the path. It had been closed for only a few years and was still used by the keepers, but it was rapidly being grown over; the blackberry brambles particularly had thrust out aggressively so that in places they almost met. I thought again what a pity it was about the pheasants. This must have been a very pretty, pleasant path between two villages. I pictured people on it, very trite pictures: little girls in spring, gathering primroses, little boys in autumn, gathering nuts, and in the long warm summer evenings, young lovers wandering with their arms about one another.

Presently I heard Rupert say, "Ah."

"Have you found something?"

"I think so. Oh yes!"

"To do with it?"

"I should say so. Stay where you are."

"What is it?" I called sharply, because now I was all curiosity.

"I'm coming," he called back, and in a moment he pushed through the bushes. He looked a little queer, half-excited and half-concerned. He had pushed back his sleeves, and his hands to the wrists were covered with soil and bits of crushed wet leaf. Holding the left one out stiffly so that he did not touch me with it, he laid his left arm over and round my shoulders while the other hand held out for my inspection what looked like a little heap of dirt with several gold coins bedded in it.

"They look like . . ." I pried one loose and rubbed it on my handkerchief. "It is the very same!" I said. What the gypsy boy had called an old woman on a stool was a queen on a throne, and his hedge rose was the Tudor emblem, exactly like the ones that were the motive of so much of the carving at Merravay.

"You were right. Elizabethan, Rupert, it says so . . ." So far curiosity and what one might call the heat of the chase had sustained me, but now I knew that I felt towards this coin as I had done towards the one in the gypsy boy's hand. "It feels the same, too," I said, and dropped it back into Rupert's palm. "Oh, was that all you found? Nothing to tell us any more, nothing to explain? That place in the hall, and by the porch, and now here . . . all connected. And all awful." The arm about my shoulders tightened.

"Darling," said Rupert, "to find so much in so short a time proves my extraordinary prospecting ability, don't you think?"

"I know. Of course. But we're no farther. I wanted something that would explain, that I could settle down with and know that it made me feel this way because of. . . . You know I went all round Merravay for days, looking for a nasty idol, or one of those horrible inkstands made out of a skull . . ."

Rupert gave me an odd swift look and I thought—Yes, now you'll think I'm morbid and hysterical.

"We'll come back when it isn't so damned wet in there. And with a spade. I'm not used to doing my own digging, you know."

"Of course not," I said penitently. I stood looking at the clump of hazels which held—I felt—the clue to the mystery.

"Let's go back," said Rupert, dropping his arm and offering me the crook of it. "I do want to wash!"

On the way back I thrust away all thought of what he had not found and we talked animatedly about what he had. He said that the coins must have belonged to a rich person, or to a very miserly one who saved small amounts and then converted them into a few pieces, for coins of such value were rare in Elizabeth's day, being worth thirty shillings apiece then, which was five or six pounds by our reckoning. He said too that he believed the little lump of stuff in which the coins were embedded were the rotted and altered remains of a leather bag and that the one piece of gold which the gypsy had found had probably been pushed out by the growth of a root, or picked up and dropped by a magpie. And that was all very interesting to me; I liked to hear Rupert talk.

VI

We did not make our second visit to Layer Wood; the weather turned cold, with a bitter wind from the east and sharp sleet storms. My papa, who within his sphere was a man of influence, succeeded in getting Archie posted to the West Indies; my mamma suffered a recurrence of migraine. So they decided that I had imposed upon Uncle Alan's hospitality for long enough, and wrote to suggest that I should go home for Christmas. This suggestion raised very mixed feelings in me. Apart from the terror I'd been happier at Merravay than in any place where I had ever been, especially since Rupert's return; the prospect of returning to take my place as a dutiful daughter in the strictly regulated treadmill of social life in a garrison town had very little appeal for me. I told myself, pretty sternly, that I had fallen victim to the comfort, the indulgences, that I had received at Merravay. And every evening, when either Uncle Alan or Rupert walked with me across the hall and up the stairs, I told myself with another kind of sternness that it would be pleasant to return to a place where I *could* go upstairs alone.

I was running all these thoughts through my mind one evening, three days before I was due to go home, when once again Rupert and I were alone, this time in the library. Because of my imminent departure the last week had been a round of gaiety with dinner parties at home, at Ockley, New Holding, and Muchanger. Rupert and I—who had reached a point where we could sit together by the fire and each read a book and look up now and then and make, or answer, a remark, and read again—had of late had no chance to spend such an evening together.

On this evening, though I was holding a book I was not reading; I was thinking my thoughts. I wished that he would put aside his book and look up and talk to me on this—this which might well be the last time we ever . . . Something swelled in my throat at the thought and tears came pushing up under my lids. I stared hard at my book until I had controlled myself.

Just then Rupert closed his book with a snap.

"Charlotte," he said, "I want to ask you something and I don't want to be clumsy. You see, from something Father said I gathered that . . ." He halted, choosing his words, and I said boldly:

"Oh, that is all ended. It wasn't *real*. It sounds a strange thing to say, but that . . . whatever it is out there"—I nodded towards the hall—"put it out of my head completely!"

"How?"

I heard myself saying, in carefully chosen, scrupulously measured words, exactly how I had known that my lovesickness was a matter of imagination. I ended with the words:

"I'm probably giving you the impression that I am utterly shallow-minded, but that I can't help. Honesty compels me to admit that your Merravay ghost, whatever it is, drove Archie clean out of my mind."

"I've been wondering," Rupert said, "whether it would make any difference if that end of the hall were walled off. You see, Charlotte, I love you. . . ." His face, the lamplight began to whirl before my eyes in a crazy fashion; his voice, saying things about being diffident in case I was still in love with Archie, about being willing to live elsewhere if I found Merravay frightening, seemed to come from a long way off. The voice, the words sounded as cool and reasonable and dispassionate as I knew Rupert to be at heart; but somehow, there we were, midway between the two chairs, locked in an embrace which wasn't cool or dispassionate at all.

"I've been in love with you, Rupert, ever since the evening when I knew I could tell you *anything*," I said. Then I thought about the haunted place and how it had shown me the truth about myself and Archie. Even at this moment when my cup of happiness was full to overbrimming, that mattered somehow. I dragged myself out of Rupert's arms.

"Wait here," I said.

I went out of the library. I closed the door behind me. The hall was lighted by a single lamp; the "bad place" lay in the gloom. I walked towards it. There was the terror; there was the despair; there was the deathly cold. I walked into it and I knew the day must come when Rupert and I must grow old, and impotent, and then die. I stood there knowing in one concentrated moment all the despair which poor human mortality brought face to face with eternity can know . . . but I wasn't frightened any more. I thought: That is how it is, how it always has been and always will be. All we can do is to snatch at this moment, the time which is ours, and make the best of it.

I went back to Rupert and said:

"It is all right. Whatever was there is gone. I'm not frightened any more."

Then he told me that on the morning when he found the coins he had also found a skeleton. He, of course, was used to ancient bones and was not much shaken, but he had feared the effect of his find on me and hurried me away. His work had led to an understanding of the importance of burial rites, and therefore he had arranged that these bones should be given Christian burial. Dear Rupert, he believes that that may have brought rest to the uneasy spirit.

He says the bones lay in peaceful, sleeping fashion with one hand under the skull and the other laid upon something which, though rotted past recognition, might have been a book; and I know that he believes that someone, when this house was young, used to sit in that window seat and read and one day went into Layer Wood to read, fell asleep, and never woke. That person set great store by Christian burial and could not rest without it.

I think otherwise. It wasn't a bookworm, it wasn't a witch who made that emotional mark on Merravay; it was a lover. I know because my false love couldn't face whatever there was there; my true love could. And those coins were somehow deeply concerned. But it is all a mystery which I accept, just as I accept the fact that I have never lost a tooth and have been blessed with six handsome, healthy children, all boys. . . .

Interlude

Strangers to Nettleton still stop to stare at and remark upon a number of cottages which, though too old and individual to be Council houses, bear evidence of having been planned and built with more taste and care than is common, and of having been erected, all twenty-four of them, at the same time.

Though their style is ornate and old-fashioned they are pretty enough and they have worn well. They stand, two by two, each with its strip of garden in front and a larger patch to the rear; each with its own washhouse, shed, and outdoor convenience; and with two wells to serve the two dozen.

In the centre of each frontage is a lozenge-shaped piece of stone bearing the letters RBS and the date 1875. That was the year when the railway went through to Bywater and Mr. Rupert Booth-Sandell sold some land profitably.

In the same year he invested money in the Great Eastern Railway Company and that was a profitable investment. In 1880 he built what is known as the Institute—used as a village hall to this day. During the following year the Tudor almshouses at Baildon, reared and endowed by the terms of the will of one Thomasin Griggs, widow, were found to be finally past repair. Mr. Booth-Sandell built new ones, single-storied versions of his Nettleton cottages because he felt that old people should be spared the effort of climbing stairs. The lozenge on the almshouses displays the initials of Mrs. Booth-Sandell.

Those were the settled, spacious days, and Rupert and Charlotte Booth-Sandell were typical of their class and generation. Until quite recently it was possible to find ancient men and women who would speak nostalgically of the "old master and mistress," of their generosity, their dignity, their family of lively handsome boys, the glory of Merravay during their régime, the way the carriage lights shone on the trees of the avenue when the Booth-Sandells gave a dinner party, the ox-roasting to which the whole village was invited when Mr. Booth, the heir, came of age. Ah, they were the days, and gone forever.

And if the wages of the farm labourers were never more than twelve shillings a week, and sometimes as little as ten, nobody was ever stood off in the winter; and the moment there was trouble in the house there was the old mistress on the doorstep, ready with an offer of help. And food was cheap, and the new houses, let for one and sixpence a week, had enough garden to grow vegetables for any family, however large.

In 1890, in the glowing mellow sunset of the century, Mr. Booth Booth-Sandell succeeded his father. Gradually the twilight descended.

Things were never the same at Merravay. For one thing Mr. Booth, for all he was so handsome, never married. Too gay and frisky in his young days, and later on too crusty. But although he was never the man his father was, and of course not nearly so rich, he was popular enough with the village people, for he could be unthinkingly generous, and he was always one for a joke.

The Heiress

O F all the self-imposed burdens under which mankind struggles, family loyalty is, I think, one of the heaviest. I notice that modern people tend to be very casual about their obligations in this respect, but those of us who are now called, somewhat scornfully, "the Victorians," were so schooled to a sense of duty towards those of our own blood that we must either perform it or suffer pangs of conscience. So I must sit down and pen the invitation which, if it is accepted, will spoil what remains of my life. I have no choice.

The exasperating part of it all is that I never liked Merravay; I never liked my Uncle Booth; I never liked my cousin Maude.

Maude and I and another cousin, a boy who died in his early teens, were the only children in our generation; of my grandmother's six sons one, the eldest, my Uncle Booth, remained unmarried, and two others were childless. Maude and I were almost of an age, she was about six months older than I, and in those far-away days visits were often arranged and long journeys undertaken because our parents thought it would be nice for us to meet. I remember her as a thin, leggy child with a mane of very curly pale auburn hair and the freckled skin which often goes with it. She had a high-bridged, arrogant nose and curiously narrow, very bright blue eyes. Her parents, who adored her, had spoiled her shamelessly and she had no fear of anything or anybody. I was rather a timid child myself, and most of our meetings seemed to end in some kind of trouble which she instigated, mocked me into, and then sailed out of, unrebuked, while I was taken aside and punished. I thought this decidedly unfair; my parents seemed to believe that they were omniscient; surely they should have seen how things were, I used to think.

One of the places where we used to meet was the family house in Suffolk, then the property of my Uncle Booth. It lay in a very remote place amongst fields and woods but it could hardly be called inaccessible, for the railway ran to within two miles of it. The shooting there was reckoned to be above average, and every year my father and Maude's and my other uncles endeavoured to get to Merravay at some time during the autumn and to arrange their visits to overlap as far as possible. So far as one could judge, this desire to get together at least once a year was not due to any deep-rooted affection; they quarrelled, they criticised one another, they took sides, but they all seemed to enjoy the reunion, and when increasing age, infirmity, and finally death broke up the family circle it was easy to look back and be rather sentimental about it all.

Merravay was a Tudor house and considered very beautiful; remarkable, they said, for having stood for three hundred years without being added to or altered. Of that fact the kitchen quarters bore witness. Uncle Booth had made one innovation; he had installed a bath. Apart from that the house remained, even to the rugs on the floor, exactly as Uncle Booth's great-great-grandfather had had it when he came from India and settled down at Merravay. The garden was delightful, but I always thought that the place as a whole was gloomy and when—as time went on—it became my duty to make occasional visits there alone, doing my duty to Uncle Booth, I always went reluctantly and left with joy.

I was never at ease, for one thing, with my uncle. He was odd and arbitrary and even in his more genial moments inclined to poke fun at one, to make outrageous statements and watch for one's reaction. His father, my grandfather, was still remembered in the neighbourhood as a liberal-minded, open-handed man. Cottages which in their day were models, and almshouses and public buildings all bear his stamp, RBS, and the date. There are boys now at Baildon school and at the universities profiting from the scholarships he founded. Uncle Booth had been known to say that his father had been extravagant in *his* way and thus curtailed extravagance in his heir.

My father died suddenly, and at a comparatively early age, when I was sixteen. We were left badly off, and I think Mother would gladly have gone to live at Merravay; but she was not asked to do so, and if she made any overtures they were disregarded. She was very anxious, however, that I should ingratiate myself with Uncle Booth. The death of my boy cousin had removed the obvious heir. Mother always knew when Maude had been to Merravay and would tell me, rather reproachfully; and I would say, "But Maude *likes* Merravay." Maude had told me so herself, times without number. She always said it was the most beautiful house in the world. I think she was sincere, too. Often when we'd stayed there together I'd seen her, before breakfast, go running to the end of the garden, scramble up onto the wall between the urns, and sit there swinging her long thin legs and just staring, and staring, as though she were in a trance. It would be no hardship for her to spend part of her holidays there, for though she got on with Uncle Booth little better than

I did, she wasn't afraid of or embarrassed by him and always had an answer.

Her parents were wealthier than mine and more worldly. At sixteen she was sent to a Paris finishing school, and a year and a half later she was presented and launched upon a London season. Everybody said that she was a raving beauty. Certainly she had got rid of her freckles and gained control of her limbs; and with that blaze of hair and those ice-blue eyes she could not help but be noticeable; but I personally thought that she was still too thin, and too tall, and too high-nosed to be beautiful.

"She'll make a wonderful match, I expect," said my mother with a little sigh.

Actually I was married first, and if getting a man as near perfection as a human being can be counts for anything, mine was a wonderful match, though it cost my poor mother many a sigh, not small ones either. I married the local doctor. That was considered little short of disgraceful, especially as he had no private money, no connections, and was only a junior partner. But I knew my mind, and for once I dug in my heels and stood up for what I wanted. Uncle Booth could not come to the wedding—he had just suffered his first slight stroke. He sent me a cheque for twenty pounds and a grumbling letter because I had not taken Ian to be looked over.

"I'm afraid you've done for yourself there," said my mother.

She said it again when, almost a year later, Maude was married and from Merravay! She said she had always hoped to be married from that house. And of course the enormous hall, which takes up such a disproportionate part of the ground floor in that house, lent itself to such an occasion. I did not go to the wedding, it was only a few weeks before I had my baby; but I heard vivid accounts of how wonderful Maude looked coming down the great staircase in her wedding dress and veil. Uncle Booth's present to her was an enormous ruby on a thin gold chain to wear as a pendant; and we were told that some old lady, a remote relative, one of the Gore Park Booths who was at the wedding, said that it was an heirloom which should never have been in our part of the family at all.

My son, my dear Angus, was born while Maude was on her honeymoon in Venice. I was perfectly content. I was very busy, too busy to bother much about anything outside my own household. In the next five years I went to Merravay only once, just for a day, to take to Uncle Booth a few things of my father's which my mother, on her deathbed, said she wished him to have. Poor mother, she was hopeful to the last; she tried to make me promise to take Angus, too; but I travelled third-class and it was hot weather; I left Angus at home in his cool clean nursery. The stroke had affected Uncle Booth's speech and made him even more difficult to talk to; otherwise he was unchanged. So was Merravay.

When Angus was five and we were in process of changing his nurse for a governess, something happened to me. To my mind. For one thing I realised that though Maude had now been married five years she had had no child; and I also realised that Ian would never make money. He was too kind, and too careless. I wanted nothing for myself . . . but for Angus, I suddenly knew, I wanted everything. We could, we would, afford a governess . . . but away ahead in the years I could see many other needful, desirable, or merely pleasant things which would be, unless circumstances changed, unattainable. And there was Uncle Booth, a man of property; and here was Angus, as handsome, well-set-up, delightful little boy as there was on the face of the earth. All suddenly I realised how *my* mother had felt about Merravay and why she had cried when she compared the twenty-pound cheque with the great ruby.

I wrote to Uncle Booth suggesting that Angus, whom he had not yet seen, and I should spend a few days at Merravay. The letter which came back was kindly enough and when we arrived our welcome left nothing to be desired. It was obvious that Uncle Booth had taken pains to ensure our comfort—even to the extent of having two steps made so that Angus could get into the high bath. But almost immediately he started making the gibing remarks which I always resented, even when they were aimed at me alone.

Angus had the grave, speculative stare which all children of that age adopt towards strangers. Uncle Booth stared back at him and then said, "Boo!" so sharply that the child jumped and backed away. I had told *him* how he was to behave, and he was trying to obey orders; he wasn't prepared for foolery on the part of a poor sick old man. To me Uncle Booth said, "Take him away, Catherine. He's a nice little boy, I'm sure, but he's got such a bedside manner I expect him, every minute, to ask have the bowels worked today."

I thought that was unforgivable; a backhanded slap at Ian, an insult to Angus. And it was rude to mention bowels thus gratuitously to me!

That was not a successful visit. On the last day of it Uncle Booth received a letter from Maude. He laughed over it.

"What a gel that is! Listen to this. 'Edward is going to divorce me. May the black sheep come and graze at Merravay before being sheared in public?' Joking about it. That damn fool of a husband of hers doesn't know what he's loosing. There aren't many with Maude's spirit. Now you can make yourself handy, Catherine. You can write for me." He sat down and dictated the letter straightway. A hateful letter. I know it began,

"My dear Maude,
I was shocked and horrified by your news. So far as I know we have

never had a divorce in the family. God knows what things are coming to when a decently bred, decently reared young woman like you can be accused, openly, of adultery . . ."

It went on like that, bitter, vituperative. And it ended by saying, "Of course you may come and hide your head at Merravay; blood is thicker than water they say; besides the thing might as well end where it began. So come and wear your penitent's sackcloth where you wore your bridal satin."

Was it all meant as a joke? He'd told me, often enough, that I had no sense of humour. I could understand and laugh at Ian's jokes; that was one bond between us, we laughed at the same things. For the life of me I couldn't see anything funny in this. In Maude's place I wouldn't have accepted such an invitation even if refusing it had meant that I had to go into cheap lodgings in London.

I went home next day. Maude went to Merravay and stayed there for several months. It was a particularly nasty divorce. Her husband was as vindictive as he had been doting; and a young, titled girl who had had what was called an understanding with the co-respondent committed suicide in a fit of disgust, so there was a great deal of publicity. Everybody expected that in the end her fellow sinner would feel compelled to marry her. Whether he ever offered to or not the family system of communication—what Ian always called "the jungle drums"—never informed me; they did tell me that Maude said the young man was a handsome ass and that his asininity was responsible for the whole catastrophe and she did not intend to marry a fool.

She had no need to. She married Sir Theodore Audley; thus gaining at one stroke another rich, doting husband, a title, a great Palladian mansion in Wiltshire, an imposing house in St. James' Square and a shooting lodge in Scotland. She also gained, and filled as though born to it, a place in that half-raffish, half-royal circle which was such a feature of Edwardian society. She remained childless.

Early in the summer of 1912 the jungle drums informed me that Uncle Booth considered himself neglected by me and mine; and that he was in failing health. In mid-July I received a letter, a formal invitation to Merravay for a month. One sentence in it roused my resentment. "Bring your husband," it said, "I have reached the state where a private physician seems to be called for." That didn't seem to me to be the right way to ask a busy man to give up his holiday.

"He's old and crotchety. Take no notice," Ian said. "You and Angus go for a month. I'll come down with you and stay a week, and then again for a week at the end."

"You probably won't," I said. "He'll insult you funnily or be funny insultingly and you'll leave and never come back. I wouldn't go near him again if I didn't feel it my duty to Angus."

"You visit your Uncle Warren . . ." Ian said.

"Because I'm sorry for him. His son died, and then his wife, and he's poor . . ."

"And dipsomaniac and dirty! Dear Cathy; at the bottom of your heart, you know, you're afraid that you might seem to be a fortune hunter. So you feel *bound* to take offence at Uncle Booth."

"Is it that? Do *you* want me to be nicer to him, about him?" I asked, a little bewildered.

"Makes no difference to me," Ian said. "I can give Angus every advantage that I ever had, and more. But it does seem to me that you're a bit mixed about your Uncle Booth. He *can't* be worse than Warren."

"All right. I'll try again. We'll all go and be nice to this poor old rich uncle of mine. . . ."

Whether age and illness had improved Uncle Booth's manners or whether Ian and Angus being there made things easier I cannot say. I only know that that was the best visit I ever had at Merravay. For one thing the weather was lovely. It is a little strange how those two or three summers immediately preceding the fatal summer of 1914 seem to glow with more than sunlight. Even Merravay seemed to lose its gloom.

Ian and Angus established surprisingly friendly relationships with Uncle Booth, and Angus was praised for the way he took to riding; he had never had much chance to acquire horsemanship, but he proved to be fearless and to have what they call "good hands." "As good as Maude at the same age," said Uncle Booth. We understood that praise could go no further.

During our last week Uncle Booth's lawyer came and was closeted with him for the best part of a morning; and after that I did permit myself a hope or two on Angus' account. There was no doubt that Maude would inherit Merravay—Uncle Booth had several times mentioned her devotion to it, as a place; "She doesn't come to see me, you know. She comes to count those houseleeks on the roof!" But Angus, I thought, had made his mark and would be remembered.

We had been home three days when I heard that Uncle Booth had had another stroke, likely to prove fatal. I went back at once, but he was dead when I got there. Maude had arrived a few hours earlier but had had, she said, no speech with him.

We were alone together there for that evening. Now and then it struck me as rather sad that we should both be so calm. Maude's manner was brittle, but no more so when she said, "I shall miss him; he was always *there*," than when she said, "This soup is almost stone-cold." I hadn't seen her since her second marriage, and to me she looked surprisingly young and almost intimidatingly sophisticated. I was almost sure that there was rouge on her cheeks and lips; she wore diamonds in her ears and on her fingers; and she smoked—absolutely naturally and with no air of bravado—cigarette after cigarette, using a long holder that looked to me as though it were made of jade.

I noticed at once that out of the confusion which inevitably follows a death, had emerged the idea of Maude being the centre and head of the house. That was hardly to be wondered at. Despite her busy social life and her travels, she had spent much more time at Merravay—though I had stayed there more recently. She was older than I; she was—if Uncle Booth could be credited with such a conventional preference—his favourite niece; and all servants being snobs to the bone, they enjoyed saying "Her ladyship this" and "Her ladyship that."

It was a lovely late summer evening, and after dinner Maude and I, by common impulse, escaped from the hushed house and went into the garden. Dusk was creeping in from the fields and the wood. Merravay had always struck me as being an unnaturally quiet place, even when allowance was made for its remoteness. Tonight the quiet seemed almost unearthly, although when one listened one could hear the soft mourning of doves, the twitter of smaller birds settling for the night, the clatter of the last train running through to Bywater.

In the rose garden the second-crop roses, which had been buds when I left three days before, were full out, wide-hearted after the day's warmth; and from the herbaceous border waves of heavier perfume from lilies, late stocks, and tobacco flowers came to meet us as we strolled. At the very end of the garden, where the urn-topped wall divided it from the field, we stopped and turned, leaning back against the still-warm bricks.

"It is," said Maude, looking to left and right and then straight ahead to the house, "the most beautiful, perfect place in the world."

Ordinarily she had a crisp, light way of speaking, just flicking her words and dropping the emphasis in unexpected places. Ordinarily she would have said, "the *most* beautiful place." But tonight her voice was deep, caressing, and she gave "beautiful" its full, brooding value.

Ordinarily I should have questioned her verdict; Merravay was solid, spacious, and had certain historically interesting features, but it was too grim and gloomy to be beautiful in my eyes—very much as Maude was too angular and high-nosed; yet the thought of Uncle Booth lying there in his vast high-windowed bedroom, dead and really unmourned, depressed me so that I didn't feel like arguing. I felt empty and forlorn; I longed for my husband, my child, my own neat, snug house and garden. All the sadness about this place, the age-old, ingrained gloom which I had always felt, seemed to rise like a tide and engulf me. On a sudden impulse I moved nearer to Maude and took her arm. Inside the billowing chiffon sleeve her arm felt hot, almost feverishly hot, and surprisingly frail.

"It's sad," I said, without choosing my words, "to die and have nobody to mourn you."

Maude jerked her arm away. "We can't all be founders of families," she said. "Who d'you expect to cry over a selfish old bachelor? And he's oblivious to whether we cry or gloat."

That struck me as exactly the thing which Uncle Booth would have said in the same circumstances.

"You and he were very much alike in some ways," I said.

"That's why we got on so badly. We saw through one another. He knew why I came here; he knew what this place means to me."

That was true. I'd heard him say so.

"That mystifies me, Maude. You have three, is it three? houses. You see and stay in all kinds of magnificent places. What is it about this place? To me it seems a gloomy old barn, it does really . . . but Ian, my husband you know, seemed terribly taken with it too."

Maude stared straight ahead towards the house, which loomed dark and menacing against the fading green of the evening sky.

"I don't know," she said at last. "It's just something . . . The first time I ever came here I wanted to stay; I asked my father to buy it. I've always come back and when I'm away I dream of it. It's my place. It is *so* beautiful. It's one of those things which nobody can explain." She fitted a cigarette into the holder, struck a match, and narrowed her eyes against the flame. "Talking of crying," she said abruptly, "I did cry, for pure happiness then, the night Uncle Booth promised to leave it to me. So if I cried now it would be hypocrisy."

So he had promised Merravay to her. That was no surprise to me; it had been understood more or less all along. Just a thousand pounds for Angus, I thought; just enough to see him comfortably through school and started in life. And there was this to be said for Merravay going to Maude; if Uncle Booth had left it to either of his brothers, Ernest or Warren, the only two left, he would have felt bound to leave money for its upkeep. With Maude that would never arise. So perhaps . . . with luck, just a thousand pounds for Angus.

Uncle Ernest arrived early next morning. He had spent most of his life in the colonial service and had retired with a knighthood and a pension. He lived in a not-very-luxurious club in London and seemed glad to get to the fleshpots of Merravay. But he grumbled, almost automatically, at everything. A damp patch and a crack on his bedroom ceiling caused him great concern.

"Well," he said, looking from Maude to me, "whichever one of you gets *this* handsome property gets a white elephant, let me tell you. Roof's in shocking condition. Ceiling over my bed! Sword of Damocles nothing to it. Have you seen it?"

"I've seen the one in my own," said Maude. "But I've been up in the roof. There's no worm or dry rot. The tiles just need relaying and re-placing in parts."

"That'll cost a pretty penny."

"Five or six hundred pounds," said Maude as though it were nothing.

"Not that *we* need worry, yet," Uncle Ernest proceeded. "Tricky chap, Booth; always was. Probably left the place to Dr. Barnardo's Homes. Short of his leaving me my father's gold watch, which I always coveted, nothing would surprise me!"

Well, Uncle Ernest had his surprise. Uncle Booth had bequeathed him not only the coveted watch but all his personal belongings, studs, cuff links, cigar cases, guns, everything in his cellar, and the sum of a thousand pounds.

That was one of the first of what seemed an interminable list of be-quests. One would have thought that this was the will of an unusually sentimental man who was either fantastically generous or prodigally rich. Dozens of servants, past and present, people for whom Uncle Booth had never had a good word to say, all remembered; the Almshouse Trust, at which he had jeered; the Scholarship Fund, which he had pretended to deplore. A veritable shower of gold fell upon all; and still there was no mention of Angus. How rich had he been? What would be left?

At last Mr. Turnbull paused, cleared his throat slightly, and read out the final phrases. All the contents of the house he left to Maude; Merravay and the garden to me.

I swallowed something sour and choking that came up from the pit of my stomach into my throat. I felt Merravay with its mediaeval kitchens and sagging roof fall like a dead weight on my shoulders. I knew a mo-ment of bitter disappointment. Then I braced myself. All right—I thought —you wanted to surprise everybody, but I am not surprised; I always thought you were a horrid old man, and now I know it. I could see that the will had been the last of his verbal quips. What perverse pleasure he must have derived in sitting down on that fine August morning and planning a surprise for everybody. Surprise a kitchen slut with a legacy of fifty pounds; surprise Angus, the obvious heir to everything, by not even mentioning him; surprise Maude, who had three houses full of furniture . . . surprise Catherine, who didn't care for Merravay. I am not surprised, Uncle Booth . . . but Maude . . . oh dear. For the first time in my life I could think, "Poor Maude."

I took a careful glance at her; she was sitting as though someone had taken a sharp sword and run her through. There was now no doubt about whether she rouged her face; the harsh colour stood out like clown's paint, her nose looked like a bleached bone. As I watched she stood up, straightened herself, and without a word to anyone stalked out of the room.

I thought to myself that I would be ashamed to make such an exhibition of feeling. After all I was equally, or more, cruelly disappointed, mocked. I was a woman who had to look pretty sharply to the butcher's bill, who had to live in a town two hundred miles away, who had a child to provide for. And all I'd got was a liability. She could have Merravay; I'd sell it to her; thank God there was one person on earth mad enough to want it and rich enough to indulge the whim.

I muttered a word of excuse and ran after Maude. She was in her room, hurriedly throwing her clothes and toilet articles into a dressing case. I was breathless from my run up the stairs and along the gallery, but I managed to gasp out,

"Maude, you can have it. I don't want it. I never did. And I couldn't afford . . ."

"Get out of my sight," said Maude. She cast at me one look in which all the hatred and accusation in the world seemed concentrated; a mad look.

"Don't take it so hard," I gasped. "I'm terribly disappointed too. But we can come to some arrangement . . ."

"I'm not going to *buy* what is mine by right. I never want to see the place again!" She snapped the dressing case and went to the bell, jerking the pull crazily.

"I'll give it to you . . ." She gave me another mad look. "Maude, you must see that it isn't any use to me. I couldn't live in it; I couldn't have the roof mended."

"Insure it and burn it down," Maude said. "Oh, Beales . . . I'm leaving immediately."

Even the rule about behaving oneself before servants was no rule to her. I said, "Good-bye, Maude," in as normal a voice as I could manage. She swept past me without a word.

Then began the terrible time during which, were I a fanciful woman, I would say that I was justified in all my feelings about Merravay, back and back to my earliest recollection when I was frightened of the place. It had seemed to threaten me, and Heaven knew it now carried out its threat in terms of near ruin. We couldn't leave it empty and uncared for and allow obvious decay to add itself to the hidden flaws; we had to find wages for a caretaker and a gardener. Upon our limited means the great house fastened like a bloodsucker.

I wrote three letters to Maude, each more beseeching than the last; she answered none. A formal letter from a firm of furniture removers, asking for access to the house for four days, informed me that she was about to remove the furniture. I shut myself in my room then and cried a little in secret. There were things of great value at Merravay; if only Uncle Booth had. . . . I know the Bible explicitly states that to him who hath shall be given and from him who hath not shall be taken that which he hath . . . but I had never expected to be obliged to interpret that so literally.

Once I knew that Maude was adamant I did everything possible to sell the place. Advertisements which stressed its historic value, the scenery, the shooting, photographs over which even Ian would brood and say, "It really *is* beautiful," appeared in all the papers. Numbers of house agents had it "on their books." But the stark fact which I had recognised before Mr. Turnbull had finished speaking just would not be gainsaid. Nobody wanted a great crumbling house in the depths of the country with nothing but a kitchen garden attached to it.

One day, when I was obliged to go there, I tried to cheer myself by playing a game. I arrived at Nettleton station and drove to Merravay in a ramshackle cab, pretending that I had never seen the place before, had been attracted by the advertisement, and had come to inspect it.

It was an experience to frighten the hardiest. Stripped of the furniture, the house was simply not habitable even in imagination. I stood in the drawing-room and looked at the walls, realising for the first time that the silk which covered them had once been deep yellow. Wherever a picture had hung or a piece of furniture stood against the wall, it was bright yellow still, with birds and sprays of flowers embroidered on it in delightful colours; elsewhere everything had faded to a dim greyish buff, marked with brown stains where the damp had crept in. In places it was frayed, in others torn. Imagine any woman standing there and thinking, "my drawing-room." That alone . . . and then there were the kitchens, grim vaults.

No, it was hopeless. I realised it then. What should I do; what could I do? I thought of Maude's remark, another one of those that old Booth himself might have made, about insuring it and burning it. Really, if I could have hoped to do so without exposure I should have been tempted. And certainly if I could have wished the place out of existence it would have vanished there and then. But it stood there fundamentally solid enough. The roof might leak, but the timber was sound. I looked at what seemed like acres of flooring, smooth and shining, honey-coloured; at what seemed like miles of panelling, much of it beautifully carved; at the staircase, as good as the day it was completed; at the roses and ships and other things which decorated the chimney breasts. Had they no value?

Then I went out into the kitchen garden. It was a wildly prolific place; Uncle Booth had employed two men and a boy, and the garden produce at Merravay had always been one of the joys of a visit. I had kept on one man, the eldest of the three, paying him a small wage and allowing him to make it up by selling what he could. I had also arranged to have boxes of stuff sent to me by rail, but that was highly unsatisfactory. Now, carefully tended, basking in the sun, the wealth of it, great plump shining strawberries, thick tender asparagus, early peas, tended to exasperate me almost past bearing.

On my way home in the train I made up my mind. Next day I wrote a letter to the Baildon agent, who, being at hand, could better deal with it. I asked him to try to find a buyer for the kitchen garden, and to sell the house if he could to a "housebreaker." Ian was very much distressed. I said, "What else can I do? Almost two years, and it's costing us money all the time. If I can just get a thousand pounds . . ."

"For almost the first time in my life," he said, "I wish I'd devoted a little more attention to money."

But it worked out in the end. A builder named Hoggett offered a thousand pounds for Merravay as it stood. The agent, shrewd and energetic fellow, took him over and persuaded him, on the strength of the staircase alone, to raise his offer to fifteen hundred pounds.

On the last Saturday of July 1914 I received a cheque for the whole, minus the agent's fees, and when I subtracted the sums I had paid out in wages and the cost of my journeys to and fro and the other expenses, I reckoned that I had almost exactly the thousand pounds for which I had hoped. I'd finished with Merravay.

Nine days later war was declared. Ian joined the Army Medical Corps and after that I had something else to worry about. I don't think I gave Merravay another thought until the other day when I heard that Maude was hard up and homeless. All her husband's houses passed to a nephew when he died, and Maude had squandered the money he left her, as well as her own, in unwise speculations and endless house-movings. They say that between 1919 and 1938 she moved house, buying and selling and losing money on every deal, no fewer than fifteen times. That must be an exaggeration.

What could I do but write and invite her to share my tiny flat, even though I am told that she once described it as "one cell in an egg box"? I suppose the whole thing would strike Uncle Booth as a most delectable joke.

Interlude

When Joe Hoggett wrote the cheque for fifteen hundred pounds and so became owner of Merravay, he was putting his name to nothing so mundane as a money order. He was signing a declaration of faith.

Several times during the past weeks he had said, "Don't you believe it. There ain't gorn to be no war. Stands to reason . . ."

He knew all the reasons and could reel them off, pat.

On the last Sunday of July he drove out from his neat villa, Jesmondene, on the outskirts of Baildon, to inspect again, this time with a possessive eye, his latest purchase. He took with him his wife and his daughter-in-law, who were always pleased to have an outing on a fine Sunday afternoon, and were today excited by the prospect of seeing Merravay, of which they had heard a great deal. It irked Joe that his son, Joe Willie, was unable to accompany them; his absence quite spoilt the day.

Joe Willie did not share his father's confidence in Germany's awe of the British Navy, in the Kaiser's blood relationship to the British Royal Family, or in any of the other things which Joe thought of when he said, "Stands to reason . . ."

Joe Willie had been, for the last two years, a member of the Suffolk Yeomanry, the Loyal Suffolk Hussars. Old Joe had nothing against that; he was proud that Joe Willie, son of a working builder, should take his place amongst the sons of farmers and gentry—and be the best mounted of the lot. Joe had taken that showy, spirited black horse as part payment of a bad debt when the Whymarks "went up the spout" as he termed it. Joe Willie, looking very smart and handsome, had gone off to what he called "exercises" on this fine Sunday.

Mrs. Hoggett and Rosie, after a glance at the outside of the house and a more prolonged stare at the hall, both of which Mrs. Hoggett pronounced "gloomy" and Rosie "romantic," went off, woman-like, to the kitchen quarters, leaving Mr. Hoggett to take—a little shamefacedly, for it was Sunday, after all—a folding rule from his pocket and just run it over, just to make sure, just to confirm . . . He *knew* that he had made a good bargain, really; but his original offer had been for a thousand . . . and though he knew and was sure, he just wanted to *make* sure.

Once, while he was running rule and eye over the panelling, the thought struck him, cold, stomach-shaking—Do that come to a war and Joe Willie go, it'll be like this a long time, me alone. . . . But then, thass daft. There ain't gorn to be a war. Stands to reason . . .

In the kitchen and pantries and storerooms the two women were having a wonderful time. Mrs. Hoggett's father had been a butcher and had enjoyed Mr. Booth-Sandell's esteemed custom; she had always regarded the family with genuine awe. Seeing the kitchen in which that meat had been prepared for table was a shock to her.

"Well, if I wasn't seeing it with my own eyes I *never* would have believed it. Swanking about like that, ever so lordly, and living so shabby. Look at that old sink. All hollowed out with wear. You couldn't clean it, not if you wanted to ever so. Well, I never did."

"I don't suppose the old man ever saw his sink," said Rosie. It was a reasonable statement, but there was just that something in her voice which made Mrs. Hoggett suspect that once again she and Rosie weren't seeing quite eye to eye. That often happened; though they were the best of friends, really. Still it was with a certain asperity in her voice that she said, in the bathroom, "He did see the bath I s'pose!" They stared at the mahogany-surrounded sarcophagus that stood high and lonely in the centre of a moderately large room.

Rosie agreed, for a moment, that the new bathroom at Jesmondene was preferable to this; then she looked out of the window and wasn't so sure.

Again Mrs. Hoggett sensed the lack of response; Rosie wasn't quite the homey, companionable daughter-in-law she'd hoped for, but she suited Joe Willie; and though she seldom said the absolutely right, cosy thing, she never said the downright wrong one.

The three met in the hall. Joe Hoggett was jubilant. He'd been right as usual. The staircase and the fireplace alone were worth the money; then there was the panelling and the flooring, all solid oak as good as new and better; and the tiles—it was curious how, these days, lots of people building a new house didn't want it to *look* new, liked the old tiles.

"Well, my dears," he said, closing and locking the great door, "Joe Hoggett weren't far off the mark there. Thass a bargain all right!"

"When I think," said Mrs. Hoggett, "how in the old days he'd come to the shop and sit there in his gig and give the window a clip with his whip to draw attention, ever so lordly and all the time . . . Well, if I hadn't seen with my own eyes . . . !"

Joe Hoggett helped the women into the high dogcart, gathered the reins, clicked his tongue to the horse, and then turned to take one last look at the house which he meant to carve up as a butcher carves up a carcass. The doomed and threatened house stared back at him.

"I call it a shame to pull it down," said Rosie in a strained, desperate voice. "It's such a beautiful house."

"Thass better; thass a beautiful bargain," said Joe easily. "You wait till Joe Willie see what his old dad've pulled off this time!"

But Joe Willie never saw the wonderful bargain; he rode away on his handsome horse, came home for one leave that was reckoned in hours, and went to meet death in the Dardanelles. Joe Hoggett's zest for money-making was quenched; there was no point in it now, for Joe Willie had left no child. There was some slight satisfaction in lending Merravay to be used as a military hospital where men less desperately wounded than Joe Willie might be mended; and when, its purpose served, the place came back into his hands he was spiritlessly relieved to sell it to the first bidder.

During the next thirty years the house changed hands seven times. A new law protecting ancient and historic buildings prevented anyone doing with it what Joe Hoggett had planned to do; a brief period in the ownership of a capricious millionaire saved it from falling into complete decay. In 1940, for a fortnight it sheltered a number of evacuees who would have stayed longer if there had been a cinema and a fried-fish shop within easy reach. Later in the war contingents of soldiers stayed long enough to write rude words on the plaster and carve their initials on the panelling.

Peace came; the old house stood and awaited the next turn of fortune. One thing only seemed certain—the time had come when Merravay must work for its keep.

The Breadwinner

IN 1946, when David was what they called "rehabilitated," we set out to look for a little place in the country where we could cultivate a market garden and bring up a family. We had about three thousand pounds between us and when we had discovered that people were asking five or six thousand for two acres of chicken-sickened ground and an asbestos-board bungalow so small that David's claustrophobia became rampant at the sight, the miracle happened and we found Merravay.

It was an old Tudor house in Suffolk; quite genuine, spacious, and beautiful. It had been modernised after a fashion some years before; it had a banqueting hall and a musicians' gallery and—what mattered more to us—a big kitchen garden and some substantial outbuildings. During the war it had suffered; as David said, looking round, "The legions have camped here," and perhaps that was one reason why it was for sale so cheaply. They were asking three thousand pounds for it. When I brooded over the possible folly of buying an historic mansion to house two adults and one child I could find three points in favour of the project; first was that even on our first visit of inspection David had stayed indoors for a full hour without making one of his pitiable little excuses to go outside; secondly I could see that—should the market-garden idea fail—there was room here for me to take paying guests; and thirdly I was a fool. "Knaves and fools all pay in the end but the fools pay first!" I was fool enough to fall for the charm of the house. Its air of having seen such better days, of falling into decay so graciously, of wanting to be loved and used gently again . . . oh, I don't know! I was just a fool!

We put down our ready money and I sold the best of the things my grandmother had left me and we bought fifty handsome Rhode Island Red pullets scheduled to begin to lay in November, when eggs, scarce and dear, command good prices. That sounded promising, and we were also encouraged by the fact that the old man who had had charge of the garden on a "sharecropper" basis while the house was empty decided to stay and work for us. He was the recipient of a pension of some kind which made it inadvisable for him to *earn* more than thirty shillings a week. His method of recompensing himself more adequately had worked well in the past and probably he saw no reason to alter it. But it broke down in September, when I went into a fruit shop at Baildon to try to sell some green figs and was informed that they always bought figs from Merravay which were better than mine. That was indisputable! The wretched old man had risen earlier and picked more discriminately. Attempts—almost pathetically well meaning on our part, at least—to reach some less cutthroat arrangement met with marked non-collaboration from him and finally, with the remark that he was used to working for gentle-folk, he left us.

However that was just at the beginning of the long spell of severe weather for which the winter of 1946–47 is memorable, and as there was nothing to do except feed the hens and wait—and pray—for eggs and look for the places where snow had penetrated the roof, we bore up bravely, saying that there was no better place to be housebound. The hall made an excellent playground for a young child, and the fireplace took kindly to a diet of wood cut from the overgrown shrubbery.

In the following spring I made my first tentative suggestion about taking in guests. David wriggled away from it. He didn't actually *say* that an Englishman's home was his castle or that it was a man's duty to provide for his family . . . that was all implied.

And there were, of course, several stones unturned, many avenues unexplored—to hell with clichés! We tried goats and bees and mush-rooms, we tried dog-breeding; we grew pyrethrum and scabious and lav-ender and potted plants. We tried everything!

And then, one day, driving in from Baildon, David overtook Ginger Whymark, whose car had broken down. Once upon a time the Whymarks had been the big noise in these parts; they'd owned Merravay and sold it and built a great new white house near by and lately sold that to an agricultural college and moved into their own lodge cottage—a bit added to. The old man had managed to retain the shooting rights and every autumn he had a big party; very favoured old friends screwed themselves into the limited accommodations at the Lodge, the others went to The Evening Star in Nettleton, and soon after David had be-come—and I had forced myself to be—friends with Ginger Whymark, the woman at The Evening Star fell ill on the very eve of one of the old man's parties and Ginger came across to ask a favour . . . would I, could I, put up four decent old chaps? Just bed and breakfast, she could man-age everything else.

I'll be honest. I didn't much care for Miss Whymark with her mar-

malade-coloured hair and her hearty voice and her abounding energy—
they said she did all the housework at the Lodge single-handed, bred
her dachshunds, looked after an old aunt across the way as well, and
still had time to hunt or go beagling when chance offered, a reputation
which made me respect and admire and . . . is there a word for it?
Resent doesn't quite do, nor does fear. . . . Anyway, that doesn't
matter. What does is that I seized on her suggestions and took in the old
men, who were perfect pets, and when David saw that the sun did
not fall out of the sky at the sight of Captain and Mrs. Stamford taking
base coinage in return for hospitality the way was opened for me to do
what I had been longing to do for months—start Merravay as a guest
house. I sold a few of my remaining treasures, a Bow clock, some bits
of Chelsea china, and a lidded wassail bowl—the only complete one, I
believe, outside a museum, in all England—and with the proceeds I
bought the necessary furniture and paid for the necessary advertisement,
and before long my guest house was on its feet and staggering along.

II

It would be ridiculous to pretend that the guest house made much
profit; what it did do was to work in very well with David's various
activities. Vegetables and fruit, eggs, rabbits and fowls I could have at
cost price, and since I could now order with comparative lavishness at the
Baildon shops their owners were more inclined to buy what we had to
sell. By May of 1950, when the lilacs and mock orange in the overgrown
shrubberies at Merravay were scenting the air for miles around and
every day ended in a kind of cuckoo-haunted dream, I could look round,
not with complacency but with some satisfaction. We were solvent;
people who had stayed once had come again and recommended us to their
friends, and Ginger Whymark had heard of someone who had two old
horses in need of a good home and we had offered to take them, "meat
for manners," so now we could offer riding as one of the amenities at
Merravay; and my main worry was that David was overworking. Since
the guest house had got going he had suffered a decline of spirits, had
more than once said something about being a failure and having made
a mistake in coming to Merravay. This I attributed to the fact that he was
working too hard as well as resenting the establishment of the guest
house.

The overwork, at least, was remedied. Early one morning, driving
back from Baildon, he saw a man sitting by the roadside, endeavouring
to hammer back—with a stone—the loose sole of his shoe. David's all-
embracing sympathy came uppermost; he stopped the car, spoke to the
man, brought him to Merravay, gave him a meal and a rather better
pair of shoes. The man was a Pole; whence he came, whither he was
bound, we never knew. When he had eaten and was reshod he looked at

the garden and said, "I dig. I am not beggar men." And he dug until the next mealtime; after which apparently his pride demanded that he should dig again. At nightfall he slept in the loft and was then so deeply in debt that he must dig all next day.

He looked harmless enough; a thin, clean-looking little man with closely cropped hair and very bright blue eyes, but, as I said to David, he might be a thief, a murderer, for all we knew.

"Damned good worker though," said David. "We could use him."

At the next feeding time David asked casually,

"Know anything about horses?"

Something happened to his tight, bony little face.

"Me. To know about horses." He dived into an inner pocket and brought out a wallet, grey-edged from wear, held together by a rubber band. He selected and held out to us a photograph of himself in the high boots and trim uniform of the Polish cavalry, seated upon a much too tall, lively-looking horse. I could think of no comment which would not—by implication at least—be hurtful, but David said, in just the right tone,

"Ha. Cavalry! Yes, I'd say you knew about horses."

"Against tanks they were no good," said the little man, replacing the photograph and busying himself with the rubber band. "Much later I have Spitfire. Was good."

"The operative words there are 'much later,'" said David with one of his brief, sudden accesses of bitterness.

"Please," he said, not understanding. But after that he was, all at once, one of us, and we were privileged to call him by his name, which was Stanislav.

Largely thanks to his efforts, Merravay was looking its best when Miss Julia Spenwood came to stay with us for a fortnight of recuperation after an operation. Somebody had recommended her; and she looked so frail, so faintly distraught, that at sight of her some Little Mother of All The World instinct rose up in me. I plied her with Bovril, Ovaltine, eggs beaten in milk, and in return she ruined me.

She arrived on a Saturday and on the following Thursday went to town to keep a pressing engagement, she said. David drove her to the station to catch the one good "up" train and arranged to meet the good "down" one in the evening. She wasn't on it; and in the morning I had a letter thanking me for my care of her and saying that urgent business had compelled her to remain in London; would I send on her belongings. She enclosed a cheque for the full fortnight.

Nobody in Nettleton was sufficiently hard up or enterprising enough to deliver Sunday papers, but they were obtainable at the station between the hours of twelve and one, and on the Sunday after Miss Spenwood's departure one of the people staying in the house who was fond of riding rode in to fetch them. I was busy getting the lunch but I did notice that all my guests had congregated in a little bunch about the papers as though something interesting was afoot. Some particularly gory murder, I thought, knowing the Sunday papers. But while I was clearing the tables the old dear who had fetched the papers lingered, hovered, hesitated, and then handed me one paper folded small and said, "I think, Mrs. Stamford, you should see this." He hurried away and I looked at the headline, which asked, in bold thick print, "Another Haunted House Near Borley?" Underneath was a small but beautifully clear photograph of Merravay. Below that was a spiel about poor Julia Spenwood, the fashion editor of the paper, who had been ill and gone to Merravay for her convalescence and who, after four days, had been forced to flee the place because it was so dreadfully haunted. There was no mention of what she saw, felt, or heard, apart from a "feeling" on the stairs, a "cold place" in the big hall, but it was a clever piece of sensational journalism. I could see exactly what it meant. It was Miss Spenwood's "comeback." Poor old dog Tray, sick and blunt of tooth, had nearly been shut out but he'd managed by chance to grab a hare and had carried it home and was now reinstated in the very middle of the hearthrug.

A cry of "Fire" could hardly have emptied the house more quickly. By Monday midday everybody—with some fatuous excuse or another—had departed. The week's post brought me several cancellations, a letter from a medium who wished to hold a séance in our haunted house, a letter from a woman whose own house had been dreadfully haunted and successfully exorcised, and an anonymous communication furiously denouncing me for trying such a cheap advertising stunt. In the next fortnight I received no requests for accommodations, and the only people who came to the house were a few sensation-seekers, hoping, half frightenedly, to find another Borley. It seemed to me that I had been ruined by an irresponsible journalist and should have some redress; so one day I put the article and the letters of cancellation into my bag and drove into Baildon to consult young Mr. Turnbull, the solicitor who had dealt with the transfer of Merravay.

At home, to David, I had always managed somehow to make light of the disaster, but as soon as I began to describe it to someone who would not be inwardly *hurt* by the implication that I needed to make a living out of paying guests, my control wavered. My voice and my hands shook, my head jerked, my eyes filled with tears.

Mr. Turnbull listened gravely and—I thought—sympathetically; then he studied the newspaper cutting and the letters.

"Most unfortunate, and, I realise, infuriating for you. But in law, I'm afraid, you have no redress. You see it would be difficult to prove conclusively that Merravay is not haunted and even more difficult to prove that Miss . . . er . . . Spenwood was not genuinely of the opinion that it was. And she could certainly produce—not evidence of haunting, but evidence that she was not alone in her opinion."

"You mean that other people have said so?"

He nodded. "As a matter of fact my attention was drawn to the subject some years ago—before the war. There was some trouble about lease-breaking. The house was rented at the time. The tenant tried to plead that it was haunted as an excuse . . . that didn't work, of course. But I looked up the story. Very interesting!"

"Tell me."

"Well, I shouldn't wish . . . though there's nothing actually frightening . . ."

"That kind of thing never frightens me," I said. I could have added that I had enough real terrors to contend with, getting into debt, finding a new and really serious leak in the roof . . .

So he told me the story of Lady Alice Rowhedge, the witch of Merravay whom some remote ancestor of his had attempted, unsuccessfully, to protect when she was tried for witchcraft in the middle of the seventeenth century. She was supposed to ride a great black horse, on windy nights at certain seasons, along a certain stretch of road; at other times she walked about in the house, brewing potions, making spells. "Three hundred years is a long time, Mrs. Stamford, but the story seems to crop up fairly consistently. Miss Spenwood wasn't being very original." He smiled and went on, "This story, you know, will either die down and all will be as before; or else you may find that your ghost is established and becomes an attraction. Then you could charge half a crown for admittance, and sell wildly expensive cups of tea."

"To a lot of stupid neurotics!"

"Oh, don't be harsh on us! I visited Borley several times; and the fact that the ghost story interested me took me to Merravay in the first place, and as a result, when somebody wanted to demolish it I put a stop to that scheme. You owe your ghost a little, Mrs. Stamford."

"Maybe," I said, getting to my feet, "it would have been better for me if it had been pulled down."

His manner grew more serious.

"The guest house really mattered?"

"Why else should I bother?"

"Well . . . of course, it's not for me to make suggestions. But if you find that people like to visit, but are averse to sleeping in, the house, you could try making it into a club. A relative of mine did that with her white elephant of a house and says it pays and she hasn't to make beds, a job she happened to abhor."

"That would mean getting a club licence."

"Which wouldn't be difficult. I could do that for you."

I thanked him for his kindness. Halfway home I stopped the car and, bowed over the wheel, gave way, for the first and last time, to a bout of lachrymose self-pity. Everything we had tried so far had come to no good and had cost money; even the bee-keeping scheme! And I had just invested in a store of sheets and towels. Now I must go marketing for glasses, liquors, and a club licence. It seemed a little too much! But by the time that I had repaired my face, stiffened my courage, and got ready a cheerful, optimistic mood in which to meet David, my mind was made up. I'd try another thing; Merravay should become a club.

The way one thing links up with and leads to another is very strange. Spite and rancour had taken me to Chris Turnbull and much resulted from that visit. Not only did he get me the licence, he made the club.

There is another strange thing—the way wars work out for different people.

My war had been dull; and because I was bored by it I had taken a course in cookery, found an unsuspected talent, and gone on and on.

David's had been disastrous. He'd just reached captain's rank when he was taken prisoner and pushed into a camp where he was senior officer. In those days, before it was proved that the Japanese intended to disregard all conventions, David, who knew the rules, often ventured upon his pitiful, futile protests. One of these concerned overcrowding and lack of exercise, and he used the unfortunate expression, "boxed up." The Japanese to whom he made his complaint said, "Bad exaggerations. I will show you boxed up. I will demonstrate to you categorically boxed up." David being six feet tall, the box they made for him was exactly five feet six inches each way, and he spent nearly two years in it. He emerged wildly claustrophobic.

Chris Turnbull's war, beginning with a wound at Dunkirk, had put him into a hospital bed next door to Jimmy Rorke the film actor, and there had started one of those apparently incongruous friendships which astonish everyone except the participants.

So now Chris could say to me, "It is nice to have somewhere to bring Jimmy and Mavis when they come for weekends!" And local people could say, "Let's run out and have a meal at Merravay. We might see Jimmy Rorke and Mavis Mallinson!"

And I could cook, especially the kind of exotic meal for which people are willing to pay a disproportionately high price. I still think that I could have made a great success of Merravay as a club and dining place had nature seen fit to endow me with cast-iron feet, a solid timber backbone, and a dozen hands. As it was I had to have help; and to need help in England nowadays is to rank with the piteous drug addict who must pay blackmailing price or perish.

Of course I could always advertise "bus passes gate." It did just that, at forty miles an hour, twice a day, making for the Nettleton post office, where it stopped. But "help" didn't like that; and after some harassed and distracted months, some comic, heartbreaking experiences, I settled down to run the place with the assistance of one good, steady daily woman and a fugitive succession of girls who thought they'd rather like to do a little waitressing, and, of course, the invaluable Stanislav, who took on voluntarily the work of bar-man. Each afternoon he would stop work, take a bath, put what looked like Durofix on his hair, and with an expression which would have become his sainted namesake—dogged resignation—get behind the bar, and proceed to act with his usual dexterity and care for our interests. Out of the tips that came his way he hoarded enough to buy what I hope is the noisiest motor cycle ever made, and often, when we had made everything tidy for the night and I had tottered to bed to lie beside David, who had been asleep for hours, I would hear that motor cycle go roaring away, lonely and raucous through the dark. Stanislav seemed to need so little sleep, lucky man. My own need was chronic and cumulative. I could have lain down at any moment and slept for a week, a month, a year, forever. Shopping, catering, cooking, making out the menus, totting up the bills, being pleasant to people; being a wife to David; being a mother to young John, who was now, thanks to the club, a weekly boarder at a decent little school and whose week ends must somehow be made to seem happy, normal interludes . . . it all took toll and sometimes I would catch a horrifying glimpse of myself in a glass; light-brown hair dusted with silver; face thin and lined, rouged and powdered too hastily into a caricature of itself; eyes too wary, too watchful. But one day—I told myself after each such glimpse—things would alter; I'd have time; one day I'd go to the hairdresser's; take forty-eight hours off and sleep . . . one day something would happen.

And one day something did. I went to answer the telephone's shrill summonses and instead of the table reservation I expected it was a personal call from London for Mr. David Stamford. A friend of his, one Eddie Blenco, much blessed by me because he had once sent me a hundredweight of sugar—he had a plantation in Jamaica—was in London and wanted David to go up to see him. I remember saying, "You go. The trip will do you good. Stanislav and I can manage." Somebody, somewhere, filed that remark away!

David went and came back to tell me that Eddie Blenco had had to have an operation which might alleviate, but could not cure, his complaint. He knew that his active days were over and he needed somebody entirely trustworthy to go and manage his plantation.

"But you don't know anything about sugar cane," I said tactlessly, and saw David's face darken.

"I am prepared to learn. Besides the place is crawling with people who know everything. What Eddie wants is somebody he can trust to go and look after *them*. And look, Jill!"

He whisked out and showed me a photograph of a long white single-storied house with a deep verandah. In the foreground was a garden, neat but luxuriant, and behind it a mass of palms.

"Ours," said David in a voice of intense gloating. "No rent, free service . . . and a thousand a year!"

It was his great moment! Man the provider had gone out and brought home the carcass and I spoiled it all. I said,

"But what about Merravay?"

He looked at me and said, "I never gave it a single thought. It was a gaff. Just a place to get away from."

That reminded me of the old David; of the dashing headlong way in which we had got married, decided to have a child, bought Merravay. And though I was glad to see this resurrection of the spirit I felt compelled to say,

"But we gave three thousand for it." And then the devil made me add, "I'm not budging from here till I see that money again."

III

Just before he left—which was three months and about thirty disappointments later—David said, "You must be the most pig-headed woman God ever made. So we paid three thousand for the damned place! Can't you see that we've lived here, three of us, for five years? It owes us nothing! For the last time, will you shut the door on it and come with me?"

"I daren't," I said. I thought of the chance of his not liking the job, not being able to stand the climate, of the plantation failing, of his falling out with Eddie. Three thousand pounds was three thousand pounds; a nest egg, education for John, food, a roof, a bridge to the next venture.

"All right," David said. "I shall go. I won't smoke or drink; I'll live on sugar cane; I'll take odd jobs and cheat and swindle everybody, and *I'll* give you three thousand for the bloody house. Nobody else will . . ."

"For the house perhaps not; but for the club as a going concern somebody might. And I just feel I must stay here until somebody does. . . ."

Stanislav promised to stay and look after everything. David promised to find him a place on the plantation. Chris Turnbull promised to keep an eye on us. I promised to take the first reasonable offer for Merravay. Even young John promised to be a good boy.

So David left and I was appalled by the sense of loss which his going inflicted. Of late we had spent little time together, rising up half asleep, utterly uncommunicative, to go about our separate chores, to meet over hasty meals, and eventually to go, at differing hours, back to our work-induced slumber, side by side. There were days when we had hardly exchanged a dozen words; but he was *there!* I could save up things to tell him when the opportunity occurred, could amuse myself by collecting, polishing up, making more amusing or significant the trivial things that happened in the course of the day's work. Now I missed him terribly; far more than I had during the war, for then our brief times together had not led me to rely upon his mere physical presence. I decided that in the past I had never been sufficiently sympathetic towards widows, especially those who had enjoyed a longish married life. . . .

The year crept up to its summer peak and then began to go down the slope which, beginning gently with August and September, would lead precipitously to the winter depths, when it would be dark in the morning when I rose and there would be no one to speak to, and dark again in the afternoon long before the most avid-for-drink member came into the bar. David wrote regularly; and every letter mentioned the warmth, the sunshine, the beauty of the country, the plentitude of things like domestic labour; every letter said, "Put on your hat and come!" And each time the temptation to do so became a little more insidious, to be balanced by the determination not to do so becoming a little more stubborn.

On the last Saturday in August my dear daily woman, Mrs. Baxter, told me that she was leaving; she was going to marry the village constable who lived next door to her. I was not surprised; she was so pink and placid and comfortable that she was sure to marry again—I would have married her myself had I been qualified to do so! But the news dismayed me.

"I'd have done it over Bank Holiday," she said, "but I wasn't sure of Annie Coote till this last week."

"A bridesmaid?" I asked, forcing myself to take interest.

"Bless you, bridesmaids! And Ager my third! No, Annie's for you. She's niece to my first, and a rare good worker. And she'll live in. She'll wait, too, trained she is. You'll be set up with Annie!"

Touched by this solicitude for my well-being I gave Mrs. Baxter the only thing I owned which had ever evoked her admiration—Granny's bow-fronted china cabinet, which still emptily mourned the treasures I had been obliged to sell. One of her husbands had been a champion winner of fairground ornaments and the cabinet would show off the prizes "a treat."

And for some time after Annie's installation I would have given her aunt-by-marriage the same thing daily, I was so grateful. Annie was about thirty-six, past the silly age, tireless, willing, quiet. A real treasure until she fell out with Stanislav.

In the beginning she seemed to like him, did little things for his comfort, spoke him very fair; and to say that he rebuffed her would be untrue; he met her overtures with the same monosyllabic courtesy which he used towards me and the club members. Annie, not understanding, felt herself snubbed and rebounded into frank hostility. I noticed the rasping little speeches which he seemed to ignore, but it was difficult for me to interfere until one morning when, carrying in some pot plants, he dropped some soil and fetched a brush and dustpan and swept it up.

"While you're about it you might as well make a job of it," said Annie. She pointed to some cigarette ash.

"When madam wish me to sweep she tell me and then I sweep," said Stanislav. His voice and the glance he shot at me were both imbued with challenge. I said—truly—that he had enough to do without sweeping. Annie, with a mutter about dirty foreigners and cheeky Poles, turned away. Best to ignore it all, I thought; but later in the day when Stanislav and I were checking supplies behind the bar he suddenly said,

"To be called dirty by that peasant! Pole I am and proud to be. Yes, despite all, proud! And never will I carry that cow on my motor bicycle. There is trouble! She wait every time and wish I should carry her. Should I take her on my motor bicycle and rape her in ditches she like me well. Otherwise I am dirty Pole. I do not forgive her. Never!"

"Well," I said, "I'm not suggesting that you should take her as passenger or anything like that, but I wish you'd forgive her and bear with her. She helps me so much. And it's for such a short time. Things are going so well. We've made twenty new members. Very soon I shall sell the club and you and I will be on our way to the Captain." (Stanislav having learned David's rank always used it punctiliously.)

"It is in my mind," he said, "that raping in ditches is not such thing as should be said to ladies. Please forgive me, madam. I was too angry!"

I forgave him. I realised that what he had said was true enough.

Our waitress at that time was a rather pretty, cheerful, bumbling little girl named Nancy Peake. I'd never been able to teach her much, but she'd taken a liking for Annie and begun to model herself on her, and very often Annie spent the afternoon in the Peake house. One morning—it was late in October but more like November weather, a day of dark drizzle—I was coming back from shopping and overtook, halfway up the avenue, a little thread of a woman who was stumping along through the wet leaves. I stopped and said, "Are you going up to the house?"

"I am," she said.

"Get in then, I'll run you up."

"But I'm Mrs. Peake. And you're Mrs. Stamford. I know you, though you don't know me. And I've something to say that on't be to your liking, so you don't want to go giving me no lifts! You go along. I'll be there presently."

I grinned. Unsuspecting, simple fool that I was, I grinned and said, "Now what could you have to say, Mrs. Peake, that would make me unwilling to give you a lift? What is it? Does Nancy want to leave?"

"She don't want to, but she's gorn to. Ah, that she is. We're poor, but we've allust been respectable, Mrs. Stamford. Nancy ain't staying in a place where there's carrying on! Oh no! There's right and wrong and how you and your husband, poor man, fix things between you is your affair and I ain't interfering; but where my Nancy is concerned, thass different. We're poor but we've allust been respectable and respectable we stay. Thass all. Thass what I come to say and I said it, to your face!"

She whisked around and stamped off in the direction of the village. I sat for a moment, feeling stunned and a little sick, and then I realised that it was Saturday; that every table was booked. Without Nancy I should be in a muddle. I turned the car and drove back to Nettleton, hoping that Mrs. Baxter . . . Mrs. Ager . . . might be free to "oblige" as she had occasionally done at a pinch.

Mrs. Baxter was pleased to see me, but it was clear that Mrs. Ager was faintly alarmed and no little embarrassed. She asked me into the parlour, where the cabinet was now a cage for a menagerie of pottery animals of unlikely proportions, and avoided my eyes as she said that Ager didn't really like her to take odd jobs. "You see, with Ager there's this, ma'am. He really do hev his position to think of; and to tell you the truth he ain't quite so easy handled as my others, so you see . . . I'm sorry. And I wouldn't like you to think that I paid any attention to that Annie and her wicked tongue. Told her straight I did, only last week, that the worst thing up at Merravay was her evil mind. But thass the Cootes all over; speak evil of somebody they must, and now they're done with me they start on you! And I'm right sorry I ever recommended her to you!" Then suddenly her wavering gaze came to rest on my face; her blue eyes were troubled, oddly innocent and yet corrupt with wisdom. "You know how it is, ma'am. For one that'll give you the benefit of the doubt there's ten that on't."

It was too late to retire into dignity and pretend that I didn't know what she was talking about; besides, it would have been utterly untrue. I knew. I simply said that I was sorry that she couldn't come and help out that evening and retreated.

IV

I suppose that anyone with a grain of sense would have gone back, sacked Annie and closed the club, admitting defeat. But at the mere thought of so doing, something—mainly panic, I suppose—rose in me and made it absolutely imperative to stay in Merravay until I sold it or died. So I said nothing; I worked side by side with my enemy and I held out until the first week of December.

There had been a long spell of fog, the worst weather for me for it made catering almost maddeningly difficult. At six o'clock I'd look out into a white blanket and resign myself to an unprofitable evening; at eight o'clock a dozen hungry people would arrive, clamouring for food. Either the fog had cleared for a bit or else some bold spirit had suggested risking it. Or again there would come an evening when the fog seemed to have lifted, and I'd cook, and nobody came; and Annie, Stanislav, and I would eat, all next day, lavishly, heartbreakingly, things like wienerschnitzel, warmed up. And David's last letter had said, "Do give it best, darling! If only you would we could still be together for Christmas." And I thought, if only I could! And I saw three thousand pounds, made visible in the shape of very black pound signs, leggitty little beasts, tearing away from me, never to be recaptured!

However, that morning, the first Saturday in December, dawned bright and clear and the weather forecast said that the fog had finally lifted. The telephone rang and rang; by eleven o'clock every table was booked. My spirits rose as I set about making the pastry.

It was Stanislav's day for having his fortnightly haircut, so with the car piled high with greenstuff and some pot plants, he had gone into Baildon early. John was paying his weekly visit of devotion to Ginger Whymark's latest litter of dachshund puppies—a fact for which I was later to be supremely grateful.

For suddenly the kitchen door burst open, and there was Stanislav, one half of his head ruthlessly clippered, the other still bristling with its fortnight's growth; his face was blue-white, his ears blazing red. Without a word he walked over to where Annie sat cleaning silver, and smacked her face twice; his palm hit her right cheek, his backhand her left, with a sound like a pistol shot.

Before he could hit her again I had him by the elbow, clutching with both hands and throwing all my weight against him. Annie saw her chance, got up, overturning her chair, and made for the door, screaming like a banshee. Stanislav jerked himself free and would have followed, but I was between him and the door and just managed to rush across, slam it, and set my back to it.

"Have you gone mad?" I gasped at him. For a moment he glared at me so savagely that I expected him to charge the door and fling me aside. In that moment I could hear Annie's screams, evenly spaced, diminishing in volume as she fled down the avenue. And I saw the madness—not the fury—go out of Stanislav's eyes.

"She is vile, wicked woman! Such things she is saying of me. I wish very much to kill her!"

"I could see that."

"If you should know what she is saying . . ."

"But I do. I've known ever since Nancy left. But she was *help!* Now look what you've done, you silly hot-head!"

"This English phlegm! This nation of shopkeeper! Never shall I understand. She is help, and so to be free to be saying untrue vile things so that barber men are winking and making filthy jokes to me. Two times he makes the joke. The first time I am not believing the ears; then I understand. I do not think he makes any further joke today!"

Apprehension seized me.

"Oh, what did you do? You didn't . . . ?"

"I am meaning to knock his teeth down the throat. But they are false teeth he is having and fall on the floor instead. Is funny!"

He gave a short, sharp bark of laughter in which I had a hysterical impulse to join. "Is funny" indeed. . . .

"Now we shall have real trouble . . . police . . ."

I could see the headline in the paper, "Pole Strikes Barber"; I could imagine the exposure of motive, all the hints and rumours which I had tried to ignore, creeping to the surface like worms after a rain.

"Can be fined," said Stanislav. "Can be in prison. Better than sit in barber chair and hear . . ." his hot little blue eyes glanced away from me, ". . . dirty jokes about me and that filthy bitch!"

The lie—and all that it implied—touched me. Suddenly something absolutely female and atavistic stirred in me. Angry, bristling, ridiculous little man, he had struck blows and would doubtless perjure himself in defence of my "honour." The clash of pennant-fluttering lance on blazoned shield, the "pistols for two" in the dawn, had narrowed down to "Pole Strikes Barber; Fined Thirty Shillings," but it was chivalrous still.

"Well," I said weakly, "all that must wait. The first thing is for you to find another barber and have your hair finished. You can't go about looking like that!"

"Will finish him presently, myself, with horse clippers. Meanwhile . . ." He snatched up the rag which Annie had dropped, plunged it into the plate polish and began to work on the silver with all the vigour of unexpended rage.

I stood for a moment, looking at all those forks and spoons which must be set out in order, collected, and washed. I looked at my unfinished pastry; at the slate upon which I had written the names of those members who had booked tables; I thought of the gallons of soup; of the mounds of vegetables. Weakness washed over me like a wave. I had tried, I had done my best, and I was beaten; why not admit it? I couldn't cook for and wait upon thirty people single-handed; nobody could. Moreover, by this time the rumour of Stanislav's assault upon the barber would be all over Baildon, lending point and substance to the scandal. Could I face the furtive, curious eyes?

I had only to lift the telephone; cable first to David, and then make a series of calls saying that, having no help, I was obliged to close the club. Let people think what they liked—they'd think the worst anyway. And I wanted, oh, how badly, to share with David the exquisite humour of "but they are false teeth he is having." After all, I thought, there are other values in the world besides material ones; why ruin your happiness trying to salvage three thousand pounds?

To this day I don't know why I didn't lift that telephone. . . .

But I didn't. And by six o'clock the tables were set and the fires made up; Stanislav with his skull shaven was behind the bar and I was in the kitchen. John, I might add, was in the Heaven of Heavens because Ginger had given him one of the puppies; its nose was a fraction of an inch too short, or its tail a fraction of an inch too long, so in this world of curious values it wasn't marketable. He'd taken it to bed with him and retired early, and willingly, because he thought it might be tired. They were asleep, curled up together when I looked in before going down to make my last stand.

Good evening! Good evening! Yes, isn't it lovely to have it clear again. Oh yes, of course you can have dinner. So difficult to make arrangements beforehand in this weather. David? Oh, he's very well, thank you. I heard from him this week. Plenty of sun there! Oh, hullo . . . if only I'd known you were coming I'd have made you one of your special dishes. An omelette will do? Of course. Cheese or mushroom? (Nothing to me, dearie, dash it off in no time.) David? Oh, very well, thank you. Yes, I hear every week; sometimes twice. A drink? That's kind and I could do with it, but I just must get back to the kitchen. Single-handed to-night. Yes, isn't it awful? Stan's hair? He does look a bit odd, doesn't he? Rather *too* short; maybe somebody "got in his hair" as they say. (Oh yes, I'm a wit, I am!)

I was back in the kitchen, having "shown" myself and faced them, or at least those who had come early, when the telephone rang. It was Chris Turnbull.

"Jill? Look, I know it's a bit late, but I've had a young American wished on me. Nice. Mad on old houses . . . so I thought. . . . But if it's awkward we'd eat at The Evening Star and then, if we survive, come on later."

"If you really had my good at heart, Chris, you'd drive out here full speed and take on the bar for an hour while Stan helped me to dish up. I'm entirely on my own tonight. If you would . . . and then eat later, I'd do you proud. . . ."

After that, what with the steam, the heat, the haste, everything melted into a kind of nightmare. I drowned in a sea of soup, potted shrimps, smoked salmon; I fought my way through a jungle of roast pheasant, filet steaks, with or without garlic, dear member? I climbed great mountains; potatoes, peas, braised celery, and what-sweet-would-you-like? I ran marathons; cheese, black or white coffee, and can-I-have-my-bill-please? There was Stanislav, useful as another pair of hands to me, never hesitating, never needing direction, never forgetful; breasting the wave, thrusting through the jungle, climbing the steeps, running the race by my side. And we did it. At about ten o'clock somebody looked out and said, "Fog coming up again," and fifty thousand people said at once, "But the forecast said . . . my bill please . . . swallow that down and let's get going . . . good night."

After that there was a great quiet.

There is something about complete exhaustion which is akin to one stage of drunkenness; time seems to skid about. I heard the last car start. I was conscious of nothing but a grinding agony in the small of my back and a peculiar feeling of being hobbled. I looked down and thought, Good Heavens! Elephantiasis! Huge bags of jelly were bulging and shaking where my ankles should have been. Another day like this and I'd have to have one of—no, two of those little carts they tie on to fat-tailed sheep.

Then, without the slightest idea of how I came to be there I was sitting by the fire in the hall. A cup of coffee and a brandy glass stood on the table beside me. Stanislav was clearing the last things from the deserted tables and Chris Turnbull and a craggy-faced young man with dark red hair were helping him.

I called to Chris and—just as in drunkenness—my voice came out peculiarly high-pitched and clear.

"Leave it, Chris; leave everything. There'll be plenty of time to clear up in. I can't go on like this. I'll just have to shut down and go to David."

"I think that would be wise," Chris said.

There, I've said it, I thought; that makes it real.

Then I lost another moment, during which somebody must have brought a stool and propped my feet on it. The place was tidy and Stanislav had gone. Chris was sitting opposite me and his friend stood by the foot of the stairs, running his hand caressingly over the almost life-size figure of Moses which stood there. The sight called to my mind the number of things about Merravay which were unique and lovely. Now that I had, by a single decision, severed my connection with the house I could afford a moment of admiration for its beauty and regret at its fate. I looked ahead and saw it deserted again, given over to the bats, the owls, the ghosts.

"It isn't my fault," I said aloud. "I've done my best. I could truly say that everything we ever tried here was doomed from the start. Chris, I believe you were right about Alice Rowhedge. She didn't want us here, so she put spells on us. Well, now she can have it, all to herself."

"Now isn't that curious," said the young American, who had been crossing the hall as I spoke. "Alice Rowhedge did you say? That was my mother's maiden name!"

Finale 1953

Between a young Cavalier named Charles Rowhedge who disappeared into the East Indies in 1662 and a Thomas Rowhedge first heard of as one of the few survivors of an ill-fated party making the overland route to California in 1841, there was a gap which nothing but imagination could ever bridge satisfactorily.

In course of time Mr. Christopher Turnbull, eager as ever for any activity more to his romantic taste than the routine duties of a country solicitor, managed to unearth the fact that a Thomas Rowhedge, in the island of Banda, in the year 1749, had added his shaky signature to a protest sent by the nutmeg growers there to the Dutch East India Company's Office in Amsterdam. That was the end of the trail in the East.

In the West the name Thomas Rowhedge occurred in a list of five people, all that remained of a party of twenty-three who had been snow-bound on Trucksee Lake for five months during the winter of 1840–41. Their trials and escape had been lent some notoriety by the suspicion—and rather more than that, since one man, almost demented by his experience, confessed to it—of cannibalism. Another survivor, in his deposition, was recorded to have said, "I went by Tom Rowhedge and he never so I never." There were a few other small indications that this Thomas Rowhedge had been a person of influence and integrity, and the family which he had founded in the sunny valley of the Sacramento had always cherished his memory.

It would have been nice to think . . . but there was the gap.

There were clues. The tendency to choose Thomas and Alice as names for first-born sons and daughters; the fact that, although the first Californian Rowhedge married a woman with some Indian blood, many Rowhedges were red-haired; and there was a mention of that somewhere in the original Alice Rowhedge's confession. Very little to go on, as Thomas Rowhedge Anderton was the first to admit. And even within his own mind he regarded his feelings with a degree of cautious scepticism. He knew that he had always been extremely, almost excessively, Anglophile; he had come to England early in the war as a member of the Eagle Squadron and he had never felt wholly at home anywhere else since then. And he had fallen in love with Merravay at first sight. Long before Mrs. Stamford had let fall the name which started his imagination leaping he'd thought that of all the houses he had seen that was the one he liked best, would most like to own.

Properly approached—Chris Turnbull had said casually—Mrs. Stamford would take five thousand pounds for it, he thought. Her husband was in Jamaica and she was very anxious to join him there.

That certainly was cheap for a house with a room still called the Queen's Chamber where the first Elizabeth had slept; for a house with a rose garden that had been laid out by a convicted witch . . . and cedars said to be brought from Lebanon seven hundred years ago.*

And Amanda, so homesick, so terribly out of place in America, would surely love it.

Also, he wanted it himself. And his experience in wanting things

* Possibly exaggerated, but one held to be 600 years old was felled at Assington, Suffolk, in 1952.

was extraordinarily scanty. His mother, once widowed and twice divorced, and the resultant circle of suitors, stepfathers, relatives, and friends had seen to it that his wishes were not only met but often forestalled. By the terms of his father's will he had attained an independent income when he was eighteen, and at twenty-one he had inherited the bulk of his grandfather Rowhedge's solid if unspectacular fortune. He was a very enviable young man, and one who might have been sadly spoilt. But his tastes had remained curiously simple. He had once quite shocked a young newspaperwoman who was gathering material for a restaurant-sponsored column of nonsense about what and where people liked to eat, by saying that his favourite food was radishes and bread and butter. The young woman, privately thinking this a facetious snub, saved her face by giving the dish the name by which she had recognised but not deigned to order it during her one holiday in France—*radis au beurre*. But it was an honest answer, and revealing. Revealing too was his certainty that Amanda, when she heard that he had bought, on the impulse of a moment, an old historic house in England, would be not merely approving but transported with delight. For he and Amanda saw eye to eye in everything.

Amanda was half-English by birth and entirely English by education, that was what had attracted him to her in the first place. Her mother, after years of unhappy marriage to a Wiltshire landowner who liked to go to sleep in a chair after dinner and finally allowed himself to be divorced so that he could do so in peace, had gone back to America and her family. She had taken Amanda, aged seventeen and just released from school. Amanda was coltish and shy, years younger, by every sophisticated standard, than her cousins and their contemporaries. Even when she had been coiffured and dressed and equipped to pattern she had failed dismally to fit in, and the chance introduction to Tom Anderton came as a godsend, just in time to save her from developing an inferiority complex.

Soon after her eighteenth birthday they became engaged; gratitude on her part, Anglophilism on his, masquerading as love. Their mothers opened the debate as to whether an Easter wedding with lilies, or a June one with roses, would be preferable. The debate continued.

One of Amanda's American uncles, who suffered from asthma, always wintered in Florida, and being fond of youthful company, and rich enough to command it, he always set out with an attendant bevy of nephews and nieces. This year Amanda was invited, and since Tom had pledged himself long ago to act as best man to a friend who was about to marry in London, it all fitted in well.

Just before he left America Tom looked in at a party where he talked for a while with a quietly spoken, shy-seeming Englishman who turned out to be Jimmy Rorke. In the course of the conversation Rorke said that he thought the really loveliest part of England was a bit one never heard about, not the famous Constable country, but the region just north of it, over the border, South Suffolk. Tom confessed that that was a part which he had never heard of.

"I go there pretty often. I have a friend there, Chris Turnbull; he's a solicitor in a place called Baildon." He went on to say that Chris was brilliant, could have done anything, but had chosen to bury his talents, in a way, because there had been Turnbulls practising law in that town for four hundred years and he hadn't the heart to break the line. If Tom should happen to go that way and cared to look Chris up and say . . .

"Maybe I will," Tom said.

And there had come a time when the wedding was over, and he was feeling lonely and yet unwilling to go home . . .

That was how it had happened.

With one thing and another he was only just back in time to keep Christmas with his mother, and immediately after he set out for Florida to see Amanda. He took with him two dozen photographs of the house. The ones of the interior, taken in powerful artificial light, were clear and dramatic; the outdoor ones, for which the photographer had been obliged to depend upon the vagrant, pale sunshine of a winter's day, were less successful; they suggested a sombreness, a look of brooding age, that was only just short of sinister. But Amanda would understand; when he said that the house was built of old brick Amanda could imagine . . .

She had no need to.

"It's the spitting image of Daddy's house. I knew it! The moment I read your letter I thought—Heavens! It sounds just like Hadwyke! Darling, what can have come over you?"

"But it's beautiful! Here, just look at this. That shows the screen in the hall. Silvery grey and so finely carved. And then this room where Queen Elizabeth . . ."

"Darling, it's always her, or Anne Boleyn! I can't believe they spent their time rushing about sleeping in different places just to give people something to talk about later on. Can you?"

Outside a voice called urgently, "Mandy! Mandy!"

"Well, we don't have to live in it, do we?" said Amanda, shuffling the photographs into a heap and standing up. "Get your bathing things, darling. The others are waiting."

He knew he hadn't even reached first base. She wasn't in the right mood. Now he came to think about it she hadn't been in the right mood ever since his arrival. There'd been a slight undercurrent . . . as though he'd offended her in some way and she was bearing a grudge. It couldn't be because he'd bought the place without asking her . . . or could it?

He probed the point at the first opportunity, which was not very soon. For something had happened to Amanda during his absence. She seemed to have become very popular. She'd always been rather out of things; now she was the centre . . . it was "Mandy" here and "Mandy" there all the time and she appeared to like it. But at last he did get her to himself and he asked his question.

She said, "Yes, I do think it was pretty highhanded."

"But, honey, there wasn't much time. This Mrs. Stamford wanted to make the sale right away and I knew that you wanted to get back there and it was the loveliest old place we'd be likely . . ."

"I can't think what made you imagine that I wanted to go back. I don't, Tom. And if I did it'd be Mother and Hadwyke all over again. It was the house that finally got her down, you know. Besides . . . I like it here. And you should have consulted me. . . ."

Fortunately the full irony of the situation escaped him. Being engaged to him had given Amanda just the confidence that she needed to make the grade in her new circumstances. Having made it, she need no more be bothered with this dull young man. And he had liked her because she was English and homesick and different.

If he had come straight home without visiting Jimmy Rorke's friend they would probably have had the June wedding with the smother of roses upon which her mother had set her heart, and a little later on some other catalystic circumstance would have revealed, more disturbingly, how little in love they were. As it was, the broken engagement hardly mattered at all. An old house, thousands of miles away, staunchly facing the blizzard-laden east wind of its four hundred and seventy-fifth winter, had merely forestalled one more divorce.

By the third week in January Tom was back in Nettleton, with the full approval of his mother, who was absolutely certain that Merravay was the Rowhedge ancestral home and that the blood of baronets ran in her veins. When the weather was warmer and he had the place comfortable she was coming, with a number of her cronies, to use the house as a headquarters for her Coronation visit.

He was camping in one room while workmen swarmed through the house, installing bathrooms and central heating. A plump, cheerful woman whom some people called Mrs. Coote, others Mrs. Baxter, others again, Mrs. Ager, and who didn't seem absolutely sure herself, came up each morning and made his breakfast and tidied his bed. He was completely happy, though at times he would have liked someone with whom he could have shared his happiness and his enthusiasms. And even that he found. . . .

One morning, after a fortnight of loneliness, he went into Baildon and was driving back when he overtook a tall girl who was plunging along through the rain. She was ill clad for such a day. A scruffed old leather jacket shed the water from her shoulders, but below it her tweed skirt hung soggily and a pair of thin, high-heeled shoes sucked at the mud;

her head was bare and her bright yellow hair, misted with raindrops, shone like a halo. She carried a parcel which looked heavy and from which the soaked newspaper in which it was wrapped was peeling away.

Tom passed, slowed down, stopped. Despite the unsuitable shoes and the parcel she was loping along at a good pace and soon drew level.

"Could I give you a lift?" he asked.

"That depends where you're going," she said crisply. "If it's only into the village it's hardly worth while mucking up your beautiful car. Thanks all the same."

"I'm going through, to Merravay."

Grey-green eyes, narrowed against the rain, widened and regarded him with frank interest for a moment.

"Oh . . ." she said; and the single word implied that she had heard a good deal about him. "Well, in that case, I should take it kindly." Before Tom could reach out and open the door she had done it for herself, had heaved the parcel into the rear seat and lowered herself into place beside him. She brought with her a faint feminine scent of cosmetics mingled with that of wet leather, wet hair, and something else dangerously near to being downright nasty.

"This is the second time this week that the car has broken down and this time they don't hold out much hope. I shall have to get a bicycle." She pushed that thought aside. "So you're Mr. Anderton. I'm Ginger Whymark—we're the nearest thing to a neighbour you have; we live in the Lodge at the end of the other avenue. Tell me . . . is it true that your folks only bought Merravay in order to rip out the stairs and fireplaces and take them off to the States?"

"Why no! My folks as you call them haven't had anything to do with it. My father's been dead nearly twenty years and my mother's quite crazy about the place, so far. She's coming over in May—if I can get it clear by then. I don't expect she'll want to stay long. But I'm staying."

"It's you then, you own it?"

"That's right. I own it."

"It was just that you look a bit young to go owning houses," she said. "Nowadays, around here anyway, you have to save hard till you're forty in order to buy a caravan. Still, I'm glad, by God, that *that* tale isn't true. I've a very soft spot for that house. I was so *relieved* when the Stamfords took it but anybody could see with half an eye that they'd never hold out. They were the nicest people, but like children, always trying out something new and never giving anything time to get going. I did try to point that out. It was just the same with my dachshunds. I mean if at the end of the first year I'd decided—as well I might—that they weren't a paying proposition and gone rushing off into great Danes or Pekes or something the way the Stamfords would, well, I shouldn't be where I am today!"

"And where is that?" he asked, matching her frankness.

"I'm recognised as one of the best breeders of dachshunds in England. Not wishing to boast—but Monarch of Merravay simply swept the board. . . . Oh!" She put a long, thin, hard-worked-looking hand to her mouth and shot him a glance. "The place was empty then, when I started, and didn't look like ever being occupied again and Merravay went so well with Maid, Matriarch, Monarch, Mischief, and Midget. Lodge wouldn't go with anything except Lousy!" She laughed, with just that touch of wryness which David Stamford had found so engaging, especially when he was having a bad day. "And," she said meditatively, "it was meant to be a bit of homeopathic magic, like African witch doctors pouring a libation to bring down the rain."

"I don't follow."

"Of course not. Well . . . there was a time when I did just hope that the Stamfords would just hold on until my great-aunt . . ." she laughed again. "Damn it, she is ninety-four! It had gone through my mind in demented moments that if the dogs did well, and if she really left me what she says she will because I mend her fuses and chase the burglars from under the bed and bully her butcher, I just might have . . . But of course that was a pipe dream. And I couldn't have left my parents. And I couldn't have kept the place up. I should just have moved from room to room, one jump ahead of the rain; and in the end the roof would have caved in on me. But how could man die better? Oh blast! I was afraid of that!"

Heaving and shrugging, she freed herself of the leather coat, then, rearing on one knee, leaned over to wrap the parcel. As she did so the unpleasant odour of which Tom had become increasingly conscious, and which had somewhat inhibited his full response to her chatter, became more noticeable. Was there, he wondered, proper bathing accommodation at the Lodge?

"Gah!" said Miss Whymark, "it's high this week! That is the one thing I don't like about my job. Even when it's fresh I have an absolute horror of horse meat."

"I once heard a professor say that all true Anglo-Saxons have," said Tom. "He said it was on account of the horse once being a sacred animal and subject to a tabu."

"That's interesting; feasible, too, I should say. Look, I wonder would you mind dropping me here. I've just remembered I must go along Goose Lane and pick up my heavy shoes. Old Farrow promised them for this morning."

"Down here?"

"Yes. But don't come. It's a vile bit of road and you couldn't turn . . ."

"I could back, I guess."

It was all too apparent that Miss Whymark was not accustomed to much consideration.

She re-entered the car, carrying, unwrapped, exactly the pair of shoes one would have expected her to be wearing on such a morning. She inspected the clumping new soles with considerable satisfaction.

"Nice neat job," she said. "How he does it I can't imagine; he's as blind as a bat!"

Was it possible that the poor girl had but the one pair of heavy shoes?

"Oh!" said Miss Whymark as they passed the mouth of the chestnut avenue which Nabob Sandell had planted. "I meant to get out here. Now you'll have to turn in *our* avenue and the College traffic has churned it into bog—tractors, you know." The avenue of limes, the cause once of so much dissension, came into view. "When my family lived at Merravay, this was the avenue up to it. There's quite a fascinating story about the family quarrel which resulted in the shrubbery being planted across its upper end."

"I didn't know you ever lived at Merravay."

"Not me; the Whymarks. Oh yes, we lived there, years before New Holding was built. Now, keep well over to this side . . . aah! Just missed it! That's grand." Once more she forestalled his effort at courtesy and was out of the car in the rain and the mud, whipping out the parcel before he had pulled on the hand brake. "Now come in and have a drink. Father has two or three friends staying; they should be shooting, but it's too wet. I bet they've been drinking for hours!"

On the inward side of the little Lodge cottage a considerable extension had been made in modern style. Tom could see a wide bay window with a bank of exotic hothouse flowers just behind it; and behind the flowers, drawn by curiosity to the window, were a number of elderly male faces, all of them, Tom thought, bearing a marked resemblance to the late Sir Aubrey Smith. The owner of one face came nearer the window, beamed at Miss Whymark, and pointed to the flowers with a gesture of exaggerated complacency and triumph.

"Lovely! Lovely!" she shouted. "That is Sir Stephen Fennel," she said, turning to Tom. "He's brought Mother some flowers. Poor old dear, it was touch and go this year but he managed to keep his hothouse going by not having a fire himself. He sits at night with his feet in a muff. . . ."

A curious, inexplicable shyness descended upon Tom.

"I mustn't come in now, thanks just the same," he said. "I've got some stuff aboard that the men are waiting for."

"Some other time then. Any time," Miss Whymark said equably. "And I've no doubt that when Mother hears you are really going to *live* at Merravay, she'll rout out a hat and pay you a formal call. That is," she added gloomily, "if they ever get the car going again. She can't walk far these days."

"Well, I'd be glad . . ." he began; but probably that wasn't quite the thing to say. "I would like very much to show you what is being done up at the house."

"And I'm all agog to see." She pondered. "I tell you what I could do. I walk the dogs most evenings. I could walk that way. I often did when the Stamfords were there. Then seeing it empty again and the rumour of the staircase being ripped out depressed me so much, lately I've avoided it."

"This evening?"

"There again, it depends. If Sir Stephen stays on, I *might*. If not they'll need me to make a fourth—at bridge."

"You might even give me a word or two of advice about furnishing. I took over a few things from the Stamfords; but for the rest, well it's all kind of new to me."

"My experience of furnishing has been confined to fitting nine-footer sideboards into rooms twelve feet square *and* leaving room for the door to open. But of course, if you really . . ."

"I do," Tom started to assure her; then he realised that she was standing, without hat, without jacket, in the rain. And he thought—I'm as bad as the rest, using her rough.

"Come up as soon as you can. I'll be looking for you," he said quickly, and drove away, followed by her voice thanking him heartily for the lift.

It was raining more heavily now, a silver-bead curtain suspended from a slate-grey sky. The men who should have been crawling about the roof had taken shelter in the kitchen and were busy with yet another brew of tea. One of them, a Nettleton man, was holding the floor.

"Mind you, I wunt want a word of this to git to *his* ears. Let him spend every duzzy dollar he got afore he wake up to the fact that this ain't a house to be *lived* in! 'Tis well known, in these parts, to be haunted. Ah, I see you grinning into yer mug, young Saunders! That don't alter fax. Why, only a year or two back there was a whole crowd of right smart people staying here and they all upped and went, saying they couldn't sleep for the moaning and groaning. Bit in the paper about it there was. Then you go back to afore the war. Lord Clumberly took it and what he warn't going to do with it . . . coo! Lady Clumberly come down once, just the once and never no more. Work stopped and up for sale again. 'Twill be the same agin now, you'll see!" He drank deeply, and looked with pleasure on his audience.

"I can remember futher back than that even. A sensible owd working chap called Joe Hoggett bought it; he come up here one Sunday arternoon, and never set foot in the place no more; and if you so much as mentioned it to him he'd blench and look at yer as if you was talking about Owd Nick. And now I bin in it I know why. You couldn't call me chicken-hearted," he said modestly (he had gone, very reluctantly, to the "old" war, and at Vimy Ridge, chiefly because no other course had seemed open to him, had held a machine-gun post single-handed and had been awarded a Military Medal) "but you wouldn't catch me spending a night here; no, not if you was to offer me a thousand quid."

"Little Mrs. Stamford slepp here all by herself," somebody contributed.

"Ah. So they say!"

"What about that there Pole?"

The conversation showed signs of drifting.

"But what is it all about? What does the haunting?" asked an electrician from Colchester.

He genuinely wanted to know, but to conceal his serious purpose he winked right and left as he spoke, pretending to be leading on this credulous Nettleton fellow.

"Ah, wink away," said the Nettleton man, who was sharper than he looked. "There's them that hev laughed for years about the walls of Jericho tumbling down when Joshua's trumpets blew and now they've dug the place up and found that they did fall down. Thass the same with this. There's the story they tell in the village, and if that ain't good enough for you go and look in Baildon museum and see the thing writ out. There was a Lady Alice Rowhedge, hundreds of years ago, and she was a witch and she made spells and bargained with the Devil to get this house for her own. And the Devil did her! So now she can't rest nor cease from tormenting till the Rowhedges hev it agin."

"Reglar Boris Karloff you are!" somebody said. "Make my flesh creep. Still, so long as I'm out afore dark."

"And not a word, mind. Don't forget the dollar gap!"

"Time he've finished here the balance'll be on the other side I should reckon!"

Tom entered—as he always did, for the sake of the joy the first sight of the hall invariably gave him—by the big front door. The lacy screen, the massive, gently mounting staircase, the figure of the old man leaning on the staff, the eighteen-inch-wide, honey-buff planks of the floor, the long taut stretch of the gallery, the Tudor roses over the cavernous hearth—he looked at them, one after another, and knew that his pleasure in them, sharp as it had been, was today increased. A little dragging sense of loneliness had vanished. It would be ridiculous and naive to bank too much on the strength of a single meeting . . . but he had been definitely attracted to her, even when he was wondering about that odd smell. And of course the setup . . . shooting parties and patched-up shoes, hothouse flowers and foot-muffs, formal calls if a broken-down car could grind out two more miles . . . that all savoured of the Deep South. But anything less like a southern belle . . .

Obviously she had the heck of a life, a very bad deal; but it hadn't got her down.

She'd wanted Merravay herself, but she didn't grudge his possession of it. She was glad. She didn't like to see it empty. When she came . . .

Yes, he'd have a fire in the big hearth of the hall—he hadn't tried that yet. He'd put his two chairs and the rug close to the fire. Drinks? He had plenty, and it might be that after the walk she'd be ready to eat, too.

And she'd come along, glad to see the lights in the windows, and he'd open the door and say, "Welcome to my home!" No, that sounded a bit pompous. He'd say, "Hi there. Come in."

But the fact remained that after the way Amanda had behaved about it, and the way that his mother had snatched at the whole thing, not because it was what it was, but because of what she chose to make of it, the idea of the arrival of someone who felt—and with more reason—about Merravay as he felt was extremely exciting and satisfactory. Probably, when she'd rested and had something to eat and drink, they'd go over the place together. She could tell him details of that family quarrel which had resulted in the closed avenue; and he could ask her—because it was quite clear that one could ask her anything—what was behind this hint of haunting. Gosh, there were so many things. . . .

Making his preparations, mental and material, for his first visitor, Tom felt he had come home.